Jessica Hart was born in West Africa, and has suffered from itchy feet ever since, travelling and working around the world in a wide variety of interesting but very lowly jobs, all of which have provided inspiration on which to draw when it comes to the settings and plots of her stories. Now she lives a rather more settled existence in York, where she has been able to pursue her interest in history, although she still yearns sometimes for wider horizons. If you'd like to know more about Jessica, visit her website www.jessicahart.co.uk.

Don't miss Jessica Hart's fabulous brand-new novel *Her Ready-Made Family*. Out in June 2006 from Mills & Boon Tender Romance™.

CHAPTER ONE

PRUE was slumped miserably over the steering wheel when the sound of an approaching vehicle made her jerk upright. At last! Scrambling out of the car, she saw a utility truck bowling along the track towards her, a cloud of red dust billowing behind it.

Too tired to realise that the car was effectively blocking the track on its own, she began to wave her arms frantically and even though she knew that no one in the outback would drive past a vehicle in trouble, she felt weak with relief as the ute slowed and stopped at last a few feet in front of her.

The driver wound down his window and leant out. 'You look like you could use some help,' he said in a laconic voice.

He had a quiet, pleasant face that was vaguely familiar. Prue groped desperately for his name. Nat... Nat *something* was the best she could do. He was one of the Grangers' neighbours, if you could really call anyone who lived seventy miles away a neighbour.

'Hello,' she greeted him, wincing inwardly at how clipped and English she sounded compared to his slow Australian drawl. Taking her sunglasses off, she bent down to look at him through the window, and Nat found himself looking back into a pair of silvery-grey eyes that bore distinct traces of tears on the long, sooty lashes.

'I can't tell you how glad I am to see you!' she said. 'I was beginning to wonder if I'd be here all night!'

Nat switched off the engine and got out of the ute. He

was a rangy man in his thirties, with the spare, self-contained look that Prue had grown used to seeing in the outback.

'It's Prue, isn't it?' he said, settling his hat on his head.

Prue looked at him in surprise. 'That's right.'

'I'm Nat Masterman.'

Masterman, that was it! 'Oh, I know,' she said hastily. 'I remember you coming to Cowen Creek. I was just surprised that you recognised me. Not many people notice a cook.'

Nat was puzzled himself to have remembered her so clearly. She was slight with a cloud of brown hair and a face that was piquant rather than pretty. He hadn't noticed that much about her on the few occasions he had seen her, only her eyes, which were an unusual silver colour, and the way she had lit up whenever Ross Granger smiled at her.

'That depends on how good the cook is,' he said tactfully. 'You made the best apple pie I've ever had.'

'Really?' Prue smiled at him gratefully. It was nice to think that she was good at something. 'Thank you!'

Yes, he had noticed her smile, too, Nat remembered. He adjusted the brim of his hat. 'What's the trouble, Prue?' he asked.

Reminded of her situation, Prue's smile faded. 'I've run out of diesel,' she said glumly.

Nat's brow rose slightly. 'Are you sure?'

She nodded. 'The red warning light has been blinking at me for miles, but by the time I noticed it I'd gone too far to go back. I was hoping to get to the sealed road at least—' she went on, kicking one of the tyres in remembered frustration '—but the engine started to cough and splutter just up the track, and then it just died.'

She blew her fringe wearily off her face. 'I've been here over two hours.'

It felt more than twice as long.

Prue saw Nat glance at her curiously and was suddenly acutely aware of what a mess she must appear. There were plenty of ways to look good, but being stuck in a car in the middle of the outback for a couple of hours was certainly not one of them.

It might not have been so bad if there had been any shade where she could sit and wait, but out here on the salt pans she had had no choice but to stay in the car. The air-conditioning had died with the engine, and even with all the windows down the sun beating on the metal roof had soon turned the car into an oven. Now, her face was red and blotchy and her curls clung limp and sweaty to her scalp.

Rubbing a knuckle under her eyes to remove any tell-tale tear-stains and hastily replacing her sunglasses, Prue could only hope that she didn't look as if she had spent the last two hours snivelling pathetically, even if it *were* true.

Not that Nat Masterman seemed to care what she looked like. He was more concerned with the fuel situation. 'These things have got pretty big tanks,' he said, nodding his head at the car, a powerful four-wheel drive far bigger than anything Prue had ever driven at home. 'It must have been just about empty before you left Cowen Creek.'

'I know—and, yes, I know I should have checked it before I left,' said Prue, forestalling him as he opened his mouth. 'It was one of the first things the Grangers told me when I came to work out here.

'The thing is, I'd had a really busy morning,' she tried to explain her carelessness, 'and I suddenly realised that we were out of flour and sugar and a whole lot of other things I need to cook the meal tonight. I reckoned I had just enough time to get into town and back before I had to start cooking, so I just jumped in the car and set off. I was thinking about…other things…and, well, I just forgot,' she admitted.

And now here she was in another fine mess. Bitterly, Prue remembered the moment when the flashing red light had finally caught her eye, yanking her out of a wonderful daydream where Ross was marvelling at how they had ever managed at Cowen Creek without her.

He wouldn't be marvelling tonight when he found out that she had spent the afternoon stranded halfway to Mathison and that there would be no pudding. She had planned to make his favourite, too.

Prue was suddenly close to tears. 'I can't believe I could be so *stupid*!' she said fiercely, knowing that there was no one to blame but herself.

'Not so stupid that you left the car and tried to walk.'

Nat's voice was calm and insensibly comforting, and Prue looked at him gratefully. He might not be the type to make her go weak at the knees, like Ross, but he had always seemed like a nice man. Not that exciting, maybe, but quietly competent. If she had to be stranded in the middle of nowhere, she couldn't ask for anyone better to rescue her.

Not even Ross, she thought disloyally. Ross would know what to do, of course, but he wouldn't have been able to resist teasing her. Nat, she guessed, wouldn't tease, and he wouldn't rush to tell everyone how hopelessly unsuited she was to life in the outback either. He was the kind of man who only spoke when he had something important to say.

'I don't suppose you've got any spare diesel, have

you?' she asked him, hoping against hope that she would be able to avoid the ignominy of having to abandon the car altogether. If Nat had enough fuel to get her back to the homestead, she could make do for dinner and Ross might not ever have to know what had happened.

But Nat was already shaking his head. 'Sorry,' he said.

Prue tried, and failed, to swallow her disappointment. 'Oh, well.'

So much for Ross not finding out. She would have to go back and confess, that was all.

Squaring her shoulders, she flashed Nat a determinedly bright smile. 'Are you on your way to Cowen Creek?' she asked, even though she knew the question was unnecessary. Once on this track, there was nowhere else to go.

He nodded. 'I wanted to have a word with Bill Granger.'

'Would you give me a lift?'

'Sure,' Nat began, but something in her smile, something in the way she turned despondently back to the car to collect her things, made him pause. 'Unless you'd rather I took you into Mathison?' he heard himself offer.

Prue stopped with her hand on the car door. She looked at him with such amazement that Nat wondered if she had misunderstood what he had said. 'You could do your shopping while I get a can of fuel,' he explained. 'I'll bring you back here, and then you can drive yourself back to Cowen Creek.'

He made it sound perfectly simple, as if it was the most obvious thing in the world for him to go back on his tracks and drive an extra forty or so miles along hot, dusty roads for a girl he hardly knew.

'But…I thought you wanted to see Bill,' stammered Prue, unable to believe that the miracle she had spent the last two hours dreaming about would turn up in the shape of a lean, quiet grazier in a hat.

Nat shrugged. 'There's no hurry,' he said, incapable of explaining his impulsive offer to himself let alone to her.

No, there would never be a hurry as far as Nat Masterman was concerned, thought Prue enviously. He wouldn't know how to *begin* flapping or fussing or panicking. You could tell by the steadiness of his gaze, by the slowness of his voice, by the easy way he moved, that hurry was quite simply an alien concept for him.

'Even so, it would be taking you so far out of your way,' she said doubtfully.

'I don't mind,' he said. 'But if you'd rather I took you back to Cowen Creek—'

'No!' Prue interrupted him, determined not to let her opportunity go. 'I mean, if you're sure you don't mind, it would be *wonderful* if you could take me to Mathison!' she admitted, and her smile was so dazzling that Nat blinked and wondered how he could have thought that she wasn't particularly pretty.

He turned to open the door of the ute. 'Hop in, then,' he said in a dry voice.

Prue grabbed her hat and her shopping list from the car. She scrambled in beside him and collapsed back into the seat.

'You've saved my life!' she told him as he turned the ute with an economy of movement that already seemed typical of him and headed back the way he had come.

Nat raised an eyebrow at her dramatic statement. 'You would have been OK as long as you stayed with the car,' he pointed out. 'The Grangers would have come to look for you eventually.'

'Oh, I know. I wasn't worried about my safety.' The cab was blissfully cool after the crushing heat in the car.

Prue leant forward to adjust the vent so that the cold air blew directly onto her face. She had never understood the appeal of air-conditioning until she had come to Australia.

'You've saved me from having to explain what an idiot I've been,' she went on, sitting back with a sigh of relief. 'I was dreading it.'

'I can't see any of the Grangers getting angry with you,' said Nat in the calm way of a man who had no idea what it was like to do anything stupid or be afraid of anything.

'I know. That's what makes it worse!' sighed Prue. 'They're so nice and kind,' she tried to explain, seeing Nat's baffled look. 'They've been wonderful to me. I'd always wanted to work on a real outback cattle station, and getting a job at Cowen Creek was like a dream come true. Mr and Mrs Granger are great—and Ross, of course.'

She had meant it to sound like a casual aside, but her voice came out ridiculously strangled instead. It was hopeless, thought Prue in despair. All she had to do was *think* about Ross and her heart clenched, squeezing the air from her lungs. She couldn't even say his name without her throat thickening.

She coughed slightly to clear it. 'Well, anyway, I just love being at Cowen Creek,' she went on, 'but I'm sure they must think I'm really stupid. They're just too polite to say so.'

Nat glanced at her. She was staring disconsolately through the windscreen, her unruly hair pushed behind her ears to reveal a fine-boned profile. He didn't think she looked stupid. Her face was warm, alert, quirky in an attractive way, but not stupid.

'Why should they think that?' he asked.

'Because I am,' said Prue glumly. 'I can't seem to do anything right. I fainted dead away once when I cut myself with a knife, and I couldn't even *watch* when they were dehorning the calves. And then the other day I nearly had a fit when I found a snake in the onion sack— they all thought that was *really* funny,' she remembered with a sigh. 'They said it wasn't poisonous but I didn't know that, did I?' she added, turning to Nat almost belligerently, as if he had been the one who had laughed at the sight of her screaming blue murder in the storeroom.

'There's no reason why you should,' he agreed gravely, and Prue subsided a little.

'I'd love to be able to ride well,' she went on, 'but all their horses seem to be half wild, and I keep falling off.' Her cheeks burned with humiliation as she remembered how Ross had grinned as he picked her up. 'I just seem to be hopeless at everything.'

'Except cooking,' Nat pointed out. 'Bill Granger told me you're the best cook they've ever had.'

'Anyone can cook,' said Prue dismissively. 'I want to be able to do the things everyone else can do out here.'

'Like what?'

'Like lasso a calf. Like mend a fence or fix a water pipe. Like brand a cow without passing out. Like remembering to check the fuel before setting out to drive to town!' She folded the shopping list sadly in her lap, turning it over and over until it was no more than a tiny square. 'I'm a liability the moment I step outside the homestead!'

'You're just getting used to a different way of doing things,' said Nat, but Prue refused to be consoled.

'I've already been here three months,' she grumbled. 'How much longer is it going to take?'

'Why does it matter?' he asked. 'You can't help what you are.'

'But that's just it! I don't want to be like me! I was born and brought up in London, but that doesn't mean I'm condemned to be a city girl my whole life, does it? I don't want people to think of me as a prissy Pom mincing around the outback, no good for anything except peeling a few potatoes or making a cake. I want to be…'

The kind of girl Ross would fall in love with. The kind of girl he would marry.

She could hardly tell Nat Masterman *that*, though, could she?

'…I want to *belong*,' she finished instead. She turned to Nat, and he was very aware of the intense, silver-grey gaze on his face. 'Do you think that's possible?'

Nat kept his eyes firmly on the track ahead. 'Why not?'

'Ross doesn't think it is.' Prue dropped her eyes and concentrated on unfolding the shopping list. 'He thinks you have to be born here to belong. I've been trying so hard to prove him wrong, and now I've gone and made a fool of myself all over again by forgetting to check the fuel in the car! If you hadn't come along, it would have looked as if I couldn't even manage to go into town and pick up a few groceries without them having to come out and rescue me. I know they wouldn't have been angry, but they're all so busy at the moment and it would have been a real nuisance…'

She trailed off, imagining the scene if Ross or one of the stockmen had been sent out to find her, and her eyes lifted to Nat's calm profile once more. 'That's why I said you'd saved my life,' she told him.

'You know, you're worried about nothing,' said Nat. 'The Grangers like you. They've told me so, and they're not the kind of people who pretend. You're fun for them to have around and, more importantly, you're a good cook. They've got stockmen to help them outside. What they really want is someone to produce meals for everyone on time, and you can do that. If they don't want you to be different, why should you?'

'Because Ross wants me to be different.' The words were out before Prue could stop them and she bit her lip, turning her head away and letting her hair swing forward so that when Nat glanced at her he could see only the curve of her jaw and the long line of her throat.

'Are you sure about that?' he asked dryly after a moment. 'When I saw the two of you together at Ellie Walker's wedding, it looked as if he liked you just the way you were.'

Surprise brought Prue's head round. 'You were at the wedding?' She frowned slightly. 'I didn't notice you.'

There had been no reason for her to have noticed him, Nat thought without resentment. He didn't have Ross Granger's famous looks or charm. He had only noticed her because of the way her eyes had shone that night. It was as if a light had been switched on inside her. She'd seemed to be literally glowing with happiness. Nat remembered wondering what it would be like to have a girl look at him the way Prue had looked at Ross.

'I got the impression you didn't notice anyone except Ross,' he said with a wry sideways look.

It was true. Prue had had eyes only for Ross that night. The other guests, even the bride and groom, had been no more than a background blur to the wonderful, glorious fact that she was with him. It had been a perfect evening. Ross had ignored all the other girls there. He had flirted only with her, danced only with her, and then he had driven her back to Cowen Creek and kissed her in the car outside the homestead.

Prue had been so certain that that night was to prove the beginning of the rest of her life. Ross was everything she'd ever wanted, and for a while she had floated dreamily through the days, imagining how happy they would be together, writing home to tell her family that she had at last found the love of her life.

And she had. It was just that Ross didn't seem to think that he had found *his*.

She smoothed the shopping list in her lap. 'I'm in love with Ross,' she said in a low voice, unable to resist the urge to talk about him, not quite sure why she had chosen Nat to confide in other than the fact that he seemed so solid and dependable. There was something steady about him, something strong and sure about his hands on the steering wheel.

She had been longing for someone to talk to. The only other woman at Cowen Creek was Ross's mother, who was very kind but not the sort you could pour your heart out to, and although the jackaroos were more or less her own age, Prue's mind boggled at the idea of trying to discuss emotions with them. Nat might not be the ideal confidant, but he wouldn't sigh or sneer or roll his eyes the way the others would. And he wouldn't gossip. You could tell just by looking at him that gossip, like haste, was an alien concept.

'I've never felt like this about anyone before,' she went on without looking at him, and now that she had started talking she couldn't stop. 'I fell in love with him the moment I saw him, just like in all the books. He was waiting to pick me up when I got off the bus from Alice Springs, and that was it. He's like a dream come true.'

Prue looked out at the heat shimmering over the saltbush, but she was seeing Ross as he had been that day, with his dancing blue eyes and his devastating smile and that body…

She swallowed at the very thought of him. 'It's not just the way he looks,' she said. 'He's funny and he's charming, but he's down to earth at the same time…oh, I can't explain,' she confessed helplessly, the tumbling words slowing at last. 'He's just…the only man I'll ever want.'

Nat's gaze flickered to Prue's face and then back to the track. What *was* it about Ross? he wondered. He was a good-looking bloke, of course, but there must be something else to reduce a girl like Prue to this kind of state. She was obviously besotted, the way every other girl in the district under the age of thirty seemed to have been besotted with him at one stage or another.

'What's the problem?' he asked.

Prue was taken aback by the sudden question. Thinking about Ross, she had almost forgotten that she was talking to Nat. 'Problem?'

'I guess you wouldn't be telling me this if Ross felt the same way.'

'No.' Her shoulders slumped and she sighed. 'He likes me, I suppose, but he doesn't love me. As far as Ross is concerned, our relationship will only last as long as my visa. The Grangers get a girl in to cook during the dry season every year, and Ross probably flirts with all of them.' It was hard to keep the bitterness out of her voice. 'I'm just the current model.'

Knowing Ross, and the succession of girls who had worked at Cowen Creek, Nat thought it was more than likely, but he didn't think that Prue would want to hear that.

'Ross is all right,' he said uncomfortably. 'He's just young.'

'He's twenty-seven, two years older than me. It's not that young.'

'It's not that old either. There's plenty of time before Ross needs to think about settling down.'

'And when he does, he's going to pick a good outback girl who'll make him a practical wife,' said Prue miserably.

Nat thought that was more than likely, too. For all his charm of manner, Ross had always struck him as having a hard head on his shoulders. 'Is that what he says?' he asked, deciding to stay neutral.

'He doesn't have to.' She looked down at her hands. 'He's made it very clear that he doesn't think I can cope with life on a station like Cowen Creek. I'm just someone else he can have a good time with, not someone he would ever think about spending his life with.'

Her voice wobbled slightly, but she was determined not to give in to tears the way she had done when the car had first spluttered to a halt and left her stranded with only the thought of how much her stupidity just seemed to prove Ross's point. She stiffened her lip. 'I don't belong,' she finished bleakly, 'and Ross thinks I never will.'

'You can't blame him for thinking about how you would manage,' said Nat cautiously. He had the nasty feeling that he was getting out of his depth. 'It's a hard life out here, if you're not used to it.'

'All I want is the chance to *get* used to it,' said Prue with another sigh.

To Nat's relief, they were approaching the turn-off onto the sealed road, where the track was marked by an old tractor tyre on which 'Cowen Creek' had been painted. He changed gear, wishing that it were as easy to disengage a conversation.

'There's no reason why you shouldn't,' he said as he

looked up and down the long, straight, empty stretch of road before pulling out. 'By the end of the season you'll be carrying on like you were born here, and who's to say Ross won't change his mind? You just need to give him time.'

'But I haven't got time,' Prue protested. 'That's just it. I've got to go home in three weeks.'

He shot her a look of surprise. 'Has your visa run out already?'

'No, my sister's getting married.' Prue's tone didn't suggest she found it much cause for celebration. 'Originally they were going to have an autumn wedding, but then Cleo decided it would be much nicer for everyone if they had it in summer instead, so I've got to cut short my trip. I promised I'd be there, and I can't let her down.'

She stared disconsolately out of the window, imagining London with its grey streets and its grey buildings and its grey clouds. Here the sky was an intense, glaring blue and the air was diamond-bright and the heat shimmered over the red earth and wavered along the vast, distant horizon. And somewhere out there Ross was riding his horse, sitting easily in the saddle, smiling that smile of his...

'I wish I could stay,' she sighed. 'It's not just because of Ross. I love it here. I suppose I always had a pretty romantic idea of the outback, and I didn't really know what to expect. When I heard about the job at Cowen Creek I was half afraid that I would be disappointed, but the moment I arrived I fell in love with the place.

'It was like coming home,' she said slowly, the grey eyes dreamy and unfocused as she remembered how she had felt. 'It was as if I'd always known the light and the stillness and the silence. I love the birds and the trees along the creeks, and the way the screen door bangs.'

She glanced at Nat, half-defiant, half shame-faced. 'That's why it bothers me so much that I don't belong, why I wish so much that I could. Does that sound stupid?'

'No, it doesn't sound stupid.' He turned his head and smiled at her, a warm smile that illuminated his quiet face and left Prue oddly startled, even breathless, at the transformation.

'It doesn't sound stupid at all,' he said again. 'That's the way I feel about the outback, too.'

'Really?'

Slewing round as far as she could in her seat-belt, Prue studied Nat with new interest. She had never taken much notice of him before, beyond registering his air of unhurried calm, but now she looked at him properly and was surprised at what she saw.

It wasn't that he was handsome, at least not in the way Ross was handsome. His hair was an indeterminate shade of brown, his eyes were brown—in fact, everything about him seemed to be brown. Brown skin, brown watch, strong brown hands on the wheel. He was even wearing a brown shirt.

But still, there was *something* about him. It was more to do with his air of quiet self-assurance than any particular arrangement of his features, Prue decided. If he wasn't so understated, he might even be quite attractive. His colouring might not be very obvious, but there was nothing indeterminate about that lean jaw, or the angles of his face, or the cool, firm mouth that had smiled with such astonishing effect.

Prue's eyes rested on it speculatively. It was a pity Nat didn't smile more often, she thought, remembering how white his teeth were, the way his eyes had crinkled at the corners and the creases had deepened in his cheeks, and for some reason a tiny, almost imperceptible tingle tip-toed down her spine and made her shiver.

Puzzled by her silence, Nat looked across to check that she was all right and their eyes met for a brief instant. There was nothing in his expression to suggest that he was aware of how closely she had been studying him, but Prue felt a blush steal up her cheeks and she jerked her gaze away.

'You're lucky,' she muttered, averting her face and conscious of a quite inexplicable feeling of shyness. 'You belong here. You don't have to go to London and wonder if you'll ever see the outback again.'

Nat didn't answer immediately. A road train was bearing down on them, and he lifted a hand to acknowledge the driver's wave as it thundered past with four long trailers.

'You'll just have to come back after the wedding,' he said when it had gone, able to put his foot down on the accelerator at last. 'The Grangers will still be here, and I'm sure they'd give you another job.'

'I'm not sure I'll be able to do that.' Prue had recovered from her momentary confusion. 'It took me ages to save the money for this trip, and I've spent it all now. If I wanted to buy another ticket, I'd have to start all over again.'

'Couldn't you do that?'

'I could, but by the time I'd got enough money together I'd probably be too old to get a work permit—and even if I wasn't, they would have had to have found a new cook for Cowen Creek.'

What was the betting that the next cook would be young, and pretty, and completely at home in the outback? Just the type to convince Ross that it was time to settle down, in fact. Desperation clutched at Prue's heart as she imagined coming back to find that Ross had given up waiting for her to get used to the bush and married someone much more suitable instead.

'So what you need,' said Nat, following his own train of thought, 'is a short-term job that will pay you enough to cover your fare back to Australia?'

Prue nodded. 'Except I'll probably need at least two jobs in order to save anything. I could get some office work during the day and waitress in the evenings, and if I stay with my parents I won't have to pay London rents, which would make a difference. It'll be all right if it's not for too long,' she tried to convince herself.

It would still take months before she could get back to Australia, she calculated in despair, and she sighed. 'Perhaps I could rob a bank or something!'

'What about a job that paid your flight back to Australia instead?'

'I can't see there being many of *those* advertised in the jobs pages,' said Prue glumly. 'Robbing a bank would be easier than finding a job like that. I might as well think about sprouting wings and flying back myself!'

'You shouldn't be so negative,' said Nat. 'Do you know anything about babies?'

Prue was momentarily thrown by the sudden change of subject. 'Babies?' she echoed uncertainly. 'As in very small people, dirty nappies and sleepless nights?'

Nat grimaced. 'It sounds as if you *do* know about them,' he said in a dry voice.

'I spent a lot of time with my elder sister's children when they were tiny. I've always loved babies,' she told him. 'They're a lot of work, but they're so gorgeous and...'

She broke off, belatedly realising why he might be asking and sat bolt upright to turn to him, her face suddenly alight with excitement. 'You don't know anyone who wants a nanny, do you?'

'Yes,' said Nat, nodding and the corner of his mouth lifted in a slight smile. '*I* do.'

CHAPTER TWO

PRUE'S grey eyes widened. 'You've got children?'

There was no reason why he shouldn't, of course, but she couldn't help feeling surprised. He seemed so self-contained that it was hard to imagine him with a wife amid the cheerful chaos of family life.

What would Nat's wife be like? Prue wondered. Probably as cool and sensible as he was himself. Certainly not the kind of woman who would forget to put fuel in the car, or cry, or pour out her heart to a virtual stranger, she decided, and felt unaccountably depressed.

'I'm going to have two.' Nat's smile was a little twisted as he thought about how much his life was going to change.

'Going to…?'

Glancing sideways, Nat caught her puzzled expression. 'They're not mine,' he explained. 'I'm talking about my brother's children, William and Daisy. They're twins, just eight months old and I'm their guardian now.' He paused. 'Ed and his wife were killed in a car accident in England a couple of months ago.'

Shocked, Prue pressed her hand to her mouth. 'How terrible,' she said, conscious of how inadequate her words sounded.

'I thought you might have heard about the accident,' said Nat after a moment. 'The Grangers knew Ed and Laura pretty well. They bought a property just to the east of Cowen Creek last year, and they'd help each other out on big musters sometimes.'

Prue shook her head. 'I didn't know,' she said. She had been too wrapped up in Ross to take any interest in the Grangers' neighbours she realised, ashamed. 'I'm so sorry,' she went on, biting her lip. 'What were they doing in England?'

'Laura was English, like you. Ed met her when he was over in London, but they married out here. Laura loved the outback, too, and she was quite happy to live here but she felt guilty about her parents. They're quite elderly, and couldn't manage the trip out to Australia, so they hadn't been at the wedding. When the twins were born, she knew they would be longing to see their grand-children and Ed promised that he would take her and the babies to London for a visit instead.

'That was in April,' Nat went on. 'It's a busy time of year, but Ed knew how much it would mean to Laura, so he asked me to keep an eye on things while he was gone. He said they would only be a month.'

The careful lack of expression in his voice made Prue's heart twist with pity, and she cringed as she remembered how she had whinged on about her own problems which were so pathetic in comparison to his.

'What happened?' she asked awkwardly.

'They'd been in London three weeks when Laura's parents offered to look after the twins for a day so that she and Ed could have some time to themselves. It was the first time they'd left William and Daisy. Apparently it was a nice day, and they decided to drive out to the country...'

He trailed off, and Prue found herself imagining Ed and Laura kissing the babies goodbye, waving cheerfully as they got into the car and drove off, looking forward to a day together alone away from the city's noise and grime. Not knowing that they would never be coming back.

'They were in a head-on collision with a van,' Nat finished. 'The police told us that they would have both been killed instantly.'

'But the babies weren't with them?'

'No, they were with Laura's parents so they're fine.' As fine as they could be when their world had been torn apart, Nat amended grimly to himself.

He was very grateful to Prue for not offering false comfort or asking him how he had felt, what he was still feeling. He didn't want to talk about that.

'Where are they now?' asked Prue, almost as if she understood intuitively that he was happier sticking to the practicalities of the situation he had to deal with now.

'They're still with Laura's parents in London,' he said. 'I went over as soon as I heard. Ed and Laura wanted William and Daisy to grow up as Australians, and they knew that her parents would be in no position to look after them, so they'd made a will appointing me as guardian. I don't think they thought for a minute that anything would ever happen to them, that I would ever need to take responsibility for their children.'

'But now that's what you've got to do?'

'Yes.' His glance flickered over to Prue. She had turned slightly in her seat to face him as far as she could in the confines of her seatbelt, her expression warm and sympathetic. 'There was no way I could bring William and Daisy back with me after the funeral,' he told her, and he found himself hoping that she would understand and approve of what he had done. 'I arranged for a nanny to look after them with the Ashcrofts—Laura's parents—until I could sort things out here and make sure that I would be able to care for them properly, but I think it's important for me to go and get them as soon as possible.'

Prue nodded understandingly. 'The longer you leave them, the more attached they will become to the nanny and the harder it will be to take them away.'

'Exactly.' Nat looked at her gratefully. 'The trouble is, I'm going to need help. I don't know anything about babies. I'm not sure I would be able to cope with one baby on a plane, let alone two. That's where you come in,' he said. 'I think we may be able to help each other. You want to come back to Australia; I want someone to help me look after William and Daisy. I'll buy you a return ticket if you'll fly back with me and the twins,' he finished.

For a moment, Prue could only stare at him, unable to believe that he could sound so casual. 'That's... incredibly generous,' she stammered, not entirely convinced that he knew what a generous offer it was.

'Not if you think about how much I need you,' said Nat with a wry glance. 'I can put a mob of cattle through the yards, and do all those things that you said you wanted to be able to do earlier, but I don't know where to begin with a baby! If you come, you're going to have to teach me how to feed them and change them and bath them and do all the other things they need. Could you do that?'

'Well, yes, I suppose so, but—'

'It's not just a question of the flight either. Eve, the nanny who's looking after William and Daisy at the moment, thinks that it would be upsetting for them to be suddenly taken away from everything that's familiar. They won't remember Australia now. She suggested that I spend a few weeks getting to know them before bringing them back, and it would make sense for you to come along too.'

'I can see that,' said Prue, nodding. 'They would need to get used to being with us.'

'And then there's the Ashcrofts,' said Nat. 'They were too distressed to talk much when I was there for the funeral, but they'll probably want to see who's going to be bringing their grandchildren up.'

'How do they feel about you taking William and Daisy away?' Prue tried to imagine her own parents in a similar situation. 'Don't they mind?' she asked curiously.

Nat thought about it. 'I think they know they can't manage the twins on their own,' he said at length. 'Losing Laura was a terrible blow for them—she was their only child—and it's hard enough for them to cope as it is, without the worry of bringing up children. That doesn't mean they're not concerned, of course,' he added, noting with one part of his mind a plane's wing glinting in the sun as it turned. The airport was just ahead, which meant that it wasn't far to Mathison, and he wanted Prue to understand the situation before they got there.

'They've never been to Australia, and the outback sounds a very strange place to them. They were worried about the fact that William and Daisy will be isolated, and that as a bachelor I wouldn't be able to look after them properly, but they were all right when I told them that I was engaged, and that the twins would grow up in a family. I said that the next time I came I'd bring my fiancée with me so that they could meet her too.'

There was a pause. 'I didn't know you were engaged,' said Prue after a moment, and wondered why her voice sounded so hollow all of a sudden.

Or why she was even surprised.

There was no reason why Nat shouldn't be engaged,

just as there had been no reason why he shouldn't have a wife and children. It was just that, having established that he *wasn't* married, she had somehow assumed that he never would be. And if he had a fiancée, why did he need *her* to help him with William and Daisy?

'I was then,' said Nat, answering one of her unspoken questions as she stole a puzzled look at him. His voice had no inflexion whatsoever and it was impossible to tell how he felt about the fact that his engagement apparently belonged to the past.

'I'm not any more,' he added when Prue continued to look blank.

In one way, it made it easier for Nat that she knew nothing about Kathryn, but a perverse part of him couldn't help wishing that she hadn't made it quite so obvious that she had never taken the slightest interest in him. He was surprised that she had even known his name.

'You obviously didn't know that either,' he commented dryly.

'No.' Prue shook her head. 'The Grangers don't go in much for gossip,' she said. 'I'm sorry,' she added, and then realised that she sounded as if she regretted not knowing about the break-up of his engagement. 'I mean, I'm sorry about your engagement.'

'Don't be,' said Nat. They were driving past the airport now, where he had said goodbye to Kathryn before she'd got on the plane back to Perth. He remembered the softness of her kiss, the swing of her hair as she'd turned, the unmistakable relief in the way she'd walked away.

'It was a mutual decision,' he told Prue. 'Kathryn and I have known each other a long time. She's got a good job in Perth, and we'd deliberately decided on a long engagement so that she could concentrate on a big project she's working on at the moment. When I got back from

London I realised that it wasn't fair to ask her to give everything up to look after two small children, so we talked about it and agreed to...postpone...the idea of marriage for the time being. It's better this way for both of us.'

He didn't sound bitter, but Prue had the impression that he was picking his words carefully, editing as he went along. He could say what he liked about it being a mutual decision, but he was obviously still besotted by her, she decided, unsure why she felt slightly peeved at the idea. Why else would make excuses for her?

She found herself disliking the unknown Kathryn intensely, and feeling obscurely cross with Nat at the same time. He *ought* to mind that his fiancée had chosen her job over him.

'It's not really better for you, though, is it?' she said, more sharply than she had intended. 'How are you going to look after the twins on your own?'

If Nat was surprised at her tone, he didn't show it. 'I'll have to hire a nanny,' he said. 'I asked Eve if she would think about coming out to Australia with William and Daisy, even if only for the first few weeks, but I've just had a letter from her saying that she's getting married and doesn't want to leave England.'

Prue couldn't imagine anyone turning down the chance to travel to Australia, marriage or no marriage. Ahead, the heat beat down on the road, creating a wavering mirage that blurred the horizon between the crushing blue sky and the sparse scrub that stretched off as far as the eye could see and beyond. It was like being in a different dimension altogether—so much space and so much light that Prue would sometimes feel dizzy and disembodied.

How could anyone *not* want to be here? Prue shook her head pityingly.

She brought her attention back to Nat, who was talking about the arrangements he would have to make. 'I've contacted a couple of agencies here to see if anyone would be prepared to travel to London with me and help bring William and Daisy back. Ideally, it would be someone who wanted to stay at Mack River on a permanent basis, but they haven't come up with anyone yet. That's why I thought of you,' he said, glancing at Prue. 'When you said how much you wanted to come back to Australia, it seemed you could be just the person I need. I know you wouldn't want to stay permanently, but it might take me some time to find someone suitable. You could stay at Mack River while you looked for another job in the area, if that's what you want. You'd only be gone about a month. The Grangers might even keep your job open for you.'

Prue sat up straighter, fired up by the mere possibility. 'I could ask them,' she agreed excitedly. 'They'll need to replace me while I'm away, but maybe they'll get someone who doesn't want to stay.'

'More than likely,' said Nat. 'There's always a high turnover of staff during the dry season. It's too hot, or too isolated, or too boring, or too much like hard work.

'There aren't many people like you,' he told Prue with a slight smile, and she found herself wishing that he'd smile the way he had smiled before.

It wouldn't take much, just a deepening of the creases on either side of his mouth, just a parting of the lips, just a crinkling of his eyes. She remembered how startled she had been, the way her heart had jolted, that odd sensation of suddenly finding herself face to face with a stranger.

For some reason, Prue's cheeks were tingling, and when she put up a hand to feel her skin she realised that she was actually blushing! Embarrassed, without knowing why, she dragged her eyes away from Nat's mouth, which had lifted into something that was almost—but not quite—a proper smile, and forced her mind back to what they had been talking about.

For a terrible moment her mind was blank, before memory kicked in. Going back to Cowen Creek...how could she possibly have forgotten?

Giving herself a mental shake, Prue let herself picture the situation. If she went back, Ross would know that she was serious about wanting to live in the outback. He would realise that she meant what she said, and wasn't just amusing herself for a few months, the way the girls who saw a stint on a cattle station as part of travelling around Australia did.

Nat's offer would mean that she would only be gone for a month or so. Surely even Ross couldn't forget her in that time? He might even miss her. The thought flickered into life, grew stronger. Didn't they say that absence made the heart grow fonder?

Prue slid a sideways glance at Nat from under her lashes. He was a bit older, of course, and not in Ross's league when it came to looks, but he wasn't *un*attractive. What would Ross think when he found out that she was going to spend a month with Nat? Might he even be jealous? Prue wondered hopefully.

Remembering how miserable she had been less than an hour ago, Prue smiled to herself. 'I'm beginning to think that forgetting to check the fuel today was the best thing that ever happened to me,' she said slowly.

'Does that mean you'll take the job?'

'I'd love it,' said Prue honestly, 'but...well, I don't have *that* much experience of babies. Wouldn't you rather have someone more qualified?' She grimaced, thinking of the catalogue of stupid mistakes she had made just since she had been at Cowen Creek, let alone the rest of her life. 'Someone more efficient?'

Nat took his eyes off the road for a moment to look at her, with her unruly curls and her wide, tilting mouth and the nose that was just a little too big. 'I'd rather have someone like you,' he said.

He didn't know how to explain that there was a warmth about her that was much more appealing than efficiency. He might not be able to imagine her keeping an immaculately tidy house, but he could picture her holding a baby in her arms, offering unlimited tenderness and security and love.

A little too vividly, in fact.

Nat frowned and concentrated on his driving once more. 'You're a nice girl,' he said gruffly. 'The Grangers like you. You love the outback and you want to come back. Those are all good enough reasons as far as I'm concerned. And then, you need to go to London just when I do...'

'You could almost say that we're meant for each other!' Prue finished for him cheerfully.

A tiny pause.

We're meant for each other. Her words echoed in the silence between them, and she suddenly realised how easily Nat might have misinterpreted them.

'I mean...job-wise,' she added uncomfortably.

Nat flashed her an enigmatic look. 'What else?' he said in a dry voice.

Nobody could say that Mathison was a pretty town, but Prue loved the old hotel, with its wide, wooden verandahs, the great iron water-tanks beside every house, and the pokey general store which had a weird and wonderful selection of goods and an eccentric taste in displays. Prue perked up as they drove along the wide street.

She had hated the thought that she might never see it again, of returning to soulless supermarkets where everything was wrapped in layers of plastic.

Now, thanks to Nat, she could stop worrying about whether every trip would be her last and just enjoy being here. Oh, and do the shopping, of course.

Nat dropped her at the store while he went off to find some fuel. Prue still had her list, although it was so creased from being folded and unfolded so much that she could hardly read it. It was better than nothing, though. Wandering around the store, Prue found it harder to concentrate on the shopping than she would have thought. She had to keep stopping and peering at the tattered piece of paper, while her mind drifted back to Nat and the fantastic offer that he had made.

The more Prue thought about it, the better it seemed. There was no way she could miss Cleo's wedding, but it had been hard not to resent the fact that she would have to leave Australia much earlier than she had originally intended. Now she would not only be a good sister, but she should also be able to spend another whole year here, and who knew what could happen in that time?

Prue could hardly believe her luck. Her momentary embarrassment had passed, and now all she could think about was how everything was turning out better than she would have believed possible. No wonder it was hard to concentrate on how much flour and sugar she needed!

She was coming back. Prue hugged the knowledge to her. Coming back to this place she loved so much.

And to Ross.

Prue's heart melted when she thought about the daredevil blue of his eyes, about the way he threw his head back when he laughed and the air of suppressed energy he carried around with him, and happiness bubbled along

her veins. Surely meeting Nat meant that she and Ross
were destined for each other after all?

When Nat found her, Prue was gazing at a pyramid of
tinned vegetables, her mouth curved in a dreamy smile.
Her sunglasses were pushed on top of her head, drawing
the tousled hair away from her face, and even in the dim
old-fashioned light of the store Nat could see that her
grey eyes were shining.

There had been a moment in the ute when something
had tightened in the air between them, but whatever it
had been it had gone now. Nat could tell just by the way
Prue smiled when she saw him, a wide, open smile that
said more clearly than words ever could that she might
think of him as a friend, or an employer, but certainly
not as a man.

Which was just as well, in the circumstances, Nat told
himself.

'You look happy,' he said.

'I am.' Prue beamed at him. 'I was just standing here,
thinking about how miserable I was when I set out this
afternoon. I was convinced that I would never have a
chance to persuade Ross to love me, that I'd have to go
home and never see him again. When that car ran out of
fuel. I just sat there and bawled my eyes out,' she confessed. 'I was really pathetic! And then—' she spread her
hands '—you came along and suddenly everything is
possible again.'

She looked at Nat with her frank eyes. 'I feel as if
today is going to prove to be the turning point of my
whole life,' she told him, 'and it's all thanks to you.'

Her face was alight with happiness, and Nat was suddenly aware of how close she was standing. She was so
warm, he thought, so vibrant, so open and uncomplicated.

So in love with Ross Granger.

He stepped away from her, unsettled to realise that he didn't want her thanks. 'Are you ready?' he asked curtly.

'Yes, the boxes are by the door.'

Prue was puzzled and a little hurt by his brusqueness as they carried the boxes of groceries out to the ute. The light hit her like a blow as she stepped out of the shade of the verandah, and she couldn't wait to hand over her box so that she could pull her sunglasses back down onto her nose.

Nat didn't seem to notice at all. None of the men she had met wore sunglasses, relying on their hats to protect them from the glare instead, she supposed, but the corners of their eyes were always creased from years of squinting into the sun. Prue could see the fan of lines at the edge of Nat's eyes now as he loaded the boxes into the back of the ute and covered them with a tarpaulin to keep out the dust.

Looking at those lines gave her a funny feeling inside—either that, or the sun was getting to her—and her gaze dropped to his mouth, which was set in a bleak line that made her frown slightly.

His expression was closed, shuttered even. Of course, Nat would be an unemotional man at the best of times, but he hadn't been like this when they drove in together. She remembered how he had smiled, the look in his eyes when he had said, 'I want someone like you.'

It was as if he had withdrawn into himself since then. As if, Prue thought slowly, her bubbling enthusiasm had made him retreat behind a barrier of impenetrable reserve. As if he didn't like her being happy.

And why should he?

Prue felt a sickening wave of shame roll over her. She had forgotten what the trip to London was going to mean for Nat. For her, the job he had offered her meant the possibility of romance, a chance to achieve her heart's desire. For him, it meant only the aftermath of tragedy.

'I'm sorry,' she said in a small voice as she got into the ute beside him.

Nat was bending to push the key into the ignition, but at her apology he straightened in surprise. 'Sorry?' he echoed blankly. 'What for?'

'I must sound absolutely heartless, wittering on about Ross and coming back to Australia when all you're thinking about is your brother.' Prue pulled the seatbelt around her and fastened it into place before turning contritely to Nat. 'It's going to be a terrible trip for you, I can see that. I wish you'd just told me to shut up,' she said in a burst of honesty. 'I feel *awful* now!'

Nat's expression was rueful as he started the engine and pushed up the gearstick on the steering column. He hadn't been thinking about Ed at all, he thought wryly. He had been thinking about her.

'You mustn't think like that,' he said, contrite in his turn. 'It's the last thing Ed would have wanted, or Laura either come to that. They were both real live-wires, and they believed in deciding what you want and going for it.

'They'd approve of you doing whatever you could to get back to Ross,' he told Prue. 'You don't need to feel guilty about being happy over the fact that I need you to help me with William and Daisy. Ed would be the first person cheering you on!'

His voice was warm when he talked about his brother. 'You must miss him,' said Prue quietly.

Nat hesitated. He wasn't used to discussing his feelings, but somehow it was easy to talk to Prue.

'Yes,' he admitted. 'I do. I miss him a lot. Ed was only a couple of years younger than me, and there were just the two of us when we were growing up. We ran Mack River together when our parents died, and then Ed met Laura, and they bought their own property. I'd got used to them not being around every day, but still…it's hard sometimes to believe I won't see him again.'

He wasn't looking at Prue, but she felt her throat tighten. 'I'm sorry,' she said again, knowing that it was inadequate, but knowing too that there was nothing else to say.

Nat's smile was rather twisted. 'I'm sorry too,' he said slowly, 'but it's William and Daisy who matter now. I've got to think about them, not Ed, and that's what I'm going to do.'

When they got back to Prue's car, they transferred the groceries into the back, and then Nat took the can of fuel he had bought and poured it carefully into the tank. He had brushed aside Prue's attempts to pay and she watched him, feeling helpless and more than a little disconcerted to discover how easy it was to accept being looked after by someone so competent.

It was difficult to imagine that barely two hours ago she had had trouble remembering his name. Already there was something very familiar about him. How much more familiar would he be after they'd spent almost a month together in London?

The thought was vaguely disconcerting, and Prue frowned. It wasn't as if they were going to be intimate, she reassured herself. It was just a job like any other. And Nat was hardly likely to show any interest in *her*, was he?

Even if she hadn't been in love with Ross, she would have little to appeal to a man like Nat. He was quite a bit older than her, for a start, and to him she probably seemed very young and very silly. Correction, thought

Prue, cringing inwardly as she remembered some of the things she had said: she must *definitely* seem very young and very silly.

Anyway, Nat himself had sounded far from over his broken engagement. Prue couldn't help wondering what Kathryn was like. What kind of woman could break through that quiet self-containment and unlock his reserve? She must be quite special, Prue decided.

Hidden behind her sunglasses, her gaze rested on Nat as he tipped the can higher to let the last drops of diesel trickle into the tank and she tried to imagine him in love. He wasn't a demonstrative man, she guessed, but behind closed doors...well, that might be a different matter...

'OK, that's it.' Nat's voice broke into her thoughts as he dumped the empty can in the back of the ute. 'Start her up and we'll see if she goes now.'

Obediently, Prue climbed into the driver's seat and turned the key. The engine shuddered into life and then settled down to a steady tick.

'Do you ever get a day off?' Nat asked, laying a hand on the roof of the car and bending his head slightly so that he could talk to her through the open window.

'I don't do much on Sundays. Why?'

'We still need to sort out a few details about this trip,' he pointed out. 'I could fly over and pick you up next Sunday and you could spend the day at Mack Creek. It might not be a bad idea for you to see where the twins are going to grow up anyway, and we could talk about things then. It would give you a chance to think about what's involved too, and change your mind if you want to. How does that sound?'

'Fine,' said Prue. 'But aren't you coming to Cowen Creek now? I thought you wanted to see Bill Granger?'

'It can wait.' Nat didn't think he really wanted to go

to Cowen Creek now and watch Prue mooning over Ross. 'I think I'll get back.'

His face through the window was very close, and his features seemed uncannily clear and detailed. Prue felt as if she could see every crease at the corner of his eyes, every minute line texturing his skin, every hair that grew in the strong brown brows. She wanted to look away, but her gaze seemed to have snagged in his somehow.

'What shall I tell the Grangers?' she managed to ask.

'Just say that you met me in Mathison,' said Nat. 'There's no need to tell them about the fuel. You could say that we got talking and when I found out that you were going to London, I offered you the job. They know about Ed and Laura and the fact that I'm guardian to the twins now, so they probably won't even be surprised.'

'Right,' said Prue, finally succeeding in wrenching her eyes away. She put the car into gear and cleared her throat. 'I'll see you on Sunday, then.'

She had the impression that Nat was about to say something else, but in the end he just stepped back, slapping the car roof in a gesture of farewell.

'See you on Sunday,' was all he said.

CHAPTER THREE

IN THE event, it was Ross who flew Prue to Mack River the following Sunday.

'He was going to Mathison anyway,' Prue found herself explaining to Nat as together they watched Ross's Cessna speed down the airstrip and lift up into the blue. He dipped his wings in farewell and headed off in the direction of the town, leaving the two of them alone together in the crushing silence of the bush.

'It seemed silly for you to come all the way over to Cowen Creek when he could give me a lift here just as easily, but if you could fly me back that would be great.'

She could hear herself babbling, but she was unaccountably shy now that she was suddenly face to face with Nat again. She had forgotten how still he was, how quietly assured, how self-conscious he made her feel.

It was stupid to think that she needed to explain anything, anyway. Even if she hadn't already outlined the situation when she'd phoned to say that Ross would bring her over to Mack River, Nat hadn't said anything to indicate that he cared one way or another *how* she got there.

His greeting had been quite impersonal, as if she were no more than a temporary nanny he was employing to look after his small niece and nephew—which was all she was, of course. There had been no reason for Prue's heart to bump against her ribs when she caught sight of him through the plane window. He had been leaning against the ute in the shade, arms folded and long legs crossed at the ankle, his hat tilted down over his eyes as he waited for Ross to bring the plane to a halt.

He had straightened as she approached, pushing his hat back and smiling that slow smile that she remembered with such unnerving clarity, and for some reason Prue had burst into speech. Now, she made herself shut up.

'I thought you'd be glad of a chance to spend some time with Ross,' Nat commented, holding open the door of the ute for her.

'Yes,' said Prue, hearing the slight doubt in her voice too late. She *had* been glad, of course, but her pleasure in the flight had been rather spoiled by her nervousness at seeing Nat again and broaching the idea that had come to her as she had driven back to Cowen Creek that day.

Still, it had been a great flight. She thought about Ross, the magnetism of his presence, the flashing smile as they'd swooped down over the bush, his eyes as blue as the sky around them. Remembering, Prue felt better.

'It was wonderful,' she told Nat, as if he had doubted her.

He got in beside her and switched on the engine. 'How does Ross feel about you coming back?'

'I think he's pleased,' said Prue cautiously.

It was clear Ross had no intention of committing himself to anything, but she was sure that there had been a definite warming in his attitude towards her since she had told him about the job Nat had offered her.

Of course, it might be wishful thinking, Prue reminded herself. It might just be that Ross was relieved to hear that she was really going and was only being so nice because he knew that she wouldn't be around for much longer.

She wished that she could have said that he was jealous of her spending a month in Nat's company, but none of the Grangers seemed to think that there was any chance—any *danger*, Prue corrected herself hastily—of Nat treating her as anything other than a nanny. They were united in believing that Kathryn would marry him in the end and that temporary help with the children was all that Nat would need. It would certainly never occur to any of them that he could ever be interested in any other woman.

'Nat's a one-woman man,' Ross had explained. 'He's adored Kathryn ever since they were kids. Everyone knew they would end up together eventually.'

'What's she like?' Prue had been unable to resist asking.

'Kathryn? She's great. Beautiful girl.' Ross narrowed his eyes appreciatively. 'Red hair, green eyes, legs that go on for ever and a smile that makes the sun look dim! She's bright too. She's got some kind of fancy job down in Perth.'

Prue didn't think he had to sound quite so enthusiastic about her. 'If she's that amazing, what's she doing with Nat?' she asked a little too tartly. 'I'd have thought he'd have been too down-to-earth for someone like Kathryn.'

Ross shrugged, obviously not seeing anything odd in the relationship at all, and it was Joyce Granger who offered an answer when she was helping Prue to wash up.

'Nat's always been able to manage Kathryn,' she said shrewdly. 'He's the only one who could. She was a very headstrong girl, but so pretty that her parents spoilt her rotten and let her do whatever she wanted. I think she needs Nat to keep her in line.'

'But if she needs him so much, why would she break off their engagement?'

'Kathryn's used to Nat looking after *her*. I think she

lost her nerve at the thought that she was going to have to take second place for a while and help him care for Ed's children, but she'll be back when she gets used to the idea,' Joyce added comfortably.

Prue scrubbed the bottom of a saucepan with unnecessary vigour. 'What if Nat won't take her back?'

'Oh, Nat will take her back all right.' Joyce finished drying a plate and put it on top of the pile. 'He'll never love anyone but Kathryn. Those two are meant for each other.'

Prue was still thinking about this exchange now, as Nat drove along the bumpy track from the airstrip to the homestead. She slid a covert glance at him from under her lashes and had to admit that he didn't look as if he were broken-hearted. Joyce Granger must be right. If he wasn't miserable, it was because he was quite confident that Kathryn would come back to him.

Which meant that her idea wouldn't work.

It had come to her when Cleo's letter had arrived two days ago, a flash of inspiration to solve her problem and Nat's, but if he were expecting Kathryn back at any minute, it might not work after all.... Prue chewed the edge of her thumb, considering. Perhaps it would be better to stick to being a nanny, and not mention the matter to Nat?

The homestead was a low, rambling house, sheltered on all sides by deep verandahs. Having been in the outback long enough to appreciate how precious the sight of water could be, Prue was disappointed to find that it wasn't right by the river that gave the station its name, but when she asked Nat why the homestead wasn't closer, Nat only laughed.

'You don't want to be anywhere near the river when

it's in flood,' he said. 'My grandfather knew what he was doing when he built the house here.'

In spite of the lack of a river view, Prue thought it was a wonderful house, cool and shady inside and set in an oasis of green. Bougainvillea scrambled over the front verandah, and a cluster of palms at the back gave the place a tropical, almost exotic feel, although it was clearly a long time since anyone had made gardening a priority.

Lunch proved to be a barbecue with the stockmen, a polite but taciturn group of men who eyed Prue curiously. She could tell they didn't think much of her. Every time she opened her mouth, she sounded more brittle and English and out of place, and she was secretly relieved when they disappeared to their own quarters and left her alone with Nat.

She helped him clear away the lunch dishes, and then Nat sent her out to sit on the back verandah while he made some coffee. She sat, enjoying the green shade and imagining what a restful place to live Mack River must be, with its tangled garden and its worn wooden floors and its air of masculine, faintly shabby comfort.

The homestead at Cowen Creek was very busy and functional in comparison, Prue couldn't help thinking. Of course, Ross lived there, and it was exciting just to be in his orbit, but sometimes it was quite exhausting to spend your day on tenterhooks, never knowing if the sound of the screen door meant that he was going to suddenly appear and bracing yourself for the crashing disappointment when someone else appeared instead.

No, living with Ross couldn't be said to be restful. But Mack River...Prue ran her hands appreciatively along the arms of the old wicker chair and gazed out at the garden…this was nice. Cool and calm and comfortable. A bit like Nat himself, in fact.

She smiled at the thought, and Nat, carrying two mugs of coffee, paused just behind the screen door.

He could see her quite clearly through the fine mesh as she sat and gazed dreamily out at the garden, her mouth curved in a secretive smile. She was wearing jeans and a pale pink shirt, and her unruly brown curls were pushed anyhow behind her ears. Nat thought that she looked relaxed and happy and disturbingly at home on his verandah.

What was she smiling about so dreamily? Ross, no doubt. Nat remembered the proprietorial way Ross had helped Prue down from the plane, and thought that the Grangers' son was a lot keener than she had admitted. She was probably planning her return to Cowen Creek already, imagining the scene where Ross swept her into his arms and vowed never to let her go again.

Nat scowled, and then wondered what he was doing. He ought to be glad for Prue's sake that Ross was showing more interest in her. Ross was the only reason that she was prepared to go to London and help him bring William and Daisy home. She wasn't doing it for *him*, Nat reminded himself. It would be a mistake to forget that.

Abruptly, he kicked the screen door open and its hinges creaked in protest. The sound made Prue jump, and she turned to see Nat coming towards her with a mug in each hand. His expression was not grim exactly, but somehow remote, and Prue was conscious of a feeling of disappointment. She had thought they had been getting on quite well.

'This is lovely,' she said politely, gesturing at the garden. If they were going to spend a month together, she had better get used to filling the silence. 'I'd like to sit here for ever!'

The thought crossed Nat's mind that he wouldn't mind her staying there for ever either, but he quashed it firmly. She was just being polite. The only way she would ever want to stay at Mack River was if Ross could be there too.

'I'm glad you like it,' he said distantly, and handed her one of the mugs.

Deliberately choosing the chair separated from hers by a small table, he sat down and leant forward, resting his arms on his knees so that he could cradle his own mug between his hands.

Somewhat daunted, Prue sipped her coffee and sought around for something else to say. In the end, the best she could manage was to thank him for lunch.

At least she could see a gleam of amusement in Nat's eyes as he glanced across at her. 'I don't think it will have been up to your standards!' he said. 'I've got a married man working here, and his wife cooks for us during the week, but, like you, she has a day off on Sunday and we have to look out for ourselves. We're not very adventurous when it comes to food, as you probably gathered!'

'I enjoyed it,' said Prue honestly. 'It's a real treat to eat anything I haven't cooked myself now!'

'The Grangers are going to miss you.' Nat looked back at the palms and tried not to sound too interested. 'Are they keeping your job open for you?'

'No.' Prue shook her head. 'They said they were sorry, but I told them when I arrived that I'd have to go back to London, and they've already promised another English girl that she can come and cook. She's a friend of a friend, I think, and she's already made arrangements to travel up from Adelaide.'

Nat frowned slightly. 'Do you still want to come back to Australia, in that case?'

'I'd rather go back to Cowen Creek, of course, but if that's not possible…well, maybe I could find another job in the district. It might even be better if I *wasn't* at Cowen Creek,' she went on thoughtfully, almost as if she were talking to herself. 'It can be awkward with us both living in the same house with his parents, and if I was working somewhere else Ross might not feel the same kind of pressure.'

Nat found it hard to believe that Ross knew what pressure was, but there was no point in saying that to Prue. She was obviously still obsessed with him. 'I haven't found a suitable nanny yet,' he said out loud. 'I'll need help with William and Daisy when I get back here and you could stay on, if you liked. Just until you found something better,' he added quickly, in case Prue thought he *wanted* her to stay. 'It wouldn't be anything permanent.'

Obviously not, thought Prue. Why would he want a permanent nanny when he was counting on Kathryn to help him look after William and Daisy? They would be a proper family then, and they wouldn't want any English nannies hanging around, invading their privacy and envying them their comfortable old homestead and cool garden.

Still, if Nat wanted to place all his faith in a girl who had already let him down once, that was his problem. Prue sat up a little straighter in her chair and pushed her hair away from her face with unconscious defiance. All *she* wanted was to be near Ross, and Nat's offer would at least mean that she had somewhere to go when she got

back to Australia. She would find something more suitable later.

'That sounds great,' she said.

'Then, if we're agreed, I'll book the flights next week,'
said Nat. 'When is your sister's wedding?'

'August the twenty-first, but I should really be in
London a week before that. Cleo wants me to be a bridesmaid,' Prue remembered gloomily, 'and I suppose I'll
have to make sure the dress fits and all that kind of thing.'

'You don't sound as if you're looking forward to it
very much,' Nat commented drily. 'I thought women
liked weddings?'

'I don't mind them if they're small, and everybody
knows each other, but this isn't going to be like that. Cleo
is determined to have a traditional wedding with all the
trimmings. At least I'll have missed most of the run-up,'
she tried to console herself. 'Judging by their letters,
Mum and Cleo are totally obsessed with all the arrangements, and my elder sister will be in there too, and they'll
all be arguing!'

Prue sighed. It wasn't the main reason she was dreading Cleo's wedding now, but it was bad enough. She
sipped morosely at her coffee.

'Cleo and Alex are both super-successful, and all the
other guests will be like them. I'll just be Cleo's odd
sister who doesn't have a career or a mortgage, and no
one will know what to say to me!'

Nat couldn't help laughing at her glum expression.
'I'm sure it won't be that bad!'

There was that smile of his again. Prue blinked as her
heart gave an odd little somersault and landed with a thud
that left her with a strange, breathless feeling. She looked
away.

'Well, anyway,' she said, clearing her throat, 'I'll be

free to help you with William and Daisy any time after the twenty-first.'

'We might as well fly over to London together in that case,' said Nat, and Prue was obscurely grateful to him for sounding so practical. 'While you're getting ready for the wedding, I can spend some time with the Ashcrofts. There are several things I need to sort out with them before the twins can come back to Australia.'

It would be a pretty grim week for him, Prue guessed. She would much rather help him through it than listen to heated debates about who would be wearing what, and which kind of canapés to serve at the reception.

'Are you going to stay with the Ashcrofts?' she asked him, turning slightly in her chair to face him over the table. It was a shame that she could only look at him when they were talking about practical arrangements and she could be sure that he wasn't going to startle her with a smile.

'No.' Nat put his mug down on the table and leant back in his chair with a grimace at the thought of the trip ahead of him. 'They haven't got that big a house, and with the twins and a nanny living with them they haven't got any extra room. In any case, I think having me to stay on top of everything else they have to deal with would be too much for them.'

'What are you going to do, then? Stay in a hotel?'

'I thought I might rent an apartment nearby,' he said slowly. 'Somewhere I could take William and Daisy during the day, and where they could eventually spend the night so they get used to the idea of being with me—and you,' he added after a moment.

'Good idea.' Prue kept her voice even, although there was something about the idea of sharing a flat with Nat, of spending the night together, that sent a funny feeling tiptoeing down her spine. They wouldn't be sharing a room, and they would only be together because of the babies, but still, there would be something intimate about the situation, she thought.

Not that it appeared to bother Nat. 'You know London,' he said. 'Do you think I'd be able to find somewhere like that to rent for a month?'

'It would probably be very expensive.' Prue was quite proud of how brisk she sounded. 'Where exactly do the Ashcrofts live?'

'In Wimbledon. It's easy to remember because of the tennis.'

'That's not far from my parents,' she said thoughtfully, pleased to have something else apart from the prospect of meeting Nat in the middle of the night to consider. 'I'll ask them if they know of anywhere. You never know, someone might be going away for the summer holidays and let you have their house in exchange for watering the plants and feeding the cat. I'll ask them, if you like,' she offered.

Nat nodded his thanks. 'That would be good.' He rubbed a hand over his face in a weary gesture. 'It would be one less thing to worry about, if it works out.'

Fascinated, Prue watched his hand moving along his jaw, and was horrified to feel her own palms prickle, as if she could feel the male roughness of his skin herself. Jerking her eyes away, she forced her attention back to the conversation.

'It...it's not going to be easy for you,' she said, and couldn't help reflecting that it obviously wasn't going to be easy for *her* either if she carried on thinking about him like that. For such an ordinary-looking man, he had an irritating ability to make her notice little details about him, like the texture of his skin, or the shape of his brows, or that intriguing shadow where his jaw met his neck beneath his ear…

'I wish Kathryn could have been there.' Nat, oblivious to her scrutiny, was following his own train of thought. 'I'm worried about the Ashcrofts,' he confided. 'They're from the generation that thinks men are incapable of looking after children. I promised that I would take Kathryn to meet them, and even though I can make some excuse to explain why she's not with me I think they're going to be disappointed.'

His mouth pulled down at the corners as he imagined the Ashcrofts' reaction. 'It's going to be difficult enough for them as it is, without them fretting about who exactly is going to be looking after William and Daisy.'

Nat had all of Prue's attention now. Very carefully, she put her mug down on the table. She had decided that her idea wasn't worth mentioning but, if Nat himself had raised the problem, surely it was worth a try? He could only say no.

'Would it make a big difference if you did have your fiancée with you?'

'Not to me,' he said, 'but to the Ashcrofts. I think it would have made it a lot easier for them to hand Laura's children into the care of a couple. They would have been able to imagine Kathryn being a mother to their grand-children but—' Nat broke off and shrugged. 'Well, it can't be helped,' he finished abruptly.

'What if it *could* be helped?' said Prue, and he looked at her in surprise.

'What do you mean?'

'I mean, perhaps you should make sure the Ashcrofts *do* meet your fiancée.'

Nat's face closed. 'I can't ask Kathryn to come with me,' he said flatly.

'I wasn't thinking of her,' said Prue. She took a deep breath. It was now or never. 'I was thinking of me.'

At least she had the satisfaction of startling Nat. She had been wondering what it would take to shake him, and now she knew.

'*What?*'

She moistened her lips. 'I could be your fiancée,' she said, quaking inwardly but determined not to show it. 'Just pretend, of course,' she added hastily as Nat opened his mouth. 'The Ashcrofts wouldn't recognise Kathryn, would they?'

'No.' Nat was watching her in wary amazement, but there seemed no reason not to answer her question. 'They were in no state to take in anything I said after the funeral. I doubt if they would even remember her name.'

'Well, then,' said Prue. 'If we told them that we were engaged, they would believe us. You could introduce me as your fiancée instead of a temporary nanny, and they would be much happier about handing over William and Daisy to the two of us, wouldn't they?'

'But I couldn't ask you to take on a pretence like that, Prue,' Nat objected. 'You'll be doing enough by helping me with William and Daisy on the plane.'

Prue got to her feet and went to stand by the verandah rail, with her back to him. She ran a finger along the worn wood. 'The thing is,' she confessed at last, 'it would quite suit me to have a fiancé myself in London.'

There was a long pause. Prue closed her eyes, hearing her words still ringing in the silence and wishing desperately that she could call them back.

It was too late for that now, though. She stayed very still, unable to turn round and meet Nat's eyes, and in the end he came to join her at the rail. To her relief, he didn't exclaim or laugh or stare. He just leant on the rail and looked out at the palm fronds.

'I think you'd better explain,' he said.

'It's my own fault,' said Prue in a low voice. 'I've been stupid, and I've got myself into a mess, and I thought you might be able to get me out of it—but I wouldn't blame you if you didn't want to!'

'Why don't you tell me what it is, and then I'll see what I can do?' suggested Nat calmly, and she turned round so that she was leaning back against the rail and didn't have to watch his face while she told her pathetic story.

'I've always been the odd one out in my family,' she began with apparent irrelevance. 'Cleo and Marisa—that's my older sister—are very alike. They're both very pretty, very clever, very popular. They're good at everything they do.' Prue smiled wryly. 'And the worst thing is, they're both wonderful. I love them dearly, but sometimes it's hard being the ugly duckling of the family.'

Nat turned his head so that he could study her profile. She had a fine bone structure, and although he could see that her features weren't classically perfect they were put together with a quirkiness that had a charm all of its own and that would last much longer than superficial beauty.

'No one could call you ugly,' he said almost roughly, and she flushed.

'Thank you,' she said, but avoided his eyes. 'I didn't really mean that I was ugly in terms of looks, though. It's more the way I never seem to fit into the family. It's not that they don't love me—I know they do—but they think I'm a bit odd. Cleo and Marisa are strictly city girls. Neither of them would know what to do with themselves in the outback. Maybe that's one of the reasons I love it here so much,' she went on slowly, as the thought oc-

curred to her for the first time. 'I know that this is one
place where neither of my sisters would come and out-
shine me.'

'They couldn't do that.'

'They could,' said Prue. 'It wouldn't be deliberate, but
they're so beautiful and such fun, and they've got a sort
of aura about them. They *dazzle*…I don't really know
how to explain it,' she admitted helplessly, 'but if Cleo,
say, was here now, you wouldn't notice me at all.'

Nat let his gaze rest on Prue's averted face, on the
dark, downcast lashes and the fine skin and the curve of
her mouth. He found it very hard to believe that he would
ever not notice her.

'I suppose I hoped that by going away I'd be the ugly
duckling who turned into a swan,' she was saying with
a rueful smile. 'I wanted to find a place where I belonged,
and I wasn't just poor old Prue with her funny ideas
about living in the back of beyond. And then one day I
had a letter from Cleo telling me all about the wedding
and how everything was perfect for her and I…well, I
wanted her to know that things could be perfect for me,
too.'

Prue risked a glance at Nat to see how he was taking
this stumbling story, but it was hard to read anything in
those deep brown eyes. At least he was listening, though.

Surreptitiously moistening her lips, she made herself
go on. 'I was so in love with Ross, and the first time he
kissed me it was like a dream come true. I had to tell
someone how wonderful he was, so I wrote back to Cleo
and said that I'd met this fantastic man, and how happy
I was.'

She flushed, remembering how she had poured her
heart out to Cleo. 'I suppose I got a bit carried away,'
she told Nat, shame-faced. 'I was so sure that things

would work out with Ross that I hinted that I'd be getting married myself and that I might not come to the wedding alone. It was just fantasy, I know, but there didn't seem any harm in it. I knew what the wedding would be like— full of cousins commiserating that my younger sister was getting married before me, and aunts assuring me that it would be ''your turn next, dear'', and all Cleo's friends wondering why I was wasting my life in the outback.' Prue pulled a face at the thought.

'And then…' She turned round and laid her hands on the rail, wondering if Nat would have any conception of what had driven her to do what she had done. 'Then I let myself imagine what it would be like if I could walk into that wedding with Ross. He would have been a sensation,' she said a little sadly, remembering how vividly she had pictured the scene.

Ross at her side, so handsome, so sexy, so different from the pallid city men. If he'd walked into the wedding he would have brought a whiff of wide horizons with him, an air of being ready to throw himself onto a horse at the slightest provocation and gallop off in a cloud of dust. No one would have thought of her as 'poor old Prue' if Ross had been with her.

Prue sighed. 'It was pathetic, I know, but there didn't seem to be any harm in dreaming. The only trouble was that I'd posted my letter to Cleo before I began to realise that Ross wasn't thinking along the same lines at all. The next thing I knew Cleo had written back, agog for more details. If I'd had any sense, I would have told her then that it didn't look as if it was going to work out after all, but I just couldn't.' Prue looked at Nat, the silver eyes pleading for his understanding. 'I couldn't admit to Cleo that the love of my life had only lasted two weeks. It was much easier to let her carry on thinking that I was blissfully happy, and tell her in a few months time that it hadn't worked out after all.'

'So Cleo and the rest of your family are still expecting you to turn up at the wedding with Ross?' said Nat carefully, not sure that he was following the precise line of Prue's reasoning.

'Yes.' Prue had suddenly run out of steam, and her shoulders slumped.

Nat was beginning to see where this was leading. 'And you can't ask Ross to go with you?'

'How can I?' she demanded. 'I can't think of a situation more guaranteed to make a man run a mile in the opposite direction than to ask him to pretend to be in love with you because you've told everyone that he already is!'

'You're asking me.' It wasn't even a question.

There was a short silence, and then Prue nodded.

'It would be different with you,' she tried to explain.

'Why?'

'Because I'm not in love with you.'

He had asked for that, Nat thought wryly.

'And you're not in love with me,' Prue hurried on. 'I was going to tell Cleo that Ross was too busy on the station to come and hope that she believed me, but when you offered me the job as nanny, and I thought about the fact that we were going to be in London at the same time, it seemed *meant*, somehow.

'I'm desperate,' she admitted, when Nat didn't say anything. 'I've got to go to the wedding, but now they're all expecting me to roll up with a gorgeous Australian bloke, and I just wondered…'

'If I would be Ross?'

CHAPTER FOUR

'WOULD you mind?' said Prue, hoping that she didn't sound too desperate. 'It would just be for the wedding.'

What was she thinking? Of *course* she sounded desperate. How did she get herself into these situations? Prue wondered in despair. Nat must think that she was absolutely pathetic, writing to her sister about a fantasy love affair, as if she were a silly schoolgirl instead of a grown woman.

And he'd be right. She *was* pathetic.

Nat's silence was unnerving. He was obviously trying to find a kind way of refusing her. Or maybe even of telling her that he didn't want her as a nanny any more! Rapidly losing her nerve, Prue gripped the verandah rail and wondered how she could ever have expected him to agree.

'Look, don't worry,' she blurted out at last, unable to bear the suspense any longer. 'It was a really stupid idea. Forget it.' Pinning a bright smile on her face, she stepped back from the rail. 'Can I go and have a look at the river?'

'Hold on,' said Nat calmly, and put out a hand to stop her as she turned. His fingers closed around her wrist, and her heart lurched alarmingly at his touch. 'I haven't said that I won't do it.'

He let go of her almost immediately, and Prue was surprised to see when she looked down that his fingers had left no mark on her skin. 'There's no reason why you should get involved in my silly little problems,' she said uncertainly, holding her wrist as if he had hurt her. 'You've got more important things to think about.'

'One of them is how the Ashcrofts are going to react when I take William and Daisy away,' Nat pointed out. 'I've been thinking about what you said. You were right. If you were to pretend to be my fiancée it would make it a lot easier for everyone, and I reckon pretending to be your fiancé in return is the least I could do. I'm not sure you've really thought it through, though.'

Prue was too relieved that he hadn't dismissed the idea out of hand to object to his implied criticism. Of course it wouldn't be the same as walking in with Ross, but with Nat at her side she would at least be spared the humiliation of having to explain to Cleo that her wonderful love affair had come to nothing.

'What do you mean?' she asked.

'I don't think I'd make a very convincing Ross, for a start.'

'You wouldn't have to be him,' she reassured him eagerly. 'I didn't trust Cleo not to ring Cowen Creek in the middle of the night and demand to interrogate him, so I never gave her a name. All she knows is that he's an Australian and that his family owns a cattle station. You could just be yourself.'

'You must have described him, didn't you?'

'I said he was incredibly attractive,' Prue admitted, trying to remember exactly what she had told Cleo. Had she talked about Ross's fair hair and blue eyes or just raved generally about how gorgeous he was?

'Oh, I see what you mean,' she said as the penny finally dropped. 'You mean that Cleo might be surprised when you turn up? I don't think it'll matter too much, though,' she added without thinking. 'You're Australian, that's the main thing. That should be enough.'

Too late, Prue heard what she had said, and her hand flew to her mouth. It hadn't been very complimentary, implying as it had that Nat had only his nationality to recommend him.

'I didn't mean...' she stammered in consternation. 'I mean, it's not that you're *not*...'

She looked so embarrassed that Nat's mouth twitched. 'It's all right,' he said. 'I know what you mean!'

He kept his face straight, but Prue was relieved to see the smile glinting in his brown eyes. 'If you think my accent will be enough to convince your sisters, I'm quite happy to pretend to be engaged to you in London.'

'*Really?*'

'I can't hide William and Daisy, though,' he pointed out. 'How will your family react to them?'

Prue wrinkled her nose. She hadn't thought about the twins. 'I'll explain the situation when I ask if anyone knows of a house you could rent for a month. They'll be a good reason for us not to stay with my parents, now I come to think of it. With any luck, they'll be so taken up with Cleo's wedding that they won't have too much time to think about us anyway and, if they do arrange anything, you can always use the twins as an excuse to slope off.'

It sounded fair enough to Nat. 'Well, if we're agreed, I'll book the flight and a hotel for the first couple of nights next week.'

'I'm...terribly grateful,' said Prue, hardly able to believe that it was all going to work out just as she had wanted. 'I can't tell you what it's going to mean to me.'

Nat looked down into her eager face. The grey eyes were shining, and he felt his throat tighten. 'It's going to mean a lot to me, too,' he said quietly.

But not the same as it did to her, obviously. To Prue,

their mock engagement meant only saving face with her family, the last cloud vanishing off the horizon so that she could look forward to coming back to Ross with uninterrupted pleasure, while to him it would mean long days in her warm, quirky presence, growing used to the way she pushed her hair behind her ears, learning what made her smile…

No, that wasn't right! Nat slammed the brakes on his drifting thoughts, and frowned. Anyone would think he was going to do something stupid like fall in love with her, which he wasn't.

Absolutely, definitely not.

He had more important things to think about, as Prue herself had pointed out. No, he was simply grateful to her for helping him out with William and Daisy, and for making it easier for him to reassure the Ashcrofts that he would be able to care for their grandchildren. That was all their so-called engagement meant to him.

Prue saw his brows draw together, and the strange expression in his eyes made her wonder if Nat was already having doubts.

'I hope that pretending to be engaged isn't going to put you in an awkward situation,' she said guiltily, belatedly realising that she had been so wrapped up in her own situation that she hadn't given much thought to what effect it might have on Nat.

'In what way?'

'Well…the Grangers told me about you and Kathryn,' said Prue hesitantly. 'It would be awful if she heard that we were supposedly engaged, and misunderstood.'

Nat looked down into her sympathetic eyes. She was really very sweet, he found himself thinking. There was something touching in her romantic belief in the power of love, and he didn't want to be the one to disillusion her.

It would be much easier for Prue to think that he was still in love with Kathryn, Nat decided. They were going to be spending a lot of time together, and she wouldn't be comfortable if she thought there was any chance of him taking advantage of their enforced intimacy. She had made it clear that she was only interested in Ross, and he would let her believe that he was still hoping for a reconciliation with Kathryn. At least that way they could be friends.

'You don't need to worry about Kathryn,' he said, tearing his eyes from Prue's face and turning to lean on the rail once more, his hands clasped loosely in front of him. 'She knows how I feel about her.'

'The Grangers are all sure that she really loves you, too,' said Prue. 'Mrs Granger said that the two of you belong together.' A wistful note crept into her voice. Somehow it was hard to imagine anyone ever saying that she and Ross belonged together in the same way. 'It must be wonderful to be in love and know that you're meant to be together.'

Nat watched a flock of cockatoos wheel in the air before settling back into the trees down by the river, and he thought about Kathryn. Kathryn with her witchy green eyes and her dazzling smile. Wilful, unpredictable, irresistible Kathryn. Kathryn who had walked away when he'd needed her most.

It still surprised him how easily he had accepted her decision. He had been so used to thinking of himself as in love with her that it had come as something of a shock to realise that he was quite happy after all to just be friends, and there had even been a slight, guilty sense of relief. Kathryn was what was known as a high-

maintenance female. She demanded a lot of attention. Nat
didn't think that he could have managed to run a cattle
station, look after two small babies *and* indulge her
whims.

'Wonderful,' he agreed.

Prue didn't hear the dryness in his voice. 'Ross says
she's very beautiful,' she said.

'Kathryn? Yes, she is.' There was no doubt about that,
thought Nat. 'She's the most beautiful woman I've ever
met.'

His voice was quite dispassionate and Prue glanced at
him curiously. Clearly he wasn't the type to wax lyrical
about the love of his life, but still, she would have expected him to have sounded a bit more enthusiastic when
he talked about Kathryn. Even Ross had been more el-
oquent. Depressingly so, in fact.

But Nat was a very private man, she remembered, and
a proud one. Kathryn must have hurt him very badly and,
although she was only offering sympathy, he might not
like the idea that she was picking over his hurts. Perhaps
he was trying to discourage her from asking any more.

'Oh, well…I hope it works out for you both,' she said
a little awkwardly. 'I'd hate it if my idea ended up spoil-
ing everything.'

'It won't do that.' To Prue's relief, he smiled. Not the
smile that made her heart behave so alarmingly, but still
a smile. 'But maybe it would be best not to tell Kathryn
or Ross or anyone else that you're going as anything
other than a nanny. Our ''engagement'', if we can call it
that, is only going to last a month, and it won't have
anything to do with anyone here. I think it should just be
between the two of us.'

'Deal,' said Prue gratefully, and held out her hand with

a smile that caught the breath in Nat's throat as he straightened from the rail.

'Deal,' he agreed, and was alarmed to hear that his voice was tinder-dry.

They shook hands, and then Prue, on an impulse, reached up to kiss him on the cheek. 'Thank you,' she said.

Nat could smell her hair, feel the softness of her face, the warmth of her lips grazing his skin, and he fought an overwhelming urge to pull her closer as his fingers tightened instinctively around hers.

Fortunately, Prue was already drawing away, but she was looking up at him smiling, and Nat found himself trapped in that clear grey gaze. He stood staring down at her, until her smile faded and he became aware too late that he was still holding her hand.

He dropped it abruptly.

There was an awkward silence, broken eventually by Nat, who cleared his throat. 'You said you wanted to see the river,' he said. 'I'll find you a quiet horse.'

Prue flicked the water from her hands and regarded her reflection in the cloakroom mirror at Heathrow with a jaundiced eye. She had been sitting in a plane for twenty-four hours, and it showed! Her eyes felt gritty, and the lighting in the Ladies gave her skin an unpleasant shade of orange. It was going to take more than washing her face and brushing her teeth—twice!—to make her feel human again.

She thought about Nat, waiting outside in the baggage claim hall, with something close to resentment. How did he manage to look as cool and uncrushed now as he had when they'd boarded the plane to Darwin at Mathison airport?

It might be something to do with his extraordinary ability to sit relaxed and patient for long stretches of time. Prue had never flown business class before and, remembering her flight out to Australia without affection, she had been thrilled with the extra space at first. But as the hours had passed she had been less and less able to get comfortable.

Fidgeting next to Nat, Prue had been very aware of how close he was. Only an arm rest away. She had shifted around in her seat, played with her headphones, tried to read and all the time her eyes had kept slipping sideways to where he sat, quiet and self-contained beside her. There had been a stillness about him that had almost been mesmerising. She had waited for him to scratch himself, or sigh with boredom, but the nearest he'd come to restlessness had been to flex his shoulders once before resettling back into his seat.

He had been wearing a short-sleeved shirt, and his bare forearm had lain on the arm rest between them. Prue had been exasperated by the way her gaze had seemed to be riveted to it, as if there was something special about the fine, dark hairs against his brown skin or the weathered leather strap of his watch. He had a broad, strong wrist, and she'd been able to see the tendons in the back of his capable hand, the faint sheen of skin over his knuckles.

It was just a hand, just an arm, she had told herself, irritated by her own fascination. Ross had an arm just like it. But it had been unsettling to realise that she had never stared at his in the same way. She had never counted the lines across the joints of his fingers and she didn't know if he had any scars like the thin, pale one running across the edge of Nat's hand. But then, she had never been trapped next to Ross for so many hours with nothing else to do, either.

Prue hadn't been able to concentrate on another thing. She had tried to sleep, but it had been impossible to relax. Nat, of course, had slept the way he did everything else: without any fuss or fidgeting or sprawling or snoring. She had watched enviously as he'd simply tipped back his seat, folded his arms and closed his eyes. In no time at all, his long body had been utterly relaxed and his breathing deep and slow.

It had been a long, boring flight, but at least it was over now. They were just waiting for their cases to appear and then they could go. Prue wished that Cleo hadn't insisted on coming to meet them. She would have preferred a long sleep so that she felt less like a zombie before she had to face her sister's inevitable interrogation.

She gave her hands a final shake and the unaccustomed glint of diamonds caught her eye. Prue grimaced as she looked down at the ring on her finger. To add the final touch to the pretence they had agreed, Nat had bought her a supposed engagement ring during their stopover at Singapore airport.

It had seemed a good idea at the time, but she couldn't get used to the feel of the ring on her third finger, and, the longer she wore it the more uncomfortable she began to feel about what they were doing. During those long, sleepless hours on the plane, Prue had had plenty of time to think about the pitfalls that lay ahead. Pretending to be engaged wasn't going to be nearly as easy as it had seemed when they had discussed it that day at Mack River.

There was nothing to get nervous about, Prue told herself, resolutely drying her hands. All she had to do was treat it as a job.

A job where they had to pretend to be in love with each other.

What could be so hard about that?

The baggage claim hall had been relatively quiet when Prue went into the Ladies but when she emerged it seemed as if at least another five long-haul flights had disgorged their passengers, and they were now milling around, jabbering and gesticulating in a babble of languages, or leaning wearily on their trolleys.

She couldn't see Nat at all. Fighting her way through the crowds to the carousel where they had been told to wait, she looked wildly around her before spotting him half hidden behind a pillar.

At the sight of his rangy figure Prue felt her momentary panic subside, and she stopped, taking a deep breath to calm herself as her eyes rested on him. He wasn't doing anything to draw attention to himself, he was just looking towards the flaps in the wall where their luggage was due to appear, but somehow he was the still, certain centre of the chaos swirling around him and, without warning, Prue's heart did a long, slow somersault, landing back in place with a thud that left her with a dizzy, oddly hollow feeling.

She stood as if rooted to the spot, staring at him as if she had never seen him before, and then the carousel jerked abruptly into life and there was a surge of expectation as the other passengers tried to manoeuvre their trolleys closer. Nat looked round and lifted a hand as he saw Prue.

'Are you OK?' he asked as she made her way to his side. 'You look a bit odd.'

'Jet lag,' she said. That was *all* it was, she told herself. 'I didn't sleep a wink on the plane.'

Nat remembered waking at one point to find Prue leaning against him, heavy with sleep. Her face had been pressed into his shoulder and a few wayward curls had tickled his jaw. He could still feel the relaxed warmth of her body, but he didn't think he would tell her that.

He turned back to the carousel, where the first cases were juddering towards them. 'It shouldn't be too much longer now,' he said instead. 'You'll be able to sleep at the hotel.'

Prue stared at a battered blue suitcase that was moving past, besplattered with stickers. 'I wish Cleo wasn't meeting us,' she blurted out.

'She wants to see you,' said Nat mildly.

'It's not me she wants to see, it's you! She can't wait to inspect you!' Prue sighed. 'I don't think you realise what's going to hit you.'

'Relax. It'll be fine.'

It was all right for Nat to tell her to relax, Prue thought edgily. He didn't know what her family was like!

She had been so taken up with getting through the ordeal of the wedding, she realised, that she hadn't really thought about what else might be involved, but now, with the prospect of coming face to face with Cleo any minute, the full realisation hit her in horrifying detail.

What had she been thinking of? Cleo's wedding wouldn't be enough to stop her mother and sisters wanting to know every detail about her engagement. They would scrutinise what Nat looked like, what he was wearing, the way he behaved, and he would face an interrogation that would put the Inquisition to shame.

And then they would sit him down and make him look at photographs of her as a baby, and tell him stories about when she was little.

Prue cringed at the very idea. Could she really put Nat through all that?

'I'm not sure pretending to be engaged is such a good idea,' she said in a hollow voice.

Nat glanced at her. She was looking tired and grumpy, but he remembered the soft warmth of her body as she had slept against him and her smile as she walked under the great gum trees at Mack River, and he felt something shift inside him.

'Do you want to change your mind?'

Did she? Prue fidgeted with the trolley. Changing her mind would mean walking out of here and telling Cleo the truth, that she had made up her engagement and that she would be going alone to the wedding. There would be no going back then.

It wasn't so much admitting that she had been stupid as what would follow, she realised. Cleo would want to know why she had roped Nat into her pretence, and there would be endless questions, and with every one she would feel smaller and sillier.

'No,' she told Nat. 'I don't, not really. It's just…do you really think we can carry it off?'

'Why not?' Nat kept half an eye on the carousel, not wanting to miss their cases when they finally appeared. 'There's no reason why your family shouldn't believe us when we say we're engaged, just like the Ashcrofts will.'

'But that's just it! Laura's parents are going to be pre-occupied by other things, and I'm sure it will be enough to turn up with a ring on my finger and tell them we're getting married, but that won't be enough for Cleo and Marisa! They'll both be on the lookout for the way we behave together, and they'll want to know *everything*. If they sense something's not quite right, they'll be on to us immediately.'

'Then we'll just have to convince them that everything is all right,' said Nat.

His calm confidence irritated Prue. 'Easier said than done! It's going to take more than a ring to convince my sisters that we're in love. I don't think you realise what you're getting into,' she said honestly.

Nat had spotted one of their cases. 'You said yourself that I'm not going to spend much time with them,' he pointed out, watching its approach.

'I know, but when you do…' She trailed off, wondering quite how to put it. 'Well, you might find yourself in an embarrassing situation,' she finished awkwardly.

Lifting the case off the carousel, Nat placed it on the trolley. To Prue's chagrin, he looked faintly amused. 'What do you mean by embarrassing?'

'You know.' Prue hesitated, twisting the diamond ring around her finger. 'We're going to have to act as if we're in love. They'll be suspicious if we don't…if we don't…' She stopped and cleared her throat. 'Look, all I'm trying to say is that you might have to be prepared to…well, to…'

'To kiss you?'

The breath leaked out of Prue's lungs. 'Yes,' she managed, although it came out as more of a gasp. 'That kind of thing, anyway.'

Nat looked at her. She was rigid with embarrassment, her chin up as she stared fiercely ahead, her cheeks flushed and the wayward brown hair pushed haphazardly away from her face, and he felt something unlock inside him.

'I think I could manage that.'

The lurking smile in his voice deepened the colour in Prue's cheeks. He thought that she was being ridiculous, but she was only thinking of him forcing himself to kiss her when he was in love with Kathryn. She gritted her teeth. 'I can see it might be difficult for you, that's all,' she ploughed on.

'What's difficult about a kiss?' said Nat. 'Look, I'll

show you,' he went on, seeing that Prue was unconvinced.

He reached out an unhurried hand and laid it gently
against her face, and for Prue it was as if everything had
stopped. The hustle and bustle of the airport, the shud-
dering conveyor belt, even the blood in her veins seemed
to freeze. She couldn't move, couldn't breathe, could just
stand there, mouse-still, with Nat's palm cool and strong
against her cheek and his thumb tracing the line of her
lower lip almost thoughtfully.

'It's easy,' he said softly, curving his hand around her
throat, sliding it beneath her hair to the nape of her neck,
drawing her slowly, irresistibly towards him.

After that first moment of paralysis, Prue's body
slammed back into overdrive. Her heart was lurching
around her chest, her pulse boomed in her ears and she
churned with a terrifying mixture of nerves and antici-
pation. When Nat bent his head, she closed her eyes
against the treacherous thrill that shot through her as his
mouth came down on hers. The touch of his lips was
warm and sure and somehow right. Prue was conscious
of a disturbing sense of recognition, as if she had always
known that his kiss would feel like this, as if her lips
were meant to part beneath his, as if her arms had been
waiting for the chance to hold him.

Her hands lifted instinctively to clutch at his chest, but
even as she leant closer Nat was lifting his head, letting
his hand fall from her neck.

'I didn't find that too difficult,' he said calmly. 'Did
you?'

Dazed and disorientated, Prue could only stare up at
him. She felt as if she had been shown a tantalising
glimpse of something deep and dark and dangerously exciting, only to have the door slammed shut again in her

face, and she didn't know whether to be disappointed or relieved.

She swallowed painfully. 'N-no,' she managed to croak. It was as if the world had slipped out of kilter during those few seconds when Nat's lips had been on hers. She could see and hear still but the world around her seemed unreal, faintly blurry at the edges, and she blinked in a desperate attempt to bring it all into focus.

Nat smiled, and his gaze flickered downwards to where her fingers were still curled into his shirt. He didn't say anything but he might as well have thrown a bucket of cold water over her. Jerked back to reality, Prue snatched her hands away, blushing furiously.

'Of course not,' she added coldly to disguise how mortified she felt.

Nat was as unmoved by the chill in her voice as he had been by the kiss, Prue realised, eying him with resentment. 'There's your case,' he said casually, and reached past her to pluck it from the carousel and put it on the trolley.

He turned back to Prue. 'Ready?'

Of course she wasn't ready! she wanted to shout. She wasn't even sure that she could stand up without the trolley to hang on to, let alone walk out of here and face Cleo, with her searching questions and her sharp eyes, but she couldn't tell Nat that. If she told him that her knees were wobbling and her heart was thudding and every nerve in her body was fluttering he would think that it was because of that brief, impersonal kiss of his, which it couldn't be, of course.

It was just the effect of a long flight. Her body was confused after passing through all those time zones, that was all it was. It was absolutely nothing to do with him.

Fixing a bright smile on her face, Prue nodded. 'Let's go.'

Nat took the trolley, and they walked through Customs and suddenly were out in the hubbub of the arrivals hall. A confusion of faces greeted them as people pressed against the barrier, watching eagerly for their loved ones to appear, and tearful reunions blocked the exit.

Overwhelmed, Prue hesitated. She was still strumming from that unexpected kiss, reeling from noise and tiredness. She had an impulse to turn back and hide, but Nat kept on walking and she had to hurry to catch him up.

'What—?' he began, with a quick glance of concern, but suddenly Cleo was there, smiling, hugging her excitedly, talking nineteen to the dozen.

'Oh, Prue, it's so good to see you! How brown you look! Did you have a good flight? I made Alex get up at five so that we'd get here in good time.'

Prue was used to her sister and didn't even try to reply to the bombardment of questions. 'Hello, Cleo. Hello, Alex,' she said, kissing them both.

Cleo was blonde and beautiful, with perfect teeth and perfect skin and sparkling blue eyes. Her fiancé was the same height as Nat, but there the resemblance between the two men ended. Alex, sleek and suave and immaculately groomed, was darkly handsome with an unmistakable sheen of prosperity about him. He looked exactly what he was: an extremely successful financial analyst. Prue had always thought the two of them could pose as an illustration of the perfect couple.

They were both looking at Nat with undisguised curiosity and he nodded pleasantly in return, unfazed by their stares.

Prue turned too, trying to see him through their eyes, a lean brown man with a quiet face and watchful eyes.

Cleo and Alex would think him unremarkable, she knew. They couldn't tell that behind his apparent insignificance lay a strength and assurance they could only ever dream of. They didn't know his calm competence, or the easy way he moved through the land as if he were part of it, or the slow smile that gathered in the back of his brown eyes.

'This is Nat,' she said weakly.

Cleo moved past her to envelop Nat in a scented hug. 'It's lovely to meet you,' she told him, giving him the full benefit of her beautiful eyes. 'Prue's been so vague in her letters that we were beginning to wonder if you really existed!'

Fortunately, she didn't wait for an answer, but flitted back to Alex. 'This is Alex, my fiancé. We're both so thrilled you could come to the wedding with Prue after all.'

The two men shook hands. Watching nervously, Prue could see that Alex was unimpressed. His eyes flickered dismissively over Nat's plain shirt and moleskin trousers and checked out his watch and boots, but there was plainly not a single brand he recognised.

'Congratulations,' he said to Nat, pumping his hand a little too heartily. 'I hear you're taking the plunge, too. Happens to the best of us, eh?'

'We're all *so* excited about your engagement,' Cleo put in, beaming. 'Mum and Marisa were very jealous that I was going to meet you first. We've all been longing to know what you were like. We couldn't believe it when Prue wrote and said that she was getting married.' She grinned affectionately at her sister. 'Somehow she's never seemed the type.'

Nat followed her gaze to Prue, who stood with her chin tilted and a determined smile that didn't disguise for a minute that she was hating every moment of this. He could still feel the softness of her hair against his hand and the piercing sweetness of her lips, and he wondered if she had any idea of how much it had cost him to break the kiss then instead of yanking her roughly into his arms as he had wanted to do.

Reaching out, Nat smoothed a stray strand of hair behind her ear. He was only acting the part he had agreed, he told himself, letting his hand linger against her throat. He looked directly at Cleo, who obviously didn't believe that Prue was the type men fell in love with and married.

'She is to me,' he said.

CHAPTER FIVE

DETERMINED to find some common masculine ground with Nat, Alex led the way to the car park talking about cars and managing to spend quite a bit of time boasting about his new Porsche.

'She's a little beauty,' he told Nat. 'I'd have brought her this morning, but Cleo insisted on the BMW instead because she thought there wouldn't be enough room for everyone. Nonsense, of course, but you know what women are like! The Porsche would have been fine, but I'll take you for a spin later,' he promised, and it was obvious he could offer no greater treat.

Following behind with Cleo, her skin still burning where Nat's fingers had grazed her face, Prue listened tensely. Alex was all right when you got past the bluff, but he was bound to try and patronise Nat.

Not that Nat showed much sign of being impressed. If the thought of being driven around in Alex's precious Porsche excited him he gave no sign of it, merely thanking him with a calmness that Alex clearly found incomprehensible.

There was a short silence. 'What do you drive?' he asked after a moment, sounding put out.

'A ute, mostly.'

Alex looked blank. He needed a label, a designer—something he could relate to. 'What's that?'

'A utility truck. It's a good vehicle for rough country.'

'Ah, yes. I forgot that you were a farmer,' said Alex

patronisingly, eyeing Nat as if wondering why he didn't have a straw sticking out of his mouth.

Prue's fingernails dug into her palm. 'Mack River is a cattle station, not a farm,' she said sharply.

'Big place?' Alex asked Nat, ignoring her.

'Not particularly,' said Nat.

'How big is that exactly?'

'About two and a half thousand.'

Prue could see Alex preparing to cap Nat's answer with tales of his grand landowning friends. 'Acres?'

Nat glanced at him. 'Square kilometres.'

Prue relaxed slightly and smiled. Nat, she thought, was more than capable of dealing with Alex.

Beside her, Cleo raised her brows in the direction of Nat's back and tucked her arm through Prue's. 'He's not very chatty, is he?' she said in an undertone.

'He's tired,' Prue bristled, instantly on the defensive. 'And anyway, he only talks when he's got something to say,' she went on defiantly. *Unlike Alex*, she would have liked to add, but didn't. She had only just arrived, after all, and it was too soon to start arguing with Cleo.

'Hmn…the strong, silent type, is he?'

'Something like that,' said Prue, knowing that it would be hopeless trying to explain Nat to someone like Cleo.

Her sister's mouth turned down in a grimace. 'I've never understood the appeal of silence,' she said frankly. 'Doesn't it get a bit boring after a while?'

Prue thought about the day she had spent at Mack River with Nat, how he had ridden patiently beside her through the scrub, pointing out birds and plants she had never seen before, how he had looked, outlined against the horizon in the crystalline light, how he had smiled beneath his hat.

And then she thought about the way he had kissed her

by the carousel, and her heart began to boom and thud at the memory. Whatever else it had been, it hadn't been boring.

'No,' she said, dry-voiced. 'Nat's never boring.'

'Oh? Well, as long as you don't think so.' Cleo was patently unconvinced. 'I must say, I'm a bit disappointed. I thought we'd be getting Crocodile Dundee!' The blue eyes surveyed Nat critically. 'I wouldn't call him much of a looker.'

Prue pulled her arm out of Cleo's and glared at her sister. 'What do you mean?' she demanded.

'There's no need to ruffle up like that!' said Cleo, amused. 'I'm sure he's very nice. I'm only saying that he's not what I expected. You made out in your letters that he was absolutely gorgeous!'

Prue bit her lip. She had forgotten for a moment that she had been talking about Ross when she wrote those letters. Cleo wouldn't have been disappointed in Ross if he'd been there with her.

But Ross wasn't there, and Nat was, and she would have to be careful that Cleo didn't get suspicious. 'Nat may not be obvious,' she said slowly, 'but when you get to know him, he's...'

She trailed off, picturing him as he had been that afternoon at Mack River: his stillness, the strength in his hands, the ease with which he'd swung himself onto his horse.

'I think he's very attractive,' she finished lamely.

Cleo laughed as she took Prue's arm affectionately once more. 'You must be in love!' she said.

Automatically, Prue opened her mouth to deny any such thing, and only just managed to stop herself in time. She was *supposed* to sound as if she were in love with

Nat, she reminded herself. If they were going to go through with this pretence, she might as well do it properly.

'I am,' she said as coolly as she could, and was then afraid that she had sounded too cool, for Cleo was looking at her with a very strange expression. 'Tell me about the wedding,' she said, hastily changing the subject. 'Are you all organised?'

Cleo needed no encouragement and chattered happily about the arrangements all the way out of Heathrow and along the M4. Bridesmaids…flowers…music… photographs… The words flowed over Prue's head, and all she had to do was put in the occasional 'Oh, really?' to make it sound as if she were listening.

It was nearly half past seven, and the early-morning traffic was already clogging up the roads. Caught in the frustrating business of stopping and starting, darting through a sudden clear patch and then grinding to a halt once more, Prue thought longingly of the empty outback roads, where you raised a hand in greeting to every vehicle that passed.

Once, not so long ago, all this had been familiar to Prue, but now it felt alien, like visiting another planet. The colours were different in London. Here, everything was grey, with sudden splashes of startling green, and even though the sky was clear it was a pale, soft, washed-out kind of blue, nothing like the fierce Australian sky.

It was all different, thought Prue. The cars around them were smaller and less rugged than the ones she was used to seeing, and their yellow licence plates looked strange. Even the road signs, marking the turn-offs to places Prue had once known well, seemed—

She sat up abruptly. 'This isn't the way to the hotel!'

she said, breaking into Cleo's reasons for choosing a finger buffet over a sit-down meal.

'We're not going to the hotel,' Cleo told her. 'I cancelled your reservation.'

'You did *what*?'

'You didn't really think we would let you come to London and stay in a *hotel*, did you? No, I arranged it all with Mum ages ago. You're staying with us.'

'But, Cleo—'

'It's all organised,' said Cleo, waving Prue's protests down. 'Marisa and Phil and the kids can stay with Mum and Dad, and you're staying with us. We've got a spare room, and it'll give us a chance to see you before you disappear back off to Australia. Besides,' she went on gaily, 'I had this brilliant idea!'

Prue's heart sank. How were they going to get out of this? 'Oh?'

'You know you asked me about house-sitting? Well, the answer's obvious! You can use my flat. We're going to be on honeymoon for two and a half weeks, so you can have it to yourselves. You can drive my car, too, if you want. It'll mean we don't need to worry about security, and you won't need to worry about getting used to a stranger's house.'

'The thing is, we're going to have William and Daisy with us,' Prue tried with a hint of desperation. 'They're the babies I told you about, and you know how much mess babies make.'

'Oh, that's no problem,' said Cleo. 'We're going to sell the flat when we get back anyway. Alex has already sold his, and if we get a good price for mine we can buy a decent house with a garden. So don't worry if the kids are sick on the carpets or anything. It might be better if they don't come and stay until after the wedding, of

course, but only because we've got a busy week coming
up.'

Swivelling round from the front seat, Cleo looked curiously at her sister. 'I thought you'd be pleased,' she
said. 'You know what Mum's like about separate bedrooms! She does try not to be old-fashioned, but the one
time Alex and I stayed there together she made such an
effort to be good about it that it was excruciating.
Honestly, I'd rather Alex had slept on the sofa! Believe
me,' she assured Prue, 'you'll be much better off with
us.'

'I'm sorry about this,' Prue said to Nat when Cleo had
shown them into the spare room with a flourish and left
them to put on some coffee. They could hear her in the
kitchen just along the corridor, sending Alex out to the
delicatessen on the corner to buy fresh croissants.

Prue stood awkwardly by the door and looked at anything except the bed. It dominated the room, a double
certainly, but not a big one, and the thought of sleeping
in it next to Nat was for some reason deeply uncomfortable.

'I couldn't think of any way to get out of it,' she apologised.

'There was nothing you could do,' said Nat understandingly. 'In any case, once Cleo had cancelled the
hotel, we had to have somewhere to go!'

'I should have known she would do something like
that,' Prue sighed with exasperation. 'I could kill her
sometimes!'

'She's only trying to make you welcome.' Nat noted
the fresh flowers on the chest of drawers and the bed that
had been carefully made and scattered with cushions.
'She's fond of you. You can't blame her for wanting to
see more of you.'

'I know, it's just frustrating the way she makes it impossible for you not to do exactly what *she* wants the whole time!'

'She reminds me of Kathryn,' said Nat, moving one of the suitcases out of the way.

Prue went very still. 'Oh?'

'Cleo doesn't look like Kathryn, of course, but she's got the same way of getting exactly what she wants.' He smiled wryly. 'You can try and refuse the Kathryns and Cleos of this world, but they're so beautiful and charming they make you feel churlish and before you know where you are you've given in, just like they knew you would all along.'

'Yes, that's Cleo. Marisa's like that, too.'

Prue was glad that Nat had reminded her about Kathryn. It helped put that brief kiss by the carousel into perspective. She had spent too much of her life in her sisters' shadow to have any illusions about her own appeal compared to the irresistible gaiety and charm of a girl like Kathryn. One little kiss was hardly going to make Nat forget his real love, was it?

Which was good, of course.

Uneasily conscious of a sinking feeling at the thought, Prue caught herself up sternly. She was very glad that she and Nat had been quite open about how they felt. Otherwise there could have been all sorts of misunderstandings when it came to things like kissing or sharing a bed.

As it was, she knew that it would take more than a quick peck to change the way Nat felt about Kathryn. Sharing a bed wasn't going to bother *him*.

If only she could believe that it wasn't going to bother her either.

The cases seemed to take up most of the room.

Stepping round them gingerly, Prue went over to the window and pretended to be interested in the garden that belonged to the flat below.

Behind her, Nat stretched out on the bed with his arms above his head and yawned. He was tired too, Prue realised and felt a bit better. This buzzing, jittery feeling was just exhaustion. She was too weary to think clearly, and as a result she had blown that stupid kiss out of proportion. Tomorrow, when she had caught up on her sleep, she would be amazed that she could have got herself in such a state about it.

The thought gave her the courage to perch on the edge of the bed, with her back to Nat. 'I shouldn't have suggested this engagement business,' she apologised, twisting the ring around her finger. 'Now look at the mess I've got us into!'

'It'll be fine,' said Nat calmly. 'This is a nice apartment, and we can bring William and Daisy here. That's all that matters to me.'

'You don't think it'll be awkward?' In spite of herself, Prue coloured painfully. 'Sharing a bed, I mean?'

Her hair swung forward, hiding her face, and her shoulders were set at a rigid angle. Nat thought about sliding across the bed and rubbing her back until she relaxed, until she could lie down beside him and let the tension evaporate. Then he thought that he had better stay right where he was. She was uncomfortable enough as it was, and he couldn't blame her. The only place she wanted to be was next to Ross, and he had better not forget it.

'It's only for a week,' he said, keeping his voice deliberately cool and impersonal. 'Like Cleo says, we'll have the place to ourselves after the wedding and we can have a bedroom each then.'

Only a week. Only a week of lying next to her, knowing she was only a few inches away. Only a week of keeping his hands firmly to himself. Nat sighed inwardly. He had a feeling that it was going to be a long week.

'I'd offer to sleep on the floor,' he went on, 'but there's not a lot of room and Cleo might think it was a bit odd if she came in.'

'There's no need for that,' Prue protested, mortified at the idea that he had picked up on how nervous she felt at the prospect of sleeping with him. She put up her chin. 'I don't mind sharing. I mean, it's not as if you're…or that we're likely to….' Floundering, she made an effort to pull herself together. 'That is, I know how you feel about Kathryn,' she tried again, a little more coherently this time.

This was clearly not the time to tell her that what he had once felt for Kathryn had gone, thought Nat ruefully. Or that what really worried him was the way he was beginning to feel about *her*.

'You don't need to worry, Prue,' he told her instead. 'I haven't forgotten the deal we made. It's not that big a bed, but there's room for both of us, and I won't…' Nat paused, searching for the right word '…take advantage,' he finished, opting for the more delicate option.

Of course he wouldn't, Prue realised. Why would he want to take advantage of her, when he was used to Kathryn with her long legs and her green eyes and her no doubt perfect skin?

She summoned a smile. 'No, I know you won't,' she said. 'I was just being silly.'

'You're just tired, that's all. You'll feel better when you've had some sleep. It's all going fine so far, isn't it?' Nat added in an attempt to cheer her up.

Prue looked at him doubtfully. 'Is it?'

'Of course it is. We've got a great flat to stay in and an ideal place to bring the twins. Cleo and Alex don't seem to have had any problem believing we're engaged, and if they don't suspect, why should anyone else? All you've got to do now is get through the wedding, and you'll have Ross to go home to.'

Nat's mouth twisted as he remembered the scene at Mathison airport, the unthinking lift of his heart when he had seen Prue walking towards him, followed by the sinking realisation that Ross was at her side. He had had to stand by and watch as the younger man gathered her into his arms for a farewell kiss.

'He seemed pretty sorry to see you go,' he reminded her. 'Or are you going to tell me that Ross kisses all their cooks goodbye like that?'

At least he had the satisfaction of seeing Prue brighten.

'He *did* say he hoped I would be able to go back to Cowen Creek, didn't he?' she remembered. 'And he asked for my number in London so that he could get in touch if he needed.'

'I bet Ross is going to miss you more than he realises,' Nat forced himself to encourage her. Hell, *he* had missed her when she had gone off on her own to buy some duty free for Cleo at Singapore, and she'd only been gone half an hour.

'Coming to London will turn out to be the best thing you could have done, you'll see,' he said.

Cleo laid on a special welcome breakfast with Bucks Fizz, freshly ground coffee and warm buttery croissants, and proceeded to lay out an exhausting week of activities she had planned for them. Prue wasn't too surprised to discover that, in spite of the fact that she had written to explain the situation with William and Daisy, Cleo was still reluctant to accept that they really had to spend so much time with the twins, but Nat handled her with an ease that was no doubt born of years of practice with Kathryn.

'Oh, all right,' Cleo grumbled, backing down at last, 'but you've got to let Prue come shopping with me one day at least! I've already arranged for her to have a fitting for her dress on Wednesday, and then she'll need some shoes. We might as well get you some decent clothes while we're out as well,' she went on, regarding her sister with a mixture of exasperation and affection. 'Haven't you got *anything* other than jeans in your wardrobe, Prue?'

'Not really,' mumbled Prue.

Nat looked at her. She was wearing a long-sleeved T-shirt with a scoop neck that showed the shadowy hollow at the base of her throat and, although her hair was tousled and her eyes looked huge with tiredness, he thought she had never looked more desirable.

'She looks fine to me,' he said.

'I'm sure she does,' said Cleo tartly, 'but she's in London now! She's going to have to have something suitable to wear in the evenings. It's not just the wedding, you know. We're having a family dinner with Mum and Dad when Marisa arrives to celebrate your engagement, and then there's Sabrina's pre-wedding party, and you can't wear your jeans to that!'

'All right, I'll come shopping with you on Wednesday,' Prue agreed, to shut her sister up. 'But the rest of the time we really do need to be with William and Daisy, Cleo.'

'I hope they'll be able to spare you on Saturday!' said Cleo huffily. 'I know it's only my wedding and that I'm only your sister, but I do think you might want to spend some time with *me*!'

It took Prue some time to charm her out of her threatened sulk, and she had to promise to go to every party the insatiably sociable Cleo had arranged that week, although her heart sank at the thought. 'Everyone wants to see you,' Cleo insisted, although Prue found it hard to believe that anyone would notice if she was there or not when her sister was in the room.

When breakfast was over, Alex got to his feet and announced that some people had work to do on a Monday morning. Prue was hoping that Cleo would be going to work too, but it seemed that her sister had taken the whole week off prior to the wedding. 'I haven't got time to work!' she said, tripping back into the kitchen after bidding her fiancé a fond farewell at the door.

'Now, Mum and Dad are coming to supper tonight, so we've got the whole day to ourselves. I need to pick up my shoes, then I've got a few jobs in town, so why don't you come with me? We could have lunch and—'

'Prue's tired,' Nat interrupted her. He had been watching her swaying in her seat, her eyes glassy with exhaustion. 'She didn't sleep on the plane.'

Cleo pursed her mouth. 'It's much better for her to stay awake, you know,' she said. 'She should keep busy and go to bed at the right time.'

'I think she would be better here with me.' There was a note of finality in Nat's voice that even Cleo recognised.

'Oh very well!' she grumbled. 'But don't blame me when she can't sleep tonight!'

Nat gave Prue nearly four hours before he judged that she had had enough. Not wanting to startle her, he sat cautiously on the edge of the bed, but she was sound asleep, her face turned into the pillow and half hidden by a tumble of brown curls.

It was a shame that she felt so overshadowed by Cleo, he thought, letting his eyes linger on the dark sweep of lashes against her cheek, the smooth, bare shoulders and the gentle rise and fall of her breathing. Prue might not have her sister's golden beauty, but he for one preferred luminous grey eyes to dazzling blue. He liked the fact that her features weren't quite symmetrical and that her hair was always untidy. He liked her elfin, expressive face and the way she always looked warm and tousled, as if she had just fallen out of bed. He liked a lot of things about her.

He just wished he could find something he didn't like. Apart from the fact that she was head over heels in love with Ross Granger, of course.

'Prue?' He ran a gentle finger down the bare arm that lay over the duvet. 'Prue, it's time to wake up.'

Prue surfaced groggily, mumbling in protest as she was dragged up through layers of deep sleep. When she finally managed to ungum her eyelids, the first thing she saw was Nat, sitting on the bed and watching her with an unreadable expression. Still swirling in sleep, it seemed too much effort to work out what he was doing there, but she knew that she was glad to see him and she smiled dreamily up at him.

Nat drew a sharp breath. 'It's half past one,' he said with an effort. 'If you sleep any longer Cleo will be right and you won't be able to sleep tonight.'

Blinking herself awake, Prue struggled up against the pillows and ran her hands through her hair. She felt worse now than she had done earlier, when she had fallen into bed in her underwear, too tired to open her case and find anything else to put on. 'Do I look as bad as I feel?' she groaned.

Nat had been trying not to think about how she looked. She had taken the duvet with her and was lying back against the pillows, her hair tumbling about her face and her honey-coloured shoulders bare except for her bra straps. He was very aware of the smooth warmth of her skin, of the huge, sleepy grey eyes and the tempting line of her clavicle, and he got abruptly to his feet.

'You'll feel fine after a shower,' he said, his voice curt.

He was right. Prue did feel a lot better once she had washed and changed into clean trousers and a fresh shirt. Almost normal, in fact.

Still combing out her hair she went to find Nat, who was in the kitchen staring in some bafflement at Cleo's gleaming chrome coffee machine.

'I was going to make you some coffee,' he said, 'but I give up! What's wrong with a jar of instant?'

Prue laughed. 'Don't let Cleo hear you say anything like that! She wouldn't allow instant coffee in the house. Here, let me,' she went on, moving him aside, and Nat watched as the machine sprang miraculously to life at her touch.

'How did you do that?' he demanded.

'Oh, we city girls have our uses,' she teased him. 'But don't worry, we'll buy a jar of instant later and smuggle it in. If we keep it in our room, and only use it when she's out, Cleo will never know!'

They laughed together until they made the mistake of looking at each other. Their eyes met and held, and for some reason their smiles faltered. With an effort, Prue looked away and concentrated on the coffee maker.

'Did you sleep at all?'

She sounded stilted, polite, the perfect hostess. Not at

all like someone who only moments ago had been laughing with him like an old friend, or who could talk casually about 'our room' as if they had been sleeping together for years.

To her relief, Nat moved away and sat down at the breakfast bar. 'I had a nap on the sofa,' he told her. 'Then I had a shower and rang the Ashcrofts to let them know that we'd arrived. I said we'd go along this afternoon to see them and the twins, but if you want to stay here and rest I'm sure they'd understand.'

Prue took a deep breath and shook her head. 'No, I want to go,' she said. She had to stop feeling self-conscious with Nat and start remembering just why she was there. Turning, she handed him a mug of coffee. 'That's what I'm here for.'

She met his gaze clearly to make sure that there would be no misunderstandings. 'I haven't forgotten that you've paid for my ticket, Nat. I'm here as a nanny, and everything else is incidental.'

Nat looked back at her, his brown eyes quite unreadable. 'I haven't forgotten either,' he said.

Having checked the Ashcrofts' address in the *A–Z*, Prue decided that it would be easiest to get the tube to Wimbledon. 'It shouldn't be too bad at this time of day,' she told Nat, who shrugged.

'You know your way around London,' he said. 'I'll follow you.'

Prue was very conscious of the grimness of the station, of the noise and the crowds and the stuffy air in the carriage. It was depressing to realise that this was her world as far as Nat and Ross were concerned. She could love the outback as much as they did, but, to them, she would always be a London girl, someone who belonged in the big city the way they belonged under the big out-back sky.

Australia seemed a million miles away as she sat on the swaying train, reading the advertisements and avoiding eye contact like everyone else. Nat sat silently beside her. He had left his hat behind, and was wearing mole-skins and a pale, short-sleeved shirt, but even in this innocuous outfit he managed to look out of place.

There was a toughness about him, Prue realised, a quiet assurance that was as unmistakable as it was hard to define. He couldn't help looking exactly what he was: a man used to riding out to distant horizons. He didn't belong in this cramped metal tube hurtling under the streets of London.

Maybe Nat had thought she looked as out of place riding through the scrub at Mack River, thought Prue despondently.

They had to change trains at Earl's Court. Nat followed obediently when she jumped out, and stood beside her on the platform, although clearly puzzled as to why they had got off one train only to stand and wait for another in exactly the same place. When the next train rattled in he glanced at Prue, but she shook her head, just as she did for the next two.

'This one,' she said as the fourth one arrived.

Nat grimaced. 'I'm glad you're with me,' he acknowledged. 'You don't seem to need to look at anything. How do you know where you're going?'

'The same way you know the best place to cross the creeks at Mack River,' said Prue, who had simply kept an eye on the destination board. 'I grew up here. It's only a question of reading the signs, anyway. You'd have been fine by yourself.'

Nat would always be fine, she thought enviously. It

was impossible to imagine him lost or bewildered or unable to cope. It was nice of him to make her feel useful but he didn't really need her, did he?

It was only a five-minute walk to the Ashcrofts' house from the station. They made their way up a hill, along a quiet, leafy street with carefully-kept front gardens. To Prue, it felt very suburban after the bustling area where Cleo lived in Fulham, but she preferred it in many ways, and she thought Nat would appreciate the respite from the constant noise of traffic that was joined every couple of minutes by the roar of planes coming in to land at Heathrow.

She turned to say as much to Nat, but he was looking so withdrawn that the words died on her lips. He was walking with his head bent, his hands thrust into his pockets, and there was a bleakness about his expression that clutched at her heart.

'Are you thinking about the last time you were here?' she asked gently.

Nat threw her a quick, surprised glance. 'How did you know?'

'It's what I would be thinking, if it was me,' said Prue, imagining Nat as he had been then, arriving alone in a strange city after that long, disorientating flight, knowing that two tiny babies were now utterly dependent on him. Thinking about them and helping Laura's distraught parents cope with their grief, he could have had little time to mourn his brother properly himself.

She bit her lip, remembering how she had sat on the tube and envied Nat his calm competence. Nat would always be fine, hadn't she decided that? Well, maybe he would be, but that didn't mean that things were always easy for him. He had broad shoulders, but the last time he had walked along the road he must have had a lot to bear.

'This week's going to be awful for you,' she said, her grey eyes full of compassion. 'Having to pretend that you're happy when just being here must remind you of Ed and Laura and everything you went through last time. It seems all wrong to be going to all these parties Cleo's got lined up and drinking champagne and celebrating when they lost everything.'

Nat was touched and more than a little disconcerted by her concern. He couldn't remember the last time anyone had looked at him the way she was looking at him now, as if they really cared how he was feeling instead of waiting expectantly for him to solve their problems.

'It's true that I was remembering what it was like before,' he said, 'but life goes on. I do miss Ed—and Laura—but I've had time to get used to it now. It's not so bad this time.'

One of the reasons it wasn't so bad was that Prue was with him, Nat had been thinking, but he couldn't tell her that. He didn't want her thinking that he needed her or anything. *You'd have been fine by yourself.* Wasn't that what she had said when he had told her that he was glad she was with him? It was almost as if she had been warning him off getting too dependent on her.

Prue was still worrying about Nat and the run-up to the wedding. 'I should have thought about how difficult it's going to be for you this week,' she said remorsefully. 'I could explain to Cleo, if you like, and get you out of some of the parties.'

'No, don't do that,' said Nat. 'Ed always loved a party. I know he'd much rather we celebrated than cried. Besides, it's good not to have too much time to think, and it doesn't sound as if Cleo's going to give either of us much of that,' he added, trying to lighten the mood.

Even so, he fell silent as they neared the house, and Prue saw him take a breath and square his shoulders as they paused at the front gate.

She had a choice, she realised. She could say that she didn't want to be a nanny after all, that she'd changed her mind and would find some other way of getting back to Australia. She could walk away if she wanted to, but Nat couldn't. His brother's children needed him, and now that he was here there would be no turning back. Reaching out to push the bell, Nat must know that his life was about to change for good.

Prue slipped her hand into his, offering the only comfort she could. 'It'll be all right,' she promised him.

Nat's fingers tightened gratefully around hers, and as he looked down into her clear grey eyes he nodded slowly. 'Yes,' he said. 'I think it will now.'

CHAPTER SIX

WILLIAM and Daisy were awake. Prue and Nat could hear
them bellowing at the top of their lungs as soon as they
stepped into the house. Harry Ashcroft had looked decidedly harassed as he opened the door.

'I'm sorry about this,' he said apologetically when Nat
had introduced Prue. He had to raise his voice to make
himself heard. 'We were hoping that the twins would be
settled before you arrived as it's impossible to concentrate when they're crying. Ruth's upstairs helping Eve
change their nappies, but her arthritis is bad at the moment so she's a bit slow.'

'Why don't I go and give Eve a hand?' suggested Prue,
seeing that Nat for once looked at a loss. 'That'll give
the three of you a chance to talk, and Eve and I can bring
William and Daisy down when they're ready.'

Nat looked at her so gratefully that she felt a warm
glow deep inside her as she went up the stairs. Ruth
Ashcroft was even more grateful when Prue appeared, to
take over Daisy's nappy, but funnily enough the older
woman's thanks didn't have nearly the same effect.

Choosing not to analyse just why that should be, Prue
concentrated instead on William and Daisy. By the time
the two babies had been changed and cuddled she was
already in thrall to their tiny hands, their warm solid bodies and the serious little faces that could dissolve into
enchanting smiles.

Both had a quiff of blonde hair and big brown eyes,
but it was easy to tell the difference between them.

William was sturdier and more placid, while Daisy had a distinctly mischievous look about her. Prue cuddled William against her shoulder, wincing as his dimpled fingers clutched at her hair, and wondered how Nat was getting on downstairs.

'They're lovely babies,' she was able to tell him later as they walked back to the station.

'You were very good with them,' said Nat, remembering the blissful hush that had fallen soon after Prue had gone upstairs.

It hadn't been an easy conversation with Ruth and Harry, who were both still shattered by the tragedy. In the face of their overwhelming grief Nat had felt hopelessly inadequate, and he had found himself wishing that Prue had been there.

And then, as if she had known how much he needed her, the door had opened and she had come in, holding Daisy naturally on her hip, and he had felt a great weight roll off him. She had known just what to do and what to say. She had sat with Ruth and let her cry for her lost daughter while he and Harry, helpless to deal with the pent-up tears, had taken the babies out to the garden.

'We're so glad you're here,' Ruth had said with a tremulous smile when it had come to say goodbye. 'It makes such a difference having met you.'

Nat was very glad that Prue had been there too. Kathryn would have been charming to the Ashcrofts, but she wouldn't have known what to do with a crying baby or a grieving mother. Prue had.

'Thank you for coming,' he said stiltedly, and then admitted in a rush, 'I don't know what I would have done without you.'

Prue thought about the expression on Nat's face when she had gone down to the sitting room. It had obviously been a difficult meeting for all of them, and it had no doubt been sheer relief at the interruption that had made him smile like that, but her heart had turned over at the sight of him. She could still feel a strange tingling along her veins.

Of course, it had probably been just the jet lag catching up with her, she realised that now, but at the time her reaction had taken her by surprise and she hoped that her smile in return hadn't been too...too revealing. Quite what it might have revealed, Prue wasn't sure. She just knew that she felt ridiculously awkward and self-conscious now.

She hugged her arms together as she walked, afraid that if left to their own devices they might start reaching towards him to offer a physical comfort that Nat certainly wouldn't want. It must have been a traumatic meeting for him, and at the very least an emotional occasion. The last thing he needed was to suspect that she was crass enough to be thinking about the way he had smiled or the feel of his lips or the warm clasp of his fingers around hers as they waited for Harry to open the door.

'I was just doing my job,' she said with would-be lightness.

She wasn't looking at Nat, so she didn't see his face close. 'Of course,' he agreed in a flat voice. 'Just doing your job.'

'It will be easier tomorrow,' Prue assured him. 'The first meeting was bound to be difficult, but now that's over we can concentrate on William and Daisy.'

She wished they could have spent longer with the babies, but there was still this evening to get through. Cleo had invited their parents round for supper and she and Nat would no doubt have to endure an in-depth interrogation as to how they met and why and when and where they were planning to get married.

As it turned out, the evening went off better than Prue had anticipated. True, her mother was inclined to be suspicious of Nat, but he and her father seemed to get on well and they seemed to have brushed through the inevitable questions without raising too many eyebrows.

All in all, Prue decided the next day, it had gone pretty well, especially considering that she had spent the whole evening feeling jittery at the thought of climbing into bed next to Nat. In the event, even that hadn't been difficult. Exhaustion had simply got the better of nerves. Nat had tactfully let her go to bed first, and by the time he'd come into the room Prue had been sound asleep.

She hadn't woken until Nat had brought her a cup of tea this morning, and now it seemed perfectly natural to lie back against the pillows while he sat on the edge of the bed and drank his own tea. They chatted so comfortably that Prue's spirits rose.

She had simply been disorientated after the long flight yesterday. Why else would she have got herself into such a state about Nat and how it felt whenever he touched her? Prue sipped her tea and reflected that she must have been even more tired than she had thought. She had hardly given Ross a thought all day!

Now, she carefully built his picture in her mind. The hunky body. The blue eyes. The devastating smile. It seemed incredible to think that she had once or twice been on the verge of muddling him up with Nat.

No, everything would be fine now that she had had a good night's sleep, just as Nat had promised. No more embarrassment, no more awkwardness. They would simply get on with what they had come to do and when they went back to Australia, with any luck, Ross would be waiting for her.

They spent Tuesday with the twins in Wimbledon, and that evening had a quiet meal with Cleo and Alex. By the time she woke up on Wednesday morning Prue was feeling confident, even cocky, about her ability to keep up the pretence. All that fuss she had made, just because of a little jet lag!

In buoyant spirits, she waved Nat off to Wimbledon on his own and headed into town with her sister. She let Cleo bully her into buying not one but three new outfits, recklessly charging them to her credit card. She pretended to like the bridesmaid's dress that had been made for her, and chose a pair of shoes that she thought she would be able to stand in all day. They had coffee out, and Prue smiled and listened to Cleo's gossip and told herself that she really *was* enjoying herself.

It was just that the thought of Nat and the twins lingered distractingly at the back of her mind. She would drift off in the middle of one of Cleo's anecdotes, or pause in the act of pulling a top off the rail, and she would find herself wondering where the three of them were and what they were doing and how they were getting on without her.

Cleo waved a hand in front of her face. 'Prue! Have you been listening to a word I've said?'

'Sorry.' Prue recollected herself hastily and realised that she was standing in front of a cosmetic counter while Cleo tried to decide what colour lipstick she needed to go with her bridesmaid's dress. 'Um…you were thinking about the pink, weren't you?' she guessed wildly.

'No, Prue, I never even *mentioned* pink!' Cleo rolled her eyes. 'Honestly, I know you always used to be in a world of your own, but you were never as bad as you are now. Falling in love seems to have softened your brain!'

'I was only wondering what Nat and the twins were doing,' Prue said defensively.

Abandoning hope of getting a sensible opinion from her sister, Cleo selected a lipstick and handed it over to the assistant behind the counter. 'They'll be fine,' she said. 'Nat seems a capable type. I'm sure he doesn't need you hovering round him every second of the day.'

'No,' agreed Prue, and a wistful sigh escaped before she could stop herself.

It didn't escape Cleo, who subjected her to a shrewd blue stare. 'I hope you don't mind me saying this, Prue,' she said carefully as she turned away to sign the credit card slip, 'but how well do you actually know Nat?'

Prue was taken aback by the question. It was true that she and Nat hadn't spent that much time together. In fact, when she did a quick mental calculation, she worked out that it came to less than a week—but somehow it felt like much more than that.

Being with Nat, Prue told herself, was like putting on a pair of old slippers. Not wildly exciting, perhaps, but familiar, *comfortable*. Almost as if she had always known him: the way he moved, the way he spoke, the way he smiled.

The way he kissed?

Prue's heart stumbled as the thought slid insidiously into her head, and she frowned. She wasn't meant to be thinking about that kiss. That had been Monday, and things had been different then. Today Nat was just…a friend.

'I know him well enough,' she said shortly.

'Don't get me wrong,' said Cleo, misinterpreting her scowl. 'Nat's very nice. Even Dad liked him, and you know how hard *he* is to please! It's just that you don't seem that close,' she tried to explain her concern as they headed towards the little brasserie she had chosen for lunch.

Prue eyed her warily. 'What do you mean?'

'Most couples are a bit more affectionate with each other,' Cleo pointed out. 'I've hardly seen you two touch each other, and if it wasn't for the way I've seen you look sometimes I'd wonder how well you knew each other. That's why I asked,' she admitted.

So much for thinking that she and Nat had been convincing! Prue was dismayed at her sister's assessment. 'We're sharing a bed, aren't we?' she said, opting for attack as a better form of defence.

'Oh, sex!' Cleo waved her hand dismissively. 'I'm sure you have a great physical relationship, but you need more than that if you're going to get married, Prue. You need to be comfortable with each other when you're not in bed as well as when you are. I just get the feeling that you and Nat *aren't*. It's as if you're really aware of each other but don't dare show it.'

Prue moistened her lips. Cleo was getting a little too close to the truth for comfort. 'Nat's not very demonstrative in public, but that's just the way he is,' she managed.

'I hope it's enough for you,' said Cleo dubiously. 'I know it's not really any of my business, but Mum and I are both worried. You've always had this dream about the outback, and we're afraid that you're getting carried away by the romance of it all.'

She stopped in the middle of the pavement and caught hold of Prue's arm, her blue eyes unusually serious. 'We don't want to spoil anything for you, Prue, but you're talking about marrying a man you don't seem that comfortable with, taking on two small children and going to live in the middle of nowhere. Are you sure you know what you're doing?'

Prue looked back into her sister's face. Cleo was practically shouting over the relentless sound of a drill which was drowning out the noise of all the idling engines as the traffic stalled, bumper to bumper both ways, belching out exhaust fumes. Trapped between the tall buildings, the fumes hung stubbornly in the muggy air, making her eyes sting. All around them office workers, heading out to get a sandwich for lunch, jostled impatiently through the crowds.

She didn't even need to close her eyes to picture the verandah at Mack River, with its shady garden blending into the scrubby trees and the river gums beyond. Prue could see it all so clearly. Nat in one of the chairs, with a baby standing on his lap—Daisy, perhaps—exploring his face with inquisitive little fingers, patting his nose, making him laugh. The shrieks and whistles of the birds. The smell of the bush. The warm weight of William in her arms as she—

Prue's imagination jolted to a sickening halt. No, that wasn't right!

Hastily, she rewound the scene and mentally replaced it with the kitchen at Cowen Creek, with Ross, tall and handsome, taking off his hat with a smile and reaching for her.

That was what she wanted, wasn't it? Her grey gaze refocused on Cleo's concerned face. 'I know just what I'm doing,' she said, although she didn't sound quite as sure as she would have liked.

'You can wear that dress you bought,' said Cleo that evening, loading Prue up with shopping bags and pushing her towards the bedroom. 'You know what Sabrina's like! Her parties are always smart and you need to look the part.'

What part? Prue wondered as she stood under the shower. She was having trouble remembering what part she was playing and what she wasn't.

She wished they didn't have to go out. She had hardly seen Nat. He hadn't returned by the time they'd got back to the flat and when he had come in, half an hour or so later, he seemed to have drawn into himself.

Conscious of her sister's interested gaze, Prue had gone to welcome him with a quick kiss. She had been hoping that Cleo wouldn't notice that she had only dared to kiss his cheek, but even that had taken Nat by surprise and he had tensed as she reached up to press her lips against the corner of his mouth.

He had practically flinched, Prue remembered miserably. It was hard to believe that she had started the day in such good spirits. Somewhere along the line her conviction that she and Nat could spend the next month as friends had deflated and she was left with the uneasy feeling that things just weren't going to be that easy after all.

She had had no chance to tell Nat about Cleo's suspicions. They hadn't had a moment alone, and she had been reduced to asking him politely about his day. He had spent most of it with Eve, he'd said, learning as much as he could about the twins' routine and drawing up a list of things he would need to buy before they came to stay.

'Ruth and Harry were both disappointed you weren't with me,' Nat told Prue, omitting to add that he had missed her much more than they had.

It had been a long day. Reluctant to admit how often

he'd found himself wishing that Prue was with him or how many times he had turned to say something to her only to remember that she wasn't there, Nat blamed his tiredness. He hadn't slept well again. Prue had been dead to the world when he'd got into bed, but he had found it harder to relax when she was so tantalisingly close.

The street light outside the window threw a weirdly orange glow onto the ceiling, casting enough light to see her face as a pale blur against the pillow and her bare arm curled across her chest. Nat had been able to smell her shampoo, a clean fresh fragrance with a faint hint of something he hadn't quite been able to identify. Herbs? Almonds? Coconut?

Without thinking, he had moved closer and lifted a lock of her hair to his face, rubbing its softness between his fingers before he'd realised just what he was doing and dropped it as if it had bitten him.

Moving firmly back to his side of the bed, Nat had set his jaw and stared up at the ceiling. Outside, he had heard the sound of traffic punctuated by a distant siren. A couple had gone by, arguing, and somehow, somewhere there had been the distinctive noise of a washing machine entering its spin cycle.

Who would do their washing in the middle of the night? Nat had wondered, half convinced that he was imagining it. He had waited for the noise to stop, but it never had. He'd heard footsteps and banging doors, cars being parked or driven away. A neighbour had had music playing. Revellers had headed home from the pub right underneath the bedroom window, unable to tell how loud their voices sounded in the night air. Did no one in London ever sleep?

Nat's eyes had strayed over to Prue, breathing quietly

beside him, and he had sighed. It looked like being a very long week.

And now they had a party to get through. Intent on organising everyone, Cleo had allowed him to shower and change and then he had been sent to wait with Alex in the sitting room while the girls did whatever it was girls did when they got ready to go out.

Nat was reassured to discover that Alex had no clearer idea than he did. Over a beer, they speculated as to what was going on in the next room, and they were getting on better than either of them had expected when the door opened and a shrinking Prue was pushed into the room.

'There!' said Cleo triumphantly. 'Doesn't she look beautiful?'

Nat hardly heard her. Pole-axed by the sight of Prue, he rose unthinkingly to his feet, perhaps hoping that it would be easier to breathe upright. He couldn't take his eyes off her. Her hair was a soft cloud, framing her pale, pointed face, and the huge grey eyes were apprehensive, sliding nervously away from his.

She was wearing a short dress that stopped just above her knees. It was made of some silvery material that glimmered beneath a layer of grey chiffon and clung lovingly to the curves of her body. Dry-mouthed, Nat let his gaze travel down from the slender knees to where her bare feet were encased in delicate silver sandals. He had never seen Prue's legs before, he realised irrelevantly. He had had no idea that she could look so…so…

'Well?' demanded Cleo. 'What do you think?'

Nat swallowed the constriction in his throat. 'You look very nice,' he said, and saw by the brittleness of Prue's smile how inadequate a compliment it had been.

'Very nice? Is that all you can say?' Cleo didn't bother to hide her disgust. 'Some fiancé *you* are!'

She turned to Prue. 'Don't listen to Nat,' she admonished her. 'You look fantastic. The trouble with you, Prue, is that you don't *try*. You could be beautiful, but because you never make the effort nobody ever notices and you just—'

'I notice.' Nat's quiet voice cut across Cleo's affectionate scolding, and something in his face made her stop in mid-sentence.

Ignoring Cleo and Alex, Nat went over to Prue and ran a gentle finger down her cheek. 'I notice you,' he said softly. 'I notice everything about you.'

Prue stared up into his face, mesmerised by the expression in his eyes. She could feel her blood beating and the nerves just below her skin began to tingle as he smoothed the hair tenderly away from her forehead so that he could hold her face between his palms.

'I notice the way the light catches your hair,' he told her, and the two of them might have been alone in the room—in the world. 'I notice your cheekbones and your eyes and the way you smile. You don't need a new dress for me to notice how beautiful you are.'

Prue was giddy and trembling inside. She felt as if she was standing on the brink of a bottomless chasm of feeling, and Nat's hands were all that prevented her from tumbling forwards and down. Her heart was slamming so painfully against her ribs that she was afraid she might actually pass out.

She opened her mouth, but no sound came out and she had no idea what she would have said. It didn't matter anyway, because the next moment Nat's mouth came down on hers and the room, Cleo, Alex, the need to think or find something to say, all evaporated. There was only the warm persuasion of his lips and the flame inside her that leapt to respond.

Prue let out a shivery sigh of release as Nat's hands left her face and his arms went round her, gathering her close against his hard body. Her bones were melting, dissolving in a golden rush of pleasure, and she clung to him with a kind of desperation, afraid of where it might take her, not wanting to know where the kiss might end, not wanting it to end at all.

That's enough, Nat's brain instructed him. Let her go.

Nat knew that he should, but she tasted so sweet and she felt so good in his arms that he couldn't, not yet.

Let her go, his brain insisted as its control slipped alarmingly. *Let her go!*

Slowly, reluctantly, Nat obeyed. He lifted his head and loosened his hold, but he still kept one arm around her. That was allowed, surely?

'That's a bit more like it!' Cleo was surveying them with a satisfied air. 'We were beginning to wonder if you two were in love at all, but I have to say that I'm convinced!'

Alex laughed. 'Either that, or they're very good actors!' he said.

His words splintered Prue's daze of enchantment and she stiffened. *Acting.* That was all it had been. Cheeks burning, she jerked herself out of the circle of Nat's arm.

'Don't be silly, Alex,' she said, and her voice was so husky that she had to clear her throat. She couldn't look at Nat. 'If we're going to this party, hadn't we better go?'

Prue had never thought that she would be glad to be going to one of Sabrina's parties, but the alternative would have been an intimate meal with just the four of them. She would have had to sit next to Nat under Cleo's disconcertingly sharp gaze and try to behave normally. How could she have done that when she was shaken and still shocked by how easily she had abandoned herself to

his kiss, when her body was still thumping and her mind
awhirl with memory?

At least the party would be a distraction for all of them,
and with any luck it would give her a chance to calm
down a bit. Nat had been so *convincing*. He had looked
down into her eyes and kissed her as if he really loved
her. No wonder Cleo had believed him. She had almost
believed him herself.

And she had been convincing as well, Prue remembered uneasily. Too convincing. She had just stood there,
staring dazedly up into his face as if there was no one
else in the world. The very model of a besotted fiancée!

Prue cringed as she sat in the taxi Alex had waved
down. Anyone would have thought that she was head
over heels in love with Nat, which was ridiculous, of
course. She wasn't in love with him. She couldn't be.

She hardly knew him, Prue reminded herself with an
edge of desperation. You couldn't fall in love with someone when you had barely known them a week…could
you?

Of course, she had fallen in love with Ross at first
sight, but that had been different. That had been wild and
romantic. Perfect, in fact, Prue told herself. She didn't
feel that for Nat at all.

He was familiar to her in a way that Ross had never
been. She had always been too dazzled by Ross's looks
or too preoccupied by the churning sensation in her stomach whenever he was near to relax and get to know what
made him tick. Nat didn't overwhelm her in the same
way, but that wasn't the same as falling in love, was it?
It was just that the better she knew him, the more she
appreciated why a girl as reputedly stunning as Kathryn
might want to marry him and the less she understood why
Kathryn had let him go.

Sabrina was a glamorous redhead with a private trust fund which she drew on for the lavish parties she loved. She always made Prue feel dowdy and dull, but Prue had to admit that Sabrina was incredibly generous, even if she was a bit over the top. She swept down on them as they arrived, kissed them all extravagantly, and promptly annexed Nat.

'So you're Prue's cowboy!' she cried. 'Come with me, everyone's *dying* to meet you!'

To Prue's consternation, Nat seemed amused rather than overpowered by Sabrina, and he let himself be borne off without so much as a backward glance. Craning her neck to keep the two of them in view, she saw Sabrina tuck her hand cosily into his arm and Nat smile down at her.

Kathryn was a redhead too, Prue remembered with a cold trickle down her spine. Perhaps Sabrina reminded him of his first love? From what he and Ross had told her, Sabrina and Kathryn were not unalike.

Prue tried to shrug off the thought. If Nat liked that rather flashy kind of beauty, there was nothing she could do about it. She just hoped he didn't think he would ever get Sabrina to the outback, she thought sourly. Sabrina felt that she was roughing it if she stepped out of Knightsbridge.

The party was just as bad as Prue had feared. The room was hot and crowded, and everyone was shouting at the tops of their voices to make themselves heard over the band in the corner. She had met most of Cleo's friends over the years, so there was no shortage of people to talk to, but most of them only wanted to ask her about Nat. Prue was soon sick of jokes about kangaroos and boomerangs and Crocodile Dundee. Paul Hogan had a lot to answer for, she decided wearily.

She kept losing sight of Nat. Sabrina was dragging him round the room like a prize exhibit—look what Prue brought back from Australia!—and whenever she did catch a glimpse of him he was surrounded by admiring girls, all running their hands through their hair and sending him flirty little glances under their lashes.

Heaven only knew what they saw in him, thought Prue crossly. It couldn't be for his looks, that was for sure, and it wasn't as if he was making any effort to charm them either. He was just standing there, as cool and contained as ever, listening courteously to their inanities and keeping his inevitable opinion to himself.

It must just be because he was different, she decided. Next to Nat, the other men in the room looked somehow pale and insubstantial. His admiring audience was simply avid for anything new. If Nat didn't watch out, he would become a craze.

Prue smiled wryly at the idea. It was ironic that Nat, the calmest and least crazy man she had ever met, should be the object of such feverish attention. Those girls hanging on his every word didn't know Nat. They didn't know what he was really like or where he really belonged.

Unbidden, a picture of Mack River sprang into her mind, and she remembered how they had ridden among the trees, how quiet it had been. The silence had beaten down around them, broken only by the gentle whicker of the horses and the jingle of their bits as they shook their manes occasionally against the flies.

Prue could still smell the hot, dry air and the dried leaves that had been crushed under the horses' hooves. She could practically *feel* the reins in her hand. So vivid was the memory that she could almost believe that if she turned her head Nat would be there by her side, looking utterly at home, his hat tilted over his eyes and his mouth

set in that cool, quiet line that snarled her senses whenever she looked at it.

The longing to be there was suddenly so intense that
Prue closed her eyes, screwing them shut as if against a
pain. When she opened them again Nat was in front of
her, looking down at her with a hard, anxious expression
in his eyes, but the trees and the horses and the diamond-
bright light had all gone and she felt a wave of bitter
disappointment wash over her.

Nat frowned. 'Are you all right?'

Prue couldn't look at him. She felt sick, shaken, per-
ilously close to tears. 'I'm fine,' she muttered.

'I thought you were about to faint.'

'I'm *fine.*'

'We can go if you want,' Nat offered.

All Prue wanted was to be at Mack River or, failing
that, in a dark room where she could lock herself in for
a good cry. But she couldn't do that because then he
would want to know what the matter was, and how could
she tell him when she didn't know herself?

She lifted her chin. 'I'd hate to tear you away when
you're having such a good time,' she snapped. 'Oh, look,
there's Sabrina! She'll be coming to find out what you're
doing wasting your time talking to me. I mean, I'm only
your fiancée!'

Too late, Prue heard the jealous note in her voice, and
her brief spurt of anger at his obtuseness died. 'Pretend
fiancée, anyway,' she muttered.

'Prue—' Nat began, but before he could finish Sabrina
was bearing down on them.

'There you are, Prue! Where have you been hiding?
Everyone's been wondering what happened to you. I'd
keep an eye on Nat if I were you,' she added. 'We're all
smitten!'

She leant confidentially closer. 'Congratulations!' she said in a stage whisper. 'That strong, silent look is to *die* for! Not that you've any need to be jealous,' she went on with a smile. 'Nat's been watching you all evening! I don't know what you did a minute ago, but he walked off in the middle of a conversation. Didn't say anything, just headed straight for you!' she said enviously. 'You lucky thing!'

'Sabrina!' said Nat quickly and held out his hand. 'It was nice to meet you.'

'Oh, but you're not going *already*?' Sabrina pouted. 'The party's only just beginning.'

'We're very tired,' said Nat, taking Prue's hand in a firm clasp. 'We only arrived a couple of days ago and you know what jet lag is like...'

'We want to be fresh for the wedding,' Prue put in, forcing a smile and trying to ignore the feel of Nat's fingers around hers.

Sabrina was obviously disappointed. 'I suppose you just want to be on your own,' she said a shade sulkily, and then recovered to smile her brilliant smile. 'Oh, well, I can't blame you! Cleo and Alex will be here to the bitter end, so you'll have the flat to yourselves,' she promised with a roguish wink.

Insisting on accompanying them to the door, she waved them off into the night. 'See you at the wedding!' she said.

CHAPTER SEVEN

IT WAS a relief to get out of the crowded house. Prue took a deep breath of night air as they walked down the steps.

Nat was holding her hand, but the moment Sabrina closed the door on them he gave it back to her like a parcel. Without the clasp of his fingers it felt cold and empty at the end of her arm, and Prue didn't know what to do with it. She tried it in various positions before folding her arms and tucking it out of sight at her waist as she pretended to look for a taxi.

'We might as well walk,' she suggested in a creditably cool voice when no yellow light appeared. 'It's not that far.'

They walked without touching through the summer night. To Nat, London seemed almost as busy by night as during the day. Plenty of shops were still open, and drinkers spilled out of the pubs to stand on the pavement in cheerful groups. The traffic continued to growl along the roads and, once, a police car zipped past, blue light flashing and siren whooping. Nat felt a long way from Mathison.

In spite of the noise and activity around them it seemed, to Prue, that the two of them were sealed off from it all, trapped in a bubble of constrained silence where there was nothing to keep the memory of the kiss they had shared at bay. It shimmered between them, unavoidable, unforgettable, making it impossible to think about anything else.

'Thank you for earlier,' said Prue awkwardly at last, unable to bear the tension any longer.

'What for?'

For kissing me. That was what she wanted to say, but her nerve failed her at the last minute. 'For saying what you did,' she said instead.

She felt Nat's quick glance. 'Don't mention it,' he said in a colourless voice.

Prue wished that she *hadn't* mentioned it, but she couldn't just leave it there. She forced a smile and tried to speak lightly. 'Did Cleo have a word with you too?'

'Cleo?' Nat sounded surprised. 'No. What about?'

'She's worried that we're not affectionate enough with each other.' Prue glanced at him. 'I assumed that she'd had a go at you too while I was in the bath.'

So that was why she had responded so willingly to his kiss. Nat was conscious of a sinking feeling in his stomach. She had just been trying to convince her sister that they really were engaged. Well, what had he expected? Had he really thought that there could have been any other reason for her to melt into his arms like that?

He watched a double-decker bus go past. 'I gathered Cleo had some doubts,' he said carefully, not quite lying. If Prue had a good excuse for kissing him so sweetly, he might as well pretend that he had approached the matter in a similarly cold-blooded spirit.

There was a pause.

'At least she's convinced now,' said Prue with a laugh that didn't quite come off.

'Yes, she is.'

Of course Cleo was convinced. Who wouldn't have been? The very air seemed to be mocking them, twanging with the memory of how they had held each other and kissed, not like two people pretending to be in love but like lovers.

Silence fell once more, awkward and uncomfortable. Prue was very conscious of the sound of her heels on the pavement. A fuzzy moon hung in the sky above the flashing lights of the planes still coming in to land at Heathrow, and the air was warm and thick, like soup, and alive with the night scent of the flowers crammed into windowboxes along the street. The streets were lined with parked cars, red lights winking on their dashboards to show that they were alarmed. To Prue they seemed to be blinking the same warning.

Be careful.

Don't make a fool of yourself.

Remember Kathryn.

Remember *Ross*.

Forget how he kissed you. It was just for show.

Hugging her arms to her, she kept her head down and concentrated on not walking on the cracks in the pavement.

'What are you doing?' asked Nat after he had been watching her careful steps for a while.

'I'm avoiding the bears.'

She saw that the reference meant nothing to him. Why should it? There were no pavements at Mack River.

'It's just a silly superstition,' she said, blushing. She pointed down at the paving-stones. 'It's supposed to be unlucky to tread on the lines, that's all. If you can keep your feet in the squares, you can make your wishes come true.'

Nat stopped, his hands in his pockets as he looked at her. 'What were you wishing for?' he asked.

What *did* she want? Prue felt as if she had walked smack into a wall in the dark and she took a step back,

inadvertently stepping on a crack after all. She had grown
so used to dreaming about Ross that it was a shock to
realise that for the first time since she had met him his
face didn't immediately spring to mind. She didn't *know*
what she had been wishing for, Prue realised. The only
thing she knew was that she felt confused and uncertain,
and she didn't like it.

'Oh, you know,' she said uncomfortably.

Of course he knew, thought Nat bitterly. Prue had
never made any secret of how she felt about Ross. It had
been stupid to even ask.

'Yes, I know,' he said, and walked on down the dark
street.

The flat felt very empty when they got in, and there
was nothing to do but go to bed. Prue longed for the
exhaustion that had made it all so simple last night, when
she had been too tired to be embarrassed, but now she
managed to feel weary and wide awake at the same time.

It was ridiculous to feel nervous, she knew. They had
shared a bed perfectly easily before, and there was no
reason why they shouldn't do the same again, but it
didn't stop her stomach looping alarmingly as she
changed in the bathroom. Pulling on her nightdress, Prue
felt the coolness of the cotton against her skin and wished
she could feel that cool inside.

She chewed her lip as she regarded her reflection in
the bathroom mirror. It was a perfectly plain nightdress,
falling from narrow straps to her calves, and although
there was nothing glamorous or seductive about it she
was conscious of her naked body beneath the thin material in a way she had never been in the past. The soft,
fine cotton was all that would be between her and Nat
when they were lying together in the dark.

Stop it! Stop it! Prue squeezed her eyes shut. She was

tired; Nat was tired. They would lie next to each other and they would sleep, and absolutely nothing else would happen. All she had to do was relax.

Relaxing, though, was easier said than done. The bed seemed to have shrunk since the night before and Prue was agonisingly aware of Nat beside her, very solid, very close. He lay so still that she was afraid to toss and turn in case she disturbed him, and had to content herself with shifting cautiously on to one side and then the other. And then back again. And again.

She was hot, then cold. Staring at the curtains, Prue let out a long sigh. They would have been better off staying at the party. She was never going to be able to sleep!

But as she listened to Nat's slow, steady breathing, her tension did in the end evaporate and she began gradually, very gradually, to relax. She must have dropped off at last, because the next thing Prue knew there was something heavy lying across her. Drifting on the edge of sleep, she let her fingers explore it questioningly.

Nat's hand. Nat's arm. They were lying like spoons, she realised, in the dream-like state where the answer seemed obvious and somehow right. She was on her side, and she could feel the length of his hard body curled against her back. His face was half buried in her hair, and his slow breath was a shivery caress against her bare shoulder.

Behind her, Nat stirred, and Prue lay very still, her eyes closed. Mumbling something she couldn't catch, he pressed a warm kiss into her neck and sank back into sleep.

Prue's eyes had flown open at the touch of his mouth and she was suddenly wide awake, her skin tingling where his lips had been. She let out a breath very carefully, without moving. It had been a reflex action on

Nat's part, that much was obvious. That mumble…had it been Kathryn's name? It could have been, but then it could have been anything—except her own name. He definitely hadn't said 'Prue'. He hadn't meant to kiss *her*.

A tiny sigh escaped Prue. She ought to disentangle herself from Nat and move away to her own side of the bed. But there was hardly any room, and if she pushed *him* away he might wake up. It wasn't that she wanted Nat to kiss her again—of course not—but she was comfortable and sleepy and there was no point in making a big deal out of something Nat hadn't even known he was doing. Prue's lashes closed. She might as well stay right where she was.

The sound of frantic barking greeted them as Cleo pushed open the gate and they walked up to the house together. 'Angus,' sighed Prue to Nat. 'Mum's dog. He's completely out of control.'

They had spent most of the day with William and Daisy, and the two babies had been so endearing that Prue hadn't wanted to leave them. Once or twice, when she looked at Nat, she had felt a peculiar sensation in her neck and she had put a hand unthinkingly to where it tingled.

She had a vague memory of waking in the night, curled up with him, his lips on her skin, but in the clear light of day Prue was more than half inclined to dismiss it as a dream. When she had woken that morning Nat had been nowhere near her. Still, like some vivid dreams, the impression had been hard to shake off, and it had left her acutely aware of him all day, as if all her senses had been set on high alert as far as he was concerned.

Her mother opened the door in response to Cleo's imperative ring on the doorbell and immediately a small terrier rushed out, wagging his tail and barking furiously. Thoroughly over-excited at the mixture of familiar and unfamiliar legs, he ran around in circles, lifted his leg on the nearest plant and completely ignored the family's attempts to quieten him.

'We'll just have to wait for him to calm down, I'm afraid,' Prue's mother apologised. 'Oh, do shut *up*, Angus!' she shouted without any expectation of being obeyed.

Nat looked down at the little dog, who was up on his hind legs and yapping hysterically for attention. 'Quiet!' he ordered, and to the utter amazement of everyone, Angus stopped in mid-yap.

'Now, sit!'

Responding to the quiet authority in his voice, Angus sank down onto his haunches and flattened his ears placatingly.

They all gaped at Nat and then at the dog, who was wagging his tail tentatively as he waited for his obedience to be acknowledged. Nat crouched down and fondled Angus's ears. 'Good dog,' he said.

Lucky Angus, thought Prue involuntarily as the others all continued to stare at Nat as if he had performed some kind of miracle.

'*Well!*' Her mother was obviously rapidly revising her estimate of Nat as a potential son-in-law. 'I've never seen him do that before! I'm impressed! Come in, Nat, and meet Marisa.'

Prue was left with Cleo and Alex to follow behind and close the door.

'Nat's well in now,' Cleo murmured in Prue's ear. 'Mum will elevate him to star status if he can handle Angus! If he can do that, he can do anything. Nat's a handy person to have around, isn't he?' she went on, eyeing Nat speculatively as he was ushered into the sitting room, Angus trotting angelically at his heels. 'Did you know he fixed the dripping tap in the bathroom, and that window I could never open? He didn't say a word. Alex would have made a huge fuss about how macho he was being, but Nat just went off and did it!'

Cleo took Prue's arm and smiled conspiratorially. 'You know, I'm beginning to see what you mean about him being attractive,' she confided. 'I noticed it at the party last night. Nat grows on you, doesn't he? And he's got a wonderful smile.'

'I know,' said Prue, who felt hollow at the very thought of it. She didn't need Cleo to remind her how Nat smiled. Right now, she would much rather that she could forget.

'Auntie Prue! Auntie Prue!' Her small niece and nephew came tumbling down the stairs to meet her, barely restrained by their father who had been bathing them.

Prue had spent a lot of time with Ben and Katie before she went to Australia and she was firmly established as their favourite aunt. Bending down to open her arms, she laughed as they hurtled into her. Delighted to see them, and secretly glad of the distraction, she let them clamber exuberantly over her before picking Katie up and carrying her into the sitting room, six-year-old Ben hanging from other hand.

Nat, cornered by Prue's elder sister and her husband, looked up in relief as Prue came in, a small child clinging to her neck and another tugging at her hand. Her hair was all over the place, but her silvery eyes were alight with laughter and Nat's heart turned over.

'Look what they've done to you!' Marisa tutted as she kissed Prue and pushed the tumbled curls back into some semblance of order, and Nat found his hands itching to slap her hands away so that he could do it himself.

'Children, this is Nat,' Marisa went on. 'He's going to marry Auntie Prue.'

She smiled apologetically at Nat. 'They're a bit shy with strangers,' she told him, but Ben was already taking the hand Nat held gravely out to him.

'Why are you going to marry Auntie Prue?' he asked.

Prue gave a tiny gasp that was half-laugh, half-embarrassment, but Nat didn't even hesitate. 'Because I'm in love with her,' he told the little boy.

'Why?'

Nat glanced up at Prue, who was clutching Katie to her, the grey eyes a mixture of appeal and apology. 'I think you might need to be a bit older to understand,' he said.

Ben considered this. 'What do you have to do to be in love with someone?' he asked, interested, and Nat's mouth twitched.

'You don't have to do anything,' he answered seriously, although all the others were laughing, except Prue, who just looked agonised. 'You just are.'

'But *why*?'

His father, Phil, rescued Nat. 'You have to kiss girls when you're in love with them,' he said, teasing. 'You wouldn't want to do that, would you, Ben?'

'No!' Appalled, Ben screwed up his face. He had reached the stage where he would tolerate being kissed by his mother in private, but that was about it. 'Yuk!'

Even Prue couldn't help laughing then. 'Sorry, Ben! I shouldn't have kissed you just now. I'd forgotten that you would have grown up since I've been away.'

'I don't mind *you*,' said Ben generously. 'I like it when you kiss me. You smell nice.'

Nat knew exactly what he meant. He straightened. 'There you are,' he said to Ben, but his eyes were on Prue. 'I feel like that too. That's why I want to marry her.'

Ridiculously, Prue blushed, which only made her wretched family laugh harder.

'Oh.' Ignoring the adults' mystifying behaviour, Ben nodded sagely. He smiled up at Nat. 'Do you want to see my super-blaster?'

'No, Ben, not now,' Marisa put in hurriedly. 'It's time for bed.'

A stormy look gathered on Ben's face, and a mighty tantrum was only averted when Nat and Prue agreed to go up and read the two children a bedtime story. 'But only if you're good now!' their mother said sternly.

Later, Prue sat with Katie on her lap, and rested her cheek on the soft curls. She was trying to read about Goldilocks, but she kept stumbling over the simplest words. She couldn't seem to focus on the page. It was something to do with Nat, sitting opposite her on the bed that had once been hers, reading to Ben in the deep, slow voice that seemed to reverberate up and down her spine. It wasn't just a sound, it was a physical sensation as real as if he was smoothing a warm hand over her bare back.

'Cold?' Feeling her aunt shiver, Katie twisted round and looked up at Prue in concern.

'No, not cold.' Prue forced a smile and cleared her throat. '"And then Baby Bear said…"'

The evening seemed to last for ever. When Ben and Katie had been tucked up, they had champagne and drank a toast to Cleo and Alex, who kissed blissfully. Prue carefully avoided Nat's eye until, to her horror, she realised that Cleo was proposing another toast.

'I think we should drink to Prue and Nat, too,' she said, gesturing to Alex to refill all their glasses.

'Oh, no...' stuttered Prue, caught unawares. 'I mean, this is *your* evening, Cleo.'

'I don't mind sharing it with you,' said Cleo gaily. 'Don't worry, I'll have Saturday all to myself, but we need to celebrate your engagement properly too.'

'I agree.' Prue's father unexpectedly entered the discussion. 'We're all very happy for you, darling,' he said, kissing her, and then turned to shake Nat's hand. 'This seems a good time to welcome you to the family while we're all here. Prue's very precious to us,' he added, a faint hint of warning in his voice. 'We hope you'll look after her for us.'

Returning his grip, Nat looked at Prue. 'I will,' he promised.

'To Prue and Nat!'

As her family raised their glasses, Nat met Prue's anguished grey gaze and he set his jaw at her obvious distaste at the idea that he might have to kiss her again. With the others beaming expectantly around them, he didn't see that they had much choice, but he tried to spare her by lifting her hand and kissing it.

It wasn't enough. They were all still waiting, and Nat could see Cleo's fine brows already beginning to rise at his hesitation. Pulling Prue towards him, he bent his head and touched his lips to her mouth. He would make it quick.

The floor tilted beneath Prue's feet as his mouth came down on hers. It was just like it had been the night before, she realised with a mixture of elation and despair. The same jolt of excitement, the same treacherous urge to forget this pretence they were committed to and let herself believe that it was real.

She had sensed Nat's hesitation too. She knew why he was kissing her, and that it only needed to be brief, but somehow their lips caught and clung and wouldn't let go, and before she knew where she was she was kissing him back and her bones were dissolving into honey, and she was pierced by a sweetness so intense that tears stung and shimmered in her eyes when he at last let her go.

And that was just the beginning. They had more champagne, and then they had to sit down to a three-course meal that her mother had spent days preparing. Prue pushed her food around her plate. She didn't think she could eat.

She worried that she might be running a fever. There was a jittery sensation under her skin and she kept going hot and cold. She felt fragile, as if the slightest touch would shatter her into a million pieces.

And she couldn't keep her eyes off Nat. She was fascinated by his hands, by the way they held his fork or lifted his glass, by how strong and brown they looked against the pale tablecloth, and she thought about the feel of his fingers against her face, about the warm press of lips against her neck last night, and she shivered again. Had she dreamt it? *Had* she?

Prue drank her wine with a kind of desperation, latching onto fragments of the conversation swirling around her but unable to make any sense of it. All she could think about was Nat's calm, quiet presence opposite. She tried not to stare at him, and her gaze skittered frantically around the table in search of something else to look at, but whenever she managed to fix it on the pepper mill or the dribble of wax down the side of a candle it would be tugged back by the gleam of Nat's slow smile.

By the tilt of his head.

By his throat as he swallowed.

There was a constriction around Prue's heart, as if all the air had evaporated from her lungs. She wanted to reach across the table and uncurl his fingers from the glass he held. She wanted to take his hand and pull him out of the room.

She wanted Nat to press her against the wall outside and to kiss her again. She wanted to wind her arms around him and burrow into the steely strength of his body, to tug the shirt from his trousers so that she could run her hands over his back, feeling his muscles flex beneath her fingers.

Oh, and she wanted him to smile against her throat, to peel off her clothes, to kiss his—

'Prue?'

Prue took a sharp, startled breath, as if someone had dashed a bucket of cold water in her face. 'S-sorry...what?' she gasped.

Her family regarded her with amusement. 'You've hardly eaten a thing,' her mother said reprovingly. 'Is something wrong?'

'I'm just...not hungry.'

'Poor old Prue! You *have* got it bad!' said Cleo, patting her sister's hand indulgently. 'I've never seen you in love like this before!'

In love.

It was all Prue could do not to clap her hands to her mouth. She stared wide-eyed at Cleo, who laughed.

'Well, don't look so appalled!' she teased. 'You're engaged to Nat. You're allowed to be in love with him!'

But she wasn't.

She couldn't have fallen in love with Nat, she told herself frantically. It was just...

Just what? Just the need to be with him? Just the wanting to touch him? Just the longing to spend the rest of her life with him?

What if Nat had guessed? Prue thought in panic. Her sisters seemed to think her expression was utterly transparent. What if he too had been sitting there, his heart sinking as he realised what a fool she was making of herself?

They were all waiting for her to say something. Prue opened her mouth, but no words came out, and in spite of herself her eyes lifted to Nat's. They held an indecipherable expression, but he smiled reassuringly at her and she relaxed slightly. Surely he wouldn't have smiled if he had guessed the truth? He would have curled his lip in disgust or turned away, wondering how to remind her about Kathryn. He wouldn't have *smiled*.

Marisa had been watching the exchange of looks across the table. 'I think you'd better have the wedding as soon as possible,' she said drily, and Prue's head jerked round.

'*Marisa...*'

'Well, why not?' Her mother picked up on the idea. 'There's no reason why you shouldn't get married before you go back to Australia, is there?'

'Good idea.' It was Cleo's turn to chime in. 'Just wait until Alex and I get back from our honeymoon!'

Prue stared at her. Only two days ago she and her mother had been shaking their heads over the whole idea of her marrying Nat, and now here they were, pushing her into it as soon as possible. And all because Angus had sat when Nat told him to!

'It's too soon,' she said, managing a brittle smile.

'But you seem so right together! Why wait?'

Because Nat's in love with another woman, Prue wanted to shout. She mumbled something about William and Daisy, but Cleo was having none of it.

'You getting married won't make any difference to them,' she pointed out. 'If anything, it'll be better for them. Give them a nice stable background, that kind of thing.'

'Yes, and I'll happily look after them if you want to have a honeymoon,' offered Marisa. 'Katie and Ben would love having them to stay.'

Prue wished they would both shut up. 'We don't *want*—'she began loudly, at the end of her tether.

'We want to get married in Australia,' Nat cut across her before she could blurt out the truth. His voice was quiet, but Cleo and Marisa subsided instantly. 'Don't we, Prue?' he added, knowing that was what she really wanted. She just didn't want to marry him.

Prue managed a nod, not looking at him. Getting married in Australia was what Nat wanted, after all. He just didn't want to marry her. He wanted Kathryn, beautiful Kathryn, who belonged with him and who everyone knew was meant to be with him.

'Oh, well.' Her mother and sisters were disappointed but not downcast. 'We'll just have to come out to Australia, then.'

Prue looked at them in consternation. 'We wouldn't expect that,' she tried. 'It's such a long way.'

'Nonsense!' Her mother disposed of that objection without any trouble. 'Of course we're coming to your wedding.'

'Besides, it's a good excuse for a holiday,' said Marisa to Prue's amazement. Marisa? In *Australia*? She couldn't picture it.

'I don't think—'

Cleo went on the attack. 'What's the matter?' she demanded. 'Don't you want us to come?'

'It's not—'

'Of course we want you to come,' said Nat firmly, seeing that Prue was looking harried. 'There's plenty of room for you all at Mack River, and you'll always be welcome.'

By the time they left, Cleo and Marisa had planned an entire trip based around the wedding they imagined would be taking place at Mack River, although their knowledge of Australian geography was hazy to say the least. If Prue hadn't been so preoccupied, she would have been amused at the very idea of the two of them in the outback. She couldn't see them tripping around Mathison somehow.

But then, they wouldn't have to. There would be no wedding, and no trip.

As it was, Prue let them plan an itinerary which involved driving from Sydney to Mathison with an overnight stop in Alice Springs and a possible detour to Perth, their increasingly far-fetched ideas flowing over her head. She felt as if she were crouched in a dark place, hugging her new knowledge of how much she loved Nat to herself and terrified in case he got so much as a glimpse of it.

Dreading being alone with him, Prue was tense and snappy as they drove back to the flat. She didn't know how to behave with him any more. She lingered as long as she could in the bathroom, scrubbing her face fiercely as if she could rub away her feelings and go back to the way she had been before, when she had innocently imagined that what she had felt for Ross had been love.

It hadn't been, of course. Prue could see that now. She had loved the *idea* of Ross more than the reality, idealising the fact that he was so good-looking and such fun, and she could live the life she had always dreamt of in a place she loved. She hadn't really known Ross, though.

She hadn't needed him or hungered for him in the way she suddenly, so desperately, did for Nat.

Perhaps it was just a passing phase, Prue tried to comfort herself. She was just obsessing about Nat because they were together, and her feelings wouldn't last any longer than her supposed love for Ross had lasted a few days' separation.

All she had to do was stay calm and not make a complete fool of herself by giving Nat so much as a *hint* that she saw him as anything more than a means to save face with her family, or by doing anything really stupid like throwing herself into Nat's arms and begging him not to let her go. That would only embarrass both of them and make the next few weeks with the twins an agony.

All she had to do, in fact, was to get a grip and wait for this new love to pass.

'What's wrong?' Nat asked when she went back into the bedroom. He was sitting on the edge of the bed, taking off his boots and watching her with a frown in his eyes. She had only spoken in monosyllables since they'd left her parents, and he could feel the tension in her twanging around the room.

'Nothing,' snapped Prue, stalking round to the other side of the bed so there was no temptation to fall weeping into his arms. 'I'm just tired.'

'You've been like this all evening. Didn't you enjoy yourself?'

'Of course I didn't! How do you expect me to enjoy myself when we're stuck in this stupid pretence?'

All of a sudden the fight went out of her, and she slumped down on the bed and put her head in her hands. 'I wish we'd never started this,' she muttered, close to tears. 'It's all so *complicated*. Now we've got my entire family wanting to meet the twins and booking flights out to Australia. Next thing we know, they'll be landing on your doorstop and wondering where I am... Where's it all going to end?' she asked wildly.

'It's going to end when we go back to Australia,' said Nat calmly. He got up and came round the bed to sit next to her. 'There'll be no problem. You can just write to your family later and say that we've decided not to get married after all.'

The longing to lean against him was so great that Prue had to dig her nails into her palms. 'They'll all be so disappointed. You've seen what they're like!'

Nat debated whether he could put his arm round her or not, but decided against it. He didn't trust himself, and anyway she was so tense he felt she might recoil in horror.

'They just want you to be happy,' he said, 'and you will be when you're with Ross again.'

Ross? How could she be happy with Ross when she needed *him*? Prue turned her face away. 'I suppose so,' she muttered.

'I thought you must have been thinking about him this evening.'

'Yes, I was,' she said dully after a moment. She might as well let Nat think that she was still hung up on Ross. Anything other than let him see that all she wanted was to unbutton his shirt and touch her lips to his chest.

Her senses snarled at his closeness. His thigh brushed hers, his arm, and she felt sick and giddy with desire.

'You mustn't let the teasing get you down,' said Nat carefully. 'They don't know how you feel about Ross.'

Prue latched onto the excuse. 'I know,' she said with difficulty. 'I just didn't realise love would be like this.' She swallowed, determined to convince him that she was in no danger of forgetting Kathryn. 'You know what it's like.'

Nat's eyes rested on her averted face. He could see the sweep of her lashes, the tantalising warmth of her skin, the hair curling under her ear. 'Yes,' he said bleakly as he got to his feet. 'I know what it's like.'

CHAPTER EIGHT

PRUE was dreaming a wonderful dream. She was lying on her side and Nat was kissing his way along her shoulder, slow, tantalising kisses to draw her deliciously out of sleep. His hand was at her knee, slipping beneath the cotton nightdress, warm, insistent, irresistible against her thigh.

And, because it was just a dream, Prue could turn with a murmur of pleasure. She could lift her arm to encircle his neck and pull his mouth down to meet hers, and oh! it was so good to be able to kiss him the way she had wanted to kiss him all evening, long, lingering, luxurious kisses that felt absolutely natural and absolutely right.

In a dream, there was no need to pretend. There was no need to think at all. There was just the taste of his lips and the enticing exploration of his tongue and the searing touch of his hands and the feel of his taut, unyielding body pressing hard on hers.

Abandoning herself to a gathering storm of sensation, Prue let her hands roam hungrily over Nat's back. His skin was sleek and supple over solid muscle, and she kissed his shoulder as his lips left hers and travelled possessively down her throat to her breast. She was unravelling, dissolving, feverish in the face of the impatient pulse inside her that clamoured to meet the growing urgency of his hands.

'Please...' she gasped, arching herself towards his touch, incoherent with desire. '*Please...*'

Her pleading filtered through the roar of sensation in

Nat's head as if from a great distance. It sounded as if she was begging him to stop and, abruptly wide awake, he stilled in the horrified realisation of what he was doing.

For one endless moment he couldn't move. He lay frozen on top of Prue, his mouth at her breast, his hand on the smooth curve of her hip, until slowly, very slowly, he lifted his head and made himself look down into her face. In the dawn light she looked bewildered, her eyes huge and dark and dazed, and her mouth was trembling uncontrollably.

With a muffled curse, Nat levered himself away from her. He swung his legs over the side of the bed and dropped his head into his hands, swearing under his breath as he fought to bring his body under control.

'What...? What...?' Prue's heart was jerking with shock as she found herself wrenched so cruelly from the dream that had not been a dream at all. She was having trouble forming the words in her mouth while her body was pumping and her mind still spinning. 'What... happened?' she managed to stutter at last.

'I'm sorry, I...' Nat trailed off. How could he explain how he had drifted awake to find his arms around her? Her body had been so warm and inviting. He had breathed in the scent of her skin, of her hair and, half asleep as he had been, it had seemed perfectly natural to kiss the shoulder so temptingly close to his mouth.

And then she had turned, sleepily smiling, and she had kissed him back, and there had been no chance of thinking after that. No chance of realising that she had been too drenched in sleep to recognise that he wasn't Ross after all, until she had begged him to stop—and by then it had been too late.

'I'm sorry,' was all he could say heavily again. He

forced himself to his feet, aware only of the need to re-move himself as far away from her as possible until he could get himself under control.

At the door, he glanced back. Prue was curled up as if from a blow, the duvet clutched defensively around her, and she looked so shocked and vulnerable that Nat flinched with shame. 'I'm sorry,' he said, because there was nothing else to say, and he went out, closing the door very quietly behind him.

Prue was too devastated to move. She couldn't accept how suddenly the glorious dream had turned to cold, hard reality. One moment she had been drowning in enchant-ment, the next Nat had pulled away from her in disgust.

He must have realised too late that she wasn't Kathryn. The only possible explanation broke bitterly through the churning fog of 'whys' and 'if onlys' in Prue's brain.

She could see only too easily how it must have hap-pened. Nat had been in love with Kathryn a long time. He must be used to waking and finding her in his arms, to kissing her awake and making love in the early-morning light. What a shock for him to find this morning that he wasn't at home, and that the woman responding so eagerly and so passionately wasn't Kathryn at all. No wonder he had leapt away from her!

Prue's whole body burned and pulsed with humiliation and unsatisfied desire, and she covered her face with her hands to keep back scalding tears. She couldn't cry. If she cried Nat would know how desperately she had wanted him, and Prue couldn't bear to see the embar-rassment and distaste in his eyes.

Moving stiffly, like an old lady, she got up and with shaking hands pulled on the satin robe Cleo had left hanging behind the door. They couldn't pretend it hadn't happened. She had to go and find Nat right now and convince him somehow that when she had begged and pleaded with him to make love to her she hadn't known what she was doing, or the next three weeks would be unbearable.

Nat was in the kitchen. Unaware of her at first, he sat at the table, his head tilted back to stare at the ceiling as he concentrated on breathing deeply and slowly. Prue could see the tendons in his throat, the clenched muscles in his jaw, the faint sheen of sweat on his skin. He hadn't waited to find a T-shirt, and was still wearing only his shorts. Prue's eyes rested longingly on his bare chest, where only minutes ago her hands had drifted so deliciously. She had gloried in the texture of his skin, the power of his shoulders, the responsive shift of his muscles, and she had pressed her lips to his warm flesh, tasting him, loving him.

And now? Now he was a stranger, out of reach. Don't look, don't touch. Prue swallowed and clutched the satin robe together at her throat.

The movement caught Nat's eye, and he lowered his head slowly until they were looking at each other across the kitchen.

'I don't know what to say,' he admitted at last.

'You don't need to say anything,' said Prue quickly. Unsure whether her still trembling legs would support her much longer, she walked over to the table and sat next to him.

Her feet were bare and her hair tumbled wildly around her face. She had no idea how alluring she looked, thought Nat, close to despair. The dressing gown she was wearing covered her completely. She was holding it firmly together at her throat, and all he could see were her hands and toes, and although that should have made it easier for him, somehow it didn't.

There was something suggestive about its soft swish as she moved towards him, something tantalising about the way it looked as if it might slide from her shoulders if she let go. The fabric was rich and red, with a slippery sheen. Nat only had to look at it to know how it would slither over her skin if he reached out and touched her.

Which he wasn't going to do, of course. His throat felt like cardboard, and he wrenched his eyes away.

'I don't know what happened,' he said. 'I was asleep one minute and the next….'

The memory of what had happened next flared between them so vividly that they both flinched. 'It caught me unawares,' Nat ploughed on past the constriction in his throat. 'I just…wasn't thinking.'

'I know.' Prue swallowed. 'I thought I was dreaming,' she said, desperate to find some way of explaining why she had responded with such abandon. 'I didn't realise that you…that you weren't…' She stumbled to a halt and looked helplessly at him.

'That I wasn't Ross?' Nat was surprised at how even his voice sounded.

He had offered her the perfect excuse, Prue realised. She longed to be able to tell him that she had been dreaming of him, but how could she do that when she had seen how he had reacted at finding her in his arms?

She nodded dully. It was easier all round if he believed that she had been thinking of Ross. 'I'm sorry,' she said in a low voice, not looking at him.

Her head was bent, and Nat could see the soft nape of her neck where he had kissed her earlier. He wished she had sat on the other side of the table instead of choosing the chair beside him. She looked so miserable that it would be very easy to put a comforting arm around her and feel the shiny robe slip and shift against her skin beneath his hand.

Too easy. Too dangerous.

He clenched his fists instead. 'It wasn't your fault,' he said harshly.

'It wasn't yours either.' Prue coloured painfully. 'We were both half asleep. It was just one of those things.'

The intoxicating sweetness of her kiss. The silken warmth of her body. The excitement blazing between them. *Just one of those things*?

Nat's mouth twisted. 'Just one of those things,' he agreed, and his voice was as dry as dust.

There was an awkward pause.

'I don't want it to change things,' said Prue hesitantly at last.

She twisted the false engagement ring round her finger. 'I know I was in a state last night, but it's been going well, hasn't it? My family are all convinced that we're engaged and the Ashcrofts seem happy.'

Her blush deepened. 'I'd understand if you wanted to tell everyone the truth,' she hurried on, 'but it's only today and tomorrow to get through. Once Cleo and Alex have gone on honeymoon we'll have the flat to ourselves and we can concentrate on the twins. We won't have to…do what we've been doing,' she added lamely.

Nat was just watching her, saying nothing. Unnerved by his silence, and terrified that he was trying to think of a way to tell her that he would rather not have anything else to do with her, Prue rushed on.

'Just now…that didn't *mean* anything. I haven't forgotten about Kathryn,' she said awkwardly. 'I know nothing's going to change the way you feel. But it won't be much longer and we'll be on our way back to Australia with William and Daisy. Once we're there, we can stop pretending and forget all of this. That's what we both want.'

She might want to forget it, thought Nat bleakly. Personally, he didn't think that it would be as easy as that.

'So you want to carry on as we are?' he said.

'Only if you don't mind.' She couldn't tell him that she only wanted to be near him as long as she could. 'I really want to go back to Australia,' she said instead.

Back to Ross.

If he had any sense, thought Nat, he would call a stop to this whole thing now. Somewhere along the line, without quite knowing how or when it had happened, he had fallen in love with Prue and, no matter how hopeless he knew it was, he couldn't find a way to fall out again.

The future stretched drearily ahead of Nat. He didn't know what would be worse, not seeing her at all, or bumping into her occasionally in Mathison with Ross, perhaps married to him, having his children. Wouldn't it be easier to make the break and start getting used to life without her now?

The longer he spent with Prue here in London the harder it was going to be to let her go in the end, Nat knew, but he couldn't bring himself to say goodbye. Not yet. He had promised her a ticket back to Australia, he reasoned. The flight was booked, and he still needed help with William and Daisy. And the next three weeks would be all the time with her he had.

'*Do* you mind?' asked Prue uncertainly as the silence lengthened, and when Nat looked into her grey eyes, he knew that he had no choice anyway.

'No,' he said slowly. 'I don't mind.'

Prue was very glad that there was so much to do that day. Caught up in a whirl of pre-wedding activity, she had her hands full calming Cleo and her mother's last-minute nerves, and she hardly saw Nat, who went off to see William and Daisy again on his own.

In a fit of tradition Cleo had decided to spend the night before the wedding at her parents' house, and Prue as chief bridesmaid was to be there as well. As Alex was to have dinner with his own family, Nat would be left on his own.

'Come home with us,' Cleo urged when Alex pointed this out to her. 'It'll be a bit cramped, but you wouldn't mind sleeping on the sofa for a night, would you?'

Nat smiled and shook his head. 'It's only for an evening,' he said, 'and I'm used to being alone.'

It was true. When Ed and Laura had moved, he had had the homestead to himself and it had never bothered him. If anyone had asked, Nat would have said that he was a solitary man, comfortable with silence and his own company, but that evening in London was one of the longest he had ever spent. He missed Prue with a physical ache. Better get used to it, mate, Nat told himself bleakly.

The sun came out for Cleo's wedding, and it was a perfect day. Prue had often thought the word 'radiant' overused in connection with brides, but it was the only way to describe how her sister looked—as she told her when she kissed her in the church porch before they set off up the aisle.

Cleo hugged her back. 'Your turn next,' she promised.

Except it wouldn't be. Prue forced a smile. 'I hope so,' she said.

She hardly recognised Nat when she saw him standing next to Marisa at the end of the pew. He was wearing a grey suit and tie and an unapproachable expression, and he looked so smart that he might have been a stranger. But then he turned to watch her pacing slowly up the aisle behind her father and Cleo and, catching her eye, he smiled slightly.

His smile was so reassuringly familiar, so *Nat*, that Prue couldn't help smiling back, and as their gazes held the church around them receded and there were just the two of them, just the smile in Nat's eyes and the warm strumming deep inside her.

Mechanically, she kept on walking, and moments later he was cut off from her view, but his smile lingered and she was so absorbed that she nearly bumped into Cleo as she came to a halt beside Alex. Jolted back to attention, Prue stepped forward hastily to take the bouquet.

She watched her sister take her vows, but she was agonisingly aware of Nat at the other end of the pew. If she leant forward slightly she could see his hands, holding the order of service, the same hands that had explored her body so enticingly, and the memory of their sureness and their strength shuddered down Prue's spine and knotted her entrails.

Straightening abruptly, she fixed her gaze on Cleo and Alex once more. What would it be like to be standing where Cleo was standing, radiating happiness, knowing that the man beside her loved her and needed her and wanted to spend the rest of his life with her? Prue let herself imagine Nat turning to smile at her the way Alex had smiled at Cleo. She imagined putting her hand in his and feeling his fingers close around hers. She imagined walking back out into the sunshine with him, going back to Mack River, staying for ever—

A sharp elbow dug into her ribs and she turned to see her mother frowning at her, while the rest of the congregation looked on in some amusement as she was left standing alone with a dreamy smile on her face.

Flustered, Prue sat down abruptly. She had to pull herself together! She had told Nat that she didn't want things to change, but it wasn't true. She wanted them to change completely. He would be horrified if he knew that being a nanny wasn't enough for her any more, that nothing less than marriage and for ever would do.

It wasn't hopeless, Prue encouraged herself. Nat wasn't actually engaged to Kathryn any more, was he? If she could just stay cool and not embarrass him, he might ask her to stay on at Mack River to help look after William and Daisy. Surely if she was there every day he would come to need her? She would make herself indispensable, Prue vowed. She would create a home for the children and cook for him and clean for him and maybe— *maybe*—Kathryn would decide to stay in Perth. And Nat might turn to *her* then. He might come to realise that he needed her, and she would be there for him.

But first they had the next three weeks to get through, and she mustn't spoil things by letting him guess how she felt. For now he just wanted her as a nanny, and a nanny was what she would be. That meant being cool, calm and capable, and *not* the kind of person who was so wrapped up in her daydreams that she had no idea of what was going on around her.

After the service there were hugs and kisses and photographs outside the church. Cleo insisted on including Nat in the family groups, and inevitably he was placed next to Prue.

'Can you get a bit closer together?' shouted the photographer. 'Prue and…Nat, is it?…squeeze up!'

He gestured with his hands to narrow the gap, and they had little choice but to shuffle together. Nat stood slightly behind Prue, so she didn't actually have to look at him, but she could feel how close he was, and the temptation to lean back against him was unbearable. She wanted to take off his tie and his stiff suit, to unbutton his shirt and press her lips to his skin…faint with desire, Prue had to close her eyes.

'OK, smile everyone!' The photographer paused. 'Prue, are you awake? You can't go to sleep yet!'

Snapping her eyes open, Prue fixed a bright smile to her face and clutched her flowers with a kind of desperation. Cool, calm, capable—wasn't that what she had decided? She was going to have to do better than this!

It was easier at the reception. Cleo had decided on a finger buffet rather than a sit-down meal, which meant Prue could avoid Nat as much as possible. If she could just stay away from him, she decided, it would be all right. So she circulated around the room, smiling and nodding and agreeing that yes, it *would* be her turn next, and if sometimes she found herself gravitating too close to Nat, she would turn sharply on her heel, make an excuse and head off in the other direction.

Not that Nat seemed to care—or even notice—*where* she was. Whenever Prue allowed herself to look at him he appeared to be absorbed in conversation, and jealousy would clutch at her heart as she caught a glimpse of his smile. He talked to old aunts and eccentric cousins and friends of the family, all of whom came up to Prue afterwards and told her how much they liked him.

'It's *such* a pity you won't be getting married here,' they sighed wistfully. 'Australia is so far away!'

'I know,' said Prue, and was seized by a longing to be there, in the stillness and the silence of Mack River, a world away from this hotel ballroom with its ornate mouldings and its swagged curtains and its glittering chandeliers.

Suddenly claustrophobic, she murmured an excuse and slipped through the French windows that opened out onto a long terrace. Leaning on the balustrade, she had taken several deep breaths before she realised that there was a knot of children in the garden below. They were clustered around Nat, who seemed to be showing them a trick of some kind, for they were all wide-eyed, their gazes riveted to his hands.

Prue leant further over to see what he was doing, and at the same time Nat became aware of her presence. He glanced up and their eyes locked.

'Have you escaped?' he asked, and she nodded.

'I needed some air.'

'Come down and join us.'

'Auntie Prue!' Ben came running to meet her at the steps. 'Nat can do magic with his hands!'

Prue knew that only too well. She smiled down at Ben. 'Can he?'

'Nat, show Auntie Prue what you can do!'

Obligingly, Nat repeated the trick. It was very simple, but the children were thrilled with it and clamoured for more, and when he had exhausted his repertoire they made him tell them about boxing kangaroos and dancing brolgas, about the flocks of brightly coloured parrots that wheeled in the sky, about spiders and snakes and the size of a crocodile's teeth.

Prue sat on the steps in her bridesmaid's dress and Katie climbed onto her lap to listen to Nat with her. He talked to the children as equals, and the sound of his slow, quiet voice was infinitely reassuring. She could feel the tension ebbing away from her. She hadn't realised what an effort it had been to avoid him earlier, and now it was bliss to give in and just be with him for a while. She didn't care that he wasn't talking to her or looking at her or even thinking about her. It was enough to be near him.

Content to sit there quietly, Prue didn't even tense when the children dispersed at last and Nat came to sit beside her on the steps.

'You're their hero now,' she said with a smile. 'Did a crocodile really take a bite out of your boat?'

Nat's eyes glimmered with amusement. 'Maybe it wasn't quite as big a bite as I said,' he admitted, 'but the tooth marks are still there! I'll show you when we get home.'

He stopped, hearing too late his unthinking assumption that Prue would be going back to Mack River with him, but she didn't seem to notice how he had given himself away.

'I can't wait to go back,' she sighed.

She rested her arms on her knees, and watched a plane on its long descent to Heathrow. 'Listening to you just now made me homesick,' she told him. 'I know I was only at Cowen Creek a few months, but it felt like home. I miss the stillness. Everything's so frantic here,' she went on. 'You rush from one thing to the next, and everyone always seems to be in a hurry and you end up so wound up you can't relax at all. I never felt like that at Cowen Creek. It's so quiet there,' Prue remembered wistfully, listening to the babble of voices in the ballroom. 'You can walk along the creek there and there's no one but you and the birds…'

And Ross, Nat reminded himself, seeing how the grey eyes were shining, how her lips curved at the memory of her happiness with him.

Did Ross have any idea of how lucky he was? Nat

wondered with an edge of bitterness. All he had to do was lift a finger and Prue would marry him. He would have a warm, vital, loving wife, a wife to smile and welcome him home at the end of the day, a wife who loved the land as much as he did.

Kathryn had never found the bush romantic. She had a low boredom threshold and, in spite of growing up in the outback, she was much more at home in the city. Kathryn liked people, action, the promise of excitement. Nat couldn't remember her ever wanting to sit and enjoy the stillness and the silence the way Prue would.

Prue would love Mack River. She had seen so little of it on the one day she had been there. Nat wanted to show her the gorge and the waterhole where he and Ed had swum when they were boys. He could ride with her through the canyons and out on the saltpans. They could take swags and camp out in the top end, and he could watch her face at sunset.

Prue had been watching him more closely than he knew. 'Are you thinking of home?'

'Yes,' said Nat. 'Yes, I was.'

Prue could only imagine how pokey and confined London must seem to someone like him. 'Don't you hate being here?'

'No, I don't hate it.' It was true that he felt alien in the city, where he seemed to be moving in slow motion compared to everyone else, and he would be lost if he had to live there, but that didn't mean that he hated it. How could he hate London, when Prue was there?

'You must miss Mack River, though,' she said, unconvinced.

Nat looked into the grey eyes that were silvery in the sunshine. 'Not all the time,' he said. 'Not right now.'

His words hung in the air between them. Prue looked

away and then back, and this time she couldn't tear her gaze away. The air leaked out of her lungs as the silence stretched dangerously, but her body wouldn't obey her increasingly frantic instructions to move, breathe, do *anything*.

'Prue?' said Nat suddenly, as if her name had been forced out of him.

'Yes?'

'I—' He put a hand out, but before he could say any more, her mother's voice was calling down from the terrace.

'*There* you are! I've been looking all over for you two! Do come in. We can't start the speeches without you.'

Perhaps it was just as well, thought Nat as he stood up. He had been about to ruin everything and tell Prue how he felt about her but, judging by the way she had deliberately ignored the hand he had held out to help her to her feet, a declaration of love from him was the last thing she would have wanted to hear.

Prue breathed carefully as she made her way to the front of the crowd gathered around the cake, where her father was waiting with Alex and Cleo, and the best man was nervously going over his notes for his speech.

It had taken every effort of self-will not to take Nat's hand, but she hadn't trusted herself to let it go again. When she looked into his brown eyes like that it was so easy to forget Kathryn and let herself succumb to every instinct in her body that told her she could lean towards him and put her hand to his cheek and kiss him.

But Prue's brain knew better than her body. It remembered how Nat had talked about Kathryn, the things he had said. How much he loved her. It reminded her how appalled he had been that morning when they had so nearly made love. It warned her not to drive him away by betraying how much she needed him.

It wasn't so good at ignoring him as he stood beside her, though.

Her father gave a short, moving speech, and then it was Alex's turn. Most of it flowed over Prue's head. She was watching Cleo, and her throat tightened at the expression on her sister's face as she gazed at her new husband. Cleo looked so happy that Prue felt ashamed, remembering how she had grumbled about coming back from Australia for the wedding. This was Cleo's special day, and she was very glad that she hadn't missed it.

'And finally,' Alex was drawing to a close, 'Cleo and I want to say a special thank you to Prue, who has come a very long way to be here today. We know you had to cut your time in Australia short, Prue,' he went on, smiling at her, 'and we both appreciate it. It wouldn't have been the same for Cleo if you hadn't been here.'

Seeing that Prue's eyes were shimmering with tears, Alex tactfully looked round at the rest of the guests. 'For those of you who don't already know, Prue is going back to Australia to get married, and Cleo and I would like to take this opportunity to congratulate her and Nat and to hope that they will be as happy together as we are.'

'And, just to be sure that you're next,' Cleo chimed in, lifting her bouquet, 'this is for you, Prue. Catch!'

She threw the flowers straight at Prue, who caught them without thinking, to a general cheer.

'To Prue!' they cried, raising their glasses.

Nat was right beside her, and the two of them were the focus of all eyes. They were both very conscious that the natural thing to do would be to kiss. It was a wedding, they were supposed to be in love, everyone was drinking to their future happiness. How could they *not* kiss?

Prue's eyes lifted to Nat in mute appeal. Resigned to his fate, he smiled slightly to show that he understood, put an arm around her, and dropped a brief kiss on her lips, his mouth barely grazing hers before he drew back.

There, that wasn't so hard after all, was it? Nat congratulated himself.

Prue didn't know whether to be relieved or disappointed that the kiss was over almost before it had begun.

Relieved, she decided firmly after a moment. It had been fine. She hadn't fallen apart and she hadn't made a fool of herself, and she could even smile her thanks to Cleo and wave the bouquet as if she had nothing more on her mind than picking a suitable date for her wedding.

'Thank goodness that's over!' said Prue, collapsing onto the sofa when she and Nat finally made it back to the flat that evening. She kicked off her shoes with a groan and lay back.

'I was beginning to wonder if Cleo and Alex were ever going to go,' said Nat, following her into the sitting room.

For some reason, things were easier between them. It was as if getting through that very public kiss had been a watershed. It had been so brief, so impersonal, that there had been no danger of either of them losing control.

Of course, it was a bit late *now*, Prue couldn't help thinking with an inward sigh. The celebrations were over, and they wouldn't be put in that kind of situation again. There would be no need for Nat to kiss her when they were just here with William and Daisy, but it was reassuring to know that if they *did* have to she could trust herself not to go to pieces the way she had done before.

Nat, too, was conscious of an easing of tension, but he

was still careful to choose a chair where there would be no danger of touching Prue accidentally.

Loosening his tie with a grimace, he unfastened his constricting collar. 'It beats me how people can wear suits every day,' he said. 'I'm not going to need it again, am I?'

'No, you've done your bit.' Prue massaged her toes and watched him as he leant back and ran his hands through his hair in a gesture of weariness. 'Thank you,' she said impulsively.

Nat lifted his head slightly and cocked an eye at her. 'What for?'

'For everything you've done this week,' she said. 'For saving my face and being nice to my family and wearing a suit and…' For not making it obvious that you wished it had been Kathryn that you were kissing. 'For everything, really.'

Nat's brown eyes were unreadable. 'It was a pleasure,' he said.

'Yes, well…' Prue cleared her throat. 'I just wanted to say how much I appreciated everything you've done. You've kept your side of our bargain, and now I'm going to keep mine. From now on, I'm just here to look after William and Daisy.'

CHAPTER NINE

'THAT'S the lot.' Nat dumped the last of the carrier bags on the table. He couldn't get used to toiling up a flight of stairs to get to the kitchen.

'You survived, then?' Prue looked up smiling from the floor, where she was kneeling with Daisy and letting her help put the potatoes away in the bottom of the vegetable rack.

It had been Nat's first solo drive through London traffic to the vast supermarket by the Thames and he had claimed to be setting off with some trepidation, although Prue knew that he would manage it in the same competent way he managed everything else. It would take more than London to intimidate Nat.

'Just,' he said, scooping up William, who had been holding up his arms and babbling for attention. 'There was a point somewhere near the cheese section when I wondered if I would ever see daylight again, but I used my tracking skills to find the checkout, and after that all I had to do was find the car again.

'Do you have any idea how many cars there are parked in that place, William?' he asked, holding him at arm's length and looking him in the eye.

William looked back, wreathed in smiles. He loved being part of a conversation. 'A—*bah*!'

'That's right...thousands. I reckon you could put the whole of Mathison in that car park six times over. The general store will never be the same again!'

Prue laughed as she got to her feet. 'I'd rather shop

there any day,' she said, brushing down her knees. 'No, darling!' She rescued the tomatoes as Daisy made a lunge for something new and more exciting. 'You stick with the potatoes and carrots. You're doing such a good job.'

Successfully diverting Daisy by shaking a few more root vegetables out of a bag, she put the tomatoes safely out of reach and began unpacking the other bags that Nat had placed on the table.

'Do you remember driving me to the store that day?' she said to Nat, who had shifted William onto one arm and was setting the bulk packs of disposable nappies to one side.

Nat remembered all right. He remembered the tears on her lashes, how desperate she had been to win Ross's approval. *I'm in love with him*, she had said. *He's the only man I'll ever want.*

'I remember,' he said, although there were times when he looked at Prue—holding out her arms to the babies, catching them to her, blizzarding kisses over their faces until they squealed with delight—and it was all too easy to forget.

'It seems ages ago, doesn't it?'

Prue found it hard to believe that it was barely six weeks since she had buried her head in her arms and wept because of Ross. She had been so sure that she loved him but now when she tried to conjure up his image, all she got was an impression of merry blue eyes and virile energy.

Whereas Nat… She could draw every line of his face with her eyes closed. She knew exactly how his hair grew at his temple, the precise point at which the crease in his cheek deepened when he smiled, and if anyone had asked her to identify just where the pulse-beat was in his throat, she could have pointed to it with unerring accuracy.

'A lot's happened in the last few weeks,' Nat agreed, rather muffled through William's hand, which was patting his mouth. 'We've come a long way since then.'

She might have moved geographically, thought Prue ruefully, but emotionally she was back where she had started, hopelessly in love with a man who was probably never going to be interested in her.

'I guess when you flagged me down on the Cowen Creek track you didn't think that six weeks later you would be knee-deep in babies,' Nat went on.

'No,' Prue admitted. She had been unable to think about anything except Ross then. It was like remembering a different person, another life altogether.

Nat hesitated. He set William down next to Daisy, who wasn't sure if she wanted her brother interfering with her game. She shouted a protest, but William ignored her. He placidly picked up a carrot and stuck it in his mouth and after a final suspicious glare, she returned to the enthralling business of putting potatoes into the rack and then taking them out again.

Having waited to make sure that William was balanced and not at risk of a shove from his sister, Nat turned back to Prue.

'I have to say that I'm very glad you forgot to check the fuel before you left Cowen Creek that day,' he said slowly.

He had spent the last few days on a very steep learning curve, and was adapting pretty quickly considering that he hadn't known one end of a baby from another before he left Mack River. Now he could change a nappy in his sleep, although he was still ham-fisted compared to Prue. She made everything look easy, even at meal times—deeply messy affairs—when she would pop a spoonful of food into the baby's mouth and wipe off the drips while the spoon Nat offered was as often as not knocked imperiously aside.

'I wouldn't have been able to manage without you,' he told her honestly.

The least sign of approval, and Prue was reduced to blushing like an idiot! 'I'm glad I forgot too,' she admitted. 'I love being with William and Daisy.'

And with you, she added mentally.

She looked down at the pair of them, each absorbed in their own play and unaware that there was anything more fascinating than the taste and texture of the humble vegetable.

'They're gorgeous babies,' she said wistfully, wondering if there would ever be a time when she would have babies of her own, babies like Daisy and William with fat, dimpled wrists and Nat's brown eyes.

'They seem to love you, too,' said Nat, thinking of how quickly the twins had accepted Prue.

She was very loving with them, cuddling them in her arms and laughing as they threw themselves against her and gave her wet sloppy kisses with their open mouths. She let them suck her nose and stroke her hair and pat her mouth until she caught their little hands and kissed their palms. Nat would find himself watching her sometimes, and was uncomfortably aware that he was jealous of his own niece and nephew.

'You're a natural mother,' he said, and Prue's eyes met his with an almost startled look.

'I'd like to be,' she said quietly, hoping that he hadn't been reading her mind.

There was a pause.

Nat cleared his throat and his mind of a picture of Prue with a tiny baby in her arms. *His* baby, not Ross's. 'I hope this girl from the agency is as good as you,' he said, and Prue froze in the middle of stacking butter in the fridge.

'What girl?'

'Didn't I tell you? I rang the agency in Darwin yesterday to see if they'd found anyone to come to Mack River as nanny and housekeeper when we get back.'

A cold hand closed over Prue's heart. 'No, you didn't tell me,' she said expressionlessly.

'It was when you were out buying those books.'

Nat had made himself ring. However much she loved the babies Prue wouldn't want to stay with them for ever, he had reminded himself, and sooner or later he was going to have to face the fact. She had made it very clear that she was hoping to be able to go back to Cowen Creek and, if that was what she wanted Nat couldn't stand in her way, however much *he* loved *her*. She deserved the chance to be happy with Ross.

By making other arrangements for someone to help him with William and Daisy he had hoped to show Prue that he wasn't expecting any more of her than what she had agreed, which was to accompany him and the babies back to Mack River. She hadn't said that she would stay, and he couldn't ask her to unless she was sure there was no chance of returning to Cowen Creek.

'I see.'

Prue had had a wonderful time in the bookshop. Nat had given her *carte blanche* to buy a whole stock of books and toys to send out to Mack River for William and Daisy as they grew up. She had imagined reading the stories to them, watching their little faces as they puzzled over their first words, and she had let herself get so carried away that she had forgotten that chances were she wouldn't be there to read anything.

Nat hadn't forgotten.

She turned back to the fridge. 'What did the agency say?'

'They've got a girl who sounds nice, but she can't start until after Christmas, so I've asked them to keep looking.'

Prue's fingers tightened around a block of cheese at the idea of a *nice* girl effectively moving in with Nat. She would try and accept it if Kathryn came back to make him happy, but she didn't see why she should let some unknown girl, however nice, make herself indispensable to him. That was *her* plan.

And it sounded as if she only had until Christmas to put it into action.

'I could stay until then if you wanted,' she said as casually as she could.

It was Nat's turn to still. 'I thought you wanted to go back to Cowen Creek?'

'I haven't heard anything from the Grangers. Their new cook must be settled in by now, and she'll probably be there until the end of the season.'

Prue risked a glance at Nat. 'You *did* say I could stay at Mack River until I found another job,' she reminded him, hoping that she didn't sound too desperate, 'and I just thought that since Daisy and William already know me, it might work out for both of us if I stayed on as their nanny for a while.'

'Are you sure?' Nat could hardly believe his luck.

'I'm sure,' said Prue. She concentrated on slotting the milk into the fridge door. 'I was dreading saying goodbye to William and Daisy,' she said to explain her willingness to throw Cowen Creek to the winds and base herself at Mack River instead.

'That would be…' Fantastic. Wonderful. Glorious. Superb. 'That would be good,' said Nat. 'I'd pay you, of course,' he added hastily. 'Whatever you wanted. And if you do get a chance to go back to Cowen Creek, Prue, then you just have to tell me. I'd let you go whenever you want.'

It wasn't quite what Prue wanted to hear, but she was elated at the thought that she would have at least another three months with him. A lot had happened in six weeks, as Nat had pointed out. How much more could happen in three months? Three months was plenty of time for Nat to forget about Kathryn and nice girls who wanted to be nannies.

And in the meantime she could relax and enjoy this strange time out of time. They had nothing to do but look after the twins, and the long, hot summer days were passing lazily. Prue would have been frantic if she had had to cope on her own, but somehow it was easy when Nat was there. He was never impatient and he never flapped or looked harassed.

It hadn't taken them long to fall into a routine. Prue had been afraid that it might be difficult being alone together in the flat after Cleo and Alex had gone, but in the event they had both been too tired to feel self-conscious at all.

They'd set up the cots in Cleo's room, where Prue now slept in solitary splendour in the wide bed. The obvious thing would have been to put them in the spare room, and give the twins a bedroom of their own, but that would have involved continuing to share a bed, and in view of what had happened the last time they slept together neither of them had wanted to suggest it.

William and Daisy had been unsettled by the change for the first few nights, and one or the other of them had woken up several times a night, generally waking the other in the process. Prue and Nat had both been up with them at all hours.

There was an intimacy about being awake together in the still of the night. London was enduring a heat wave, and Prue was too hot and too tired to bother with a robe. It was bad enough wearing a nightdress, and she envied Nat, who wore shorts to preserve the decencies but could hold a baby to his bare chest as he walked up and down. Prue was sure that William and Daisy picked up on his slow heartbeat and were soothed by it.

Cradling the other baby, she would sometimes watch enviously and wish that she could relax against him and be held that securely, but generally Prue had felt that she was coping pretty well with being alone with him in the dark with hardly any clothes on. It should have been an awkward situation, but there was no time to think about awkwardness when you had two screaming babies on your hands and when desire came a long way down the priority list after the longing for a few hours of uninterrupted sleep.

By the time the twins had settled down into sleeping through the night, Prue had convinced herself that things would be fine. And they *were* fine, most of the time. As long as she didn't brush against Nat by accident, or make the mistake of looking into his eyes when they laughed, or notice how strong and gentle his hands were when he held the babies.

If she avoided all of these things, getting through the day was no problem at all. Daisy and William woke her with their singing in the morning, and she lifted them out of their cots to play in the bed with her. Nat would bring her a cup of tea, which she never got a chance to drink, as the twins lurched precariously between them, demanding to be kissed and cuddled and bounced on their knees.

It was impossible to be constrained when they wanted to play peek-a-boo behind their hands or to have their tummies tickled until they chuckled with glee.

After their morning nap, Prue and Nat would take them out. Sometimes they went back to see their grandparents and to play in the garden there, and a couple of times they visited Prue's parents.

The days Prue liked best, though, were the ones when the four of them were alone and they caught a red bus into the great parks at the centre of the city. 'You might as well see London while you're here,' she'd said to Nat, although sometimes when they sat with the twins gurgling on their laps and drove past the famous landmarks it felt as if she was the one seeing London properly for the first time.

The parks were littered with people stretched out and enjoying the sunshine, but Nat had a much warier attitude to the sun and insisted that William and Daisy wore floppy hats and sat in the shade. Propped up against them, the babies were fascinated by everything going on around them. There were so many people for them to look at and so much going on that they were never bored.

Prue lay in Green Park one day and looked around her. It was another beautiful day, with just a few cirrus clouds adrift in the sky, and a soft breeze carrying the smell of cut grass and sunshine lifted her hair. Daisy nestled against her, happy to rest for a moment, and William was sitting between Nat's knees, absorbed in stroking the grass. Prue couldn't remember ever feeling as relaxed in the city before.

'London doesn't seem so bad on a day like today,' she said, closing her eyes with a contented sigh.

Absently steadying William, who was wobbling as he reached for a leaf, Nat watched the way the dappled light from the broad leaves above fell across her face. Daisy lay on her stomach, her head on Prue's breast and Prue's hand on her padded bottom, holding her securely. The two of them looked utterly relaxed. The corners of Prue's mouth were curved upwards and the long dark lashes swept her cheek, hiding the beautiful grey eyes.

Nat made himself look away. 'I hadn't realised there were places this green in the middle of London,' he said. Picking a blade of grass, he chewed it thoughtfully. 'We could do with grass like this at home.'

'They were muttering about drought on the news last night,' said Prue without opening her eyes.

'Drought?' Nat looked incredulously around him at the sweeping, freshly cut grass and the lush green trees, and he remembered the bitter times at home when the rains failed and the dust blew over the empty paddocks. 'They don't know what drought means!'

He was silent for a while, thinking about Mack River and imagining what was happening on the station. 'They should be mustering this week,' he said, half to himself.

Prue opened her eyes to look up at him. He was holding William between his hands and gazing down to where the traffic roared ceaselessly past Buckingham Palace, but she knew he was seeing something very different: a place where there were casuarinas and gums and boab trees instead of sycamores and chestnuts, and where there was no traffic and no tourists and no men in suits striding briskly past, barking orders into their mobile phones.

'It's not a good time for you to be away, is it?' she said.

Nat shrugged slightly. 'It can't be helped. The ringers know what they're doing, and Bill Granger promised he'd keep an eye on things while I'm away. Right now, William and Daisy are more important.'

'It won't be for much longer anyway,' said Prue. 'Cleo and Alex will be back from their honeymoon soon, and we can go home.'

She had spoken without thinking but now her words with their implied intimacy seemed to echo around them. *We can go home.*

But Mack River wasn't her home, Prue reminded herself sadly. Biting her lips, she glanced at Nat to see if he had noticed her casual assumption that she would belong at Mack River with him and found herself looking right into his deep, brown eyes.

He had noticed all right, she thought with a tiny jump of her heart. He was watching her with a strange expression and as he opened his mouth, Prue was suddenly convinced that he was about to point out that she was going to Mack River as a nanny and nothing else.

'Back to Australia, I mean,' she said quickly, before he could speak.

What else? Nat turned away dully, shaken by how close he had come to revealing exactly how he felt.

We can go home. It had sounded so right when Prue said it, as if the two of them were meant to be together. As if she belonged with him at Mack River, as if there was no question that she would go back with him and stay for ever.

'We'd better tidy the flat before Cleo and Alex get back,' was all he said.

Prue heard the constraint in his voice without understanding what had caused it. 'We'll need to have packed by then anyway,' she said, sounding as awkward as he did now. 'We fly out the evening after they come back.'

Now was not the time to remind him that they would have to share a bed again for the night they overlapped with Cleo and Alex, but the prospect clanged in Prue's brain.

An uncomfortable silence fell. Nat gazed unseeingly at a girl who was managing to roller-blade and talk on the phone at the same time, and tried to forget the image of Prue at home at Mack River.

He wished he couldn't picture her there quite so clearly. He could visualise exactly how she would look sweeping the verandah, stopping to smile a welcome as he came up the steps, waking in his bed. If only she hadn't looked so right amongst his furniture.

'Ga!' William's shout made Nat start. He had forgotten his nephew was there for a moment.

The baby was waving his arms excitedly, and when Nat looked around he saw instantly what had attracted his attention. A police horse was making its way slowly along the path and, glad of the diversion, Nat hoisted William up and carried him over so that he could see better.

Easing the sleeping Daisy gently onto the grass, Prue sat up and watched them. She couldn't hear what Nat was saying to the policeman but she saw him run a hand down the horse's nose and whisper to it. The horse stood still, its ears flickering as if it were listening. It was a huge animal, but William was quite unafraid. He reached out a chubby hand and stroked its coarse mane, and then Nat let him feel the horse's velvety lips and warm breath.

When the policeman moved on with a smile, William let out a wail of disappointment. 'Don't worry, Will,' said Nat as he carried him back to join Prue and Daisy on the grass. 'There are plenty of horses at Mack River. You'll be riding your own one day soon.'

Together they watched the horse moving sedately away, its tail twitching. 'You and Daisy will each have a pony of your own,' Nat promised William. 'Would you like that?'

'Baba!' William's shout sounded so much like enthusiastic agreement that Prue couldn't help smiling.

'You would?' Nat turned his nephew round and held him between his strong hands so that they faced each other. 'Then when you're big enough, you can help muster the top end,' he said, talking to him as seriously as if William could understand every word. 'It's rough country up there, and nothing beats a man on a horse when it comes to tracking down those scrubber bulls.'

'Gah, gah, ma?' said William, so thrilled at participating in a real conversation that his intonation rose just as if he had asked a real question.

'Too right,' said Nat. 'Daisy'll come too. We'll take our swags and sleep on the ground, and we'll build a fire and make damper and drink billy tea, just like your dad and I did when we were kids.'

Prue's heart twisted. She could imagine them so clearly, the man on his horse with the two children riding beside him, their faces bright and alert. She could see the firelight on their faces and the glimmering stars above them, but she couldn't see herself.

She wouldn't be there.

Beside her, Daisy stirred and knuckled her eyes. Prue picked her up and cuddled her on her lap until she woke properly and then let her have a drink, kissing the top of her head while she guzzled thirstily.

Daisy's wispy hair was clean and soft, and Prue breathed in her baby smell. Daisy wouldn't be riding for a while yet. For now, she still needed Prue.

Glancing up, she caught the eye of two middle-aged women who were passing and they smiled at her. 'What lovely babies,' one said, looking from the unusually angelic Daisy to William, who was clambering happily over Nat. We must look like a perfect family, thought Prue wistfully.

'You are lucky,' the other woman said, and all she could do was smile weakly back at them as they walked on.

Lucky? Perhaps she was at that, Prue decided. The future might be unclear, but this time next week she would be at Mack River with Nat. When William and Daisy were in bed, and the men had eaten and gone back to their quarters, she and Nat would be alone in the dark outback night.

Things could be worse, Prue reminded herself, and felt much better. Things could be a lot worse.

The phone rang when they were giving Daisy and William their lunch the next day.

Expecting her mother or Marisa, Prue tilted back in her chair and groped for the cordless phone which she had left on the worktop behind her with one hand, while with her other she deftly slipped another spoonful into an unsuspecting William.

Nat shook his head in admiration. He was engaged in a battle of wills with Daisy, who was being particularly naughty, and the resulting mess was smeared and splattered over both of them, not to mention the floor around her highchair.

'Behave yourself, Daisy,' scolded Prue as she pressed the 'receive' button on the phone, but she was smiling as she lifted it to her ear. 'Hello?'

'Prue? Is that you? It's Ross.'

Prue nearly dropped the phone. Abandoning William's lunch, she had to put both hands up to hold the receiver. 'Ross?' she croaked, and Nat looked up sharply.

'Yeah, it's me! I called your parents and they gave me this number.' Ross's vigorous voice came surging down the line, so clear that he might have been in the next room. 'How are you doing?'

'Fine,' stammered Prue, who was totally unprepared for this. 'Fine,' she said weakly again.

'I bet those babies are a handful! Nat's not working you too hard, is he?'

'No...no, everything's...fine.'

It wasn't very original but it was the best she could do under the circumstances. She glanced at Nat, but he was carefully scraping around the edge of Daisy's bowl and apparently not paying any attention to her conversation.

'That's great,' Ross was saying. 'Listen, Prue, I rang to ask when you'll get back to Mathison.'

'Next Thursday, I think.'

William was mindlessly shoving an empty spoon in his mouth. Prue leant forward and automatically filled it for him. Pleased, he took it and proceeded to wave it around energetically. Most of the food fell onto his bib but the spoon made it to his mouth eventually, so he seemed to be getting the idea.

'Why, there's not a problem, is there?' she asked, trying to keep her mind on the conversation.

'We've got a bit of a crisis in the kitchen,' Ross confided. 'You know that girl who was so keen to come and work in the outback when you left? She lasted a couple of weeks and then got fed up and went off to Cairns. We're all hoping that you'll come back, Prue. You're the best cook we've ever had.'

'I don't know, Ross...'

Prue was finding it difficult to concentrate, what with William's erratic spoon and Daisy, who was banging her hands in her dish and vociferously protesting at Nat's attempts to get some food down her.

And Nat, with that wooden expression, pretending he couldn't hear what Prue was saying.

'Don't say no!' Ross was at his most charming. 'We all want you back.' He lowered his voice. 'Especially me.'

'I...it's a bit difficult.'

Leaving William to it, Prue pushed back her chair and got up so that she could turn her back on all the distractions. 'I did say I'd stay on to look after William and Daisy, and I don't want to leave Nat in the lurch.' She tried to explain to Ross without letting him or Nat know how desperate she was to go to Mack River. 'He can't manage two babies on his own.'

'Oh, he won't be on his own,' said Ross cheerfully. 'That was another reason I rang—to drop a word in Nat's ear that a certain someone close to his heart is very keen to get back together with him again!'

Unaware of Prue's heart splintering at the other end of the line, he chatted on confidentially. 'Kathryn's been asking when Nat's coming home, and I think she wants to meet him at Mathison. She made me promise to ring her with the flight details as soon as I had them. Between you and me, I reckon she's come to her senses at last and realised that she won't find anyone like Nat down in the city.'

Every word was like a knife turning inside her. Prue felt sick. Why, why, *why* had she let herself carry on dreaming about Nat when she had known about him and Kathryn? Why had she let herself believe that Kathryn would stay conveniently in Perth? Of *course* she would want Nat back in the end.

'I see,' she managed past the constriction in her throat.

'So, what do you say, Prue?' said Ross eagerly. 'Nat won't need you if he's got Kathryn to give him a hand, will he?'

'No,' said Prue in a voice dull with pain. 'No, he won't.'

'But *we* need you at Cowen Creek. I tell you, meals haven't been the same since you left! You did say you wanted to come back if you could,' he reminded her when she didn't jump at the offer.

Prue couldn't deny it. There had been a time, a lifetime ago, when it was all that she had wanted. She wouldn't be here now if she hadn't dreamt and hoped and prayed that Ross would ring her up and say just what he was saying.

'Yes, I did,' she agreed.

It seemed that she had little choice. As Ross had pointed out with such unintentional cruelty, Nat wouldn't need her any more. Even if he asked her to stay on for a while to ease William and Daisy into their new life at Mack River, Prue didn't think she could bear to see him happy with Kathryn. At least Ross was offering her a chance to keep her pride intact. It wasn't much of a comfort, but it was all that she had.

With an immense effort, Prue forced a smile. 'When you put it like that, how can I refuse?' she said. 'I'd love to come back.'

'Great! I'm looking forward to seeing you again. I missed you, you know.'

'I've missed you, too.' What else could she say?

She heard Ross give a muffled exclamation. 'Before I forget, can you give Nat a message from Dad when you see him?'

'You can tell him yourself. He's right here.'

Pinning a bright, brittle smile to her face, Prue turned and offered Nat the phone. 'I'll finish feeding them if you want to take it in the other room,' she said. 'Ross wants to talk to you. He's got some good news for you.'

CHAPTER TEN

'THAT was good news, wasn't it?' Prue flashed Nat a brilliant smile as he came back into the room and put the phone very carefully back onto its cradle on the wall.

'Yes, very.'

Once Nat had got rid of the phone, he didn't know what to do with his empty hands. He stood by the wall, looking down at them and trying to remember exactly what Ross had said. There had been something about Kathryn, but all he had taken in was that Prue wasn't coming back to Mack River with him after all. She was going to Cowen Creek, and to Ross.

So, yes, it was good news for her.

Nat knew that he should make the effort to sound pleased for her, even if his own future did yawn bleak and empty. 'Ross sounds very keen to get you back,' he managed.

'Yes.' Prue wished that she could sound more enthusiastic.

She finished wiping up the mess around Daisy's chair and straightened. She didn't want to look at him and see the happiness in his face at the thought of seeing Kathryn again, so she went over to the sink instead and rinsed out the cloth with unnecessary vigour.

Nat saw the unconscious slump of her shoulders and sudden hope flickered. She didn't seem *that* happy. Maybe she wasn't as desperate to go back to Ross as he had thought. 'Are you OK?' he asked.

Prue's betraying back snapped back to attention, and

by the time she turned she had her smile in place once more.

'Of course,' she said brightly. 'Ross has missed me and they want me back at Cowen Creek. It's just what I wanted to happen when we left.'

It wasn't what she wanted now, though, but she couldn't tell Nat that. It wouldn't be fair on him to complicate matters when he was about to sort things out with Kathryn.

Nat's brief hope died, and he was left with a dull, empty feeling inside. 'I'm glad it's worked out for you.'

'I'll miss William and Daisy, though,' said Prue, in case he had seen past her smile to the desperation in her eyes. He obviously expected her to be over the moon, and the babies provided a good enough excuse for not doing handsprings around the kitchen.

It was true, anyway. Picking up William, she hugged him against her shoulder and kissed the side of his head. The thought of saying goodbye to him and his naughty sister made her heart crack.

'You're going straight back to Cowen Creek from Mathison, then?' asked Nat after a moment.

'I might as well.' Prue put William on the floor and turned to lift Daisy, who was leaning out of her high chair and protesting loudly at being left behind. 'After all, you won't need me if Kathryn's there to give you a hand.'

How could he tell her that he would always need her? It would only make her feel guilty about leaving him with the twins, and that wouldn't be fair. She had done what she promised to do, and now she deserved the chance to be happy with Ross.

'No, we'll be fine,' said Nat a little too heartily, and was unable to resist adding, 'The kids will miss you.'

But not as much as he would.

'They'll soon get used to me not being there,' said Prue. She swallowed. 'I'm sure they'll love Kathryn.'

Kathryn... Nat remembered the cryptic message Ross had passed on. Ross seemed to believe that Kathryn was ready to throw up her life in Perth and come back to live with him at Mack River, but to Nat, who knew Kathryn better than anyone, it sounded highly unlikely.

He couldn't even imagine Kathryn at Mack River now, and he certainly couldn't see her giving up her career to wipe dirty faces or change nappies or clear up after Daisy had finished eating. She would play with the babies, and no doubt charm them the way she charmed everyone else, but Nat was pretty sure that she would lose interest the moment they became less than adorable.

Still, Ross had said that she was determined to meet him at the airport, and he might find that he was glad of her help. However fastidious she might be, Kathryn was a friend, and she wouldn't let him down if he needed another pair of hands. She would make it easier to say goodbye to Prue, too. He could pretend to be glad for her if he had Kathryn as an excuse for not throwing his pride to the winds and begging her to stay with him.

Prue was never sure how she got through those last few days in London. She kept a fixed smile on her face, but inside she felt as if she were shrinking away from her bones as misery churned in her stomach and clawed at her heart.

There were endless goodbyes to get through, too. Her father hugged her and told her that Nat was a fine man, her mother sent her off with much grandmotherly advice about dealing with the twins, and Marisa made her promise to let them know the wedding date as soon as possible so they could book their flights to Australia.

It was even harder leaving the Ashcrofts for the last time. Ruth clung to her when it came time to say goodbye.

'I can't tell you what a difference it makes to know you'll always be there for Laura's children,' she said tearfully. 'Harry and I know we're doing the right thing letting Daisy and William go back to Australia with you and Nat. You'll be a good mother to them. We can trust you and Nat to love them and look after them for us.'

Harry Ashcroft hugged her tightly as well. 'If Laura could see you, she would approve,' he said gruffly. 'She would have liked you very much.'

Prue swallowed the hard lump in her throat. 'I'm glad,' she said.

'You'll come back and see us some time with William and Daisy, won't you?'

There was the tiniest of pauses and then Nat spoke. 'Of course we will,' he said.

Prue wiped her eyes as they drove away, the twins babbling cheerfully in the back, oblivious to all the emotion. 'I hope we did the right thing,' she sighed. 'Ruth and Harry are going to be devastated when they found out that we lied to them. When will you tell them the truth?'

'What truth?'

'That we're not really in love.'

'Oh, that truth,' said Nat. His voice was remote, the way it had been ever since Ross had rung. 'I'll leave it a few months and then write to them. I'll just say things didn't work out. If the twins are safe and happy I don't think they'll mind too much.'

Cleo, brimming with happiness and brown and glowing from her honeymoon, took them to the airport.

'I wish you could stay longer,' she said. 'I've hardly had a chance to talk to you since we got back.'

Knowing how quickly her sister would sniff out anything wrong, Prue had deliberately avoided spending any time alone with her. 'I'm sorry, Cleo,' she said as she hugged her goodbye. 'We have to go back.'

'I know.' Cleo held her tightly. 'Thank you for coming, Prue. I used to think that you were making a terrible mistake going to live in the outback and taking on two small babies, but I was wrong. You and Nat are absolutely right for each other.'

At last it was over. They handed over their passports to be checked, passed through security control and there was no more need to pretend.

They barely spoke on the long flight to Singapore, and what conversation they had was limited to the twins. The airline provided sky cots for the babies, and they slept most of the way, which left Prue nothing to do but be achingly aware of Nat, silent and withdrawn beside her. For someone returning to his first and only love he was very subdued, Prue thought, but then he had always been a private man. Perhaps he had always worn that unapproachable expression, and it was only now that she was sensitive enough to notice?

Prue remembered the last time they had boarded a plane together, how hopeful she had been, how thrilled at the prospect of returning to Ross. Didn't they say that you shouldn't wish too hard for what you wanted in case you got it?

She sighed and turned to face the window. Outside there was only darkness and the monotonous drone of the engines. Maybe she could recapture that longing, she told herself.

Maybe she would take one look into Ross's blue eyes and fall in love with him all over again. He was much more suitable than Nat, anyway. He was her own age, he was handsome, he was fun. She got on well with his parents and loved his property. What more could she want?

Maybe in a few days' time she would marvel that she could ever have thought that Nat was the one she loved.

Maybe.

As the jumbo began its slow descent to Singapore, Prue looked down at the ring on her finger and remembered how little it had meant when Nat had bought it for her during the last stopover. It had taken her ages to get used to seeing it on her hand, but now it seemed to belong there.

Not any more. Taking a deep breath, she tugged the ring off her finger and held it out to Nat. 'You'd better have this back,' she said. 'I don't need to wear it any more.'

'You might as well keep it,' said Nat after a single, curt glance.

'Oh, but I couldn't—'

'What use is it to me?' he interrupted harshly. 'I'm not planning on any more pretend engagements. It's just a cheap ring,' he dismissed it. 'Keep it as a souvenir.'

Prue's fingers closed around the ring so tightly that the stones dug into her flesh. 'Thanks,' she said bitterly.

Nat clearly had no wish for a souvenir of the time they had spent together, but then, why would he? He had Kathryn to go home to, and she probably already had a beautiful engagement ring. Kathryn wouldn't be interested in the cheap little diamond that had been good enough for *her*. Prue wished that she had the pride to throw the ring away, but she knew that she would keep it. Soon it would be all of Nat's that she had left.

It was an interminable journey, but part of Prue didn't want it to end. When it ended she would have to face the hardest goodbye of all, and every hour that passed was an hour less she had to spend with Nat. Secretly, she hoped for a delay somewhere along the line, but they made all their connections easily. The Darwin flight left bang on time, and by the time they had shuffled through immigration at the other end the local plane which would take them on to Mathison was already waiting on the tarmac.

Both William and Daisy were fed up with travelling by then, and unimpressed by the smaller, noisier plane that linked a number of small outback towns. They grizzled and wriggled and cried at the pressure on their ears as the plane landed.

Mathison was the third stop. As they took off for the last time, Prue held a struggling Daisy in her lap. Only half an hour left. Her heart was drumming and there was a cruel band of steel tightening around her throat and making it hard for her to breathe.

Twenty five minutes…twenty… The seconds ticked inexorably away, and all too soon the plane began its descent over the familiar scrub. Prue could see Mathison below her, a cluster of buildings squeezed together by the vast, empty red country around it. There was the hotel, there was the store where Nat had driven her that day they had met, and now there was the airport….

The plane was sinking fast. Seconds later, it had bumped down onto the Tarmac and was speeding along the runway, its engines screaming, while Daisy provided the counterpoint.

Trying in vain to shush her, Prue looked out of the window. She could see the tiny terminal building and the cluster of people waving behind the rail. Ross would be there, and Kathryn.

This was it then. It was over.

Numbly, she carried Daisy, still yelling, down the steps. The heat hit her like a blow. Mingling with the aircraft fumes, it wavered over the Tarmac and refracted the light so that the terminal and the waiting people seemed to hover above the shimmering ground.

Nat had William in one arm, and their cabin baggage in the other. Without speaking, they walked across the Tarmac towards the barrier.

A beautiful girl with long legs and a mane of auburn hair was smiling and waving. Prue knew without being told that it was Kathryn. She made everyone else look faded and dowdy, and her smile was dazzling. Bitterly, Prue remembered how she had dreamt of making herself indispensable to Nat, of being there when he turned to her, of replacing Kathryn in his heart. How presumptuous she had been to imagine that he could forget someone like Kathryn!

Kathryn's face was alight, and she pushed her way towards him as he came through the barrier, calling his name. Prue had to watch as, not thinking how William might feel at a strange woman throwing herself at him, Kathryn flung her arms round Nat's neck and kissed him.

'Oh, Nat, I couldn't wait see you again!' she cried.

William's little face puckered and he burst into tears. Disentangling himself from Kathryn with a muttered apology, Nat put down the bag and joggled the baby against his shoulder. His heart sank as he saw Kathryn's slightly hurt expression, but he couldn't deal with her and a crying baby. Instinctively, Nat looked around for Prue.

He was just in time to see Ross put an arm round her and hug her to his side. 'Welcome back,' he was saying, smiling down at her with his dancing blue eyes.

Wiser than Kathryn, Ross made sure that he didn't

crowd Daisy, but he tickled her on the tummy with a grin. 'G'day, there!'

Daisy was so surprised that she stopped crying abruptly and stared at him, and, under Nat's jaundiced gaze, she dissolved into smiles. She was obviously no more immune to Ross's charm than any other female, Nat thought, watching sourly as his niece flirted her lashes and chuckled as he tickled her again.

Seeing that William had redoubled his cries, Prue handed Daisy to Ross. 'Would you mind holding her a minute, Ross? I think Nat needs a hand.'

'Hi!' Kathryn turned her warm smile on Prue as she went over. 'You must be Prue!' She winked. 'Ross has been telling me *all* about you!'

Prue managed a brief smile before turning to Nat, who was still trying to quieten William's wails. 'Why don't I take him?' she said, holding out her hands. 'That'll give you two a chance to say hello properly.'

Without waiting to see Nat take Kathryn in his arms, Prue carried William into the shade and found a quiet corner to sit down with him and cuddle him reassuringly until he calmed down. He had subsided into hiccupping little sobs when Kathryn came to join her on the seats. She had apparently inherited a smiling Daisy from Ross, and sat jiggling the baby on her knee.

'Ross has gone with Nat to sort out the luggage,' Kathryn told Prue with another friendly smile. 'Nat was muttering something about putting special seats in the car, so I guess they might be a little while. He said I'd frightened William too,' she said contritely, and chucked his chin. 'Sorry, William!'

From the safety of Prue's arms, William was prepared to concede a smile.

'It's just a bit confusing for them,' Prue apologised.

'I know, it was thoughtless of me. Nat's always told me I don't stop and think,' said Kathryn cheerfully. 'I was just pleased to see him again. I've got so much to tell him! I must say,' she added, cocking a curious eyebrow at Prue, 'he does seem a bit uptight. I've never seen him so grumpy before. Has he been like that the whole time?'

'It's been a long flight,' said Prue stiffly.

She wished Kathryn wouldn't be so nice. She wanted to hate her, not to find her warm and open and confiding. Kathryn was chatting about Ross now, asking how long she had known him and saying how much she would be envied by the other girls in the district.

'He certainly sounds very keen!' she said with a wink. 'When we were waiting for your plane to arrive he didn't stop talking about you and what a wonderful cook you are, and you know what they say about the best way to a man's heart…!'

It had obviously never crossed Kathryn's mind that she might have any reason to be jealous, or that there could be anything between her and Nat, Prue thought sadly. And there wasn't anything. They had made a deal, and they had both kept their side of the bargain, and now it was over.

Nat and Ross reappeared at last. Ross was grinning, but Nat had a set expression that only hardened when his eyes fell on Prue. 'Sorry about the wait, but we're ready now,' he said almost brusquely. 'Only one more leg, kids, and then we're home.'

He stood in front of Prue and looked down at her. 'I think it would be better if you and Ross went first. I'll take William.'

Nodding dumbly, Prue got to her feet. She held William tightly against her for a moment, kissing his chubby hand. She wanted to say goodbye but she couldn't speak, so she just gave him to Nat and bent to kiss Daisy on her wispy curls, wishing that there was some way of telling them how much she was going to miss them.

Now all she had to do was say goodbye to Nat. Straightening, Prue drew a ragged breath and made herself look at him. 'Will you let me know how they're getting on?' she asked unsteadily.

'Of course.'

She managed a wavering smile. 'I'll say goodbye, then.'

'Goodbye, Prue.' On an impulse Nat bent and kissed her cheek, a warm, fleeting kiss that seared her to the soul. 'Thanks,' he said. 'Thanks for everything.'

Somehow, Prue made herself turn and walk away beside Ross, but she had only taken three steps when Daisy and William, belatedly realising what was happening, set up a wail. It took everything Prue had not to turn back to them, and she had to cover her ears with her hands, unable to stop the tears spilling down her cheeks.

'They'll be fine once you've gone,' said Ross hearteningly. 'Out of sight, out of mind.'

Out of sight, out of mind. Prue only wished that it were true. The Grangers had welcomed her back with flattering warmth and put down her subdued spirits to jet lag. They were so kind that Prue felt guilty that she couldn't be happier to be back. She threw herself into the cooking to try and keep the pain at bay but, far from fading out of her mind, the longer she was away from Nat and the twins, the more she ached to see them again.

She tried everything to forget Nat. She told herself that it had been the equivalent of a holiday romance, that it hadn't been real, that she had only fancied herself in love because they had been thrown into such an intimate situation. She reminded herself that he was happy and didn't need her. She did her best to fall back in love with Ross.

None of it worked. Ross, intrigued at first by her preoccupation, soon lost interest once it was obvious that the days of her uncritical adoration were over. When she had an hour off, Prue would walk down by the creek where she had used to go and dream about Ross. Now she dreamt about a very different man, a quiet man with slow hands and a slow smile.

She yearned to see him again. Several times she picked up the phone to ring Mack River just so that she could hear his voice, but each time she put down the receiver before she had finished dialling. She could have asked how Daisy and William were, but he had promised to let her know, and if he hadn't contacted her it must be because he had better things to do. When was it going to get any easier? Prue wondered in despair. She couldn't spend the rest of her life with this raw ache inside her. Sometimes it felt as if someone was pulling her entrails out of her, loop after loop.

It was nearly two long, bleak weeks before she had any news from Mack River. Prue was drearily setting out the lunch and wondering how much longer she could stand it when Joyce Granger came back from Mathison, big with news.

'I met Bev Martelli in the store,' she said, unpacking the groceries Prue had asked her to get while she was in town.

'Who's she?' asked Prue without much interest.

'I thought you'd know her,' said Joyce, surprised. 'Her husband is the married man at Mack River.'

Prue's head came up abruptly. 'Oh?' she said, dry-mouthed.

'She reckons Nat Masterman is having a bad time with those babies.' Joyce shook her head. 'He can't get a nanny to stay. The first one left after three days, and the next only managed a week, so now he's trying to cope on his own until he can find someone else. Bev does what she can, but she's got three kids of her own and all the cooking to do.'

'But…what about Kathryn?' asked Prue, clutching the knives and forks to her chest. 'I thought she would be there.'

'Well, so did we. We were all sure that the engagement was on again, but I don't think it can be. Bev said she went back to Perth as soon as the first nanny turned up.'

Prue could only stare at Joyce, unable to take in what she was saying. Kathryn had *gone*? Why? What had happened?

'Of course, I got on the radio to Nat straight away,' Joyce was saying. 'I said why didn't I send you over to help him out, since it sounded like he needed you more than we did, but Nat wouldn't hear of it. He said he could manage.'

'Manage?' said Prue in slowly gathering wrath as Joyce's words sank in. 'How can he possibly manage the two of them on his own and run a cattle station?'

'You know what men are like. They won't accept they need help.'

Prue slammed the cutlery down on the table. 'He should be thinking about William and Daisy, not his own stupid pride!' she said furiously.

Two weeks she had endured the agony of not seeing him, and all the time she could have been at Mack River! All Nat had to do was ask, but no! He had let her break her heart with wanting him and rung up his stupid agency instead!

Prue was so angry she didn't know what to do with herself. All those tears, all that pain he could have spared her if he had simply picked up the phone and asked for her help! She didn't know whether it was Nat's lack of consideration for the twins' comfort that enraged her or his refusal to turn to her when all she had wanted was a chance to love him but, whichever it was, it had jolted her out of her misery.

'I must say, it's not like Nat,' Joyce commented mildly. 'He's usually so level-headed.'

'He's just being stubborn and stupid and pig-headed!' snapped Prue, invigorated by the rage scalding through her. She untied her apron and threw it over a chair. 'Mrs Granger, can you manage without me for a few days? I'm going to ask Ross to fly me over to Mack River right now!'

'Does Nat know you're coming to stay?' Ross grinned as she threw a small bag into the back of the plane and climbed into the seat beside him. The propeller of the small Cessna was already whirring.

'No,' said Prue, tight-lipped, 'but I'm staying whether he likes it or not!'

No one knew that she was coming, so there was no one to meet her at the airstrip but it wasn't far to the homestead. Clutching her bag in one hand, still buoyed up by anger, Prue marched along the track.

She could hear the bawling before she got halfway across the yard. Stalking up the verandah steps, she slammed through the screen door, dumped her bag and headed straight down the corridor to the source of the noise.

William and Daisy's combined lung power drowned out the sound of her footsteps and Nat was unaware of her presence as Prue paused in the open doorway. She derived some satisfaction from seeing that the calm, controlled Nat was looking distinctly harassed at last.

He was struggling to change William's nappy and casting increasingly desperate glances over his shoulder to the cot where Daisy had whipped herself into a pitch of screaming frustration.

'Hold on, Daisy,' he pleaded. 'I'm just coming.'

Daisy's face was bright red and screwed up with misery, her eyes piggy with tears. She looked, thought Prue, exactly the way *she* had been feeling for the last two weeks.

And that was Nat's fault, too.

Exasperated, Prue went over to the cot and picked up the screaming baby. 'Shh, shh, sweetheart,' she whispered.

Nat, fumbling with the nappy and still deafened by William's bawling, had yet to notice her, but he registered the diminution in the volume as Daisy responded to the familiar feel of Prue's arms and burrowed into her, the screams subsiding to mere heart-wrenching sobs.

'Good gi—' Nat stopped as he risked a glance over his shoulder and saw Prue, cradling Daisy in her arms.

'It's all right now, it's all right,' she was murmuring soothingly. 'I'm here now.'

'Prue?' he croaked, half afraid that he might have conjured her up out of his imagination. '*Prue...*!' She had to be real. She *had* to be. 'Prue, what are you doing here?'

'What does it look like I'm doing?' she snapped. 'I've come to help.'

She seemed angry, thought Nat, still reeling with shock

and consumed by the sheer joy of seeing her again. He couldn't take his eyes off her as she carried Daisy over and laid her on the changing mat next to William's.

'Prue...' He couldn't seem to say anything else. He wanted to pull her to him, to run his hands all over her to convince himself that she was real, to devour her with kisses, but she was deftly stripping Daisy of the dirty nappy and her expression was decidedly stormy.

'How long have things been like this?' she demanded, jerking wipes out of the box.

Nat didn't pretend not to understand her. 'Three days,' he said. This wasn't the way he had imagined seeing Prue again but, as she was being so efficient with Daisy, he might as well finish changing William.

'The last nanny couldn't cope. She said Daisy and William were too much for her, although I was doing as much as I could. I asked her to stay until I could find someone else, but she wouldn't. The agency is supposed to be sending another girl out in a few days. I thought I could manage.'

'Do you call this managing, with both of them screaming their heads off?'

'I'm doing my best,' said Nat, faintly defensive.

'It's not enough!' Prue's hands moved automatically while inside she was shaking with a mixture of fury and emotion at just being near him again. 'Why didn't you ask me to help, Nat? You must have known I would come!'

Jaw set, Nat finally managed to fasten William's nappy. He snapped the Babygro together and lifted his nephew against his shoulder, patting his back until his outraged screams subsided like Daisy's, although he continued to snivel into Nat's neck.

Nat was very tired. He had hardly slept for the last two

weeks. It had been a nightmare trying to deal with the two of them single-handed. He hadn't realised how much he had relied on Prue. William and Daisy were miserable and unsettled without her, and so was he. He had missed her desperately.

'Why didn't I ask you?' he repeated, an undercurrent of anger stealing into his voice. If she only knew how many times he had reached for the phone! 'I didn't call you because I didn't want you to feel that you had to leave Ross as soon as you'd got back. You went on and on about how much you loved him and how all you wanted was to go back to Cowen Creek. I thought the last thing you'd want was to be dragged away to help me.'

'I'd have done *anything* to come!' Prue was so angry at his obtuseness that she was almost shouting. 'I only went with Ross because I thought Kathryn was going to be here. Couldn't you *see*…?'

There was an astounded silence, broken by the last hiccuping sobs of the babies. Appalled at how badly she had given herself away, Prue stared into Nat's shocked brown eyes for a long moment before her fury evaporated without warning and she began to cry.

She put her hands up to cover her face and gave in. 'Oh, Nat, I've missed you so much!' she wept.

Nat's first reaction was helplessness. Now he had three of them in tears, and only two arms. He was looking between them, wondering which of them needed him most, when he belatedly realised just what she had said. She had missed him.

'Prue,' he said in a shaken voice.

'I'm sorry, I'm sorry.' Prue turned hastily away and was trying to change Daisy and wipe her cheeks at the same time, but the tears wouldn't stop. 'I didn't mean to tell you like this, but all I wanted was to come here and be with you, and then Mrs Granger said you didn't want me.' Her voice broke again.

'Not want you?' Nat almost laughed. 'Prue, I've wanted you ever since you kissed me on the verandah here.'

Prue's hands stilled on the nappy and her head turned to him very slowly, as if it had been pulled round on a string. 'You have?' she whispered.

Nat shifted William into one arm, and reached out his free hand to pull her gently towards him. 'Come here,' he said softly, and she leant into him with a sigh of release, circling him with her arms and pressing her face into his throat. 'Shall I tell you how much I want you, Prue?' he said into her hair. 'Shall I tell you how much I've missed you too?'

His arm tightened around her. 'Shall I tell you how much I love you?'

'Yes,' said Prue, lifting her face to his. 'Oh, yes, please!'

Their mouths found each other in a kiss that was honeyed with promise but all too short. It wasn't easy to kiss the way they both wanted when William was smacking Nat's hair crossly and Daisy was objecting equally loudly to the loss of attention.

Reluctantly, Nat let Prue go. 'How do you tell a nine-month-old to shut up?' he asked with a resigned sigh, and she laughed, high on the enchantment that was fizzing and flooding through her.

'You don't,' she told him. 'I'll finish Daisy and then we'll give them a drink. Perhaps that will keep them quiet for a bit.'

They sat on the double seat on the verandah, a baby on each lap. William and Daisy guzzled contentedly and at last a blissful hush descended. Nat put his free arm around Prue. 'Tell me again how much you missed me,' he said with a smile.

Frustratingly one-handed as it was, it was a much better kiss this time, deep, and hungry and intoxicatingly sweet. Breathless at last, Prue kissed her way along Nat's jaw and down his throat before resting her face there and breathing in the scent of his skin.

'I love you,' she said, muffled against him, and Nat slid his fingers under her chin so that he could tilt it and kiss her again.

'I wish I'd known,' he said when he could speak. 'Why didn't you tell me?'

Prue leant her head against his shoulder and thought how right it felt to be there, with his arm around her and the warm, solid weight of a baby in the curve of her body. 'I thought you were in love with Kathryn.'

On Nat's lap, Daisy choked and spluttered and Nat sat her upright, rubbing her back. 'I only let you think that because I thought it would be easier for you,' he said.

'*Easier*?'

'You were so full of Ross,' he explained. 'I thought you might feel awkward if you knew that I was falling hopelessly in love with you, so I pretended I was hoping that Kathryn and I would get together again, but it wasn't true. Kathryn and I have always been good friends but I've never loved her the way I love you, and she knows that.'

'But Ross said—'

'Ross got the wrong end of the stick,' said Nat. 'He was right about Kathryn wanting to see me as soon as I got back, but it was only because she wanted me to be the first one to know she was getting married to a man she met in Perth. We'd been engaged for a while, and she wanted to tell me herself so that I didn't hear about it through the grapevine. It was typical of her to come all the way up here, but she got more than she bargained for—if she wasn't dealing with babies she was listening to me talk about you! I'm not surprised she headed back for Perth as soon as the emergency nanny arrived!'

'We've wasted so much time,' sighed Prue, snuggling happily against him. 'I was so certain you were in love.'

'I was,' said Nat, smoothing her hair behind her ear and kissing it. 'With you.'

They shared another blissful kiss.

'You'd better ring your family tonight and tell them to book their tickets,' he murmured against Prue's lips. 'Say we'll get married as soon as they can get here.'

Prue laughed softly as she kissed him back. 'We don't need to get married straight away,' she pointed out. 'My visa lasts a year and I'm not going anywhere now!'

'I'm not waiting any longer than I have to,' said Nat firmly.

Removing Daisy's bottle from her slack grasp, he propped her against his shoulder and patted her gently to wind her. 'Besides,' he went on, rewarded by a burp, 'do you have any idea how hard it is to get nannies to stay in a place like this? I want to make sure you're on a permanent contract!' His brown eyes were teasing. 'After all, I reckon I'm getting a bargain—a cook, a nanny and a wife all rolled into one. There's no way I'm letting you go now!'

Prue's eyes shone silver with happiness. 'So you'll tell the agency you don't need that nice girl they've booked for you any more?'

'I'll ring them this afternoon,' promised Nat. 'I'll say I've got the only nice girl I need. There's only one cook I'll ever want and only one nanny' He kissed her again. 'And absolutely, definitely, only one wife!'

ADOPTED: TWINS!

by

Marion Lennox

Marion Lennox was born on an Australian dairy farm. She moved on – mostly because the cows weren't interested in her stories! Marion writes Medical Romance™ as well as Tender Romance™. Initially she used different names, so if you're looking for past books, search also for author Trisha David. In her non-writing life Marion cares (haphazardly) for her husband, kids, dogs, cats, chickens and anyone else who lines up at her dinner table. She fights her rampant garden (she's losing) and her house dust (she's lost!). She also travels, which she finds seriously addictive. As a teenager Marion was told she'd never get anywhere reading romance. Now romance is the basis of her stories, her stories allow her to travel, and if ever there was one advertisement for following your dream, she'd be it! You can contact Marion at www.marionlennox.com.

**Don't miss Marion Lennox's new
Medical Romance™**
The Doctor's Proposal
in June 2006 from Mills & Boon.

CHAPTER ONE

THE marital order in Bay Beach was thoroughly satisfactory for all concerned. Matt was marrying Charlotte. Erin, with her five unwanted children, was happily single.

Then the twins' bomb exploded.

Matt McKay was one of Australia's best known cattle breeders. He was also running late, but he wasn't so late that Charlotte would be annoyed. He'd been paying a visit to a friend in hospital. Now he was headed to Charlotte's for dinner.

He was also headed for commitment.

Well, why not? Charlotte was beautiful, immaculately groomed and extremely pleasant company. She understood his farming needs. Acclaimed as the best hostess in the district, she'd been loyal to Matt for almost twenty years.

Back in Bay Beach hospital, Matt's friend, Nick Daniels, was recovering nicely from his appendix operation. Matt had left him comfortably settled, Nick's wife and children pandering to his every whim.

The visit had made Matt think. Life should include pandering, he'd decided. He'd avoided it so far, but it was hard not to feel jealous of Nick's domestic bliss. Despite his lost appendix, Nick couldn't be more content.

Which was why Matt had detoured via the jewellers.

Something schmaltzy came onto the radio—something about love and snow-white hair and faithfulness forever.

Matt glanced down at the velvet box tucked into his map compartment, and he pushed away the last of his qualms. Marriage to Charlotte…

It had always seemed logical, and maybe that's why he'd taken so long to get around to asking. He'd had a few flings in his youth, but Charlotte was always calmly waiting for him to return from what she teasingly called his nonsense. Ten years ago her possessiveness had driven him nuts. But now… Maybe she was right. Maybe they were suited.

And he wouldn't mind a kid or two.

Nick was managing fatherhood beautifully, Matt decided, thinking of the family group he'd left at the hospital. With two gorgeous kids and another on the way, Nick and Shanni were blissfully happy.

Could he and Charlotte be the same?

Would Charlotte even want children? Charlotte wasn't a baby sort of person, but if she could produce little Charlottes… Children who were neat and practical and knew what was right…

That might be a problem. He wouldn't mind a bit of spirit in any child he had. He grinned to himself, acknowledging that he hadn't been a childhood angel. In fact he'd driven his mother to distraction.

But kids were a fifty-fifty gene split. He'd spent most of his childhood with his father, and if Charlotte thought she could breed children who'd wipe their feet and read their story books quietly, then maybe he could persuade her to give parenthood a try.

They could be hers indoors and his outdoors—which would be a childhood just like his had been.

So…

So tonight he'd finally ask her to marry him, he decided,

as he drove Charlotte-wards. After all, it was an excellent night.

Apart from a bomb waiting in the wings...

And at Home Number Three of Bay Beach Orphanage, things were also excellent.

Erin Douglas, Home Mother, had all her charges in bed by eight, which was no mean feat.

The baby, Marigold, had gone out like a light, bless her. She was showing every sign that she'd make her adoptive parents blissfully happy.

Five year old Tess and eight year old Michael, a brother and sister who'd been placed in the Home while their mother was ill, had gone to sleep on cue. No problems there.

And—amazingly—the twins had gone meekly to bed when told. When she'd checked ten minutes ago, they had their eyes closed and seemed out for the count.

This was truly amazing!

It was worth a glass of wine to celebrate, Erin decided. There weren't too many nights in a house mother's life when all her charges went to sleep this early, and it *never* happened when she had the twins.

Her hand stilled on the refrigerator door, survival instincts surfacing. It was almost too good to be true, she thought, and her well-honed nose smelled a rat. She tiptoed to the twins' bedroom yet again, and opened the door a crack.

But her instincts seemed wrong. They looked beautifully asleep.

How could she doubt them? she wondered as she gazed down at their intently sleeping countenances. How could anyone doubt them?

At seven years old, Henry and William were gorgeous. They had bright, curly, carrot-red hair, smatterings of freckles on their cute, snub noses, and a look on their faces that said they were the work of angels.

That look, Erin knew to her cost, was entirely misleading. There was a solid reason they were in care. Their mother couldn't control them, and by the time they were four, with no husband and seven other children to look after, she'd abused them unmercifully and then simply abandoned them to foster care.

That hadn't worked either. Up until now, no foster parents could cope with their trouble-making, and after each effort to find them a home, back they'd come to the orphanage every time. If it could be organised, they were placed with Erin. Erin could usually control them, but even Erin found it tough.

She sighed. What would she do with them? They were holy terrors, but as she looked down at their sleeping faces her heart twisted with pain for the two little boys she was starting to love.

They shouldn't be in the orphanage. They were sharp as tacks—maybe clever enough to be categorised as intellectually gifted, Erin thought, remembering a few of the truly amazing spots of trouble they'd landed themselves into. As well as that, they were engaging and lovable, and they desperately needed a mother and a father to love them.

If only they weren't intent on destroying the world!

Still, for now they were asleep and she was feeling as if a miracle had occurred! She took herself back to the kitchen, kicked off her shoes and put her feet up in bliss.

'Here's to a miracle,' she told herself, raising her wine glass in a toast to the evening. 'Here's to an excellent night.'

* * *

Back in their bedroom, Henry and William's plan was working like a dream.

They'd strung thread from the kitchen door to the top of their bedroom door. Then they'd tied their stuffed toy, Tigger Tiger, to the thread, and they'd frayed it so it'd break at the first movement of the kitchen door.

The plan was perfect. If Erin left the kitchen, the thread snapped and Tigger fell to the floor. Unless the thread tangled in Erin's feet—which would have been really, really unlucky—she'd never notice.

As Tigger landed, there was just enough time for the boys to shove what they were doing under the bed, grab Tigger, scramble under the bedcovers and flick off the light before Erin appeared to check.

So to Erin, all was beautifully, unnaturally normal, and they concentrated fiercely on looking asleep as she tiptoed over to them.

'Goodnight, you rascals,' she'd whispered, and they'd both had to concentrate even harder not to giggle.

Then, with Erin gone, they picked up the end of the thread and retied Tigger in his warning position. And then they retrieved what was under the bed.

Brilliant! Absolutely excellent.

But the bomb wasn't meant to go off when it did.

The plan was for Henry to carry it outside in the toe of his slipper. It was scary to carry it in his bare fingers, and a slipper should hold it safe. Their bomb was a hand-taped ball stuffed with matches and fire-crackers, designed to go off when thumped on the ground. They knew how volatile it was, but they weren't stupid.

After carrying it carefully outside, the plan was to lob it over the next-door fence.

It was eight at night. At eight *every night*, just as the

news ended on the telly, their next door neighbours, Helmut and Valda Cole, let their pet poodle out for her evening run.

Pansy Poodle never went more than two feet into the garden so there was no fear of hitting her. But she might just about turn inside out with the bang, and Mr and Mrs Cole would go berserk. Which would be very interesting indeed!

Henry and William disliked the Coles, and they knew exactly what the Coles thought about them—and orphans in general. The Coles were raising a petition to have all the orphanage houses put together. 'To put all the trouble-makers in the one spot!' They were even nasty to Erin, which was unthinkable.

Henry and William mightn't always do as Erin wanted, but she gave the best cuddles of anyone they knew, and even when they were in serious trouble she just sighed, ruffled their hair and said, 'What am I going to do with you, you twerps?'

And Pansy Poodle yapped so much she woke the baby, and when Henry poked his finger through the fence—just to say hello—she'd bitten him! It had taken fifteen minutes of Erin's cuddles before Henry had stopped shaking.

The Coles, therefore, had to be got rid of before they upset Erin further, or before Pansy bit someone else, and the only thing that might make them move was if they thought their poodle was in danger. Hence the bomb, the construction of which had been learned from spying on the bigger kids at school.

Only then...

Well, Henry was pushing the bomb into the slipper and William was holding the slipper up so it'd slide in, and it wouldn't quite fit—and then Henry got nervous and the slipper sort of fell sideways.

The tape-wound ball, stacked really, really tightly with matches and firecrackers, fell heavily onto the floor and rolled under the curtains by the bed.

Henry and William stared at it for one horrified moment—and then dived for cover under the opposite bed.

The explosion reverberated through the house and into the night beyond. Instantly the lights went off as the electricity safety switch cut in, and there was the sound of crashing glass from along the veranda. The smell of smoke swept into the kitchen, and then the fire alarm in the corridor ceiling started to scream.

Bay Beach Orphanage, Home Number Three, was on fire.

Matt heard the fire alarm before he rounded the corner. That was no big deal, he thought. His smoke detector at home went off every time he burned his toast. Which, he had to admit, was often.

But Matt was driving with his truck window down, and the alarm was loud enough to make him glance sideways. He was now right out front of one of the Bay Beach Homes—and what he saw made him slam his foot on the brake and pull to dead halt.

He left his truck sitting where it was, engine still on, and he started to run.

'Take the baby.'

Matt knew Erin Douglas. Of course he did. Everyone in Bay Beach knew everyone else, and these two had gone to school together.

Not that they'd got on. Erin was three years younger than Matt, and maybe he still thought of her as the bossy, forthright kid she'd been way back in third grade. Over the years he'd danced with her a few times at local functions, but she definitely wasn't his type.

It didn't stop him appreciating her. With a lovely figure; with a clear, almost luminescent complexion and huge blue eyes, she'd always had her share of boyfriends. She was definitely attractive, he'd decided, in a blonde, curvy sort of way, but she was a bit…well, sassy, and inclined to laugh at the world—and at him in particular.

Matt was wealthy and his family were descended from the landed gentry. Normally that stood him in good stead with women, but with Erin it was almost as if she was mocking him because of it.

And she always looked frazzled, he thought. She didn't fuss if her shoulder-length curls were tangled, and her make-up was always scant and looked like it had been applied in haste. Yeah, he knew all the Home Mothers looked like that—they had such little time to themselves— but it wouldn't hurt her to take a bit more effort.

She wore brightly coloured dresses, nipped in to a neat waistline and then blousing out in soft folds to mid-calf. They looked home-made, Charlotte had told him, and he could see that they were.

The last time he'd seen her had been at the local school fête. One of her kids had painted her face as a butterfly, and her blue eyes were orbs under enormous, colourful wings, the paint reaching right out to her ears.

Good grief, he'd thought, as he and Charlotte had paused for a second, stunned look. No, she definitely wasn't his type. She wasn't groomed and elegant as he liked his women. She wasn't like his mother or like Charlotte.

And now… Well, she certainly wasn't concentrating on appearances, but she was looking more frazzled than he'd ever seen her. As he reached the veranda, she burst through the screen door and she was carrying a baby. The little one couldn't have been more than four or five months old.

Erin didn't say anything more than, 'Take the baby,' before thrusting the child into his arms and disappearing again into the house.

What was he supposed to do with it? He stared down at the baby in indecision. He couldn't just dump it, but there were things that were more urgent here than baby-holding.

A face appeared over the side fence. Well, it would. The explosion must have been heard for blocks, and Valda Cole was into everyone else's business before it happened. Usually Matt avoided Valda like the plague, but now, burdened with the baby, he was even grateful to see her.

'Take the baby and phone the fire brigade,' he snapped, and thrust the infant over the fence into her startled arms before she had a chance to protest. 'And contact the police and ambulance. Fast.'

And then he dived into the house after Erin.

She'd found Tess and Michael.

The children had woken and stumbled to their doors in the increasingly smoke-filled dark. Calling and feeling her way, she found them and grabbed their hands. Five years old and badly frightened, Tess stumbled in the gloom. Still holding eight-year-old Michael's hand, Erin lifted Tess and fumbled her way out toward the door.

The smoke was so thick she couldn't see anything. Her eyes were streaming as she called to the twins.

'Henry? William?'

There was no answer. Ventilation slits were built in above the bedroom doors and the smoke seemed to be coming from the twins' room, but she couldn't investigate. Her first priority must be to get Tess and Michael out.

And then she barrelled right into Matt in the hall.

This time she acknowledged his presence. She needed help—any help!—and she knew enough of Matthew McKay to know he was capable.

'Matt, there's these two, but the twins are still inside.' She propelled her children forward and choked on a lungful of smoke. 'Take them out.'

He took them all out. Grasping her arm without a word, he pulled her back out of the door before she could argue. There, standing on the porch, she fought to regain her breath so she could speak again.

Her panic was threatening to overwhelm her. The smoke seemed almost impenetrable, and she could see flames shooting from the side window. It was definitely coming from the twins' room.

'Dear God, the twins...' It was hard to make her voice work. The smoke had seared her lungs, so every breath hurt.

'How many more are inside?' Matt's voice was harsh with authority. 'How many and tell me where they are. Now!'

Somehow she hauled herself under control and made herself heard. She couldn't have asked for a better assistant than Matt McKay. Sure, he was wealthy and too good-looking for his own good, and he moved in circles she didn't belong too, but his competence was never in question.

'Just the twins,' she told him. 'Two seven-year-old boys. They're in there together.' She choked on another lungful of smoke, but she had enough sense to thrust the children off the porch as she motioned toward the twins' window. The curtains were billowing out through the smashed glass, flaming outward in the night air. 'Please look after the kids. I'll go—'

'Stay where you are!' Matt's brain was in overdrive as he sorted priorities. Helmut Cole was running across the lawn with a garden hose, while Valda watched horrified from a distance. She was holding the baby like she was holding something unclean.

It couldn't matter. At least the baby could come to no harm where she was, and Helmut was doing the right thing.

'Have you called emergency services?' he yelled and, as Valda nodded, he turned back to her husband.

'Helmut, point the hose in that window and keep it there.' Then he turned and headed back inside—back in the direction of those shooting flames.

'Please be careful.' Erin was close to collapse. 'The smoke…'

'We can't get in through the window,' he told her. 'Let's just hope the whole bedroom isn't ablaze.'

The house was in pitch darkness, but even if it had been daylight he couldn't have seen anything. The smoke was so dense it was threatening to choke him. Matt dropped to his knees and crawled, but the smoke was too thick…

Then his brain kicked in. Finally! Damn, he should have thought of this outside. He paused, hauled off his sweater and tied it round his face. It wasn't much protection, but it was better than nothing.

The twins' bedroom was the second window from the front. He needed to turn right through the kitchen and head for the second door along the passage to the closed door…

He had to work fast, whatever was behind that door. If he was met with a wall of flame he didn't have a chance—but then, neither did the twins.

With a silent prayer, he felt the knob, but it wasn't hot to touch. That was his first good sign. There was therefore only smoke hard against the door. There was nothing to do now but...

He took a deep, smoke-filled breath, opened the door and forced his eyes to see. The curtains across the window were blazing, and the bed against the far wall was well alight. Outside, Helmut raised his hose and he was hit in the face by a jet of water.

Thank God for Helmut. The water wouldn't put the fire out, but it helped keep him alive. The soggy sweater across his face made breathing possible—just—and he kept his face in that direction until the sweater was completely soaked.

Then he took another breath and somehow managed to make his voice work.

'Kids, where are you?'

'H-here...' The muffled gasp came from the side of the room away from the window—low down. A piece of burning curtain landed in his hair. He thrust it away, unconscious of the pain, and groped under the second bed.

'Grab hold,' he managed, and small hands reached out and gripped his arms. As he counted contact hands—four!—he could have sobbed in relief.

There was no time for sobbing. Now what? Somehow he had to get them back through the house, and the smoke was building every minute.

'T-Tigger,' one of the children was saying, and the kid was pulling away.

'What?'

'Tigger.'

Matt found his hands full of sodden fur as the thing was thrust at him. A toy? Good grief! He shoved it down his shirt and grabbed a blanket.

'Wait.' His voice came out as a hoarse croak. More of Helmut's water hit the blanket, but not enough. He held it up and let it soak, and then threw the cloth over the boys' heads.

'We're crawling out of the room,' he croaked. He had them cradled against him, but he pushed them towards the door. 'You crawl first. If I stop, then you keep going. That's an order. Now!'

And he shoved them forward out of that burning room, along the passage, into the kitchen and the hall beyond.

'Henry... William...'

Erin met them in the hall. Like Matt, she'd wrapped her sweater over her head. She'd come in as far as she dared and was waiting, crouched at the kitchen door. As they crawled from the passage, she hauled them into her arms and tugged them outside.

Matt followed. He crawled four feet from the front door and collapsed unconscious onto the porch.

The most beautiful pair of blue eyes was gazing down into his.

'Do you think he'll live?'

There was something over his mouth and nose—something plastic and hard, and he tried to push it away.

'Keep it there, Matt.' He recognised the voice—Rob McDonald, the local police sergeant. 'You've got a lungful of smoke and we're giving you oxygen. Yes, Erin, if he's capable of fighting off a mask, then I reckon he'll live.'

Matt thought that through, and it seemed to make sense. The gorgeous eyes were still looking at him. It was funny how he'd never noticed them before. Erin was grimy and smoke-stained and still looking frazzled, but suddenly he thought she looked the most beautiful woman he'd ever seen. Just like that butterfly at the fête, he thought dazedly. Gorgeous!

Life was gorgeous!

If she hadn't come in to find them, he never would have got the boys out, he acknowledged. It had taken all his strength just to crawl those last few yards and he couldn't have propelled the twins any further.

'The twins?' It was a muffled whisper under the mask, but Erin knew what he was saying.

'They're scared out of their wits but they're fine. I need to go back to them. If you're sure you're okay...'

'He's tough,' Rob growled. 'The ambulance boys are just bringing the stretcher across.'

That roused him. Hell, no. He didn't need a stretcher. He pushed the mask away, coughed and coughed again, and finally managed to sit up. Rob stayed by his side, uneasy.

'They told me to hold the mask over your face. Do you mind not getting me into trouble?'

'I don't need it.' Matt coughed again, grabbed the mask and took two deep breaths to prove it. The improvement was immediate.

Then he took a look around, and was astounded by what he saw.

People were everywhere. The fire engine was parked almost beside him; there were men running, hoses uncoiling; the police car was there with its blue light flashing...

Half of Bay Beach was here, he thought dazedly, and then he turned to the house.

Helmut's hose hadn't been enough. The house was well alight and they'd be lucky to save anything. The bedroom where the twins had come from was now a charred shell, and the rest of the house was roofless and smouldering. There was little for the fire-fighters to do but to play their hoses over the ruin to stop sparks causing trouble elsewhere.

Matt looked at the charred remains of the twins' bedroom, and a shudder ran though his entire body. He'd been in there. The twins had been in there!

The man beside him saw what he was seeing and guessed his thoughts. 'You got the kids out,' Rob said in a voice that was none too steady. His big policeman's hand came down and grasped Matt's shoulder. 'I don't know how you did it, mate, but you did. You're a bloody hero.'

'I don't know how I did it either,' Matt said. He gulped in two more takes of oxygen and focussed some more.

There was something heavy and soggy in his shirt and he suddenly remembered the kids' toy. Or whatever it was. He peered down his shirt in the combined firelight and floodlights, and was relieved to see a pair of grimy glass eyes staring up at him.

It *was* just a toy, then. Great! For a minute there he'd thought maybe it was an unconscious pet, and mouth-to-mouth resuscitation on a dog or cat didn't really appeal.

Back to important stuff.

'The kids...they really are okay?'

'They really are okay. Thanks to you.' Rob looked up as the ambulance officers approached and he gave them an apologetic grin. 'He's giving me trouble.'

'He would.' The ambulance officers were locals and they were mates of both Rob and Matt. Their smiles were wide as houses.

In truth as they'd rounded the bend and seen the fire their stomachs had tightened in horror. Fire casualties were awful, and kids were the worst. Now, they were having trouble containing their delight that their only patient was a stroppy mate—a mate who looked like he had every intention of making it to old age.

'Let's get you loaded up and off to hospital,' they said cheerfully. 'Hey, we hear Nick Daniels is in there without his appendix. You can keep him company.'

'I'm not going to hospital.'

'Too right you are, even if we have to tie you down.' Then they glanced up as a young woman came hurrying across the lawn toward them, her doctor's bag at her side. 'Doc, he's saying he won't come to hospital.'

'Lie down, Matthew McKay,' she said firmly.

'But—'

'Shut up and let me examine you or I'll put you out for the count.' Dr Emily Mainwaring knew her stuff, and she knew her patient. 'Hurry up, Matt. They say you're the one worst affected but I have five kids and Erin to examine, so let's get this over fast.'

He was fine. Excellent, almost.

'You'll live,' she told him, tucking away her stethoscope and casting a brief yet horrified glance at the still-smouldering house. 'Just don't push your luck any further. You need antiseptic and a dressing on that burn on your head, but it's superficial.' Then she peered closer under his shirt and saw what he'd stuffed there. 'What on earth is that?'

'It's a toy of some kind.' Matt managed a grin. 'It's not a patient—thank Heaven.' He put a hand down to haul it out but she stopped him.

'No. If it really is a toy, leave it there and see if you can clean it up when you get home. If you leave it here it'll get lost in this mess, and it just may be important. These kids have lost everything, and I suspect I'm not looking at long-term physical problems here, but psychological ones.'

He thought that through and it made sense. 'Okay.' The toy could stay, soggy or not.

'Can you dress that burn yourself? It's not too bad.' She was flustered, worrying about Erin and the kids and wanting to move on. 'Good. Okay, you don't need hospital, but

I do want you supervised tonight. No going home to that farm alone. What about going to Charlotte's? Shall I have someone ring her?'

'No!' For some reason that was the last thing he wanted. 'I'm fine.'

'You hear what I'm saying?' she said fiercely. 'Home with someone with you—or hospital. Choose.'

'I…'

'I don't have time to waste,' she said firmly. 'Think about it while I check the rest. Though, thanks to you, I gather I hardly have a patient to contend with.' She turned to the ambulance officers.

'Hold him down, boys, and don't let him go until he can give me a plan for this evening that doesn't involve going home by himself, forgetting the antiseptic, having three stiff whiskies and passing out without anyone there to watch.'

She meant it.

Matt knew Emily well enough to accept that she was quite capable of trussing him to a stretcher, and he had enough wit—and he was feeling bad enough—to acknowledge that she was talking sense.

So what were his alternatives?

She'd suggested Charlotte's, but the idea was distinctly unappealing. Sure, she'd put him up for the night, but she'd fuss.

All he wanted was his own bed, he thought, and suddenly he wanted it very, very much. Shock was starting to hit home, and he had to clench his hands into fists to stop Rob seeing the sudden tremor that ran through him.

But Rob wasn't noticing. His mind had moved on.

'What can we do with the kids?' The police sergeant was still beside Matt, but he was speaking to Erin. The doctor and the ambulance officers were attending the children.

With immediate health fears eased, it was time to concentrate on the next problem, which seemed, Matt gathered, to be accommodation for Erin and the children.

Erin was tightening her lips, thinking it through. Or, she was trying to think it through. She looked like her mind felt full of smoke.

'I don't know,' she managed, and then she looked up as someone else darted through the jumble of fire-hoses and fire-fighters. Her strained face slackened in relief. 'Wendy…'

Wendy was an ex-House Mother, now happily married and immersed in domesticity. She was followed by her husband, Luke. Luke strolled languidly through the chaos, lifted a trembling Michael into his arms almost as an aside—marriage to Wendy meant that Luke and the Orphanage kids had met each other heaps of times before—and he hugged the little boy close.

'Hey, Michael. Been having some excitement, then? Wow! It's great that you're all okay. And this is a great fire engine.'

Then he looked down at Matt in admiring amusement. 'And here's our Matthew out for the count. Been playing heroes, have we, kids?'

'Shut up, Luke.' But Matt grinned. It suddenly did feel good. Heroic even. The feel of those four little hands clutching his arms from under the bed came sweeping back, and he knew where they'd be now without him…

His grin faded and the tremors swept back. He'd been lucky to get them—and himself—out alive.

'The other homes are all full,' Wendy was saying. She was right back in House Mother mode, as though she'd never left. She was hugging Michael's little sister, Tess, to her breast as if she was her own. 'Erin, Shanni was at the hospital with Nick when the call came through. The nurse in charge told her what was going on, so she rang us first thing. I rang Lori on Luke's cell phone on the way here. Lori's on her way, but we need to sort the kids out.'

'Yes.' That made it through Erin's fog. Lori was House Mother at Home Number Five, and the only one without tiny tots to care for. They'd need her, but Erin was in no state to concentrate.

Wendy recognised it. She came forward and gave her friend a hug like her husband was giving Michael, then she kept right on holding her, Tess somehow squashed in the middle. Which Tess didn't seem to mind at all. 'Hey, kid, you and Matt got them all out,' she told her friend. 'Everyone's safe. You did good.'

'The twins…they must have been making something.' Erin was trembling in her friend's arms, and, from where he was lying on the ground, Matt had an almost unbearable urge to rise and take over. He wanted to hug her as well.

Which was crazy. He grabbed the oxygen mask and took two more deep breaths. He wasn't himself here.

'I've been thinking,' Wendy said into her friend's hair. 'Tess and Michael are only with you until their mother gets out of hospital at the week-end. Luke and I talked about it as we drove here and we can take them until then. They know us.'

Tess and Michael's mother was on her own, and she was a severe asthmatic. She was in and out of hospital often, and Tess and Michael were frequent visitors to the Homes. They'd be happy with Wendy, Erin knew. But…

'That still leaves Marigold and the twins.'

'Tess and Michael will be shocked,' Wendy said gently, gathering Tess closer as she spoke. The doctor was check-

ing the twins, and the little girl was starting to tremble.
'They'll need lots of care, so I don't think Luke and I can
do much more than take them. I talked to Lori and she
said the same. She's thinking about the baby and the twins
now. And speaking of Lori…'

Lori arrived then. Thirtyish and competent—as all the
house mothers were—she might be shocked, but she took
right over where Wendy left off.

'It's fine for Michael and Tess to go with Wendy,' she
said directly. 'It makes sense. But the other Homes are
packed. Maybe we can use the hotel as an interim measure.'

'Erin can't look after Marigold tonight,' Wendy told her.
'Look at her. She's shocked to the core. The last thing she
needs is two o'clock feeds. She needs to sleep. And the
twins—'

'No one but Erin can control the twins,' Lori said
bluntly.

'Yeah, look at how I controlled them,' Erin retorted.
'That's control?' She gestured to where the flames were
dying and leaving a charred and smoking ruin, and she
shuddered.

'And the publican's heard of the twins,' Lori added. 'I
guess we might have trouble persuading him to take you.'

'You bet we'll have trouble.'

'But the baby's up for adoption and her placement's due
on Monday,' Lori said, brightening. 'I guess I could
squeeze Marigold in with me until then. She's such a great
baby.' She glanced around to where Valda was holding
her at arm's length, a look of complete disgust on her face.
The baby, it seemed, had started to smell.

They all knew it didn't matter. Lori had decreed
Marigold was a great baby, and so had her prospective

parents. She'd survive a few more minutes of Valda's disgust. 'That just leaves Erin and the twins.'

'I don't know about the hotel,' Erin said doubtfully. 'Maybe we could stay with Shanni.'

'Shanni has two kids, is pregnant and has a sick husband.' Wendy was suddenly in charge again. 'And I can't take any more than Michael and Tess.' Then she looked down at Matt and her brow grew thoughtful. 'Hmm.'

Hmm?

Matt gazed upward and he didn't like the way Wendy was looking at him.

Wendy, Erin, Shanni, Lori… Even Doc Emily. They were all the same. They were organising, bossy women, in a sensible, non-Charlotte type of way that you couldn't just ignore by going outside and heaving a few hay bales until it was time for dinner.

Frankly, they scared him to death.

He took two more breaths of oxygen from his mask and tried to look pathetic. It didn't come off. In fact, it seemed to make things worse.

'Doc says you're not to go home alone, and I know you live in that great rambling place all by yourself.' Wendy was onto her good idea like a hound on a scent and she wasn't to be distracted. 'What could be more appropriate than Erin and the twins coming home with you to keep you company?'

'The twins?' He'd seen enough of the twins!

'You saved their lives,' Wendy said, her voice softening, as she crouched beside him. Her eyes met his. They were inches apart and he couldn't argue if he wanted to. 'And maybe you saved Erin's, too, as I know she'd have tried to get them out herself if it wasn't for you. So you can't just turf them out on the street, now can you?'

'I…' It was too much. 'No,' he said weakly. 'I suppose I can't.'

'So you can have them?'

He forced himself to think. He wouldn't make much of a host. 'I need to be away occasionally, for cattle shows and things…'

'But they can look after themselves with ease. So that's that,' Wendy said triumphantly, and she rose and hugged Erin harder. 'It's all sorted, my love, so you can stop shaking this very minute. All of you. Drama over. All we have is one burned house to rebuild and we'll be back to normal. Now as soon as the doctor's cleared the lot of you then you can go out to Matt's. I can see the Welfare Shop lady over by the fire chief. Good old Edna. She's always armed with a stockpile of emergency clothes. I'll see how she can help and then we'll send you all home. Together.'

CHAPTER TWO

FOR how long?

All we have is one burned house to rebuild and we'll be back to normal.

It occurred to Matt as they started out to the farm that this might be no short undertaking. The Bay Beach Home lay in ruins, and finding accommodation in this town was next to impossible. Rented houses were taken by tourists at big dollars, and everything else…

Everything else would have to wait. 'Worry about tomorrow tomorrow,' he told himself, glancing back at the cavalcade behind him. Rob was driving him home in Matt's truck—'because there's no way you're driving tonight,' the doctor had decreed, and Matt could only agree. He didn't even feel like driving.

Behind them was the police car, driven by a police constable and containing Erin and the twins. Behind that another helper was driving Erin's Home car. That car held enough Welfare donations to clothe a small republic.

Heck!

He glanced back again and Erin was sitting in the passenger seat of the car behind. They were just turning out of town, and as they passed under a street lamp she looked right back at him, raised her eyebrows and gave him a quizzical look that said she knew exactly what he was thinking.

That this was a disaster.

This was just great!

He had a mind-reading, bossy tenant, with twins and

27

trouble attached. His nice bachelor existence looked like it was being threatened in a much more dire way than when he'd thought earlier that he might—just *might*, mind you, definitely not *would*—ask Charlotte to marry him.

Charlotte was one thing. Married to Charlotte, he knew he'd be free to carry on with life as normal, and his emotional involvement would be minimal.

But life with Erin and twins?

Life could just be chaos.

Then he twisted back to face the road ahead as Rob applied the brakes. Behind them, the cavalcade slowed as well.

'I think this might be someone wanting to speak to you,' Rob said, and he gave him the same quizzical look that he'd just received from Erin. 'If I'm not mistaken, it's your Charlotte.'

His Charlotte…

Once more he had that sensation of entrapment—the sensation he'd had since he was about thirteen and Charlotte had told the district he was the man she intended marrying. Of course it was Charlotte, driving her smart little red BMW and pulling to a halt as Rob steered Matt's truck to a halt on the grass verge. Then she was out of the car and darting across the road toward them.

Charlotte was looking immaculate. Of course. When had she not? She was wearing her signature, beautifully cut, white slacks and white silk blouse, her long, blonde hair was carefully braided into a chignon, and she looked all ready for their intimate dinner.

Except she was no longer expecting her special dinner. Bay Beach had a very effective communication system, and it hadn't let Charlotte down. She'd heard of the fire. Hauling the truck door open before Matt could do it himself, she practically threw herself into his arms in relief.

'Matthew... Oh, love, you could have been killed.' But emotion or not, her eyes were taking everything in, including Rob—and including the red velvet box lying forgotten in the map compartment. Sensibly, she ignored it. Almost.

'Sally rang and she said you dived into that burning building and pulled out the orphans all by yourself. She said you were burned!' She stepped back and saw the nasty red blister on his forehead and the grime of smoke all over him—and then, instinctively, she looked down at herself.

Whoops. Her pure white ensemble was now smudged grey.

House fires, however, required courage. Matt had been brave and she could be, too.

'It'll wash off,' she told her beloved. 'Not to worry. But, Matt, Sally said the doctor said you're not to stay alone.' She turned to Rob. 'Bring him to my place.'

It was time Matt put a word in, but it was tricky to do. However, Rob was made of sterner stuff.

'We can't,' Rob said, and thumbed back to the cavalcade. 'Matt's got all the company he needs.'

Charlotte looked back—and then stared in horror as she saw who was in the police car. 'Not the orphans!' she gasped. 'You're not taking the orphans home with you. Matt, you're burned!'

'I can cope.'

'You can't.'

'Charlotte, there's only two kids needing a place to stay, and Erin will take care of them.' Matt was growing uneasy now. Erin had emerged from the police car and was walking over to see what was happening. From where she was now, she could hear every word Charlotte said. 'Erin's been through a lot, Charlotte.'

'I'm sure she has.' Charlotte shook her head in disbelief

that this could be happening. 'But darling, so have you.'
She turned her head and raised her voice. 'Erin, Matt's
coming back to my house. He needs to be looked after.
Your organisation can look after you.'

Whoa...

Erin took a deep breath. Count to ten, she told herself.
This is important.

Charlotte was *not* one of Erin's favorite people. Lovely
and gracious, and generous to people she considered the
'right sort', her graciousness had never extended to Erin.
Erin was three years younger and about a million miles
below her on the social ladder. As she'd grown older,
Charlotte had grown more adept at hiding her distaste for
those she considered beneath her, but somehow Erin always knew exactly where she stood. Right on the bottom
rung!

But, like Charlotte, Erin could be ruthless when she
needed to be, and she needed to be ruthless now.
'Charlotte, Matt's offered us accommodation.'

'I don't care if he has.' Up until now, Charlotte had had
a wonderful feeling about this evening. The sight of that
tiny crimson box confirmed she'd been right, and now all
it had come to was *this*! 'Anyone can see he's unwell.'

And so was Erin. She'd been through enough without
Charlotte's arguments. Back in the police car were two
subdued little boys who needed a bed, fast. She knew well
enough that at Matt's house she would find one—and one
for herself, too.

There wasn't an alternative.

'Matt's offered to take us in and I've accepted,' she said,
and there was a certain amount of grit in her voice. 'I'm
sorry, Charlotte, but we've been through too much tonight
to stand on the road and argue. If you could just let us
go...'

'Matt's hurt.'

'Then follow him home and fix him up,' Erin replied wearily. 'I'm sure I can't do it with your style. A sticking plaster and a push in the direction of bed is all I'm capable of, believe me.'

Charlotte glared. She didn't like this one bit.

But what was the alternative? Charlotte was thinking on her feet, and she was thinking fast.

Firstly—naturally—she was thinking that Erin was attractive and unmarried and she didn't like the thought of such a woman staying with Matt. But then, Matt had known Erin for ages—since childhood in fact—and he hadn't seemed attracted in the past. So maybe that was okay.

Her eyes moved imperceptibly sideways. He'd already purchased the contents of the box, so she needed to concentrate on priorities.

Which were, secondly, that Erin was saddled with the twins. They might be subdued now but the whole town knew their reputation. Matt would be driven crazy before he could get used to them in the house.

The only alternative open to her now was to invite them all back to her place, and that didn't bear thinking of. She had a perfect little horse stud in the hills; the house was immaculate and children would destroy it.

What else then? Create a scene? No! She knew Matt would hate it. She'd worked so hard to make him see her as the perfect wife that she'd be a fool to mess it up now.

The velvet box was there, like a tantalising promise. She could concede a little.

'Okay, sweetheart,' she said softly, ignoring Erin totally and turning back to her intended. 'You go ahead. I'll bring your dinner over.'

'My dinner?' Matt was still too befuddled to think.

'You were coming to my place for dinner. Quails with the most gorgeous sauce... I've kept it hot for you.' She gave him her most loving look, and he responded with gratitude. But he didn't want her quails.

'Eggs on toast is all I'm capable of tonight,' he said wearily. 'I'm sorry, Charlotte. Freeze my dinner. It'll have to wait for some other time.'

This wasn't going to work.

Erin had never been inside Matt's house, but she walked through the front door and she darn near walked out again. This and the twins? No and no and no.

'You'd best take off your shoes,' Matt said, through force of habit. 'The carpet shows every mark.'

'I'd guess it would.' Erin stared at the floor in doubt, but obligingly removed her shoes and then turned to the boys and slipped theirs off too.

The twins let her do what she wanted and they hardly moved as she did. The Welfare lady had dressed them— sort of—but they were so subdued they hadn't said a word. Now Erin badly wanted to get them alone. She wanted them bathed and tucked up somewhere warm and safe and alone, where she could cuddle the shock and fear out of them.

Matt was stooping to help with their shoes, and she was grateful for that at least.

'Did...did you choose this carpet—or did Charlotte?' she managed. It was a stupid conversation starter, but it was something.

'My mother chose it,' he said stiffly and that made her blink in surprise, memories flooding back.

She'd known Matt's mother—not that they'd ever spoken, of course. Matt's family owned one of the wealthiest farms in the district. Not so Erin's. As one of eight kids in a big, loving and decidedly impoverished family, Erin was considered by Mrs McKay to be a nobody.

Which suited her nicely, she acknowledged. Erin had no wish to move in Matt and Charlotte's exclusive world. She and her friends—and their respective parents—used to check out Louise McKay's perfectly tailored white suits and think how impractical they were. Only Louise thought they were perfect.

'Didn't your mother die five years ago?' Erin managed, thrusting away memories of the perfect Louise. 'This carpet looks unused.'

'I usually use the back door,' he told her. Then he managed a grin. 'I guess Mum trained me well—or I got sick of taking off my boots.'

'I can see that.' She stared at the white carpet, and then through to the white leather lounge suite in the sitting room beyond. 'The boys and I had better get used to the back door as well.'

'I guess it'd be best.'

Hmm.

The situation here was decidedly strained. Erin was standing in the front hall of the great McKay family home. Alone—apart from the twins—with Matt McKay. The feeling was…weird?

But she didn't have the time to examine her personal feelings. The boys' needs were too great. 'Show me the bathroom and where the boys can sleep,' she said wearily. 'They need to be in bed.'

So did Matt. He gave himself a mental shake, trying to sort priorities. There were two bathrooms. He could clean up in one while she coped with the twins in the other. Maybe he could help her, but first he had to clear his head. It still felt fogged with smoke and the aftermath of terror.

'This way.' He led them, minus their shoes, to the back of the house. Here were two bedrooms side by side, with a bathroom between. To Erin's delight, the beds were freshly made, as if he'd been expecting guests any day.

'It's another legacy from my mother,' he told her, seeing her look of surprise. 'The bedrooms stay immaculate at all times in case of unexpected visitors. That's you. Unexpected visitors.' He managed another of his smiles, and even though it was crooked and weary it was a smile that made a girl want to take a backward step.

Or a forward step?

But he was talking in a dragging voice that had Erin suddenly looking sharply up at him. She needed to focus here. The burn on his forehead was blistering badly and his eyes were red-rimmed from the smoke. He might be hero material but he was badly shocked and he'd inhaled a lot more smoke than she had.

'I'm afraid they won't stay immaculate if my twins are sleeping in them,' she said apologetically, and then, propelling her charges into the bathroom, she turned back to him with decision written all over her. House mother personified. 'You go and take a shower yourself,' she said. 'And then go straight to bed.'

'We'll see. I do need to eat. I'll meet you in the kitchen when the twins are settled.' He managed a rueful smile. 'That is, if you dare leave them alone.'

'They'll be good tonight,' Erin told him, and she smiled as she ruffled the twins' soot-blackened hair. The children were so tired they were sagging on their feet. 'Won't you, boys? I think any mischief has been blasted right out of you.'

'We're sorry, Erin.'

It was the first whisper she'd had out of either of them.

She'd run a bath, washed them to within a whisker of their lives, rubbed them dry on Matt's mother's sumptuous white towels—and still managed to leave a streak or two of grey on the gorgeous linen—and then cradled them into bed. They shared the one bed, despite there being twin beds in the room.

In times of trouble these two stuck together and they were sticking together now.

And all the time they'd stayed silent.

Now, dressed in some very strange and ill-fitting pyjamas, they looked up at her from their shared pillow, and their eyes were still glazed with shock and fear and remorse.

'We only made the bomb to scare Pansy,' William said, trembling, and if he hadn't sounded so pathetic Erin might have been tempted to laugh. Oh, heck... Pansy Poodle?

'Why on earth would you want to scare Pansy?'

'So Mr and Mrs Cole would move away and stop being nasty to you.'

That was all she needed! She was overtired and overemotional and now she had to blink back tears. They were such terrors but there was always a motive. They had such good little hearts.

Somehow she schooled her features into sternness, and hugged them both.

'Well, we were very, very lucky that Mr McKay came to save us. You'll promise me you'll never, ever play with fireworks or matches again? Not even to scare Pansy?'

'We promise,' Henry told her and she looked down and knew that she had their word.

It wouldn't be a bomb next time. Something else for sure, but not a bomb.

She tucked them in, hugged them again for good measure and wondered where Tigger was now. They loved

Tigger, and when they realised he'd been burned... It didn't bear thinking of.

Then she looked up at the sound of footsteps in the hall. Matt was standing in the doorway. He was clean now, big and bronzed and capable, dressed in clean jeans and an open necked shirt and with only the burn on his forehead to show any damage had been done.

He was back to the farmer she knew.

Charlotte was one lucky lady, Erin thought suddenly. A class above the likes of her or not, Matthew McKay was not bad as husband material.

Not only was he extremely good looking, with his thatch of sun-bleached brown curls, his weathered skin and his strongly muscled frame, but his deep brown eyes were twinkling with kindness. In his hands he held two mugs, and he carried them carefully over to the bedside table for the boys.

'My Grandma always used to say a glass of warm milk is the best cure in a crisis,' he told the twins. 'So I brought you boys one each. There's another for Erin when she's had her shower.' And then he smiled at Erin—a smile that somehow had the capacity to knock her senses reeling. 'Off you go, and I'll meet you in the kitchen when you're clean.'

Darn, she must be more exhausted than she thought, Erin decided. She really was very close to tears, and his kindness was almost her undoing.

'I've also brought my very favourite story book from when I was seven,' he told her, motioning to a book tucked under his arm. 'It's all about fire engines. So I propose that you go and clean up while I read to the boys.'

'Your throat...'

'Hurts,' he finished for her. 'Well guessed. I'd imagine yours does, too. Luckily my book's mostly pictures so the boys and I just have to look. So scoot.' He smiled down at the two nervous little boys in their shared bed, and his smile was encompassing and kind. 'Is that okay with you guys?' he asked them. 'It seems a bit unfair that we're clean and Erin's not.'

The boys considered in silence—and then slowly nodded in unison.

'Great.' Matt's smile widened and he sank down onto the bed beside Erin. It was sort of crowded down there—four on the bed—but it was familiar and very, very comforting after the fear of the last hours. 'I don't know about you,' he told Erin softly, 'but I'm pooped and the sooner we get this lot asleep the sooner we can get to bed ourselves.'

Absolutely.

He was perfectly right.

So why did his words bring a blush to her face as she rose and headed gratefully to the bathroom?

And those tears were definitely still threatening.

By the time she'd showered, the twins were solidly, absolutely asleep. Wrapped in one of Louise's vast towels, Erin checked them from all angles and decided it'd take another bomb to wake them, and even then it wasn't a sure thing.

She didn't blame them. She was exhausted herself, but Matt was nowhere to be seen.

He'd meet her in the kitchen, he'd said, but she couldn't go and find him wrapped only in a towel. Her own clothes were disgusting, so she hauled on an enormous dressing gown she found in the donations pile and made her way through the house to find him.

The house was huge. Vast! It must have six or seven bedrooms, she thought as she padded barefoot down the passage, and when Matt emerged from a door in front of her she practically squeaked in fright.

'Hey, I'm no ghost.' Still those eyes twinkled as he put his hands on her shoulders to steady her. 'Uh, oh. You're done in.'

'You must be, too.' She looked up at him and saw that his eyes were still reddened slightly from the smoke and the burn on his forehead had blistered further. 'You look a darn sight worse than me.'

'I'd have to agree there.' The laughter lines deepened as he took in her total appearance. 'But only just. What you're doing in a bathrobe that looks like it was designed for Mother Hubbard...'

That brought a chuckle. The robe was enormous. She swam in it, and it trailed out behind her like a flannelette bridal train.

His voice softened as he realised why she was wearing it. 'Hell! I guess you'll have all lost your own clothes.'

She had. She'd barely had time to take it in yet, but it was something she'd have to face. Most of her belongings were back in the blackened, smouldering ruin. However...

'They were just things,' she said resolutely, trying not to think of her mother's seed pearl necklace that she'd loved so much. 'Things can be replaced.'

'You're one brave lady.'

'No.' She shook her head. 'I've never been so frightened in my life as I was this evening. I thought I'd lost them.'

'The boys.'

'Yes.' He was leading her into the kitchen as they spoke, and at last she relaxed. Unlike the rest of the house, this felt like a proper home. The kitchen had ancient polished floorboards, big comfy furniture, a huge wooden table and cushioned chairs, and a settee than made you want to bounce and sink out of sight.

A gleaming Aga was sending out its gentle warmth across the kitchen, and an ancient collie dog looked quizzically up at her as she entered. He thumped his tail gently against the floor and then went straight back to sleep.

This was home, she thought. This was a real home.

Damn, she had to blink back tears again. The waterworks were surely ready to pounce tonight. The fear had driven every ounce of strength from her.

Bed.

She should go to bed, but...

'Hot chocolate and a brandy,' Matt was saying. 'I know I told the kids warm milk, but you and I need something stronger. I've eaten toast. Do you want something to eat? No? Then just a drink and then bed.' He turned away to fetch mugs and glasses, and while he was faced away his voice changed.

'You love them, don't you?'

'Who?' She leaned against a chair to steady herself—her legs seemed to have lost all their strength—but she knew instinctively who he was talking about. His next words confirmed it.

'The twins.'

The hot chocolate made, he turned back to her and gestured for her to sit. There was nothing for it. In her ridiculous night wear she sat, sinking into his squishy chair like she was drowning. She took the chocolate and cradled it, drawing strength from the warmth of the mug.

She thought of the twins and her mouth twisted. 'I'm pretty fond of them.'

'You're a House Mother,' he said, thinking it through. 'I thought you're not supposed to get attached to your charges.'

'You mean I'm not supposed to care if they go up in flames?'

'I didn't mean that.' He was watching her face. 'The boys are different, though, aren't they? To you.'

She shrugged. 'I guess.'

'Why?'

That was harder to answer. She thought about it and gave him the easy answer. 'It's probably because they've been with me more than most. Kids don't tend to stay in orphanages any more. They get adopted or fostered out as soon as we can find someone who'll take them. Fifty years ago we used to have scores of orphans. Now we have kids like Tess and Michael who are in for short-term crisis care, or the baby Lori's taken for me. She's been with us while her mother made the decision to allow her to be adopted.'

'And the twins?'

'That's the problem. We can't find anyone for the twins.'

There. It was said—the stark reality that hurt just to think of it.

'Why not?' Matt said, watching her face.

'I don't know.'

'Liar.'

She shrugged, and then gave him a weary smile. 'No. I'm not a liar and I do find it hard to understand. They're adorable. But the twins push people away, you see.'

'I don't see.'

'You may well see it soon.' She sighed. 'Look, they were the product of a one-night stand. Their mother doesn't remember who their father is, and she has seven other kids to look after. To be honest, the twins reached their mother's IQ level when they were about three. I'd reckon whoever fathered them wasn't lacking in the intelligence quotient and they're smart as paint. Anyway, she can't cope with them, she rejected them absolutely and she threw them at us for adoption. Unfortunately they were old enough to understand what was happening.'

'And they're taking it out on the world?'

'Only on whoever is deemed to threaten them. And now they expect to be rejected. They won't let anyone close because they know it'll end.' Erin sighed. She was bone-weary and the comfort of the hot chocolate and the sympathy in this man's eyes was more than enough to push her over the edge. He'd poured her a brandy but she wasn't game enough to drink it. Her eyes wanted to close so badly...

'Sleep,' he said, and leaned over and took the mug from her hands before she dropped it. 'You'll find toothbrushes and everything you need in the bathroom.'

'I already have.' Her tired eyes smiled. 'Your mother must have been the best hostess in the district—and you haven't let her standards slip one bit.'

'I'm not allowed to.' He smiled back at her and his weary smile touched something in her insides which hadn't been touched in a very long time. If ever. 'Charlotte's trained the redoubtable Mrs Gregory for me, and she sees to it that everything's pristine.'

'Uh, oh.'

'Don't worry.' Before she knew what he intended, he reached forward and took both her hands in his. He pulled her to her feet and then stood for a moment, looking down into her troubled eyes. 'I'm sure you and me and the twins and Mrs Gregory will get along just famously.'

And Charlotte? Erin added under her breath but she didn't say it. Instead she looked up at Matt, a crease of worry still behind her eyes.

'Doc Emily said I should keep an eye on you tonight. You did lose consciousness.'

'I did,' he agreed gravely. 'But I don't want checking

every hour, thank you very much. If I promise not to die in the night, will you promise to go and put your head down on the pillow and let tomorrow's worries wait until tomorrow?'

Those dratted tears... Damn, they threatened to be her undoing.

She blinked and sniffed and then blinked again.

'Fine then. Um...you *have* put something on that burn?' She was under no illusions that Charlotte would kill her if it got infected.

'I have at that,' he told her. 'It's cleaned and it's nicely antiseptic. So we can both go to bed with a clear conscience. Goodnight, Erin.'

'Goodnight, Matt. And...thank you.'

And then, because she looked so rumpled and lost and forlorn he couldn't help himself. He leaned forward and let his lips brush her forehead.

'It was all my pleasure,' he said softly. 'Now stop thinking about twins and burns and belongings and worries. Think only about yourself for a change. Sleep!'

And she did.

There was simply no choice.

CHAPTER THREE

'WHERE are we?'

Erin planned to wake the minute they woke, but she must have been too exhausted for her normal House Mother instincts to work. She'd propped open both bathroom doors so the twins could see her as soon as they opened their eyes, and now they landed on her bed in a tangle of legs and arms and astonishment.

'Did the house really burn down? Did we really ride in a police car?'

That was easy.

'It did and you did and you're now at Mr McKay's farm,' she said, hugging them to her and hauling them in to lie under the covers. She was wearing an oversized T-shirt, and in their oddly assorted pyjamas they looked just as disreputable as she did. They were like something out of a charity bazaar, she thought and grinned to herself and hugged harder. She didn't mind. They were safe.

'The policeman won't arrest us?' It was Henry, ever the anxious one.

'Now why would he arrest you?'

'Because we made a bomb.'

'But you've promised faithfully never to make another one,' she said.

'Mmm.'

She fixed Henry with a look. 'You did promise.'

'Yeah.' He gave her a feeble smile. 'Okay. We did.'

'Then I think we might persuade him not to arrest you—this time.'

Apparently this was satisfactory. They snuggled down beside her and then snuggled some more.

But then William asked what was apparently super important in both their minds.

'Erin, where's Tigger?'

Oh dear. Erin thought back to the last she'd seen of the house. There seemed not one snowball's chance in a bushfire that anything could have been saved. There was nothing to do but tell them the truth.

'Guys, I'm afraid Tigger was burned.'

That silenced them completely. They lay, taking in the enormity of it, and then Henry sniffed.

One sniff was all he allowed himself, but Erin's heart wrenched. Tigger had been given to the boys by one of their first foster families—a sort of sop-to-conscience-at-taking-them-back-to-the-orphanage gift—and they'd been so young they'd mixed him up with leaving their mother and their bothers and sisters. Tigger had become their only constant, a toy never fought over, never discussed, but simply there.

Apart from each other he was all they had—and now they'd lost him.

Erin knew enough to acknowledge he was irreplaceable. She thought of the impossibility of saying they'd find another Tigger, and she simply didn't know what else to say.

She was saved by a knock. There was a light rap on the door and it opened to reveal Matt. Unlike Erin and the boys, Matt was fully dressed in his farmer's moleskins and khaki shirt. A sticking plaster lay across the burn on his forehead, but otherwise he looked completely unscathed. He was bronzed, strong, capable and ready for the day's work.

'Good morning,' he said gravely enough, but his deep brown eyes twinkled at the sight of the three in the bed.

'That's a single bed and you guys look squashed. Didn't you find the other two? Is something the matter?'

'We just came into Erin's bed now—to keep her company,' William said with dignity, casting a doubtful look at his twin. Henry was looking dangerously close to tears, and the twins' code of conduct decreed it didn't do to show emotion in front of strange adults.

They'd learned early to keep themselves to themselves.

But after one knowing look at Henry, Matt mercifully changed the subject, seeming not to notice the one errant tear sliding down Henry's cheek. He chose the one subject that might make them think of something other than loss.

'I've made pancakes and I thought you might like them in bed. How about it?'

'Pancakes?' William said, resolutely putting aside the vision of a burning Tigger. 'I...I guess...'

They were very upset about something, Matt realised, but he could only go on from here.

'I'll bring in a tray, shall I?'

'Yes, please.' Erin was so grateful she could have hugged him. How had he guessed that the last thing they needed was a formal breakfast? 'That'd be lovely.'

'Coming right up.' He left them to it, and Erin never knew what an effort it had been for him not to sit down and hug the lot of them.

It had cost to get them breakfast.

Matt had come in from the paddocks to find his weekly housekeeper, Mrs Gregory, hard at work. He had a cow in calf in the home paddock and, after a sleepless night, he'd decided he'd be happier checking on her than staring at the ceiling. His cow now safely delivered, he'd come in to find Mrs Gregory already sniffing lugubriously over the marks on the carpet.

'Charlotte rang me,' she said before he could say a word. 'I knew how it'd be, so I decided it was my Christian duty to get here early. Those dratted children. You saved them, didn't you? Why you had to offer to take them in…'

'I guess it was my Christian duty,' he told her and she didn't even smile.

'Hmmph. Those twins. And that mother of theirs. Oh, you don't need to tell me a thing about that woman. The whole of Bay Beach knew her before she disappeared with the last of her string of men. If ever there was a no-good, two-timing—'

'Hey, you can't place the sins of the mother onto the children,' Matt interceded. 'She threw the twins out.'

'Which is saying a lot about the children,' Mrs Gregory said soundly. 'That woman's a slut, and if even she couldn't put up with them…'

Hmm. 'Mrs Gregory, how would you like a holiday,' he said thoughtfully. This wasn't boding well for the future at all. 'Erin's here and, with two adults, she and I can surely do the housework.'

'She won't. She won't even notice if the house is a mess. I know her kind.'

'She will.' His lips tightened. Heck, his mother and Charlotte and their set had truly branded Erin. Just because of her father…

He finally wrung pancakes out of Mrs Gregory—by throwing in a few more Christian duties and an agreement to take an extended break for as long as they could manage without her—and now he carried the tray toward the bedroom with the air of one who'd achieved a major triumph. When he saw the grateful smile in Erin's eyes the feeling grew, so his chest felt a whole six inches broader.

There was still something wrong, though. Something

majorly wrong. The twins were polite—sort of—about the pancakes but they sat up in bed with the pancake tray on the table between them and they poked at Matt's offering as if the end of the world was nigh.

'You didn't yell at them because of the fire?' he asked Erin, frowning as she crossed to the window with her pancake plate. She'd done it as a deliberate ruse to talk to him without the twins hearing and it worked. He'd figured it out and followed her. Now they stood with their backs to the twins, as if the cattle grazing in the paddocks was taking all their attention.

She took umbrage at his suggestion. Yell at the twins? 'Of course I didn't,' she told him. 'They feel dreadful enough without me yelling at them. What do you think I am?'

'Far too kind,' he told her promptly, and she smiled but in an absent sort of way as she munched her pancake—which told him her thoughts were still on the twins.

'I'm not.' She glanced back at the twins. 'Sometimes I feel I'm not kind enough. They need so much…'

'Why the sad faces? Are they still scared?'

'No.' She shrugged, After all this man had done for them it seemed stupid to let him see how upset they were about one small Tigger, but there was something in his eyes that said he really wanted to know. He cared. 'It's just that they had a stuffed toy that they loved. They've now realised it's been burned.'

He stared.

Then…

'Wait right here,' he told them soundly, and without another word he strode from the room and left them gaping after him.

And then he was back, and in his hands—at arm's

length because it was so disgusting—he carried the blackest, filthiest soggiest *Tigger* they'd ever seen. But it was…

'Tigger!'

Erin barely got the word out before the boys were out of their beds, upending milk as they went and heading straight for Matt. They clung to what he held out to them— one to Tigger's snout, one to Tigger's tail, and all the grime in the world wouldn't have made one ounce of difference to the love that shone from their eyes.

Their Tigger…

Erin was looking at him as if he'd produced a miracle, and the feeling was just great. His expanding chest almost popped the buttons on his shirt. 'How on earth did you rescue Tigger?'

'I never meant to,' he told her and managed a shamefaced grin. 'They thrust it at me in the fire and, to be honest, I thought it was a dead cat. I just shoved it down my shirt and kept going.'

'A dead cat!' Her lips twitched. 'And do you always go around shoving dead cats down your shirt during house fires?'

'Before anything else. They're excellent for curing warts,' he told her. 'All you need is a graveyard and a full moon. Everyone tries to find them, but this time I got there first.'

He was ridiculous. She chuckled and suddenly things were just fine. The twins were inspecting their disgusting toy with relish. It appeared that the grime and general dishevelment made not the least difference to their affection.

How could it?

Matt grinned, trying to ignore the warm feeling Erin's pleasure was giving him. 'Doc Emily deserves some credit, too,' he admitted. 'She saw it when she was listening to my breathing and told me to hang on to it. Then I forgot it—until I took a shower, opened my shirt and it fell out. The damned thing nearly gave me a heart attack.'

'I imagine it might.' Erin's smile was a mile wide. 'We're so lucky you didn't toss it away.'

'I could have.' Matt's eyes were resting on the twins. They'd sat on their shared bed again, one end of Tigger on each of their knees. 'But by last night both Doc Emily and I had an inkling that whatever could be saved might be important.'

'You have no idea how important,' she said warmly. 'Oh, Matt…' Her eyes were glowing.

Whew! Her eyes were doing something to his insides which was truly spectacular. He needed to be grounded here.

He was.

The admiration session was interrupted before his chest buttons could finally pop from the strain. Just as Matt was starting to feel very peculiar indeed, another knock sounded through the room.

Visitors were coming thick and fast this morning, Erin thought, but what the heck. They had Tigger. With Tigger, they could save the world! They could cope with anything.

But it was Charlotte, and suddenly Erin wasn't so sure if anything included Charlotte.

She was amazingly early, Erin thought, and then she glanced down at her wrist-watch and stared in disbelief. It was after nine o'clock. Help!

And she looked like this!

'Charlotte,' Matt said warily, and the tone of his voice summed up all of their feelings.

Charlotte gave him her most sympathetic smile—heroine racing to save hero!—and then she moved straight to practicalities.

'Mrs Gregory told me you were feeding the children

their breakfast in the bedroom,' she said briskly. 'Why on earth don't you do it in the kitchen? At least you can wash the floor there.'

And then she looked again—and saw Tigger. She physically flinched.

'What…what on earth is *that*?'

'It's Tigger,' Erin said, and beamed her joy with the world. Even Charlotte couldn't burst her bubble this morning. 'He's a bit fire-stained. As we all are. Hi, Charlotte. Isn't it the most wonderful morning?'

Erin's greeting startled Charlotte out of her composure. 'I suppose it is.' She looked Erin up and down—aristocrat to a low life form somewhere under the level of porriwiggle. 'What on earth are you wearing?'

'At a guess, I'm modelling old Mr Harbiset's hand-me-down dressing gown,' Erin told her, refusing absolutely to be ruffled. 'He's the only local I can think of who's fat enough to own a dressing gown this size, and Mrs Harbiset's always giving things to charity.' She gave a fast twirl, ballerina-like, and the flannelette dressing gown swung out almost full circle around her bare legs. 'Isn't it great? You think the style will take off?'

Charlotte somehow managed a smile. Then she turned to face Matt, excluding Erin and the twins nicely from her ordered world.

'Matt, darling, I've talked to my parents,' she told him sweetly, in a tone that said she'd solved all his troubles. 'And they've been terrific. They say the orphanage can have the use of the stables until the Home is rebuilt.'

'The stables?' Matt blinked and Erin raised her eyebrows politely. Stables?

'I don't mean the stables proper, silly,' Charlotte said, giving him the benefit of her delicious, tinkling laugh. She threw the twins a look that said she wasn't so sure that stables wouldn't be the best place for them, but then went bravely on. 'No. There's living quarters directly above the horse boxes. We used them for the men when I housed all my horses there, but now I've moved out they're empty. They're still quite liveable.'

'That's very generous of your parents,' Matt said, thinking it through. 'But the living quarters were built for use by the stable lads, weren't they?'

'Yes.'

'Then they're pretty basic.'

'Yes, but it's almost summer.' Charlotte beamed. 'There's a little kitchenette and a dormitory and a bathroom. Everything they need.'

'One dormitory?'

'Yes.'

'So Erin would be sharing the dormitory with the children?'

'That's what she does, sweetheart.' Charlotte gave Erin her very nicest smile. Her beam widened, all her problems solved and she reached out to take Matt's hand. 'She won't mind, darling. Caring for children is her job. Isn't it, Erin?'

Hmm. Erin might have continued to twirl but she had also been listening. And thinking—fast.

'It is,' Erin said thankfully. 'And I'm very grateful. But I'm afraid I can't accept any offers before our director comes down here and sorts things out. Meanwhile, if Matt's offer still stands...'

'When's your director coming?'

'This morning, I imagine,' Erin said dryly. She glanced at her watch. Tom Burrows had been in Sydney this week, but she'd imagine news of the fire would have him down here by lunch time. 'I'll pass on your offer to him and he'll come out and see your parents—and the stables.'

'Hey, hang on a minute!' Matt wasn't having a bar of this. 'The kids are staying here.'

'You must see that's impossible.' Charlotte was still at her sweetest.

'Why?'

She lowered her voice, just enough to make the twins aware that they were being discussed without them hearing.

'Because they're juvenile delinquents, that's why. They burned down the last place they stayed in. Heaven knows what they'd do here.'

But that was enough for Erin. Her hackles had well and truly risen. Juvenile delinquents? *At seven years old?*

If she didn't get rid of this woman soon she'd lose her temper—which maybe wasn't such a good idea, she thought, as she'd really, really like to stay here for a while. This set-up was perfect for the twins. They had a farm where they could be relatively isolated from the rest of the community.

If Tom agreed—and he surely would—then she could stay here, too. The farm was beautiful, nestled right on the river mouth and overlooking the sea. It'd be like a beach holiday. There'd be no other children for her to look after—the Homes couldn't ask Matt to look after any more—and they'd have her sole attention.

Which was just fine by her. These were badly traumatised children, and most of the trauma had been inflicted well before last night.

'Matt, would you mind if you continued this conversation with Charlotte outside?' she managed. Juvenile delinquents indeed! 'I...I need to get dressed.'

'I noticed your donated clothes pile is still out in the hall,' Charlotte said pointedly. 'You'll have to go and forage. Unless you're planning on wearing what you had on last night.' She smiled.

'Charlotte!'

Whoops! She'd gone too far. Charlotte's self-preservation instincts surfaced then, as a look on Matt's face told her that he wasn't seeing things as she was. And this crazy woman wasn't any real competition. Matt was only being charitable, after all, and it behoved Charlotte to appear the same.

'I'll fetch you something, shall I?' she asked. She looked at Erin, assessing. 'You're a couple of sizes larger than me or I'd lend you something of mine.'

'I'm quite happy with our charity pile,' Erin said through gritted teeth. Anonymous charity, that was. Not Charlotte charity. 'I'll fetch something myself.' She pulled open the door and stopped short.

Last night, when they'd come here their toes had sunk into the lush white carpet. It had still been here and squishable when she'd come to bed.

It still was now—but there was plastic over the top.

Lines of plastic. Erin recognised it. She'd seen it last at the home of a super-fussy aunt. Purchased by the yard, the stuff was transparent and it had tiny pointy teeth on the back to hold it to the carpet. People used it to keep homes immaculate against any who might sully their precious flooring, and it felt just horrid.

Urk! What was the point of having carpet if one had to look at it under plastic and walk on the coldness of the stuff?

She took a deep breath and counted to ten under her breath. She had to take this in her stride. Okay, it was insulting, but if Matt wanted to protect his home, then who could blame him?

But it wasn't Matt who'd laid the plastic. 'Where the

hell did that come from?' he demanded, staring. He stalked
out into the passage and stared some more. The plastic
tracked off in both directions, a path for anything unclean.

'I had heaps stored at home,' Charlotte said, not hearing
the low growl of displeasure in his voice. 'I bought it when
I went overseas last year and my grandparents borrowed
my house. Grandpa is such a grub—he just refuses to take
his boots off and Grandma doesn't insist. It was just the
thing, I thought, and it worked beautifully but now
Grandpa's gone and I don't need it. So I brought it over.'

She sounded immensely pleased with herself—but Matt
had had enough.

'Well, you can just roll it all up and take it back where
it came from,' he managed, embarrassed to his back teeth.
Hell, of all the insensitive, unwelcoming acts. What would
Erin think of this? Charlotte might be gorgeous and a great
hostess and cook, but sometimes she was impossible. She
really was just like his mother!

But…

'Um…no.' It was Erin.

'No?' They both turned to stare at her.

'Leave it. The kids and I will hardly notice.' The kids
certainly wouldn't. A floor was a floor as far as the twins
were concerned and Charlotte was right. This way Erin
wouldn't sully Matt's precious carpet, and she wouldn't
have to worry about the twins doing it either. Which was
one less worry—and she had enough worries as it was.

But Matt was implacable. 'The plastic goes,' Matt told
her. 'Now.'

'Matt, it's fine.'

'Erin, it's not!' His temper was rising now, and there
were memories flooding back that were making everything
worse. His mother standing at the kitchen door yelling at

his father in the voice of a fishwife. *'Get those boots off right now or I'll walk out and never come back.'*

It was her ultimate threat made over and over again, it had scared the young version of Matt stupid, and only later had he wondered whether maybe he and his father would have been a whole lot happier without her.

Which might be why he was still a bachelor.

So no, the plastic went. And the image of marriage that he'd had last night faded a little as well. Maybe he was meant to be a bachelor. He'd bought the ring, but he hadn't done the asking.

But this was hardly the time for dredging up old memories and future plans. Now was the time to take the well-meaning but misguided Charlotte by the shoulders and steer her out of the room.

'We'll leave you in peace,' he told Erin. 'Charlotte, Erin's right. We need to continue this discussion outside.' He gave Erin and her crazy, wonderful dressing gown one last glance and then he propelled Charlotte outside.

'I'm going into town,' he told Erin over his shoulder as he left. Then he turned back to the lady he was propelling. 'Charlotte, I could use some help. Do you have time to come with me?'

Charlotte was surprised but instantly gratified. 'Of course I do, sweetheart. When do you want to go?'

'Now,' he told her. 'Erin, just make yourself and the twins at home. Mrs Gregory will be here until lunch time, so anything you need, just ask. Charlotte and I will probably eat in town so I'll see you mid-afternoon.'

Charlotte visibly sighed with relief. This was much better. A lunch date with Matt, with Erin nicely excluded. She turned and gave Erin her sweetest smile, because she could afford to be charitable to one who was so clearly a charity case—and then she allowed herself to be propelled from the room by the man she intended to marry.

There was no threat here, she decided.

There was no threat at all.

CHAPTER FOUR

MATT arrived home at about three and he couldn't find them. There were no kids in sight, and there was no Erin.

He walked from living rooms to bedrooms. No one. He went outside and checked the out-buildings. He checked that Erin's car was where it had been parked the night before and still he couldn't find them.

Finally he checked the house once more, and this time his old collie, Sadie, decided to join him. As they passed the laundry, Sadie whined and put up a paw. He pushed the door open—and there were the three of them, sitting on the floor with three noses pressed hard against the glass of the tumble dryer.

They were watching the tumble dryer?

'Isn't the television working?' he asked dryly, and they swivelled to face him.

They really were the most ill-assorted trio! The charity bin hadn't been good to them, he thought. Nothing fitted anywhere.

Yet Erin looked amazing!

He hauled his eyes from her with an almost Herculean effort. Concentrate on the twins! he told himself.

The twins were wearing jogging suit pants that were way too big, and T-shirts that were far too small. Their sea-green eyes were over big and over bright in their anxious faces and, as they looked up at him, he felt his heart give a thump of sympathy. They looked such waifs!

But Erin...

He failed. Try as he might, he couldn't turn his eyes from her. She didn't look much less waif-like herself.

She was wearing someone's cast-off crimplene dress— pale blue with pink spots, buttoned to the waist and belted with a cheap and nasty plastic belt. The dress looked as if it was meant for a woman of sixty. The bust size was about five sizes too big for her and it looked ridiculous. How she managed to still look beautiful was beyond him.

'If you so much as smile, you're dead meat,' she said, reading at least some of his thoughts, and he wiped the tentative smile from his face, hoped she hadn't read the rest and tried for a look of innocence.

'Now why would I smile?'

'Because this is—or was—Beverly Borridge's second-best Country Women's Association dress, and it's the only thing I can fit into. Her breasts must be…'

She faltered as his eyes fell immediately to the points in question. She blushed bright pink, she folded her arms defiantly across her chest and she turned back to the dryer.

'Huge,' she finished, but she was no longer looking at him.

He couldn't help it. He grinned—which was exactly the wrong thing to do, because she sensed it. She turned back and caught the grin full on and retaliated just like Erin had retaliated as a kid at school. No one teased Erin Douglas without copping it right back.

A sodden towel was lying by her side. How convenient. Her lips twitched into a smile, she lifted it and she threw with deadly accuracy. It whacked him with a soggy thwump; slap across his face.

She was some shot.

She was some lady!

But, soggy or not, he still didn't know what they were doing. Matt removed the towel from around his shoulders, laid it aside, wiped the grin from his face and crossed to the dryer. Once more, they all had their backs to him and they were staring at the dryer.

There was nothing for it but to see for himself. He crouched down beside them and stared at the glass.

'What's the program here?' he asked. 'Something good? *Days Of Our Lives*—or *General Hospital*?'

The twins simply ignored him. After that one brief glance they'd gone straight back to watching the glass window. Their anxiety was palpable and they were watching the glass as if their lives depended on it.

So Matt watched, too, and he saw a pair of eyes flash past the glass. And also a tail.

All was suddenly clear. 'That's Tigger,' he said in amazement.

'Of course it's Tigger.' Erin nodded and went right back to Tigger-watching. 'I rang the manufacturer. I hope you don't mind me using your phone but it was important to get his washing instructions right. They said he'd never dry naturally, even if we hung him out in the sun—he'd go mouldy inside. Their advice was to wash him in soap and water—and you can't imagine how much soap and water we had to use to get him clean, then squeeze him dry in a towel. We hung him outside in the sun long enough so the fur fabric was dry enough not to shrink, and then we put him in the dryer. But...'

'But?'

'But the boys are still a bit anxious,' she told him. 'We sat outside with him while he hung on the clothes line and now we thought we'd just stay here and watch.'

'I see.' The whole process was crazy. He repressed the grin, though. One look at the little boys' faces was enough to make that easy. Then he looked at the dial. It had twenty minutes to go. 'How long have you been here?' he asked.

Sitting watching tumble dryers going around ad infinitum was hardly his idea of a great afternoon's entertainment.

'An hour and a half. He should be almost done.' Erin had a twin on either side of her and she hugged them hard. She was acting like she had all the time in the world and this was the world's most pressing problem. 'And he's doing just fine.'

It might just as well be television's *General Hospital* they were watching, Matt thought. Drama had nothing on this. *Here we have the patient on the operating table and anxious relatives fearful of the worst...*

'He doesn't like it in there,' Henry whispered, and Tigger's eyes flashed past the glass again. Matt almost had to pinch himself back to reality. Good grief! This was a stuffed animal, yet the tremor in Henry's voice had him imagining agony within.

Twenty minutes to go...

'I brought back ice-creams,' Matt said helpfully, but no one moved.

'I'll fetch them, shall I?'

'That'd be great,' Erin told him, but all eyes were on the glass. They had no time for him at all.

If anyone told Matt he'd spend twenty minutes watching a stuffed animal go round and round in a tumble dryer— and almost enjoy it—he would have said they were crazy, but that was just what happened next.

He placed a chocolate ice-cream in the twins' hands, gave one to Erin and settled back with his. He should have brought popcorn, he thought. He hadn't realised they were into movie-watching.

They certainly were. There was hardly a word spoken. Every ounce of the boys' concentration was directed at

Tigger—as though by watching him they could get him through this ordeal.

They were amazing kids, Matt thought, and began to see what Erin was fighting for. Once you had the loyalty of these two, you'd have it for life. They licked their ice-creams, but they licked them absently and one flicker of doubt that things weren't well in the Tigger department and the ice-creams would have been abandoned. There was no doubt of that at all.

The ice-creams demolished, Tigger spun on and on, and then the timer clicked off. Tigger thumped three more times around the drum and Erin opened the door.

'He might be hot,' Erin warned but, hot or not, they'd waited long enough. The twins had him out of there and were checking him from snout to tail.

'He's perfect,' William breathed.

He wasn't, actually, Matt thought, looking at the battered toy that had seen years of loving service. Patches of Tigger's fur were completely worn off, his eyes were decidedly crooked, there was a piece missing from one ear and a bit of stuffing was coming out of his rump.

'Absolutely perfect,' Erin agreed, grinning from ear to ear. 'And I've never seen him so clean.' She poked the stuffing back into his rump. 'Wasn't it clever of Mr McKay to save him? I'll sew his bottom up tonight but meanwhile…'

'Meanwhile, now he's fixed, can we see the farm?' Henry said, bounding up and turning pleading eyes from one adult to another. With Tigger restored to glory, things were obviously okay in his world and he was ready to move on.

'Yes, please,' breathed William, and Matt looked into their combined eyes and could no sooner deny them than fly.

Plus Erin was watching.

'Haven't you been outside yet?' he asked.

'Apart from sitting under the clothes line, no. We had to fix Tigger first,' Erin told him, as if he was a little bit thick for not realising it. 'But now Tigger's better so maybe we can explore. If it's okay with you, Mr McKay?'

Okay?

Of course it was okay, and suddenly Matt was very, very pleased that they hadn't explored without him. He very much wanted to show off his farm to this woman.

And these boys, he told himself hastily. Not just Erin.

Of course not just Erin.

'What have you done with Charlotte?'

They were walking across the yard toward the machinery shed. The boys were whooping ahead, the traumas of the night before forgotten completely as Tigger circled victoriously above Henry's head.

'She's gone home to make dinner for me.'

'I see.' Erin didn't see. She was feeling acutely uncomfortable in her ghastly crimplene, but there was nothing else for her to wear. At least she had her own sandals, she thought gratefully. The twins hadn't even got those, and were now wearing wellingtons two sizes too big.

'I was supposed to be going there for dinner last night,' Matt said, and he also was feeling uncomfortable. After all he'd asked Charlotte to do in town, and the effort she'd put into doing it, he'd felt obliged to accept her dinner invitation.

There was also the issue of the little velvet box…

Whatever he decided about that damned box, he *was* putting Erin and the boys up only because they had no place else to go. That was the *only* reason. Therefore, as

Charlotte had carefully explained, he surely couldn't be expected to play host. And Erin wouldn't be lonely.

'Tom Burrows is coming out to see you,' he told Erin, and if his voice was a bit too gruff she appeared not to notice.

'Tom?' Tom was the director of the homes and Erin could only be grateful. She needed his advice 'You saw him in town?'

'I went to find him,' Matt said. 'He has heaps to do, you understand, but he said he'd bring pizza out from town at about six. He says he needs time to talk to you and that seemed the best way. He's caught up with insurance assessors until then but he wants to…' Then he caught his breath. 'Uh, oh.'

The machinery shed door was open. The twins had darted in and they were up on the tractor before Erin and Matt reached the door. Matt could only feel the keys in his pocket and think gratefully that nothing worked without those keys.

Unless…

They weren't old enough to have learned hot-wiring? he thought uneasily, and Erin looked up at his face and grinned. She really was a mind reader.

'No, they don't know how to hot-wire machinery. You know, they're not as bad as they're painted. It's just that they're two active, enquiring little boys, they haven't had the supervision they've needed in the past, and they need to be kept busy.'

'So my tractor is safe?'

'I didn't say that exactly,' she admitted—and grinned. 'Keep your keys locked up.'

'Yes, ma'am.' He smiled down at her, and something stirred within. She looked ridiculous, he thought, as the weird feeling kept right on stirring within his chest. Crazy in her oversized crimplene and curls that he suspected would tangle two minutes after brushing.

But she also looked sort of vulnerable. And underneath the crazy crimplene and riot of fair curls, she looked very, very lovely…

'You were saying about Tom Burrows?'

'What?' It was a big effort to make his mind work on that one when it was thinking about crimplene. Tom Burrows. Who was Tom Burrows? His mind was wandering all over the place—or maybe it was just wandering to one place…

Tom… Oh, right. Orphanage Director. Tom Burrows, the guy who was coming here tonight with pizza while he was having dinner with Charlotte.

Why on earth had he ever agreed to have dinner with Charlotte?

Business! Plans! Future! Get your head screwed back on, McKay, he told himself sternly. He had things he had to tell this lady, rather than stand here like a dummy and try to remember why he'd agreed to have dinner with the best cook in the district—and the lady he'd bought a velvet box…

'I told Tom you're welcome to stay here long-term,' he told her gruffly. 'Until the Home is rebuilt.'

She paused at that, and turned to face him. Good grief! Had he any idea of what he was offering here?

'Matt, that's really nice of you but have you thought it through? Rebuilding might take six months.'

'That's no problem. There's heaps of room, the house is underused, you need a roof over your heads and I'm not putting you out on the street.'

'The twins can always go into one of our Sydney homes.' But she sounded doubtful at that.

'You don't want them to, though. Do you?'

There was only one answer to that. 'No,' she told him. She sighed and looked up at the twins on the tractor.

Which was unusual in itself, Matt thought. He was looking at her, and really seeing her, crimplene and all, but she was totally focused on her responsibilities.

This was a bit of a new thing, as far as Matt was concerned. Good looking and eligible—extremely eligible—Matt wasn't accustomed to young women looking straight through him.

But there was no doubt about it. She was only seeing the twins.

'They haven't had much security,' she was saying. 'Bay Beach is mostly *it*, really. It's the only place they know. A big city would scare them.'

'And you'd miss them?' Still he was focused on her.

She took a deep breath. 'I only have them between trials of new foster parents,' she told him. 'I can't... I shouldn't get too attached. Maybe Tom will have organised another couple to give them a try.'

Maybe he would. The thought should have pleased Matt—but then there was a tiny part of him saying that just maybe having this woman and these kids around for a while would be fun.

And suddenly the thought hit home that life wasn't much fun any more.

Sure he had a great existence, he told himself, surprised by the drab thought that had just entered his head. He had one of the best farms in the district. His stud cattle were internationally renowned, and he had more money than he knew what to do with.

And he had Charlotte.

But...

But what? He really couldn't say. He could only react to what was going on right now.

William was in the driver's seat of the tractor and Henry was standing beside him. Tigger was propped up on the windscreen. They'd pushed every button in sight without result, and now Henry was hauling the gear stick, just aching to make something go.

Their aching was irresistible, and so was the need to give them what he wanted himself. Fun.

'I need to check the cattle in the bottom paddock,' he called up to them. 'I'm taking the tractor. Do you want to come for the ride?'

Would they ever? They stared down at him, their eyes as round as saucers.

'Is it okay with you?' Matt asked Erin. Maybe he ought to have asked her first.

But her eyes were glowing and he knew straight away that he'd done the right thing.

'Sure, it's okay,' she said, smiling her approval. And then she added a rider. 'But only if I can come too.'

'You...'

'It's a very big tractor and we can squash,' she said.

'There's no need. I really will look after them.'

'I'm sure you will.'

'Well, then...'

'Well, then what?' She put her hands on her hips. 'What, Mr McKay? Why can't I come?'

'You mean you *want* to come?'

'Of course I want to come. It looks great!'

It looks great... He tried to think of his mother—or Charlotte, for that matter—ever wanting to ride on his tractor and the thought just wasn't there to conjure. They never would in a million years. 'I guess you can,' he said at last. 'I just didn't think you'd want to.'

She gave him a look of blank amazement. 'Why on earth would I want to be left behind? It looks really, really fun.' She swung herself up into the tractor cab and beamed down at him, a twin at each side. A conspiratorial trio, ripe for adventure, he thought, and he felt stunned.

There were four if you counted Tigger...

'Can I have a go at steering?' Erin asked. 'Please?'

They all had a go at steering.

Matt had to take the long way down to the bottom paddock because a couple of minutes' steering wasn't enough for any of them. The tractor was huge. Matt usually used it for hauling heavy harvesting equipment, not for ferrying passengers, but these passengers were entranced and he couldn't figure out who was the most excited to be in the driver's seat—the twins or Erin.

The twins went first, of course, with Matt standing behind them carefully controlling their attempts at driving. Then Erin took the seat, and his arms had to lean over her shoulders, just as they had with the twins. But it felt...different.

It was the crimplene, he told himself sternly, feeling just a trifle dazed. He'd never been so close to a woman wearing crimplene.

But the crimplene wasn't exactly sexy. So why did it feel that it was?

Concentrate on cattle...

The cattle in the bottom paddock were fine. The tractor circled them three times, just to make sure. They circled the cow with her new calf twice, and then, reluctantly, Erin turned the wheel to return to the house.

She was enjoying herself so much! The ride had been wonderful. It really was the most gorgeous day, and they'd been stuck inside with Tigger-washing for most of it. The twins' faces were glowing, and she didn't want to usher them back to the white carpets quite yet.

'Maybe you could drive the tractor back to the house and we could walk,' she told Matt, but he shook his head.

'Nope. Not unless you want to walk the long way round. The paddock between here and the house is due for first hay cutting next week and I don't want you walking in it. There's too many Joe Blakes.'

'Joe Blakes?' The twins were fascinated, as they'd been fascinated by everything Matt said. In their eyes, Matt had achieved almost cult status—not by saving them last night, but by saving Tigger. They thought, simply, that he was the greatest, and they hung onto his every word. Now they waited with bated breath to hear what he had to say about Joe Blakes, and he didn't let them down.

'Snakes,' he said deliciously and they shivered. 'We breed great big slimy ones hereabouts, and they'll be all through that paddock.'

Instinctively the boys moved closer to Erin and looked nervously down at the ground around the tractor. But their small boy need for ghoul meant that it was fine—as long as they didn't have to get off the tractor!

'It's safe enough to walk through when it's cut,' Matt told them. 'But not when it's two feet high.'

'No.' They breathed the word as one and Matt grinned. And suddenly he, too, was reluctant to end the day so soon. There was still an hour and a half before Tom was due, and he was expected to leave for Charlotte's.

He did have things to do. This was a working farm, but...

'Tell you what,' he said expansively. 'Let's take this baby down to the river and have a swim. Henry, it's your turn to steer. Erin—give up steering. It's Henry's turn!'

She was like a big kid, he thought, and grinned. She gave a comical grimace and pouted as she relinquished her seat to Henry. 'Aw, rats!' But... 'A swim?' she said, and looked a question at him.

'Now, I know we haven't brought our costumes and we're all wearing our very best clothes.' That brought a chuckle from all of them. 'But the river here is the safest swimming hole for miles. You want to do it?'

Once again he thought of his mother and Charlotte—and then didn't think of them at all as Erin's face lit up with laughter and delight.

'I can't think of anything we'd like more,' she said definitely. 'Thank you, Mr McKay. That would be very nice indeed.'

It was.

'You mean we really can swim in our clothes?' the twins asked, as the tractor slowed at the river bank. Here the paddock dropped to a sandy curve—a gorgeous, golden beach leading down to the water's edge. The river flowed gently here, having almost reached the sea. It'd be tidal this close to the coast, Erin thought. The water was turquoise and glittering, sandy-bottomed and clear as crystal.

And the need to swim was now irresistible to all of them.

'I really mean you can swim in your clothes,' Matt said. 'Though you might be more comfortable in your knickers.'

'Are you swimming in your knickers?' the boys demanded of Matt, and Matt remembered enough about being a small boy to know they intended to do exactly what he did.

Matt eyed the lady. She eyed him back and, hell, he could see what she was thinking. She knew exactly what he normally wore when he swam here, and the thought was enough to bring a blush to a grown man's cheeks.

Hell!

'Um… I think I'll leave my jeans on,' he told them, and that decided it as far as the boys were concerned.

'Then we'll leave our pants on, too.'

'Fine by me.'

Which left Erin.

Erin was looking doubtfully down at her crimplene. There'd been no bra to fit her in the donations pile. The bra she'd been wearing the night before was still hanging on the washing line, so she had no cover underneath her dress at all. Heaven knew what crimplene would do when it was wet.

But there was no way in the wide world she was not going to swim in this magic place.

'What are we waiting for?' she said, laughing and shrugging her shoulders. Okay, she was taking a risk with her modesty, but what the heck? 'Come on, twins. Last one in gets to wash up after pizza.'

To Matt's surprise, the twins could swim like little fish, and Erin was like a dolphin circling around them.

'It's my one life skill,' she told him, surfacing but only up to her neck. Very carefully up to her neck. Her fears about the crimplene were justified the moment she hit the water. 'You can't be brought up in Bay Beach and not swim, and I take a personal pride in teaching every one of my charges to survive in water.'

They could do more than survive. The twins were doing handstands under water, their toes just breaking the surface as they competed to see who could stay under longest. It was a game that looked like it could go on for hours.

Matt stayed until he saw that they were safe and then he swum away from them, stroking his usual two hundred yards up river and then down again. In a way it was a relief—to get away from the lady with the responsibilities.

And the transparent swimwear!

As for Erin, she would have liked to join him, he knew, guessing instinctively that she'd long to stretch out for a good, long swim, but she didn't. She stayed and supervised her boys, taking her duties very seriously. He watched from a distance, liking more and more of what he saw.

There was a boat, an old wooden rowboat, moored on a roughly made jetty a hundred yards from where they were swimming. It fascinated the twins, and Matt watched as Erin laid down the rules. She could see their fascination, and she knew trouble when she saw it.

'The boat is out of bounds when Matt or I aren't with you,' she told them as their gaze swung instinctively and longingly toward it.

'I'll take you out prawning in it one night,' Matt called. 'That's what it's for.'

'When?' The twins were nothing if not direct and Matt had to smile. He'd been like this at seven himself.

'When the moon's right. You can't prawn with a full moon.'

'So meanwhile it's out of bounds.' Erin fixed the two children with a look. 'Promise me you'll leave it be.'

'Why?' They glared back at her, and Matt's grin broadened. Yep, these two were trouble, but you had to admire their spirit. And Erin was their match.

'Because it's dangerous to be in without adult supervision. The tide could take you out to sea.'

'But we wouldn't—'

'You might. And while you're living with me you obey my rules,' she finished, and she glared at them right back. They tried meeting her look head on, but finally they conceded. How had he known that they would?

'Okay, we promise,' William whispered reluctantly.

One down, one to go. Erin's gaze shifted. 'Henry?'

'I promise, too.' And Matt knew that the promise would

be kept. Trouble, he thought. Yep, they were trouble but they weren't bad kids at heart. It was just a matter of guessing what the risks were before they took them. And Erin was some guesser.

She was some lady!

Finally he swam back to her as the twins whooped and dived away, the boat forgotten—or at least put on the back-burner. As he reached her, she'd just surfaced from a dive herself. They were nose to nose, a yard apart, and suddenly the whole set-up was intensely…

What?

He didn't know what. He had no experience to describe the way she made him feel. She looked amazing, he thought, completely free of make-up, her blonde curls hanging in wet tendrils over her face and to her shoulders, and her eyes bright with sunshine and with happiness.

And this was a lady who'd lost everything only the night before?

Maybe her belongings had been in another place, he thought. He asked her, and her face momentarily clouded, the pleasure of swimming dissipating.

'Nope. The Home has been my home for years. I guess everything I had in the world was burned.' But then her face was deliberately cleared, blocking pain. 'But they were just things. I told you before, they can be replaced. We have the kids and we have Tigger. Who can ask for anything more than that?'

She wouldn't mourn if her white carpet was stained!

The thought crept in subtly at the edges and held. His house was full of beautiful things. How would he feel if they were destroyed?

Probably gut-wrenchingly dreadful, he decided, thinking of the paintings his mother had so carefully collected over her lifetime. To not care about things was an entirely new concept—as was the way he was looking at Erin now.

'Hey.' She was laughing, her lovely blue eyes twinkling at him over the water. 'You're looking at me like I just landed from Mars. I'm not that bad.'

She surely wasn't. Different, yes. A world apart from the world he lived in.

That, too. But not bad.

The boys had dived through the water to shore, and were up on the bank. Instinctively Erin turned toward them. She'd learned early never to take her eyes from them. Not for a moment.

True to form, they'd headed straight to the only threat as far as the eyes could see. There were two long pieces of wood on the shore, driftwood brought in by the tide. The sticks were worn by the sea to smooth, white poles.

'Hey, these'd make great swords,' Henry yelled, and lifted one up. William was almost as fast, and Erin dived away from Matt and was at the river's edge almost before the poles had touched.

'No,' she said sternly, but they tuned out as if they hadn't heard her. The poles clashed in salute and clashed again.

And then the fight was on in earnest. Robin Hood and Sheriff of Nottingham—without the finesse.

And without the Hollywood blunted swords. These sticks were big enough to hurt!

'*I said no!*' Erin was out of the water now, stalking toward them. She couldn't get close—the sticks were flailing wildly enough for her to be injured if she got in the way. 'William. Henry. You put those sticks down this minute or you will walk home. The long way or through the Joe Blake paddock. Take your pick.'

There was one more clash, but they'd heard her. The sticks slowed and their eyes grew thoughtful.

'You know I mean it,' Erin said, as if she didn't particularly care what they decided. 'You choose.'

They turned and stared at her, and Matt, who'd swum to the shore, watched the battle of wills with some surprise. This was a side of the twins he hadn't seen. They were being crossed, and they didn't like it.

He could have intervened, but he didn't. This was Erin's territory after all, he thought. She was the child expert, and she was facing them down with a sternness that told him she had every intention of following through with her threat.

'We want to fight,' Henry said, his voice mulishly stubborn.

'And one of you will win and one of you will be hurt. Those sticks are heavy enough to hurt badly,' Erin said. 'You heard me, Henry. Put them down.'

Henry turned to William. Their eyes locked and Matt knew they were asking a question of themselves.

And finally Erin won.

But not happily. As if of one accord, the boys glowered, then turned and threw the sticks as hard as they could across the beach toward the paddock beyond.

It was just unfortunate that Sadie chose that moment to appear from behind the tractor.

The old dog hadn't been with them during their tour—there'd simply been no room for her in the tractor cab—but she must have watched the tractor's progress from the house. When it stopped she'd plodded on down to the river to find them. Just at the wrong time.

William's stick caught her right across the foreleg. She gave one stunned yelp and collapsed. She tried to rise, yelped again and lay still.

No!

Matt launched himself up the beach like he'd been shot. His dog! His Sadie....

With one incredulous look at the twins, Erin followed him, her heart sinking to her toes. Dear heaven, just when everything was going beautifully...

It was always like this with the twins, she thought, her heart sick with dread. It was why no foster family would have them. Disaster followed them like sunshine followed rain.

'Is she hurt?' Erin couldn't see. Matt was crouched over his dog, his whole body tense, and all Erin could see was one black and white tail. It lay ominously still. She took those last few steps around him, and then sagged in relief as she saw the collie lift her head and look pathetically up at her owner.

It *had* been her foreleg, then. For one awful moment Erin thought maybe she'd been mistaken in what she'd seen, and the stick had caught her head.

Her leg was bad enough, though. It was bleeding sluggishly at the point of impact, and Matt's face was grim as death.

They'd be out of here tonight, Erin thought bleakly, as she looked down at the lovely old dog. And they deserved it. Oh, no!

'Matt, I'm so sorry.'

'So am I, but it's not you who should be apologising.' Matt's voice matched the grimness of his face. One hand was cradling the old dog's head, the other was carefully examining the injured leg. 'Maybe it's not so bad. I can't feel a break, and she's holding it up.'

She was, too. When Matt released the leg—just half an inch from the ground so it couldn't be further hurt if it fell—Sadie kept it up, as much as to say, *'Look at this, it hurts.'*

'She really is a bit of a hypochondriac,' Matt told Erin in an undervoice, so the twins couldn't hear. 'But it was a fair whack. She'll have to be checked.'

'I'll pay the vet's bill.' Heaven knew her wages weren't sufficient to cover all she'd have to buy in the next few weeks but this…

It was her fault, she thought bleakly. She should have seen the sticks. She should have moved faster.

She'd let herself be distracted by Matt…

'Erin, don't! I told you before, it's not you who should be apologising.' Matt cradled his dog and looked up at her. She looked so distressed that he couldn't bear it. Damn, she'd been through enough because of these kids.

She was so lovely. Standing there in her crazy crimplene that had turned totally translucent with the water, she looked…

Actually she looked naked.

Maybe he'd better concentrate on his dog—and on the twins, he told himself firmly. As Erin was so distressed, then it was time for him to take a hand in the twin-control stakes.

What these kids needed to learn was consequences.

But what?

The twins were standing side by side, ashen-faced and flinching. He looked up at them, and he knew instinctively that these kids had been beaten in the past. Beaten beyond reason. They weren't in an orphanage for nothing. Nobody loved this pair, and they knew it.

So now their faces were stoic, expecting pain. They were expecting the world to come crashing down around their ears, as it had so obviously done in the past.

What had Erin said of them?

They expect to be rejected.

They expected it now. They were waiting for a good thrashing and to be sent away, and a glance at Erin's face said she thought the same. Oh, not the thrashing—because she was here—but she was surely expecting him to toss them out.

'Come here,' he told them and then, when they didn't move, he lowered his voice a notch. 'Henry. William. I said come here. *Now!*'

With an uncertain look at each other they came. Slowly, their shoulders touching, they came, waiting for what was to come, but waiting together.

Erin's whole body tensed.

She was like a mother hen, Matt thought. If he laid a finger on these boys, no matter how justified he was, he'd have her to contend with, and he just knew that taking her on would be some task.

He was doing no such thing, but the boys had to face up to what they'd done.

'You've hurt Sadie,' he said, and waited for what most kids would say. *William did it*—or *We didn't mean to*, or *It wasn't our fault*.

They said none of those. Instead their faces fell to Sadie and the knowledge that had hit home when he'd watched them with Tigger in the dryer was reinforced yet again. These kids weren't bad. They cared. Their loyalty, once won, was won forever.

So no, he wouldn't thrash them, and he wouldn't throw them out.

'We…we're sorry,' Henry whispered and one glistening tear slid down his cheek. Only one. These kids had schooled themselves not to show emotion and it didn't show now.

'Being sorry won't help Sadie,' Matt growled, immeasurably moved despite his anger. 'You need to do something that will.'

'Like…' It was Henry again. William was trembling, and the urge to lift the child and give him a hug was almost overwhelming. Erin, though, was managing to hold her hug instincts in check. She was leaving this to him. 'Like what?' Henry whispered.

And Matt made a snap decision.

'We need to take Sadie to the vet to make sure the leg's not broken. I'll call first, but before that we need to get her back to the house. That means we all have to squeeze on the tractor because I'm not leaving Erin behind. You two climb up behind the driver's seat, sit down and make your knees as flat as you can. Then I'll hand her up to you. You'll carry her on your knees. You'll be uncomfortable but I can't help that. Erin, can you ride on the step?'

'Sure.'

Of course. Anything.

'Right. Let's move.'

CHAPTER FIVE

IT DIDN'T stop there.

Back at the house, Matt carried his dog inside to her basket, he telephoned the vet and then he turned to the boys. 'Okay, you have two minutes to get changed because you're coming with me.'

'But…' It was Erin and he turned to face her. His face was still implacable, but then she saw the tiniest glint of laughter behind his eyes and her own widened with astonishment.

'I'm pretty sure the leg's just bruised,' he told her as the boys disappeared toward their bedroom and dry clothes. 'But I've pre-warned Ted, our local vet. He'll play it up—as I suspect Sadie's playing it for all she's worth. She was hit by a car when she was a pup. I pandered to her dreadfully while she recuperated, and now every time she'd like a little snack—say when I'm eating a nice juicy steak—she'll look pathetic and limp.'

'Oh, Sadie…' Erin stooped down and hugged the big dog lying pathetically in her basket, her leg just slightly raised as if to say, *What a thing to suggest!—I'm fatally wounded here.* 'You wouldn't do that, would you?'

'She would.' Matt knelt, too. Which was sort of nice, he decided. Erin was still gorgeously transparent—literally—and kneeling beside her was quite an experience. 'That's not to say the whack by the stick didn't hurt, though. I bet it did. And now…' He patted his old dog's head. 'She likes the vet, we'll buy her some rump steak on the way home and the boys just might have a lesson in consequences.'

Erin took a deep breath. 'Thank you for not yelling at them,' she said softly, and he smiled at her.

Mistake.

She smiled back, and something strange happened. Something indefinable.

But real. Incredibly real.

'It's… It's my pleasure,' he told her in a voice that was suddenly none too steady. 'Now, if you'll excuse me, I'll go put some dry clothes on as well.'

That'd be good, Erin thought inconsequentially. He'd been swimming bare-chested, he was still bare-chested and crouched beside her he was suddenly far too large and far too…far too male!

And far too something she couldn't define in the least.

'Do you want me to come, too?' she asked. She should. They were her charges.

'No,' he told her, breaking the moment finally by rising and backing a step or two. 'This business is between me and the boys. You stay here and wait for Tom. There's enough on your plate without worrying about my dog.'

He was right, only…

'I should stay with the twins.'

'Delegate responsibility,' he told her, and just for a fleeting moment he touched her damp curls. That was a mistake, as it happened, because the 'something' that was between them intensified a hundredfold.

He caught his breath, and tried for a dignified exit. 'Just for an hour or so,' he told her. 'Just for a while, I want you to think of yourself and let me worry about the twins.'

He left her, but he didn't leave her thinking about the twins—or herself for that matter.

All she could think of was Matt.

* * *

'There was no harm at all in letting them go with him.'

It was Tom. The head of the Home Service had arrived at Matt's farm before Matt, Sadie and the twins returned from the vet, and Erin was feeling dreadful.

When she'd finally got her muddled thoughts back into order she'd gone straight back to concentrating on the twins, and now she was imagining the worst. What sort of chaos could they cause in a veterinary surgery? However, when she told Tom what was happening, his eyes grew thoughtful and he nodded his approval.

'Don't worry. Matt's a sound man, Erin,' he told her. 'I spent some time with him this afternoon, and by the end of it I decided he's the sort of person who, if he applied as a foster parent, I'd be approving in a flash.'

'There's not much chance of that.' Erin gave her boss a half hearted smile. 'You take one look at this house and you can see that. And when you meet the lady he intends to marry…'

'Was that the woman he was with this afternoon?' Tom's craggy eyebrows raised in surprise. 'Charlotte? I didn't know he was engaged.'

'I don't think he is yet,' Erin told him. 'But I gather marriage to Matt has been Charlotte's intention for years. She's knocked back perfectly good offers while Matt went out with other women. Faithfulness personified, is our Charlotte, and I can't see him letting her down now. In fact…'

She took a deep breath and wondered why there was a strange constricting feeling around her heart. 'I have a feeling there's an engagement ring in the truck right now. I saw something that definitely looked like a ring box. Maybe he was planning on popping the question last night.'

'I can't see it happening.' Tom shook his head. 'I took

to Matt right away, but I didn't take to her. She's a cold piece of work.' Then he smiled, relegating Charlotte to his list of the least of his worries. 'Nevertheless, she's useful for some things.' He motioned to the back of his car. 'She's great at shopping. She did all this.'

'All what?' Erin followed his gaze.

'Clothes shopping. None of the rest of us could do it. Lori's flat out taking care of the baby, all the other house parents have their hands full with problem kids and Wendy's taken in Michael and Tess. We knew you'd be desperate for a change of clothes, and you can't go shopping in welfare handouts. Matt remembered you were Wendy's bridesmaid, so he rang her to find your size, and we had the boys' on file. We bullied an emergency contingency cheque from the insurers, then Matt sent Charlotte shopping—and there you go.'

Erin stared. 'There I go?'

'More clothes than you can poke a stick at,' he told her. He lifted the pizzas from the passenger seat. 'Clothes courtesy of your Matt's organisation and his Charlotte's happiness to shop, and dinner courtesy of me. I hope this place runs to a microwave so we can reheat these when the twins return.'

'It runs to everything,' she said, staring at the parcels and itching to undo them. Matt had organised this? Was this why he'd had to take Charlotte into town? The thought warmed her to her toes, and made it difficult to concentrate on anything else.

Somehow she had to manage it. What were they talking about? Oh, yeah. Matt's house. 'Honestly, Tom, it's a display home,' she said at last. 'I don't see how we can stay here.'

'I don't see how you can do anything else,' he told her. 'It's an answer to a prayer. There's nowhere else I can put you. The only alternative is me laying you off for six months, leaving you unemployed and me sending the boys to Sydney.'

That was some choice! It sure took her mind off parcels. But even so...

'You're prepared to keep paying me as a House Mother if I stay on here?' Erin was incredulous.

'I am. I had an emergency briefing with the board before leaving Sydney this morning,' he told her. 'The problem's the twins and I told them that. They're getting too old to place. No one wants to take on two seven-year-olds with a history of trouble, and I won't separate them.'

'No.' The very idea was dreadful.

'Everyone wants babies,' Tom said sadly. 'I could place a hundred Marigolds. Littlies are easy but, once they're over six, people believe that the damage has already been done.'

'The twins are still...salvageable.' Erin said softly. 'They're still capable of attachment.'

'That's why I put your case so strongly to the board,' Tom told her. 'If we take them to Sydney they'll have to go into one of the bigger homes—even if it's only for a short while—and I hate the idea. It could do so much damage. We may have these kids on our hands for the long term, Erin. House Mothers are supposed to be short-term parents while we find foster homes or adoptive parents but it's not happening here.'

He shook his head, but he was watching her face and seeing acceptance of what he was asking. Even more commitment to the twins! 'It's asking a lot, and separation at the end will be more difficult, but the alternative's worse,' he told her gently. 'If you can care for them here for a while longer I'd appreciate it. I'll do my damnedest to find them some other couple as soon as I can, but it's looking bleak.'

'I don't have a choice then, do I?' Erin asked, and Tom shook his head again.

'No. Matt's offer is far too good to knock back. He's said he'll take you for the full six months.' He fixed her then with his all seeing look. Tom had been around, and he knew his staff. As he watched the trouble washing over her face, a sudden thought occurred to him.

'It's not putting you into an awkward position, is it?' he demanded. Then he brightened. 'I guess it can't be if the man's engaged to be married. There'll be no hassles.'

'No.' But she sounded doubtful.

He picked up on her doubt straight away, and he pounced. 'You don't trust him?'

'I trust him, all right,' Erin said, as she turned away with the pizza boxes. And then she added a rider that was meant for her ears only. 'I'm just not sure I can trust myself.'

'Her leg's just badly bruised. We didn't break it.'

They burst in like miniature time bombs, exploding into the kitchen with their news. Momentarily they paused as they saw Tom, but they'd been dealing with Tom all their lives and apart from lowering their voices a notch, it didn't stop them telling Erin what was important.

'The vet says it's just grazed and bruised, but he's wrapped it up in a great big white bandage and he says she's not to walk on it for a week.'

'Which is just what is going to happen.' Following the twins was Matt, carrying Sadie in his arms. He lay the big dog down in her basket, she looked pathetically up at him—and then she wagged her tail.

The wag destroyed the pathetic image completely and Erin had to grin.

'Not mortally injured, huh?'

'Not.' The boys had spotted the pizza which demanded their immediate and undivided attention—which left Matt free to speak to Erin and Tom. 'I'm glad to see you again,' he told Tom.

'It's my pleasure to be here.' Tom beamed at what was happening around him. A man, a woman, two kids and a dog. This was a great family situation. Perfect. If he'd tried to engineer a better placement for the twins, he couldn't have done it.

A sudden idea flashed into his head, his eyes grew thoughtful and his smile widened as Erin shooed the boys out to wash their hands before eating. Hmm.

Double hmm.

'I brought enough pizza for the lot of us,' he said expansively. He was suddenly feeling expansive. He was a man who liked a good happy ending if he could possibly arrange it. 'There are four different types. Help yourself.'

Then he watched Matt's face with interest—and he liked what he saw.

What he saw was confusion.

The pizzas smelled great, Matt had decided, but that alone was really, really strange. Matt was a bachelor and pizza was his staple food—except he'd become fed up to the back teeth with pizza. Normally he'd run a mile to avoid it, and something gastronomically wonderful was waiting for him at Charlotte's.

But suddenly all he wanted to do was haul up a chair, sit down beside Erin and eat pizza.

'Um…no.' He gave a half hearted grin. 'I have a date.'

'With Charlotte,' Erin told Tom, and Tom nodded politely. But his eyes were still thoughtful. His idea, once planted, refused to be dissipated by a small obstacle like a fiancée.

His idea was wonderful!

'Well, off you go, boy,' he told him. 'I daresay Erin won't wait up for you.'

'She certainly won't.' Erin's eyes creased into laughter. 'I'm pooped already. Too much excitement last night and then a swim on top of it... I wonder how you can face a night out.'

'But he's going to see the woman he loves,' Tom said, watching Matt's face and getting answers to unspoken questions that were most satisfactory. 'I expect he won't find that tiring in the least.'

The woman he planned to marry was waiting for him. She'd been ready for hours, and the cooking smells hit him before he opened the door of the truck.

Wow! They were great smells. And then Charlotte was running lightly down the front steps of her house, greeting him with a hug as he pushed open the door, and he had to acknowledge that she looked just beautiful.

'Matt. Darling. I thought you'd never come. No more house fires tonight?'

'No more fires tonight.' He put her away from him and smiled down at her. She really was incredibly lovely—and those smells...

But it wasn't quail.

'I thought you were reheating last night's dinner,' he said, suddenly uneasy. 'That's why I agreed to come—so it wouldn't be wasted.'

'Well, yes.' She blushed and fluttered her eyelashes at him. 'But...' Her eyes slid sideways. 'I sort of thought... Well, I saw the box when I was in the truck this afternoon, you see, and I thought lobster thermidor was the very least I could produce—and Dom Pérignon champagne to go with it.'

The box.

Hell, the box!

It was still sitting where he'd left it last night. Two thousand bucks' worth of diamond and it had completely slipped his mind. He'd had it sitting in the truck all day, and he hadn't even locked the truck! Or thought that whoever sat in the passenger side would see it.

And now...

Charlotte was looking at him with eyes that glowed, then looking past him to where the damned velvet box was still sitting in the map compartment. She was expecting him to ask her to marry him.

Well, why not? he demanded of himself, and wondered why he felt so reluctant to move further. This was what he'd planned to do all along, he told himself. He'd thought about it long and hard. It was the sensible decision.

But...the twins.

'Charlotte, I've offered to take the twins for six months,' he told her hastily.

'That's fine.' Apparently it wasn't an impediment.

It wasn't. Charlotte had heard Matt make his offer to Tom this afternoon and her mind had been working in overdrive since then. There was no way she wanted *that woman* living with Matt—but maybe she could cope with the twins. Just for a few months. If she must. All they needed was a little discipline!

'Tom didn't like our idea of the stables,' she said, in a voice that hinted at her opinion of orphanage directors who weren't grateful for any charity they could get. 'But I've been thinking about it. If Erin stays with you, there's a

Home Mother completely taken up with only two children. So what if we get married quite soon and look after them ourselves?'

For Charlotte this was a definite possibility. Unknown to her beloved, she'd had her wedding gown and her wedding plans ready for years. This would not be a rush.

'We could go away for a lovely honeymoon,' she told him, taking his hands in hers and smiling her most beautiful smile. I'm sure my manager here would take over your farm while we're away, and we'd be combining the properties anyway. Then we can come back and Erin could leave.'

He was stunned. 'You have it all figured out.'

'Mmm.' She beamed, and then looked into the truck again. The box was irresistible. 'It's so sensible.' She leaned in, lifted the box from where it lay, opened it and stared down at the solitary diamond. And gasped. 'Oh, Matt! It's just beautiful.'

But he was still uneasy. 'Charlotte, I don't know—'

'Look, let's not worry about the twins and Erin tonight,' she said, sliding the ring onto her finger with a triumphant flourish and tucking her arm in his with proprietorial ease. 'In truth, I don't know when I can organise the wedding, but I'll try to do it as soon as possible. For now, let's just concentrate on being engaged—and tackling our lobster and champagne. It's cost me a fortune and I refuse to let it spoil. For now we're celebrating our engagement. The rest can all be sorted out over the next few days.'

Hell!

How had he managed that? he thought as he drove home three hours later.

He was engaged to be married!

Well, he'd made the decision when he'd bought the ring. He might have known. Charlotte probably had spies in the jewellers. This town was too small for secrets, and even if he hadn't left the damned ring in the truck she would have known he'd bought it.

It was impossible to back out now.

And why would he want to?

He thought that through, forcing his confused mind to be sensible.

This was a sensible, well thought-out decision, he told himself firmly. Charlotte was a lovely woman and she'd been faithful to him for years. She'd make a loving wife and a wonderful homemaker.

She'd never appear naked in wet crimplene!

And he'd never want her to, he told himself but he knew deep down that he was a liar. Or maybe he wasn't.

He wouldn't want Charlotte in wet crimplene—but Erin was a different matter.

Hell!

He'd expected them all to be in bed. Erin wasn't. She was sitting at the kitchen table, surrounded by opened parcels. She was sorting clothes into piles, and as he walked in, her eyes lifted to his and glowed with pleasure.

'Matt, these are excellent. Charlotte's been so good. They're great, sensible clothes, the sort that we can really work in around the farm. They're just what we need.'

He walked forward and fingered the clothes. Yep, they were sensible. Jeans, T-shirts, windcheaters, sneakers… Great for the boys.

Sensible for Erin.

But he sort of liked the crimplene.

Yeah, and he knew why. He grinned at himself and

thrust the memory of Erin in wet crimplene onto the back-burner. There'd be no more of that now. Charlotte had outdone herself. These were quality clothes, carefully chosen. Erin would look practical in these clothes; like a sensible, hard-working Home Mother. A woman who knew her place in the world. They wouldn't turn transparent when wet. They were built to cover everything!

Charlotte wouldn't be seen dead in these clothes.

That was an uncharitable thought, he decided hastily, pushing it away with a definite shrug. Charlotte wore quality linen blouses, and tailored skirts or slacks. He knew instinctively that Erin wouldn't like Charlotte's style of clothes, and these were much more…well, sensible. So she'd done the right thing. To criticise Charlotte's choice of clothes was to be unfair to the woman he'd just promised to marry.

Or…she was the lady he'd just seen put his ring on her finger, he thought suddenly. He'd never actually said the words, 'Will you marry me?'

He'd never actually promised anything.

It didn't matter, he told himself harshly. She was wearing his ring, and she'd wear it now for ever. Tomorrow she'd tell the world, and he should, too.

Starting now.

'Charlotte and I are engaged,' he told Erin.

Her eyes flew to his, there was the merest fraction of hesitation—and then she rose. Her pile of denim fell back onto the table. Erin's face creased into a smile of delight for him—she really did seem delighted!—and she walked forward, took both his hands in hers and kissed him lightly on the forehead.

'Matt, that's wonderful. I'm very, very happy for you. The whole town's been expecting it for ever.' Then she stood back a little, her eyes twinkling with understanding. 'It was supposed to happen last night though, wasn't it?'

This lady had the knack of knowing things he'd rather she didn't, but there was no point in denying what was obvious. It just disconcerted him. 'Yes.' He thought for a moment of telling her the rest of Charlotte's plans and then thought better of it. Weddings took ages to organise.

Please let it be six months....

Erin's thoughts were still on Charlotte, unaware of the threat the marriage posed to her boys. A Charlotte mother!

'Poor Charlotte,' she was saying. 'No wonder she looked so downcast yesterday. Matt, I'm so sorry we messed with your plans.'

He wasn't, and he wouldn't let Erin be sorry either. 'Hey, it got me lobster instead of quail,' he told her, and she chuckled.

Erin had the most delicious chuckle...

'And to think you missed out on pizza. Poor old you. Lobster and a new fiancée. Tch. And our pizza was Bay Beach's best!'

He grinned at her. Erin's laughter was infectious. 'Yep. It's a real shame.'

'Mmm.' Still she was smiling, and he suddenly could think of nothing else to say. All he could think of was how blindingly attractive her smile was.

Funny he'd never seen it before.

Maybe it was because he was engaged, he thought. Erin was now forbidden fruit. He was engaged to be married.

He was *happily* engaged to be married! Forbidden fruit indeed.

So he should leave. He should go to bed. Instead he stood, stupidly fingering the pile of new clothes.

'Charlotte's bought you everything you need?'

'Yes.'

'She should have brought you something pretty,' he said inconsequentially. 'You can't just wear jeans and windcheaters.'

'There's not a lot of call for me to wear anything else,' she told him bluntly. 'These are just fine.'

'But you go to dances and things.'

'Only when I'm off duty. I don't expect I'll be off duty for a while.'

'I can look after the twins sometimes,' he told her. 'If you want to go out.' He took a deep breath. 'Like tomorrow... Go to town tomorrow. There's still plenty left from Tom's insurance cheque. Go and buy yourself something nice.'

'I hardly need pretty things tomorrow.'

'You never know.' He stared down at the jeans with distaste, and noticed a pile of flannelette pyjamas. He looked more closely and discovered they were all the same. Charlotte had bought three sets of red flannelette pyjamas, two small pairs and one larger set. His mouth tightened in distaste as he lifted them for inspection.

'And these,' he said shortly. 'They're wrong. I don't know what Charlotte was thinking of buying matching sleepwear. They'll make you and the boys look like something out of an institution.'

Erin agreed, but she was forced to defend Charlotte. She had to be grateful. 'Matt, they're new and clean and the boys won't notice. They'll be fine.'

'They're not fine and I'll notice,' he growled, and her gorgeous chuckle rang out again.

'Oh, no, you won't. These are pyjamas, Mr McKay. Worn in bed. You need never see them.'

'I don't want to. They're dreadful.'

'They're sensible.'

'They'll be hot as be damned. It's almost summer. You're not wearing them.'

'Tonight I'll wear them.' Her eyes were defiant—but still twinkling. 'It's them or nothing—and I'm definitely not wearing nothing.'

Erin in nothing…

Where had that thought come from? Erin not in her crimplene. Erin in less…

Hell! He had to get out of here. He was a sensibly engaged man.

Just as well, or anything could have happened.

'We'll talk about it in the morning,' he told her. But he grabbed the package. There was no way he was letting her wear those pyjamas. 'Meanwhile, wear a T-shirt or something. These are going back to the shop.'

'Yes, sir.' Her tone was half mocking and he grimaced. Did she know what he'd been thinking—and what he was feeling right now? Somehow he knew that she did.

He glowered and glowered some more. 'Good. I'm glad you agree.'

'It doesn't mean I'm not grateful for Charlotte's thoughtfulness.' She wasn't, but she wouldn't admit it for worlds.

She turned to gather her clothing together, and he stood watching her for a couple of moments. Erin was wearing the dress she'd been wearing the night before when the home burned down—one of her Charlotte-decreed homemade jobs. It was pale blue with lemon swirls, with a couple of fire stains she hadn't been able to remove by scrubbing. Stained or not, it made her look…

It made her look as if the jeans and windcheaters Charlotte had chosen were totally unsuitable.

Suddenly he had a thought. This was one thing that was suitable, at least.

'Erin?'

'Yes?' She paused from her clothes gathering and looked up in enquiry.

She was expecting him to go to bed and leave her, he thought. She was expecting nothing from him at all.

He felt his midriff clench in sudden pain. Hell, he wanted to do something for her so badly, and all he had was this. He shoved his hand into his back pocket and found what he'd been searching for.

'Tom showed me the layout of your house and which was your bedroom,' he told her, his suddenly gruff voice failing to hide his inexplicable emotion.

'Yes?'

'There were a few things we were able to salvage.'

Her face stilled. 'It wasn't all completely burned?'

'The roof burned and the ceiling caved in,' he told her, seeing her sudden look of hope and wanting to dispel it before it started. 'The weight of the ceiling, and the soot and smoke and water effectively destroyed most of your stuff. But the base of your bedroom didn't actually catch fire. The roof caved in while it was still smouldering, but it was doused fast. So the lads from the fire brigade and I made a really good search and we found these.'

And he lifted up what he was holding—a string of seed pearls.

As pearls went they were what he'd been brought up to believe were inadequate. Both his mother and Charlotte would have scorned these as trumpery, he knew. But to Erin...

To Erin they weren't trumpery. She stared at the string dangling from his fingers, then took a tentative step forward as if she couldn't believe what she was seeing.

'My mother's necklace.' She whispered the words. It was as if she wasn't able to believe what she was seeing, and any minute they'd be snatched back from her.

'It's the only trinket we found that was recognisable,' he told her. 'Did you have much jewellery?'

'That's all I had.' She lifted it from his fingers and stared down at it, still disbelieving. 'Oh, Matt…'

'I'm sorry we couldn't retrieve more stuff,' he said awkwardly, but she lifted her face to his and her eyes were bright with unshed tears.

Then, before he knew what she was about—before he could take one step to defend himself—she threw her arms around his neck, raised herself on her tiptoes and kissed him soundly on the lips.

It was a kiss of thanks—nothing more. It was a kiss of gratitude.

So how it had the capacity to knock him sideways—to have him catch her waist in his hands and pull her in to him and kiss her back—to feel like his world was shifting on its axis and shifting forever—who could say?

Matt couldn't.

He could only feel, but feel he did. He felt the way her body felt delicious under his hands. The way her mouth yielded to his and the touch of her hair against his, the moulding of her breasts to his chest—the fragrance of her….

He didn't understand this in the least. He could only feel and feel some more, and when she finally pulled away he could only regret her parting, and regret it with every inch of his being.

'Oh, Matt, thank you,' she whispered, and the tears in her eyes were real now, threatening to slide down her cheeks. She blinked them back, fast and furious, and then made a grab for her pile of clothes. Carefully sorted heaps

were ignored. They were crumpled into one vast mound
of clothes, gathered against her breast almost as a defence.

'Goodnight, Matt.'

And then she fled, taking her clothes and her necklace
twin-wards, before her tears finally were allowed to run
free. She left Matt staring after her, wondering what the
hell he'd just done.

He'd just restored a necklace to its owner.

And now something else needed restoring but it was
nothing tangible. In fact, he didn't have a clue what it was.

But it was a long time before he slept that night. And
when he slept, he didn't dream of the lady he was about
to marry.

He dreamed of seed pearl necklaces, and he dreamed
of Erin.

CHAPTER SIX

DESPITE the emotions of the day, Erin slept soundly. In fact, she slept more soundly than she remembered sleeping for years.

It was because Matt was here, she thought as she drifted toward unconsciousness. As House Mother she always slept on the brink of waking. There was always a child in need. And before that...

Her mother had died when Erin was just fourteen. Erin had been the oldest of the kids. Her father had crumpled with her mother's death so she'd reared her siblings with love and also, she had to admit, with pleasure. When the last child left home she moved on to being an orphanage House Mother, but her choice of career meant that from the time she was fourteen there'd always been a child dependent on her.

There was no one else to share her load.

But here, at the other end of the house, slept Matt. She wasn't totally in charge. The feeling was novel, and she shouldn't indulge it, but in truth it was also wonderful.

She indulged it. The twins slept soundly and Erin totally relaxed. She slept on dreamlessly, and she couldn't guess that at the other end of the house Matt stirred and tossed and fretted because he couldn't get her out of his head.

Erin woke at dawn when Matt crept silently into the room next door.

She might have been sleeping soundly, but she was still a House Mother. Some things were instinctive, and protection was one of them. The moment the twins' bedroom door opened, her eyes were wide and she was pushing herself up in bed wondering what was wrong.

She'd propped the bathroom doors open between the two rooms so she could see, and she could see clearly straight through. Matt was in his working clothes and he was tip-toeing towards the twins.

'What's wrong?' It came out as a whispered croak of surprise.

He cast her a look of annoyance—annoyance with himself for waking her. 'Hell, Erin, I'm sorry. You go back to sleep. I'm after the twins.'

She found her right voice. 'What on earth for?'

'The twins hurt my dog,' he explained. 'So I told them last night that they need to accept responsibility for what they'd done. Sadie needs to rest for a week, and therefore the twins need to take over Sadie's workload.' He reached the bed the boys were still sharing and touched two small shoulders. 'Okay, guys. Wake up. It's six a.m. You know what we need to do.'

And, amazingly, they did. They opened their eyes, they smiled shyly up at Matt as if this had been expected, and to Erin's astonishment, they moved straight into dress mode.

'What on earth are you doing?'

'Tell her, boys.' Matt smiled at her—and then he carefully diverted his attention elsewhere.

Hell! What was happening here?

Following orders, Erin was wearing one of the welfare shirts as sleepwear. It was buttoned to the neck and it was a man's shirt to boot, but the sight of Erin fresh from sleep, tousled and rumpled, with her curls flying free and her gorgeous blue eyes wide with enquiry somehow had the power to make something inside him kick.

Hard.

Luckily a twin spoke, giving him time to gather his wits.

'We're rounding up the cows,' Henry told Erin solemnly, hauling on the ill-fitting trousers he'd worn the day before.

'You have new clothes to wear now,' Erin told him, and then took on board what Henry had said. 'Rounding up cows?'

'The boys don't need new clothes to do what they need to do,' Matt told her, still carefully concentrating on the twins. 'In fact, new clothes would be completely wasted. We're cutting Cecil out from where he's been serving the cows. He's due at the Lassendale Cattle Show tomorrow.'

'The Lassendale Show...'

'You're still half asleep,' Matt told her kindly. 'William, that windcheater's inside out. Surely you know the Lassendale show, Erin? And you a farmer's daughter and all.'

Right. Of course she did. The whole farming world knew the show he was talking about, but she'd never been there. Well, why would she? Lassendale was a show-case of the cream of the country's pedigree cattle, and a prize from the Lassendale judges meant the making or breaking of a stud farmer. Of course Matt would be showing.

'You're putting Cecil in the show?'

'I surely am.'

And then Erin started feeling strange, too. Matt was adjusting William's windcheater and the sight of him dressing the little boy—a job she should be doing herself—did strange things to her insides. Things she didn't understand in the least. She hauled her bedclothes up to her neck in an instinctive act of defence, but for the life of her she couldn't think what she was defending.

'And the boys?' she managed.

'I can't cut a bull out of that herd without a good dog,' he told her, his eyes twinkling. He'd overcome his unease in the face of her discomfort—or maybe it was because she'd hauled the sheet up so far. 'Or, failing a dog, then two obedient twins. Which I have here, don't I, boys?'

'Yes.' William said the word solemnly and Henry nodded his agreement.

'Now there's no need for you to get up,' Matt told her. 'I'll give the boys some milk and a piece of toast each and we'll have a proper breakfast when we're finished. You go back to sleep.'

Back to sleep? Such a thing was unheard of. Go back to sleep when the twins were awake...

'No!'

'You're not wanted,' Matt told her, making his voice severe. 'Is she, boys? Cutting out bulls is man's work.'

'But Matt,' She was bewildered by the plan. 'A bull—'

'Cecil is a pussy cat,' he told her, seeing what her major worry was. 'Don't fret yourself. You know I wouldn't let the boys near anything I considered dangerous. With these two to help me, we'll have him back to the yard in no time. Then we'll scrub him down, make him beautiful and then we can introduce him to you personally.'

'But—'

'Stop arguing and go back to sleep.'

'Matt—'

'Sleep!'

Sleep? Ha!

Go back to sleep, he'd said, but it was just plain impossible. Erin lay in bed and listened to the sounds of the boys in the kitchen. She heard Matt talking, and she heard the boys giggling in response.

Giggling?

They sounded just like they did when they were plotting trouble, Erin thought, but the difference here was that Matt was plotting trouble for them. Excellent trouble. Cutting a bull from the herd was just the sort of adventure they craved, and to do it with such a wondrous person as Matt...

He was wondrous, Erin thought sleepily. He knew instinctively how to act with the boys.

Take responsibility for your actions...

She'd tried and tried to drum that into them, and here was Matt doing exactly that. Yesterday they'd hurt Sadie, so today they were doing Sadie's job.

She desperately wanted to join them, but she knew that to do so would spoil it for them. This was men's work, Matt had decreed, and for Erin to interfere... To have their House Mother hovering over them, fussing and bossing while they did it, would spoil it in a way she instinctively understood. So somehow she forced herself to lie still.

Then the bedroom door opened again and it was William, carefully balancing a cup of tea.

'Matt said you'd like this.'

Behind him was Henry, carrying a plate of toast with marmalade. Erin blinked and blinked again. Breakfast in bed! Good grief!

And Matt was in the doorway behind them, watching his charges with pride as they wobbled their responsibilities to her bedside table—without a single spill.

'Well done, boys,' he told them. He looked at Erin and he winked. 'Okay, lady. Wrap yourself around your breakfast, then put your head on the pillow and sleep—while we men go off and organise the world. Okay, men. Let's go round us up some beef cattle.'

She couldn't do it.

She physically couldn't lie in bed and do nothing. It

nearly killed her. She drank her tea and ate her toast, then lay and stared at the ceiling for all of half an hour. Then Sadie sidled in and put her nose on the bedcover, and Erin fondled the old dog's ears and smiled in sympathy. She knew exactly what the dog was thinking.

'We've been made redundant, girl,' she said softly and Sadie waved her silky tail in agreement. 'How does that make you feel?'

Sadie flopped down on the mat beside the bed, put her head on her forelegs and sighed.

'It makes you feel funny, too?'

Another sigh.

'I suppose I could just go see what they're doing,' she told the dog. 'From a distance.'

Sadie looked up at her with hope, and Erin shook her head.

'Not you, girl. You have a sore leg to look after.' Then, at the look on Sadie's face, she burst into laughter. 'Oh, you fraud. You pulled a con and now you're feeling like you'd like to change your mind.' She leaned down and lightly touched Sadie's bandaged leg. 'I'm sorry, girl, but you're going to have to put up with it. I have a feeling your leg might be more important than you know.'

There was another sigh at that, and Erin was starting to feel like the dog understood every word she said. Which was good, because Erin surely needed someone to talk to.

'I know how you feel,' she told her. 'But for more reasons than one, you need to keep your nose out of it.'

But Erin wasn't keeping her nose out.

If she stayed in that bed any longer she'd bust something.

If there was one thing being brought up on a farm with seven siblings had taught her, it was how to hide. Years of hide and seek had made her a master of the art. Erin washed and dressed with speed, and then made her way down the paddocks, moving from the concealment of one clump of river gums to another with the ease of a master.

The mustering team—Matt and his dog-cum-twins—were easy enough to find. The boys were whooping and yipping loud enough to wake the fishermen back in Bay Beach. Their targeted herd of cows was moving uneasily away from this unknown quantity, and by the time she reached the edge of the paddock where they were, Erin had a clear idea of what Matt was doing.

He was using the boys just like he'd use a working dog. Maybe they didn't have as much finesse as Sadie possessed, but his team strategy was effective all the same.

It was simple, really. Matt would send the twins into the herd, whooping at the top of their lungs and effectively splitting it down the centre. Half the herd would move one way, and Matt would concentrate on keeping the half containing Cecil the bull packed tight into the fenced corner. Ignoring the rest, they then had a smaller herd to work with.

Once the herd was where Matt wanted, the twins moved in again to split a smaller herd. With each foray of yipping and yelling, they made the controlled group smaller.

And finally there was just Cecil, a confused-looking beast but a magnificent specimen of Hereford Bull all the same. He stood in his corner, a twin at each side and Matt before him. While Erin watched from her safe distance, Matt slipped a rope through the ring in the bull's nose. The huge animal looked up at Matt in a resigned sort of way, and then he started plodding steadily toward the house before Matt so much as tugged on the rope.

He'd done this a thousand times before, his body language said, and while he might have tried his darndest to escape, now that he was cornered, like Matt had said, he was a real pussy cat.

So much so that Erin wasn't surprised when Matt slipped the rope into Henry's hand so he could lead him, and then scooped William up to ride on the bull's broad back. The twins were so light the bull would hardly notice his burden.

He didn't. Cecil plodded on without changing stride.

'You ride halfway, and then swap with Henry,' Matt told them, and from where she stood in the cluster of gums by the paddock's boundary, Erin could see the twins' collective shoulders expand a notch or six.

They'd be so proud of what they were doing!

All their attention was on the bull. Henry was leading the bull with the solemnity of an undertaker leading a funeral procession, and William was clinging on as if he expected Cecil to buck.

And, as she watched, Matt fell behind, then turned his head toward the trees where Erin was hiding, and he waved. And grinned.

Caught!

For a split second Erin hesitated, then she grinned and waved back. Drat the man, he had eyes in the back of his head.

She wasn't wanted, though. She could see that. She left them to it, and went quietly back to the house.

She was a House Mother without charges, and it felt very peculiar indeed!

By the time they finished doing what they were doing, she was fed up with being a House Mother without charges. She desperately wanted to be part of it.

The urge to go out to the sheds was almost overwhelming. Instead somehow she made herself organise the boys' clothing, make the beds, prepare another breakfast, talk to Sadie, talk to herself...

'I'm going nuts,' she told the dog. 'I don't think I'd be very good at living alone.'

She'd been alone for three hours and it felt weird.

'What are they doing out there?'

She didn't know, and Sadie couldn't help her. So they sat in the kitchen and waited, and it was hard to know which of them was more frustrated.

Finally they reappeared.

They were filthy! The twins were mud splattered, soaking wet and they were beaming from ear to ear. They stood at the back door and fought for the rights to tell her everything. All at once.

'We've cleaned him and soaped him all over and now he shines and shines.'

'He's beautiful.'

'I rode on his back.'

'William squirted Matt with the hose but he didn't mean to, and Matt didn't mind...'

Then Matt appeared behind them, and he was just as filthy as the twins were—and his grin said he was just as happy with his morning's work. He smiled at Erin and then looked doubtfully down at himself.

'We're a bit dirty to come in,' he told her.

She nodded, trying not to laugh. They were all so pleased with themselves, but that mud...

'I think you should stay outside,' she told them.

'Aw, Erin...' Both twins howled a protest and then saw she was laughing. Their small faces relaxed and they took a tentative step over the threshold.

'Stop this minute!' She stopped them in their tracks, in

a voice that Charlotte or Matt's dead mother would be proud of. 'Go not one inch further.' Matt blinked. He hadn't thought it of her.

And he was right. She wasn't worried about her kitchen floor. She was concerned about something else.

'Do you have a camera?' she asked, and when he nodded she made him tell her where to find it.

'Because you're not getting rid of one spot of that gorgeous mud until I've documented this moment,' she told them. 'I want a photograph of you guys standing next to a beautiful Cecil so I can remember this moment for the rest of my life.'

It wasn't just a memory for Erin.

She took the photograph from three different angles, with Matt standing proudly, one hand on each twins' shoulder, and all beside Matt's magnificent, gleaming bull, and she knew this photograph would be precious for many reasons.

The boys had so few memories. So few possessions.

If she took copies of this and framed it, it'd become as valued as Tigger the Tiger, she thought, and she finished taking the shot and raised her eyes to Matt in gratitude.

'Thank you,' she said and her words held a whole wealth of meaning.

He got it in one.

'My pleasure,' he told her and if his voice wasn't quite steady it wasn't for the want of trying.

Then they trooped through the kitchen, showered, the boys inspected and accepted and donned their new clothes and they breakfasted properly. They sat at Matt's big kitchen table and wrapped themselves around bacon and eggs, and toast and cereal, while Erin watched with amazement at what they were demolishing. The boys were normally picky eaters. Now they ate and talked and ate and talked like there was no tomorrow.

And all the time Matt watched, like a benevolent genie who'd wrought this change with a wave of a magic wand.

They were great kids! he was thinking. The best!

'Do you like your new clothes?' Erin asked, and they nodded over slices of watermelon. Matt had done a vast grocery shop the day before, and he'd done them proud. He'd had to do a few things since he'd granted Mrs Gregory her holiday, but he was finding that he didn't mind in the least. The house was the cosier for it.

It was also messier. Matt looked ruefully down at the tracks he and the twins had made across the kitchen floor which Mrs Gregory wouldn't have tolerated to stay while she cooked breakfast. But it was definitely cosier.

Nice.

'But we don't like your clothes,' Henry was telling Erin, and Matt agreed entirely.

'What's wrong with mine?' Erin looked down at her beautifully fitting jeans and long-sleeved shirt. 'They're great.'

'You wear dresses,' Henry said stubbornly and William tilted his chin in agreement.

And Matt found himself with the kids. Yep, Erin wore dresses. She looked great in dresses, even the crimplene.

'Go into town and buy yourself something decent,' he growled. 'Now. Today. I can look after the twins.'

'My dresses are home-made,' she told him.

'So? My mother's sewing machine is still here. Buy yourself what you need and I'll twin-sit while you sew.'

'We'll help,' the twins announced, and Erin grinned at the thought that conjured up.

'Oh, great. I can see a twin sewed into each side of the zipper—with Sadie's nose at the bottom.'

They chuckled at that, but Matt wasn't to be side-tracked. 'Seriously, Erin...'

'Mmm?' It was time for her to tilt *her* chin.

He tilted his right back. He could be obstinate, too. 'The clothes Charlotte bought were just to tide you over until you got a wardrobe you liked.' He glanced at his watch. 'The draper's open on Saturday afternoon. You could go in now.'

'But the twins—'

'The twins and I have more work to do,' he told her. 'And I'm more than capable of looking after them by myself.' Then he paused at the sound of a car pulling up outside. He knew that sound. 'And maybe I don't have to,' he continued. 'Here's the help I need.'

It was Charlotte.

Of course it was Charlotte, and Erin schooled her face into an expression of pleasure. After all, Charlotte had shopped for her, and she was Matt's affianced wife. The fact that Erin had never been able to stand the woman should be irrelevant. So as Charlotte walked into the kitchen—without knocking—she found Matt and Erin smiling a welcome, and the twins looking up from their bacon with expressions of distrust.

The distrust was nothing new or personal. The twins distrusted the world.

'You're still eating breakfast!' Charlotte, as beautifully presented as ever in her smart slacks and blouse and beautifully arranged chignon, stopped on the threshold and stared at them all in amazement. Her eyes fluttered to the delicate silver watch on her wrist. 'Matt, darling, it's ten o'clock!'

And then she saw the mud on the floor, and her breath drew in horror. 'What on earth has been going on?'

'They've been cleaning Cecil,' Erin told her, rising and crossing to the woman at the door. She kept her smile straight, took Charlotte's hands in hers and kissed her lightly on the cheek before Charlotte could pull away. 'I hear congratulations are in order. You're engaged to be married! That's lovely news, Charlotte. And you're not to be disgusted with us. This is our second breakfast—and the mud is Cecil mud.'

'Cecil…' Charlotte thought this through and her face cleared. 'Oh, the bull. Of course. You've been cleaning your wonderful bull for tomorrow's show. But, Matt, you know you should have stripped at the door—or made the children do it at least.'

She regarded the twins as one might regard two interesting but slightly disgusting creatures from the sea, and it took an almost Herculean effort for Erin to keep her smile pinned on.

'It'll only take minutes to mop, but the troops were hungry,' she told her.

'Well, I guess it was in a good cause,' Charlotte said reluctantly. 'As long as you do intend mopping, Erin. I don't see that Matt has the time. We're leaving at the crack of dawn tomorrow.'

'You're *leaving*?' It was Henry, his eyes swivelling toward Matt. His face was horrified.

'I'm taking Cecil to the show,' Matt told him. 'It's a two-day affair so I'll only be away for one night.' His brow creased. 'I didn't think you were coming, Charlotte?'

'I've managed to find a place at the hotel,' she told him. 'The Royal's very expensive, but it still has places.' She gave her tinkling laugh, the laugh that made Erin shudder. 'I thought…now that we're engaged we should do things together.'

Urk. The boys winced, and inwardly Erin winced along with them. Charlotte's sweetness was almost repelling.

And it seemed Matt found it almost as distasteful. He dredged up a smile and rose, carrying his plate across to the sink.

'Well, that's great.' Then he turned back to Erin, and his face was under control again. 'Erin, now that Charlotte's here, I want you to hop it. Go into town and do your shopping.'

'But what for?' Charlotte looked from Erin to Matt and back to Erin. 'I did all the shopping you could possibly want yesterday.'

'And it was wonderful,' Erin told her, but Matt shook his head.

'Charlotte, if everything you owned in the world was destroyed by fire, could you imagine another woman supplying you with everything you need on one shopping trip? Without even discussing it with you first? You don't think that Erin might just want to buy a couple of things herself?'

'I guess…' Charlotte faltered at Matt's logic, but she obviously didn't. In her view, Erin was a charity case, and charity cases deserved what they got.

But Matt was no longer listening. 'Go, Erin.'

'I'll just clean up—and the boys can come with me.'

'No.' Matt's voice was implacable. He took her shoulders, steered her to the door and forcibly propelled her out. 'Charlotte and the boys and I will clear up, and then we'll take hay around the cattle. We'll be so busy we'll hardly miss you. I don't expect you back here before four o'clock. So go.'

She cast one worried look at the twins, but Matt wasn't taking no for an answer.

'If you're sure…'

'I'm sure. And so's Charlotte. Aren't you, sweetheart?'

Charlotte was stumped. There was nothing for a well brought-up young woman to say to that but yes, and she rose to the occasion with fortitude.

'Of course.' Charlotte gave them all her very sweetest smile. 'You go and do your shopping, Erin. I'll look after your responsibilities.'

Drat the woman!

Erin's hands clenched on the steering wheel all the way into town, and by the time she got there she was still having trouble calming down. What Matt saw in that cold-blooded barracuda... Couldn't he see what she really was? She was so nice to Matt, but so darned nasty to those she didn't consider important.

It was nothing to do with her, she told herself, as she drove into Bay Beach. Matt's love life was Matt's business, and that was that.

She was here to shop.

And then she saw Shanni emerge from the greengrocer. Her face brightened. Shanni was a really good friend. Like Erin, she was a local girl from a farm where money wasn't in oversupply and so, like Erin, she'd been given the cold shoulder by Charlotte from a very early age. What Erin needed now was a coffee, a chat with her friend and a very long whinge.

'Where are the kids?' she called, and Shanni beamed as she dumped her shopping in her car and headed across the car-park to her friend.

'They're at Mum's. Oh, great. I was just going to head out to see you. You want a coffee and a chat?'

'Do I ever,' Erin told her. 'If you don't mind a bit of bitchiness thrown into the gossip.'

'That's my very favourite kind of gossip,' Shanni said, and tucked Erin's arm into hers. 'What gives?'

Back at the farm it was Matt's temper that was giving. He'd loaded the trailer with hay, the twins had helped cheerfully enough but when they headed out to the paddocks Charlotte decided she was coming, too.

Then, as William heaved his first bale off the trailer—no mean feat for one so small—she told him how to do it right.

'The cattle trample it if you put it down in full bales,' she told William sharply. 'Wait until Matt cuts the twine and then throw it off a quarter at a time.'

William's small face fell, he dropped behind the trailer and Henry, after looking at his twin, decided to do likewise.

They stumped along unwillingly, waiting to go home. Charlotte scolded. Matt tried to make things right but the more that was said the more the twins turned stubborn and mute.

'You'll be glad to get away tomorrow,' Charlotte told him. 'Kids are okay in small doses—in very small doses.'

'They're good kids.'

'If they were good kids they'd have been adopted long before this.'

'Hush!' Charlotte's voice was carrying. Matt cast a glance behind him. He didn't think the twins had heard, but... 'Be a bit careful of what you're saying.'

'I'm only telling the truth,' Charlotte said stubbornly. 'For heaven's sake, they actually burned down a whole house. They should be a bit grateful for what you're doing instead of grumping along like two spoiled brats.'

Yeah. Right. But they didn't look like spoiled brats, Matt thought as he tried to cheer them up. They just looked like kids who knew they were hopeless and expected to be told that at every available opportunity.

'Come and help me brush Cecil,' he told them as they finally fed out the last of the hay. 'He'll be dry by now, and he needs to be brushed like he's never been brushed before if he's to win.'

'Oh, Matt, really...' Charlotte again, unable to resist putting in her oar. 'As if they know the right way to brush a bull. I'll help.'

'Boys...'

'I want to watch TV,' Henry said, and William chewed his bottom lip and said nothing.

'I'd really appreciate it if you could help me.'

Silence.

Erin arrived back at the farm feeling very much better. There was nothing like venting a little spleen with a friend, she thought cheerfully as she turned into the gate. That, a couple of bolts of material, a really gorgeous ready-made dress, new shoes and a bottle of her favourite perfume supplied by Shanni had made her feel she was ready to face the world again.

Or ready to face Charlotte.

They were in the kitchen. Erin pushed wide the door and knew they'd been talking about her. The conversation stopped dead as she entered, and Matt bit his lip.

It wasn't anything good, Erin thought, but then, when had Charlotte ever said anything nice about her? Or anyone who had less money and influence than Charlotte?

'Hi,' she said brightly, determined to be cheerful. 'I had to come home. Bay Beach ran out of things I could buy.'

'Did the insurance money run to all this?' Charlotte asked incredulously, looking at Erin's parcels. She sniffed.

'That's the same perfume as Sally wears. It costs a mint. And you've never bought a dress from Della's!'

'I do get paid,' Erin said gently. 'I'm not exactly a welfare case, Charlotte.' She dumped her parcels and somehow kept right on smiling. Then, because she knew it'd cut right to the bone, she couldn't resist. 'I even had money left over for lacy knickers. Because a girl just never knows...' And that was enough of that! 'Where are the boys?'

'They're watching television,' Charlotte snapped, watching Matt's face and not being reassured at all. He'd definitely heard what Erin said, and there was definitely a level of interest there. 'They've been distinctly unhelpful.'

'I expect they're tired,' Matt threw in, trying to appease—and trying not to think of Erin in lacy knickers—but Erin was no longer listening. She left them to each other.

If Matt was stupid enough to believe he loved Charlotte, then they deserved each other.

The twins weren't watching television.

Erin went from there to the bedrooms. Then she searched the house, but there were no twins. Finally she returned to the kitchen.

'They're not in the house,' she told Matt, and watched as his eyes widened. 'Where else could they be?'

'They're watching television.' He walked forward as if he thought she just wasn't looking hard enough, and flung open the sitting room door. The television was blaring, but there were no twins.

They looked at each other—and they started to run.

She checked the river first.

It was Erin's golden rule. Check out worst-case scenarios and work backward. The most dangerous places for the twins to be were the machinery shed and the river, so while Matt checked the sheds, she ran down along the track they'd used to go swimming.

They weren't there, but something else was there that made her suck in her breath in dismay.

Oh no!

She looked back up at the house, and her fears were confirmed. There was Matt, emerging from the shed where Cecil had been groomed. He was holding a twin by each hand. Erin couldn't see his face, but she could guess it'd look like thunder.

Because as soon as he saw the empty stall, he'd have guessed.

She turned around again and she sighed.

The river flowed on golden sand, and then curved away inland. As it did, the sand turned to mud.

That was where Cecil was. He was no longer confined, brushed and beautiful in the shed, ready for tomorrow's show. He was rolling full length in the mud, doing what every self-respecting bull would do, given all the peculiar odours they'd put on his body.

He was getting it all off.

And he was now disgusting!

CHAPTER SEVEN

'THEY deserve to be spanked. I'll do it if you won't.' Charlotte was at her vitriolic best and Erin silently counted to ten before she put herself between Charlotte and the boys. Somehow she forced herself to think fast. She needed a defensive weapon here, and luckily she had one, just granted to her by an indignant Shanni.

'You touch them and I'll... I'll publish the poetry you and Bradley Moore wrote to each other when you were teenagers!'

What a threat! Erin's voice was whisper-quiet and desperate, but everyone knew she meant it. Matt's eyebrows flew up in astonishment. Charlotte gasped and took a step back, allowing Erin to crouch protectively before her two white-faced little boys.

Now what? Erin thought desperately. The boys knew exactly what they'd done, and how naughty they'd been. Now they flinched, but they met her look, defiant and expecting the worst.

Why did she always want to hug them?

She couldn't. Matt was still holding them a hand apiece. He was angry, she knew. He'd been distracted momentarily by her stupid threat to Charlotte, and she could see her threat would surface to haunt her, but meanwhile he had every right to be angry.

'What the...?' Charlotte was shocked to the core. 'You never...'

'You used Rob McDonald as a go between,' Erin said, and managed a smile. This was kids' poetry they were

116

talking about. It was only teasing, after all. Wasn't it? 'Silly move, Charlotte. Rob might be a police sergeant, but at fifteen he wasn't so law-abiding. The dratted boy copied them and Shanni found them a couple of weeks ago when she was cleaning up out at her parents' farm.'

It might be crazy, and wholly unethical, but as a desperate ruse it worked brilliantly. As a distraction, this was a beauty!

'That's ridiculous,' Charlotte managed, right off track.

'Yep!' It was, but Shanni had laughingly suggested it as a weapon, and it had been in Erin's head at the wrong time. Bay Beach was a very small town with a very long memory!

'Poetry,' Matt said blankly. *'Bradley?'* and Erin had to choke back laughter and concentrate on the important issue here.

'Do you know where Cecil is now?' she asked the boys gently. She was more dismayed than angry. Heaven, it was as if they tried to drive off anyone who was good to them. They'd all put in so much work to make Cecil splendid, and to undo it all now didn't make any sense. 'He's down in the mud by the river, and he's filthy,' she continued. 'All the work that you and Matt did is wasted.'

'We don't care,' William whispered.

'Now Matt won't be able to go to the show,' Henry added. He was scared stiff, but still there was a whisper of defiance. 'With her!'

And there was the crux of the matter. They wanted Matt to stay right here, so they'd taken matters into their own hands.

Help! Erin thought bleakly. They needed to be punished—but how? She couldn't let them off scot-free, and here was Charlotte ready to thrash them. All of them. Erin included.

The woman looked at explosion point. Maybe Erin's threat hadn't been such a good idea.

Concentrate on the twins, she told herself. 'You'd better go to your room,' she said wearily, trying to block out Charlotte's fury and think what was best. Her head was spinning. 'Oh, Matt, I'm so sorry.'

'There's no need for you to be sorry.' Matt's face was still grim, but there was a trace of understanding behind his eyes. Now they'd given their reason, he could see it and, damn, he'd had fun with the kids himself. He could see why they didn't want it to end. He hadn't thought it important—he'd assumed they'd be fine here with Erin while he was away for the night—but looking at it from a kid's perspective he could see where they were coming from.

And he could see the problem Erin had with them now. They needed consequences, but where were the consequences in this one? He stay home and they'd won? That'd achieve nothing except trouble next time. Or he'd work until midnight getting the bull ready again, and leave them all to be upset in his absence. Erin feeling guilty and the kids feeling bad.

Consequences...

Charlotte was quietly having kittens by his side. What had Erin said? Bradley Moore... Well, well.

Consequences!

'This is a real shame,' he said, and made himself look gravely at the twins instead of at Erin. He still had their hands. Now he gave them both a gentle tug so they were facing him. Unlike Erin, he didn't stoop. He stayed looking down at them from his great height, and he schooled his features into sad instead of angry.

Or...sadness instead of laughter?

'I can't believe you did this—just when I'd made the extra bookings,' he told them, and they stared.

'Bookings?' The twins knew they were expected to respond but they didn't know how. They didn't know what the word meant.

'For accommodation,' he told them. 'Since you'd done such a fine job helping me with Cecil, and since he needs a lot of grooming at the show, I'd decided you needed to come with me. I've just booked hotel rooms for you and Erin, so all of us could come.'

Erin blinked. Had he?

He hadn't. He'd only just thought of it, she decided as she watched his face, but it was a great idea. The boys faces dropped to their boots, and their look of incredulous disappointment was stunning.

'You were going to take us?' Henry whispered and Matt nodded.

'Yep. But it's no use now. We have a filthy bull.'

Charlotte's jaw had dropped in disbelief. 'You didn't...'

'Hush, Charlotte,' Matt told her kindly. Bradley Moore, eh? Brad was a bachelor farmer living not five miles away. The man was horse mad, and had the brains of a peanut.

But he couldn't think of that now.

'I guess none of us can go, now,' Matt said.

Silence. Erin was looking stunned, as well she might. She couldn't think of a better punishment for the boys than this if she'd thought for a week. To miss out on something as brilliant as the Lassendale show...

She felt a stab of disappointment herself, and had to remind herself that he'd only made it up to punish the boys.

'What if we catch him again?' Henry asked. 'We could wash him.'

Matt glanced at his watch. It was four-thirty already.

'I have things to do,' he said. 'A lot if I'm to get to the show. I haven't even started feeding yet.'

'If he's in the mud all by himself then we could catch him.' William was right there with Henry, and their two active little minds were in overdrive. 'If you gave us the rope…'

'And we can wash him. We know how to.'

'We helped the first time, and now we can do it ourselves.'

Erin compressed her lips, trying not to smile. Now what? Had Matt backed himself into a corner?

But no. He rose to the occasion with fortitude.

'I don't have the time to do it myself,' he told them. 'But if Erin's willing to supervise and you're willing to try—'

'They'll never do it,' Charlotte snapped, but Matt simply raised his eyebrows and smiled.

'They can try. I don't want to miss out on showing Cecil unless I must. He's a champion but I won't get the highest stud fees for him unless he's shown.'

'Can we try?' The twins were turning to Erin, their eyes a mixture of hope and despair. They knew they couldn't do it without her help, and they needed her.

So what was new? Kids always needed Erin.

And she was a farmer's daughter. Supervising the cleaning of one docile bull should be a piece of cake.

'You really have booked us accommodation?' she asked suspiciously. If she did let the boys go to this effort, Matt couldn't let them down at the end of it.

'I really have,' Matt told her. His eyes met hers and held, and something intangible passed between them. Some assurance that wasn't all about accommodation.

There was a moment's pause.

Then…

'What are we waiting for?' Erin asked. 'Come on, boys. Let's go find us a bull.'

And four hours later, once again they had a fine looking bull. Cecil was brushed and groomed to within an inch of his life, and the three of them had never worked so hard to make him that way. He was some bull, Erin thought. To have put up with it all twice in one day…

He had, and the boys had worked themselves to the point of exhaustion to make him perfect. They'd stopped briefly for dinner—sandwiches eaten on the back step so they wouldn't have to clean up—and then gone straight back to work until they'd finished. They gave Cecil the final brush-strokes right on eight, just as Matt strolled in for final inspection.

He'd kept far away from them all evening, knowing that was what was right, but it had cost him some resolution to do so. Charlotte had gone home an hour or more back, and it had been an almost superhuman struggle to stop his feet making their way to the shed.

Now though, it was all worthwhile as he entered to find three beaming faces, proudly displaying what they'd done.

And Cecil was practically beaming, too. He looked magnificent!

'What do you think?' Erin asked, and he heard the note of anxiety behind her words. She still thought that maybe he couldn't keep his word. That he'd say the bull wasn't good enough or there was a problem with accommodation.

But Matt was a man who was owed a few favours. As soon as Charlotte had gone he'd made some phone calls, and everything was set. Except Charlotte's temper, he thought ruefully. She'd slammed off home in a vile mood, and he could see all sorts of problems looming ahead.

Erin had overstepped the mark with her threat, but then,

he knew that Charlotte had been perfectly capable of slapping the boys, and he also knew how urgent it had been to stop her. She didn't understand what he instinctively did—that a slap to kids who'd been kicked around in the past meant the undoing of all of Erin's work.

So, in Matt's eyes, Erin was forgiven. And who couldn't forgive her now? She was wet and mud-stained and there was a soap bubble in her tangled curls that he just wanted to reach out and...

'What do you think? she asked again, this time more urgently, and he practically had to slap himself to get his attention back where it was supposed to be.

Right. The bull. Cecil.

'I think our Cecil's never looked so good,' he told them, and he included the boys in his broadest smile. 'Well done, all of you.'

'Does that mean we can come to the show?' Henry demanded, and Matt nodded.

'Of course. I promised, didn't I?'

Yes, but they'd hardly believed him. William and Henry exchanged significant glances and Erin could tell Matt had gone up another notch in their estimation. Here was a grown-up who meant what he said, and there hadn't been too many of them in their lives. In their eyes Matt was reaching hero proportions.

And in Erin's?

Cecil was quietly munching from his feed-box, and Erin ran a hand down his glossy back, forcing herself to think of practicalities rather than thinking of Matt. It was hard, but necessary. Matt was engaged to Charlotte, she reminded herself bluntly and, even if he hadn't been, he was way out of her league. Even if her errant heart was starting to think otherwise.

It was just the way he smiled, she thought, and the way

he made her smile right back. His gentleness, and his intuitive knowledge of little boys...

Cut it out, she told herself harshly. There were still things that needed to be settled.

'I'll... I'll pay for us for the hotel accommodation,' she told him, but he shook his head.

'Nope. The boys worked hard for this. This is their payment.'

'But—'

He held up his hand. 'No buts. Just say thank you kindly, and go to bed.'

She grinned at that. 'Thank you kindly and go to bed,' she said, and the twins giggled.

It was a great sound. She looked down at their exhausted but happy faces, and she could have kissed the man who'd made this happen.

She darn near did—but she remembered all too well what had happened last time she'd tried something like that.

Once was enough.

Any more might be a disaster.

So at nine the next morning she was in the car, following the truck which was towing Cecil.

They had to go separately. The truck didn't fit five bodies and Erin's car wasn't strong enough to tow the trailer.

Charlotte's BMW could have done it, but Matt had enough sense not to suggest it. Charlotte was angry enough already, and to have the twins sitting on her gorgeous leather upholstery would be unthinkable. She hadn't suggested it herself, although he knew she didn't like travelling in his truck.

This way, though, she had Matt to herself and Erin was forced back into her place.

Behind her betters.

Which Erin didn't mind at all, she decided as she watched the trailer disappear around the first bend. They were moving fast. Let them go.

As the boys snoozed contentedly in the back, she turned the radio up and she sang along to schmaltzy songs at the top of her voice.

She was taking her boys to the Lassendale Show. They were happy, she was happy and not even Charlotte could spoil this one for her.

It was hard to say who was more impressed—Erin or the boys.

The show was an agricultural paradise. It lasted for two weeks. Matt had only come for the two days of Hereford judging and showing, but there were exhibitors there who'd camped the entire time.

As an exhibitor Matt had passes and he'd given one to Erin before he left. Therefore she parked her car easily enough, at the foot of the mountain that overlooked Lassendale, and then strolled with her two dumbstruck charges through the throng of people out to enjoy themselves.

Lassendale had started off a century before as a tiny country cattle show. Now, it was the biggest show in Australia, in the most gorgeous setting. The natural bushland had hardly been disturbed. Apart from the show ring and the cattle pavilions, the displays and side-shows were set up under clusters of spreading gums. Crowded or not, the place retained its natural beauty, and the sound of the distant sea could be heard whispering beneath the hubbub of the crowd.

Erin looked around her and felt a frisson of excitement building. It was gorgeous!

'We can afford to take our time,' she told the boys.

There were things here the boys would boggle at—amazing machinery, scary ghost rides and clowns where you poked ping pong balls into their mouths because 'every player wins a prize'.

Matt and Charlotte would already be here with Cecil, but they wouldn't need Erin or the twins. The judging was not for an hour. There were so many things to keep the boys entertained that she could take her time to find them.

But... 'We need to see Cecil straight away.' The boys were tugging her hands with urgency. 'What if Matt needs us to help? He might not get him looking beautiful in time. What if he lay down in the straw and messed his coat? And we want to see the judging. Erin, hurry.'

Erin grinned. They felt totally responsible for the bull, and she could only hope he didn't let them down when it came to judging time.

Not that it really mattered. If the judges didn't think Cecil was magnificent then the boys would simply decree him an idiot and do their own judging. In their eyes, Cecil was simply the best.

As was Matt, and Erin didn't take much persuading to turn her feet toward the cattle pavilion. Even if he was with Charlotte...

The boys were right. Cecil did look magnificent. Standing in his stall he seemed to have gained an aura of winner about him that hadn't existed at home.

'He's a born champion,' Matt told them as he stood back and admired his bull with pride. 'See how he holds his head? He never does that at home. He knows there are people looking at him, and it's all he can do not to preen.'

'Oh, for heaven's sake...' Charlotte had been jolted to bits in Matt's truck, she'd been stuck here for an hour while Matt groomed his precious bull and she wanted to be off to see the horses. But she couldn't go because Erin and the boys were coming, and some basic instinct told her she'd best stick around. But she didn't need to be gracious about it. 'The way you talk about him, you'd think he was intelligent!'

'You're saying my bull's not intelligent?' Matt teased her with his eyes but she didn't smile back. She wasn't in the mood for smiling.

'I know he's worth a fortune, but he's a bull, Matt.'

'Now you could put it much more diplomatically than that,' Erin told her, while the boys petted and fondled Cecil as if he was a very large and dopey dog rather than a pedigree bull. 'You could say you're sure he's almost as intelligent as his owner, and Matt would have to take it as a compliment.' Then, as Charlotte paused to work that one out, she scooped the boys back from the bull. 'Leave him be, boys. Matt has to take him through for judging now.'

'We want to watch.'

'It'll take an hour or so before we know the outcome,' Matt warned. 'The judges look at everything.'

'We'll wait,' Henry said firmly, and Matt and Erin exchanged looks. What harm could they get into? Matt's raised eyebrows asked, and Erin's imperceptible shake of her head told him she had the utmost faith in the boys to be on their best behaviour.

As they were.

No one was allowed near the cattle during judging. Only their owners stood by their side as the judges went over every inch of each beast.

Most family and friends took this time off to visit the fairgrounds—for something far more exciting than watching men watch cattle—but for all the interminable judging time the boys stood with bodies leaning over the fence that divided the public from the judging ring.

They were too far away to see what was happening, but it was as if they were willing Cecil to win, Erin thought as she watched their intent, silent faces. They watched and watched, as if part of themselves was being judged.

As indeed it was. They'd done the hard work. They'd paid their consequences, and when the blue ribbon was placed around Cecil's neck it was as much as Erin could do not to burst into tears at the look on their faces.

William did. He buried his face into Erin's breast and sobbed, while Henry just stood and stood, dumbstruck and silent.

'Well done, us,' Erin said in a voice that shook, gathering Henry into her as well as William. She found a tissue and mopped William's soggy face. 'Well done, all of us. And well done, Cecil.'

Then she looked up, and Matt was at the fence, leading Cecil away from the judges and beaming fit to bust. He'd seen them all. They'd been small figures in the distance, but he'd been so aware of them that the longing to win was no longer purely about what he could earn from his magnificent bull.

He knew how much the boys wanted this.

He'd wanted this ribbon for them—and for Erin.

He looked at her face, and he knew the trouble to get Cecil here—to get all of them here—had been worth it. She stood, her twins still tucked in beside her, and her eyes glowing with happiness. She was wearing Charlotte's sensible clothes—jeans and a checked shirt—and her normally unruly hair had been tied back in a sensible ponytail. She wore no make-up, but her face was lit with joy, and he wanted to hug her so badly...

Instead, he contented himself with hugging the twins,

grabbing them and swooping them over the fence, while Cecil looked on with placid bovine approval.

'This calls for a celebration,' he told them. He pushed a hand in his pocket and handed a note over to Erin. 'Here you go, cola and chips, fairy floss and a ride on the tunnel of death, courtesy of me.'

'Can we do that in reverse order?' Erin said faintly, thinking this through. 'Gee, Matt, thanks very much.'

'There's champagne for the grown-ups later,' he told her, and his smile was so warm she almost melted.

He was only being kind, she told herself sternly. Cut it out, Erin. Stop imagining things!

'We don't want to celebrate by ourselves,' Henry told him, casting a look for reassurance at his brother. 'Can you come with us?'

'I can't leave Cecil.' Matt's voice was sure, and Erin nodded. The farmers didn't leave their cattle. There were living facilities in the cattle pavilion. No one brought a bull as valuable as Cecil to a show and left him to the mercies of the general public. Even at the small shows around Bay Beach she'd learned that. No matter what they'd do tonight, Matt would be with his bull, sleeping on a camp stretcher beside him.

'Tell you what,' she told the twins. 'Why don't we go and buy a feast? A celebration feast. As much fairy floss, hot dogs, chips and fizzy drinks as we can find, and bring it back to share with Matt.'

Now it was Matt's turn to say, 'Gee, thanks,' and Erin's blue eyes danced.

'It'll be all our pleasure. Is there anything you'd like to add to our list?'

He thought about it. Fairy floss, huh. 'A beer would do nicely.' Before or after fairy floss? Good grief!

'Coming right up,' she sang, and they trooped away, leaving Matt and Cecil staring after them.

'She's quite a girl,' he told Cecil, and Cecil pushed his great head against Matt's chest, and nudged him sideways, as if reminding him of his duties.

He got the point. 'You're right. I have a woman. I'm an engaged man.' Matt shook his head as if dispelling a dream. He looked down at his bull and he grinned. 'Not like you. You can have thousands of them. In the human world we're restricted to one, and a very suitable one she is, too.'

Charlotte had gone to inspect the horses, and he badly wanted her here now, to see Cecil's ribbon and to share the moment.

Or maybe he didn't.

Maybe it was enough that Erin had seen it and was coming back to celebrate.

'Where are you going to sleep?'

It had turned into a party. The twins were working their way through mountains of junk food, Erin had had the forethought not to bring back one beer but a crate of two dozen, and half the cattle pavilion seemed to be crowded into Cecil's stall.

Not Charlotte, though. She was off doing her own thing.

Which was how it should be, Matt thought doubtfully as Henry questioned his sleeping arrangements. That was why he'd decided she'd be a suitable wife. She'd lead her own life and he'd lead his...

But it was sort of nice being surrounded by kids—and by Erin.

'Where are you sleeping?' Henry's small hand was in his, clutching him urgently as he repeated his question. 'Erin says we're staying in a hotel but you're not.'

'I'm staying here.'

'Where?'

His eyes met Erin's for a fleeting moment over Henry's head. She was laughing at something one of the cattlemen had said, but he knew by the sudden stillness of her body that she'd heard what was being said, and was gently mocking him. See if you can stay uninvolved, her body language said, and for the life of him he couldn't.

'Matt gets to sleep in the nice comfy straw with Cecil and all these great people and these wonderful animals,' she told Henry, making her voice mournful. 'While poor old us get to sleep between sheets in a really comfortable hotel.'

Silence while the twins took this on board. Then came the inevitable—'We want to sleep on the straw, too,' Henry said.

'Yes,' said William.

It would be sort of fun, Erin thought. Staying here with these down-to-earth farmers instead of going back to the hotel, putting the boys to sleep and then spending the evening with Charlotte.

No! Spending the evening alone!

'Matt's booked us into a really great hotel,' she told the kids. 'With a swimming pool.'

'It'd be better here. We don't want a swimming pool. Matt's river's better.'

'Yes, but we don't have sleeping bags—and I'll bet Matt's already paid a deposit for the hotel.' She was all with the kids on this one, but it wouldn't work. Even if their sleeping bags hadn't been burned in the fire, which they had, sleeping in the cattle pavilion—with Matt—was probably unwise. In more ways than one.

But bad news had a habit of travelling fast in country communities. Even though they were now a hundred miles from Bay Beach, most of the people in the pavilion knew exactly who Erin and her boys were. They were receiving sympathy from all sides, and they received more now.

'Bet your sleeping bags and stuff were burned in the fire,' the cattleman she'd been talking to growled, and when she nodded he chewed his bottom lip.

'There you go then, boys,' he said to the cattle shed in general. 'Kids and the lady want to stay here. We've been thinking of a way we could help and here it is.' He hauled his hat from his head and tossed a twenty dollar bill into it. 'Here's a start.' He passed the disreputable Akubra on to his neighbour.

'This is a whip round, and when we have enough my Bert'll go downtown and fetch what you need. Three full swags with our compliments. No arguments, girl. The hotel room Matt's booked will be snatched up by any of a score of people who need accommodation and who don't figure, like us, that the place we have here is fit for kings. And as for the swags... It'll be our pleasure to buy them for you.'

The generosity was immediate and almost overwhelming. It left Erin with nothing to say but thank you. Despite Erin's protestations, there was no resisting the wave of generosity passing through the shed, and the hat with the money disappeared out the door before she could see it.

Bert returned half an hour later, laden with swags—padded sleeping mats, sleeping bags, mosquito nets and pillows. Following him in was Charlotte, and, to Erin's surprise, she appeared delighted with the new sleeping arrangements.

'That's wonderful,' she told a bemused Matt, tucking a proprietorial arm through his. 'It means Erin can stay here and look after your beastly bull and you can stay at the hotel with me.'

There would now be a free room, Erin thought, and then thought, they're engaged, why would Matt even need a spare room? The thought, for some stupid reason, made her feel ill.

It didn't suit the twins, either. They'd been checking out the sleeping bags with whoops of delight, but now they paused, mid whoop.

'Matt's sleeping with us,' William said uncertainly and Henry stuck his thumb in his mouth in affirmation. The little boy looked up at Charlotte as if she was some slug-like creature who even his small boy's interest in slug-like creatures would still find repelling.

For once, Erin was in sympathy with his sentiments entirely.

But she couldn't admit it.

'Of course Matt can stay with Charlotte,' she made herself say. 'It makes sense.'

'Of course it makes sense,' Charlotte snapped, resentful that Erin felt she had any influence at all on Matt's sleeping arrangements.

But Matt had other ideas. He knew by now exactly what the twins were capable of. Not that they'd worry Cecil, he thought. He knew them well enough by now to accept that if he told them they were guarding Cecil then they'd do it as if their lives depended on it, but what else they might do…

No! Erin's job was to look after her twins, and his job was to look after Cecil. He couldn't ask her to do both.

'I'm sleeping here,' he told Charlotte and watched her face darken. Damn, now he had to feel guilty!

'Don't you trust me with your bull?' Erin teased, and he cast her an exasperated glance.

'You have enough on your hands.'

'I normally look after five kids,' she told him, and her

eyes were still teasing. Damn, they had the ability to mes-
merise a man. 'Two kids and a bull should be a piece of
cake.'

'Erin…'

'Darling, don't be stupid.' Charlotte's hand was still
resting on his arm and he had to fight back the urge to
shake it off. 'You know you can come.'

'Do you know how much this bull's worth?' he demanded, driving her against the ropes. If there was one
thing Charlotte understood it was money.

'But Matt…'

He didn't trust them completely, Erin thought, watching
the affianced couple, and who could blame him? If it was
her priceless bull, would she leave him with the twins?

Yes, but then she knew her twins!

'Look, let's compromise,' Erin suggested. Goodness,
here she went again. This was what being a House Mother
was all about—finding compromises before there was a
scene, and the cattlemen listening around them meant that
a scene would be quite spectacular.

'Matt, what if you take Charlotte out for dinner while
we care for Cecil? Then you can come back here to sleep.
I guess we'll probably be dead to the world by the time
you return, but we'll set up our bags right by Cecil and
we promise we won't leave him alone for a moment. He'll
be safe—won't he boys?'

'Yes,' said William, and Henry took his thumb from his
mouth long enough to say,

'Yes, if he really has to go out with *her*…'

'He really does. Don't you, Matt?'

And, with the eyes of the entire pavilion on him, what
was a man to do but agree?

CHAPTER EIGHT

As RESTAURANTS went, Charlotte would have rated this one as entirely satisfactory.

Show time was Lassendale's biggest two weeks of the year. The hotel Charlotte was staying in was five star, and the restaurant chefs had pulled out all the stops to impress a clientele which, for these two weeks, was international and wealthy. Therefore Matt—who'd packed a suit as he always did, for business meetings with those who were interested in what Cecil could provide—escorted Charlotte into the dim recesses of the dining room and he knew he was in for a gastronomical treat.

He wasn't disappointed. The waiter took one look at the sleek and svelte Charlotte and her handsome companion, and he ushered them to the best table, gave them the best service and they were treated to the best food Lassendale could offer.

Matt had an appetiser of some sort of tiny goat's cheese souffle. Entrée was ginger chilli prawns cooked to perfection, and then steak...

Steak!

Cecil.

Matt found his thoughts wandering right back to his bull—and to the people who'd be guarding him. All through appetiser and entrée he'd fought to keep his attention on Charlotte's small talk, but he could ignore the pull of his conscience no longer.

'Maybe we should give sweets a miss,' he told Charlotte tensely. 'I'm a bit unhappy about Cecil.'

He wasn't. He just…

He just didn't know, but it didn't seem right that Erin was back there and he was here.

'Oh, for heaven's sake!' Charlotte gave a soft laugh and put her hand over his. Curiously the motion made him flinch. It was all he could do not to pull away, and the sensation was starting to worry him. This was the woman he intended marrying, he told himself. To flinch was ridiculous.

He forced himself to return the pressure of her hand as she continued.

'Darling, Erin does come from solid farming stock. I remember she used to take her father's herd droving through the drought years when she was little more than a child herself. My parents were horrified, but I gather she coped very well.'

She had, too, Matt thought. Droving… He'd forgotten that.

Matt let Charlotte chatter on, but his thoughts flew elsewhere. In his late teens there'd been a drought which had left every farm in the district low on feed. Farms like Matt's and Charlotte's, where there'd been money to spare, had brought in food from interstate. But the Douglas family hadn't been in that position and Jack Douglas, bereft from the loss of his children's mother, simply didn't care.

That had been the end of Erin's formal schooling, he remembered. With seven siblings to feed and clothe, she couldn't afford to let the farm go under. Aged all of fifteen years old, she'd taken herself out of school and driven her cattle around the dusty district roads, letting them graze on any roadside where there'd been any growth at all.

It was a desperate measure to keep her breeding stock alive. Somehow she'd managed it, and managed it alone, though he still didn't know how.

And he remembered his mother's fury when she discovered his father had taken Erin a pile of hay to let her stay in the same place for a while.

'If the drought keeps up much longer we'll need it ourselves,' she'd hissed. 'You don't have to feel sorry for every destitute little tramp in the district...'

Destitute little tramp...

He looked into Charlotte's flushed face and he knew she'd felt exactly the same. Erin had been very much alone then, and she was very much alone now.

'I'll go back,' he said flatly, and the hand in his suddenly stilled.

'Matt, don't be stupid. I'd like sweets, and there's dancing afterwards.'

'But I have responsibilities.' And then he looked up as a man he recognised appeared in the entrance. Bradley Moore. Of course. Bradley always stayed in the finest establishment, and he was always looking for someone to talk with about his horses. Charlotte was just the woman. She even liked horses! He lifted an arm. 'Hi, Bradley. Over here!'

'Matt!'

'You like Bradley, don't you?'

To his amazement, Charlotte blushed from the tip of her manicured toenails to the roots of her sleekly chignoned hair. 'Yes, but...'

'There you go, then,' he said amiably. Why had he never seen how suited these two were? 'Bradley, I need to go back to my bull. Could you keep Charlotte entertained on my behalf?'

'Why...' Bradley, the sort of half-wit who couldn't decide whether to look like a Really Important Person or a half-baked kipper, looked stunned but incredulously delighted. 'Of course.'

'Of course.' Matt beamed. 'I'll leave you be, then. Will you come out and watch Cecil in the grand parade tomorrow, Charlotte?'

'I might,' she said peevishly. She was seriously annoyed. 'It depends on what Bradley's doing.'

'Right ho,' said Matt, with all the amiability in the world, and made his escape.

They hadn't missed him a bit. That much was clear the moment he walked into the cattle pavilion.

While he'd been wining and dining Charlotte, the cattlemen had set up a barbecue. The aroma of seared sausages and steak hit him the moment he entered the doors, and he thought fleeting of the grossly overpriced steak back at the hotel and wondered how much better it had been.

A hundred bucks better? he wondered, and he knew darned well it wasn't.

He'd missed out on sweets back at the hotel, but he needn't have worried. The moment he was sighted, he was handed a plate of pavlova.

'Get that into you, Matt McKay,' a cheerful young matron told him. 'You almost missed out. And then get into a set. Your family have been at it an hour or more, and if you don't join in soon they'll have danced their legs off without you.'

His family...

It was the strangest feeling, but that was exactly how it felt. He stood on the sidelines absently spooning in pavlova—which was a shame because the crisp meringue and the gorgeous sun-ripened strawberries deserved all his attention—and he watched his 'family' dance.

'Swing your partners, round we go.'

The square dancing was at a frantic pace. One of the

cattlemen had produced a fiddle, another a mouth organ, and the centre of the pavilion had been cleared for the dancers. Now it was a mass of whirling, laughing, cattlemen and women, teenagers, kids and even the odd dog.

And Erin and her twins were in the middle of everything. They were part of a set, the twins were obeying the caller's instructions as if their lives depended on it, and Erin...

Erin was being swung from one appreciative cattleman to another. And what she was wearing...

It was the new dress she'd bought in town with Shanni and it was gorgeous! All the colours of the rainbow, with a full circle skirt that flew out like a whirling, flaming hoop around her, it was a dress that had to be seen to be believed. Her hair was flying free, her gorgeous blue eyes were sparkling with laughter and her face was flushed with exertion.

She looked so desirable that it almost killed Matt to stay on the sidelines and eat his pavlova. But to join the set you needed a partner, and there were no spare women. Except...

Except the pavlova lady who'd just handed over her last piece of pavlova. With a whoop of triumph, Matt cast off his coat and tie, seized the unsuspecting lady and whirled her onto the dance floor before she had time to object.

Now it was just a matter of working his way up the line to Erin...

'Hey, William, Matt's here!' Henry was doing his darnedest to whirl around a very fat lady of advancing years—and not doing such a bad job of it either. The lady was whirling as required, though Henry, trying valiantly to clutch her around the waist, merely had an armful of thigh, and her breast was threatening to crush him at any moment.

William was doing better. He was paired at the moment with a young lady not much older—or bigger—than he was, but the responsibility of the occasion didn't give him time to respond. There was a twirly bit coming up and he had to get it right....

But Erin had heard.

'Matt!' She was flying past him as she threaded in and out of the dancers. Darn! Matt hadn't realised this wasn't a 'change your partners' set. She was threading and so was a stud of a cattleman who he didn't recognise but disliked on sight. 'What have you done with Charlotte?' she called, and he dredged up a smile.

'Left her with Bradley.'

Her eyebrows hit the roof. She gave that delicious chuckle and then someone else swung her away, she flew back to the arms of her cattleman and she was lost to him.

There was no more contact then for about five minutes, until it was time for Matt and his partner to take their turn threading to the lead. Then, as he whirled Erin around to change to the other side of the set, she laughed up into his face.

'You must have the utmost faith in her,' she teased, and he glowered.

'Why wouldn't I?'

'With your bank balance?' Still she was laughing. 'No, indeed.'

And then Erin was gone, leaving him to glower some more and then regain his composure as he joined his partner again and found she was looking up at him in mute enquiry.

She really was bouncy and pretty herself, he told himself. The twins were having the time of their lives and the whole pavilion was having fun. Even the cattle were watching with bovine approval.

There was no earthly reason—or even a logical one—for a man to sulk just because Erin was dancing with someone else. He gave himself a huge mental shrug and decided to have fun.

Which he did.

They danced on. The music went on into the night. The twins decided it was more fun whooping around the cattle stalls with other kids than being squeezed from bosom to bosom. The cattlemen ended up with their wives or lovers. And Matt…

Matt finally ended up with Erin. They danced on. The music slowed, and maybe he should have stopped, but Erin felt sort of nice, with her hands in his, then sort of closer, her breasts against his chest, his mouth nuzzling her soft curls, the scent of some faint perfume drifting upward and making him feel…

That was enough of that! Enough! This was tantalising, unwise, unplanned, thoughtless, and hopeless.

The music stopped as the musicians finally ran out of puff, and Erin and Matt were left looking at each other in the middle of the dance floor-cum-cattle shed. They were still holding each other. Still sort of feeling…

They had twins!

As the music stopped, the kids in the pavilion returned reluctantly to their respective parents. Most were heading off with one or both parents to a hotel, but a few were camping with the cattle tenders, as Matt and Erin were.

'It's time to go to bed,' William announced importantly for what must surely be the first time in his life he had ever asked voluntarily to go to bed. He was head-butting Erin's thigh to get her attention. Totally unaware of the currents of sexual awareness between the two adults, he was onto the next thing on the twins' agenda. Which was sleeping in the straw.

'We need to set up our beds,' Henry told them, and reluctantly, Erin's hands were released and the twins were included in between them. There was a sandwich of adults with kid filling, and the frisson of warmth and linkage remained the same. It felt so right!

'So we do,' Matt said, but his eyes were still on Erin. There were matters here that were unresolved.

And that had to remain unresolved, he thought fiercely, forcing himself to remember Charlotte back at the hotel and all the logical reasons why he'd decided to marry her. Charlotte was a sensible choice, he told himself harshly. Good grief! If he married because of a spur-of-the-moment attraction, he could have married fifteen years ago, and where would he be now? Burdened with school fees, chaos, change to his mother's lovely, ordered house...

Marry with your head, not your heart, his mother had said over and over, until it had become almost a mantra.

There was more of his mother in him than he thought, he decided ruefully. Fifty-fifty gene split? Yeah, there he had it. He was half his father who loved the farm and didn't mind a little chaos occasionally, and half his mother who liked order and beauty and...

'Hey, Matt, we're just organising somewhere to sleep.' Erin's voice was chiding him gently, and her blue eyes were full of laughter. She could see exactly what he was thinking! Damn her!

'Do you think we'll all fit in with Cecil?' William was asking anxiously, and somehow Matt tore his mind from where it definitely wanted to go and forced himself to think of sleeping arrangements.

And there were dangers there, too.

'Of course we'll fit,' Erin said soundly. 'We just have to persuade Cecil to move to the back of his stall.'

Hmm. Easier said than done.

The stalls weren't huge, but they were all the space allocated to them which was why at most, one or two people were bedding down beside each animal. If Cecil lay widthways at the back of the stall the thing was possible, but if he'd done that his rear would be against one wooden division and his nose would be pressed against the other. Cecil was nothing if not large!

So Cecil, being the sensible animal he was, was lying full length on the hay, his nose poking out onto the walkway so he could gaze his fill at the dancers. He was one sleepy bovine, and he looked as if his intentions to shift were at about nil.

'I suppose if we all shoved,' Erin said doubtfully and Matt grimaced.

'Yep. You and a two-ton crane might do it.'

Which left two strips of hay three feet wide on either side of Cecil, stretching back the eight feet or so to the rear of the stall.

'We can take a twin each and sleep on either side,' Matt said slowly. But it wasn't the arrangement his gut wanted—and he might have known it didn't suit the twins either.

'We want to sleep together.' Of course.

'You will be sleeping together,' Matt told them without much hope of being heard. 'Except instead of a pillow between you there'll be Cecil.'

'We can't share Tigger. And Cecil's as big as a mountain.' Henry put a finger on his nose. 'See? He's up to here.'

Erin choked, and Matt frowned her down. Didn't the woman realise there was no alternative?

Apparently she didn't.

'Of course you must sleep together,' she told them. 'You can't cut Tigger in half. So, into the bathroom, into your pyjamas and then into these wonderful sleeping bags. Now!' It was her command voice and the boys responded accordingly.

'Okay.' They hesitated just long enough for William to ask; 'But where will you sleep?'

'Matt and I will top and tail on the other side, of course,' she said—as if the matter had never been in doubt.

'Top and tail?' Matt was frowning and she grinned.

'Easy to see you haven't slept in a family with eight children,' she told him. 'You fit two in a bed this way, and it minimises fights. It doesn't stop them entirely—' another grin '—but I'm sure we can fight quietly. You sleep with your head near Cecil's head and I sleep with my head near Cecil's butt. We'll be cosy as two bugs in a rug. The only thing is…' She looked down at her toes and grimaced.

'Yes?' he said resignedly. This woman was nuts. Nice, but definitely nuts!

'After all that dancing and carting cattle around all day, maybe you'd better not take your boots off, Mr McKay. If there's one thing I can't bear sleeping with, it's a man with stinking socks!'

Matt's socks weren't the problem.

There wasn't room for Matt's camp bed or Erin's blow-up mattress—not both—but the hay was thick and fresh. Matt hauled his sleeping bag up to his chin, tossed his pillow beside Cecil's head and lay down. Erin did the same, lying in reverse, but nobly Matt had left her the side against the wood partition.

On the other side of Cecil, the twins snuggled in with plenty of room. Their noses barely reached Cecil's neck, and their toes didn't reach his rear end. Once assured Erin and Matt were settled for the night right on the other side of Cecil, they closed their eyes on their shared pillow, snuggled Tigger and were out for the count. Two exhausted but perfectly content children.

As Erin was content. Matt's legs were distracting, and she was absurdly aware of the presence of his body so close to her, but this was a way of sleeping she'd been brought up with. She could cope.

'Erin?' It was a hoarse whisper and Matt's toes nudged her shoulder to gain her attention. He had it!

'Yep?' She had to whisper back. The entire pavilion was settled to sleep now, and the lights had been turned low. Cattle and cattle carers alike were purposefully sleeping.

Not Matt. 'Erin, Cecil's chewing.'

She choked on a bubble of laughter. 'He's what?'

'He's chewing.'

She thought about that, and nodded into the dimness. 'I wouldn't worry. Cattle do.'

'Not right in my ear, they don't.'

'Take away his feed, then.' Honestly!

'He's not chewing his feed,' Matt told her, and there was a trace of desperation in his whisper. 'At a guess, he's chewing yesterday's feed, or even…' His toes nudged her shoulder again as if to emphasise the awfulness of it. 'By the smell of it, even the day before's!'

'Are you saying,' Erin asked, trying not to laugh out loud, 'that your champion bull has halitosis?'

'If halitosis means breath that stinks like rancid garlic, then yes,' Matt told her, forgetting to whisper and being shushed from about six different stalls for his pains. 'That's exactly what I'm saying. And he keeps trying to lick my face.'

'He loves you.'

'Oh, right.'

'You want to swap sides so I'm against Cecil?'

'All that means is that he'll lean over your feet to lick my face.'

'So…'

'So I'm shifting!' Matt was nothing if not a man of decision, and some decisions were easy. Cecil or Erin? Erin won every time. He rose, sleeping bag and all, hopped until his feet were with Erin's and then flopped down again onto the straw.

Which meant that now his face was level with Cecil's tail. And Erin's nose.

There was no room for two pillows. They had to share.

Uh, oh… Maybe this hadn't been such a good idea after all.

The intimacy which had been building during the night had dispersed a little while putting the twins to bed and settling themselves. Now however it slammed back like a lightning bolt. Unconsciously Erin found herself hauling her sleeping bag zipper higher, right to her chin. As if that could protect her from what she was feeling…

'Hey, I'm not into seduction mode here,' Matt told her, seeing her movement and trying to make light of it. 'It's just if I have a choice of being kissed by you or by Cecil…'

Being kissed?

He'd meant to say licked!

No. That wasn't right either. Hell, his whole body was going rigid with the strain of having her so close.

'You prefer me to Cecil?' Like Matt, Erin was trying desperately to keep things light. She chuckled and rolled over to face him—which was another mistake as she hadn't realised how close he was. His nose was inches from hers. Major mistake!

'You…' Her voice cracked and it was only after a couple of desperate swallows that she made it work again. 'You mean it? Matt, it's the very sweetest thing to say, but I'm very sure you don't mean it. One of the guys I was dancing with tonight told me what Cecil is worth. That'd make ten of me and then some.'

Maybe.

'But only one of Charlotte,' she teased gently. 'She's a lady who knows her worth.'

'She is...special,' Matt said grudgingly and tried like crazy to conjure up Charlotte's image. The image refused to be conjured. All he could see was a smattering of freckles, one pert nose and gorgeous, laughing eyes. And lips that were so soft...

Hell!

'She's a lucky lady, too,' Erin whispered warmly into the dark, seemingly unaware of the sensations he was feeling. 'To be marrying you. You're one fantastic guy, Matt McKay. To have given the twins today... It was just great.'

'And it'll stay great as long as Cecil doesn't roll over and squash the pair of them.'

He must stop looking at her lips. He must!

'As if he would,' Erin said indignantly. 'As well as expensive, he's also intelligent.'

'He is at that.'

And it was the truth. Matt's pride in his bull was almost overwhelming. Cecil was the result of years and years of careful planning and selective breeding. Up until now, he'd been Matt's pride and joy. He still was! But up until now, Cecil was the first thing he thought of when he woke in the morning, and his last thought as he slept at night.

And if he'd had to choose between Cecil and Charlotte, the choice would be obvious and absolute.

Cecil or Erin, though....

No! This was ridiculous. He liked a simple and ordered existence, he thought desperately. He wanted an existence where he farmed and Charlotte kept the house and his social life nicely ordered.

That was how he'd been raised, with his mother and father living together but in separate worlds, and that was the way he believed the world worked. As it would continue to work.

Except…there was this woman right before his nose!

But this woman came with complications, and they weren't just minor hiccups. They were major. She came with a pair of troubled twins, and he just knew wherever Erin went it wouldn't be just the twins that'd follow.

Get involved with Erin Douglas and he knew there'd be more kids, his and others, every lame duck in the district, every hard luck story…

And the boundaries between house and farm would cease to exist. He knew it. There'd be a riot of kids and dogs inside and out, and Erin herself wouldn't know her place. She'd be out heaving hay or grooming cows or…or somewhere he couldn't get away from her.

Like now. He was trapped two inches from her cute nose, and hell, all he wanted to do was kiss her.

'Would you stop looking at me like a rabbit caught in a floodlight?' she said suddenly, and there was no way he could escape the gentle mockery in her tone. Could she really know what he was thinking?

Apparently, yes. 'Matt McKay, you are very, very cute, but you are an engaged person and I am not the least bit interested. I take the lust I'm looking at in your eyes right now as a compliment, I am exceedingly grateful for all you've done for me and the twins but I want nothing more from you than enough space to go to sleep. So you can stop looking at me like I'm going to lunge at your body any minute and you can go to sleep. Now!'

'Hey, I'm not expecting anything!'

'And neither am I,' she said firmly. 'So there's nothing to stop either of us from sleeping.' And without another word she rolled over and put her face to the wall.

He rolled over, too, which left his nose pressed against Cecil's butt. The comparison to what he'd just been looking at was ridiculous.

And her butt was against his. There was simply no room for it not to be.

Sleep? Ha! All he could feel was her. All he could think of was her. She was so…

So right out of his league! In every single way he could think of.

As for Erin? She'd said she was going to sleep, but it wasn't quite that easy. He was too darned close. Too darned male.

Too…too everything!

'I am not interested in Matt McKay,' she told herself fiercely. Not. Not. Not!

But he was the most gorgeous male she'd ever slept with in her life! That wasn't saying much, she thought ruefully. Erin had always been so involved with her kids that men usually ran a mile, sensing that commitment with Erin meant commitment to a whole lot more.

But Matt was certainly gorgeous.

And he was so darned nice! He was so nice that she wanted to turn right over and…

'That's enough of that,' she whispered into the dark. 'Go to sleep!'

CHAPTER NINE

ERIN slept late. Late, that is, in cattle terms. It must have been three a.m. or later before she'd finally fallen into an uneasy slumber, she was dog tired and she was accustomed to noise. So maybe it wasn't surprising that when she finally woke, the rest of the cattle pavilion was bustling.

As were Matt and the twins. Erin rolled sleepily over and found herself looking at ten legs. Four belonged to Cecil who was standing looking regally around as his minions worked over him. Four belonged to the twins, who, armed with a brush apiece, were intent on making Cecil look even more regal.

And two belonged to Matt.

'Well, well. Sleepy-head's finally decided to grace us with her consciousness. Good morning, Miss Douglas.'

'Good…good morning.' She brushed the sleep from her eyes and sat up, then gasped and hauled her sleeping bag up to her neck. She must have pulled the zipper down in her sleep, and her nightdress wasn't exactly decent…

'Have a coat,' Matt said, and tossed a waterproof down to her, though by the glint in his eyes she knew he'd seen—and approved of what he'd seen. 'Bathroom's thataway, lady, but you'd better scuttle or you'll miss breakfast.'

'Breakfast?' She was still befuddled by sleep and totally bewildered.

'Pancakes at two o'clock,' he told her, doing a sweeping circle of the pavilion until he was pointing to a barbecue at the far end. 'Courtesy of the Country Women's

149

Association. But the dress code's a bit rigid. Nightgowns with unfastened buttons don't reach their standards.'

She gasped. Enough!

She clutched his waterproof to her while awkwardly escaping from her sleeping bag, then bolted, tinglingly aware that his eyes stayed on her until the door closed behind her.

It was a silly, happy, busy couple of hours before the Grand Parade.

Breakfast was delicious—steak and sausages for those with strong constitutions, but pancakes and honey for those with a bit more finesse. 'Which is me,' Erin declared, watching Matt chomp into his beef. 'And in front of Cecil, too. Honestly, Matt, have you no sensitivity?'

'If you think for one minute that Cecil will end up as beef steak…'

'His cousins might.'

'They'd have to be pretty inferior cousins.'

'I don't care. I'm sticking to pancakes. What about you, boys?' And although the twins desperately wanted to be like Matt, honesty prevailed and pancakes won the day.

'Weaklings,' Matt declared but the boys looked up into his twinkling eyes and knew he was kidding them.

Honestly, Erin thought. For a man to get away with calling the twins weaklings—and for the twins to love it…

She could seriously fall for this man—if he wasn't already spoken for. Or if he wasn't rich. Or… If a million other things that weren't going to happen!

Breakfast finished, the whole pavilion settled down to the serious business of making their animal the most magnificent. The animals left here now were all winners, but none looked as great as Cecil, Erin thought, but she knew she was biased. The four of them worked as a team, going way past the necessary preparations for a bull who'd already won champion of his class.

'Do you think I should tie a big blue bow around his ears?' she asked as she stood back and admired their handiwork. 'And maybe a matching one on his tail?'

'Over my dead body.' Matt stood beside her and grinned. 'I'll have you know my bull's a he-man and I want him to stay that way. His testosterone level would plummet at the first bow.'

'And that would never do,' she said mockingly. 'A McKay male with suspect testosterone...'

'We try to keep it above the run of the herd,' Matt said smugly.

'Brains or balls.' Erin nodded sagely as she gazed at Cecil's amazing appendages. 'Yep, I can see the choice has been made here.' Then, as Matt drew in his breath, she took a wise step away from him. 'Come on, twins,' she said, choking back laughter at the expression on Matt's face. 'There's no way you can get Cecil more beautiful than he is right now. It's time for Matt to take him out.'

'Wait a bit.' Matt had control of himself now—almost— and he was thinking. He was enjoying himself enormously, he thought, and the realisation was hitting home that his enjoyment was coming to an end.

It shouldn't be. The Grand Parade here was the ultimate achievement. Already he'd had a steady stream of potential customers, national and international, pass by Cecil's stall and assess for themselves his stud potential. In the parade, they'd be watching from the stands, making their final decision on which stud farm to choose.

Cecil moved magnificently. In the stalls he looked great, but out in the open he swayed with a majesty that had to be seen to be believed. For potential customers interested in Herefords there was now no choice, Matt knew, and he also knew his income for the next twelve months would skyrocket.

So, for Matt, the parade was the culmination of years of hard work. This was what he, his father and his grandfather had spent years achieving.

Why then, did he feel reluctant to take the rope attached to Cecil's halter and tug the giant beast toward the parade ring?

Because this year showing Cecil and winning first prize wasn't the highlight, he thought suddenly. It was working side by side with others; with this funny, warm and lovely woman and her two troubled charges.

This was pure novelty factor, he thought harshly, trying to bring himself back down to earth. He had no intention of working side by side with a woman. He worked alone. That was the way he'd been brought up. It was the order of things, now and forever...

'Matt! Oh, darling, he's wonderful!'

It was almost a relief to look up and see Charlotte bearing down on them—a Charlotte refreshed by a good night's sleep in the hotel, and wearing her signature apparel of white on white. White slacks. White linen blouse with collar that just stood up the right amount. A white on white silk scarf, casually knotted. The very epitome of casual elegance in a wealthy farmer's wife.

She didn't have straw sticking out of her hair like Erin did. She hadn't stepped in a cow pat in her only pair of shoes, forcing her to wear borrowed gum boots three sizes too big—as Erin had.

She was a much more suitable woman, Matt told himself.

The trouble was, she might be more suitable, but she wasn't nearly as much fun.

Life wasn't fun, he told himself. Hadn't his parents

taught him anything? Work wasn't fun. Fun was something you had intermittently with your mates, when the women weren't around. Fun was…

Hell, he didn't know what fun was any more.

Wasn't fun what they'd had this morning?

'He's a fine-looking beast.' With a jolt, Matt hauled himself out of his strange line of thought and realised Charlotte wasn't alone. Bradley was right behind her, his portentous tones echoing through the pavilion. 'I hope you don't mind me escorting Charlotte back here?'

Yep, the weed still remembered the drubbing Matt had given him at school when he'd paraded his self-importance from age ten, and he wasn't risking anything here.

'But when I found Charlotte had no one to drive her…'

'You brought her from the hotel. Very kind.' Matt was suddenly feeling almost overwhelmingly claustrophobic. 'I'm sorry, Charlotte. I have to go. Cecil's required in the ring. Bradley, could you look after Charlotte for me?'

'Creighton Bow is also required in the ring,' Bradley said stiffly. 'The horses come in straight after cattle. My lads are grooming him for me now.'

'Creighton Bow.' Oh, right. Bradley's wonderful horse. 'Um…right. Did he win, then?'

'He gained a second placing. I felt the judging overlooked—'

'I'll look out for him,' Matt said hastily. 'Well done.' But inside he was cringing in repugnance. To let his lads groom what he knew was a magnificent stallion, without even supervision… To stay the night in the hotel while his precious bloodstock was here… The claustrophobia was rising by the minute.

'I need to go.'

But then there were two urgent little hands tugging his

shirt. 'Can we come, too? Please, Matt? Can we come, too?'

Matt hesitated—and was lost. A thought hit him, and it was as if a thunderbolt had crashed into his solar plexus. Good grief!

'Matt, please...'

Why not?

He'd seen this happen. Livestock had been led into the ring by youngsters before, and he'd always thought, how the hell could you put all that work into breeding and preparing an animal and then let someone else show it?

It was like Bradley letting someone else groom his horse.

But it wasn't like that, he realised suddenly. Bradley let someone else do the hard work and then would take the glory himself. He'd lead Creighton Bow into the ring. Matt looked down into the two desperately eager little faces and he knew that if he let his bolt of lightning idea have its way he'd have two levels of pride. Not one.

He'd never seen it before, but there it was. All those years of watching kids...

His father would never have dreamed of such a thing, he thought, and if he did his mother wouldn't have allowed it.

But he wasn't his father, and the idea was like slicing the past from the future. He cast an uncertain glance at Erin, unsure how she'd react, but there was no chance of taking her aside and sounding his idea out.

She looked ridiculous, he thought. She looked unkempt, frazzled, over-booted and underdressed beside Charlotte's perfect dress code, but his lips twitched at the sight of her and it was only with difficulty that he turned his attention back to the twins.

They were waiting to be turned down. He could see by

their eyes that they'd asked to come, too, but they were accustomed to knock-backs. As Erin was accustomed to knock-backs on their behalf.

'I have a proposition,' he said, and they stared in incomprehension.

'A...a propos...'

'An idea. If you're willing.'

'What's your idea?' They were all looking at him. Charlotte and Bradley. William and Henry.

And Erin.

Mostly Erin. Or maybe it was mostly Erin he was aware of.

'You've seen how quiet Cecil is?' He was talking more to Erin than the twins, aware it was she he had to convince rather than them.

'Yes.'

'Then if I take him to the entrance and get him into position in the parade, would Erin allow you to take him around the arena for me?'

There was an audible intake of breath from every last one of them—including from Matthew himself. Was he mad? Trusting his precious bull to two urchins?

But he looked down into their incredulous faces and he knew that he had nothing to fear at all. Cecil would be as safe as houses. They considered him theirs, and he was as precious to the boys now as their Tigger.

Heaven help anyone or anything that threatened their Cecil!

Bradley was the first to find his voice. Of course.

'You'd trust your beast to these...' He paused, stuck for words, and then found what he was looking for. 'These brats?'

'They're not brats,' Matt said evenly. 'They're my right hand men, and I'd rather trust my bull to these two than to hired hands—as you have your precious horse.' It was impossible to keep the disdain from Matt's voice. Bradley might come from a family who bred champion steeple-chasers, but you'd never catch Bradley doing anything as menial as grooming.

And as for calling his kids brats!

Erin's kids, he reminded himself hastily. Not his. Erin's.

'Matt, you're not serious.' It was Charlotte, putting in her two-bob's worth, but Matt's eyes were on Erin.

'Erin? Is it okay with you?'

Erin thought about it for a whole two seconds flat. For her precious twins, to be given such a trust at the focal point of the most prestigious show in the country....

She met Matt's look head on, and the eyes looking back at him were bright with tears.

'Of course it is,' she managed. 'If you want to, boys.'

'If we want to?' The twins could scarcely breathe for the enormity of what they were being asked. 'You mean....lead him around the ring...all by ourselves?'

'All by yourselves,' Matt said solemnly, still watching the wave of emotion washing over Erin's face. 'If I didn't think you were capable I wouldn't ask it of you. I'll be standing at the pavilion doors, waiting for you to bring him back, but once he's out in the arena he's all yours.'

Charlotte was not impressed! In fact, Charlotte was about as seriously annoyed as Erin had ever seen her.

Bradley had disappeared to take charge of his horse—his lads had done the work but there was no way *he* intended handing over the glory to anyone else. Matt and the twins took themselves off to place Cecil in his parade order, and Erin and Charlotte were left together, to do whatever they wished.

Charlotte didn't wish.

'If I hadn't come in Matt's blasted truck I'd go home now,' she muttered as the last of the menfolk disappeared from view. 'I only wanted to see Matt in the grand parade.'

She did, too, Erin thought as she followed her through the door to the stadium. Matt was a man who stood out in any crowd, and to sit in the stadium and casually let all around her know that there was her fiancé… Well, for Charlotte it was the culmination of twenty years of effort.

Instead of which, she had to content herself with two seven-year-olds leading the bull of her fiancé—and it hardly had the same impact to say; 'Those children are leading my fiancé's bull!'

'I guess you can always watch Bradley,' Erin told her, determined to be good-humoured with the woman. She was feeling so cheerful herself she felt like doing a little jig on the spot. For her twins to be given such responsibility… She tucked her arm into Charlotte's and refused to withdraw it even as Charlotte tugged sharply away.

Maybe she had to be even nicer. 'Hey, Charlotte, I'm sorry for saying what I threatened about your poetry,' she told her. 'You know I'd never really tell anyone—and, in truth, Shanni burned them.'

'We were only teenagers,' Charlotte said, displeased to the core. As well as having to put up with the absence of Matt in the parade, she also had to put up with this disreputable member of the lower orders acting as if she was her friend. Her friend!

Charlotte plumped herself down on a seat and huffed. Not put off in the least, Erin plumped beside her. 'It was just childish stupidity. I'd forgotten all about it,' Charlotte added.

'Bradley hasn't,' Erin told her thoughtfully. 'You must know that. He's always thought you were the ant's pants.'

'There's no need to be coarse!'

'Why have you always refused to go out with him?' Erin said curiously, and got an angry glance for her pains. When Erin still looked an enquiry, Charlotte thrust out her diamond-adorned ring finger, as if that explained all.

'Because Matt and I—'

'Not at fifteen,' Erin told her flatly. 'Or even at twenty-three. If I remember rightly, Matt didn't go out with any-one until he was seventeen, and then it was with Sally McKinley.'

'How on earth do you remember that?'

'I was three years younger than you and Matt,' Erin told her simply. Her eyes twinkled. 'Come to think of it, I still am. But then…well, Matt was school captain and a hunk even then, so whatever he did was the cause of major school gossip. He and Sally—'

'I don't want to hear.'

'No.' Erin chuckled her agreement. She paused, scanning the cattle starting to emerge from the pavilion, but there was still no sign of Cecil and the twins. More to keep her mind off what the twins might or might not be doing, she kept right on probing. 'But I seem to remember that Bradley was good-looking, too. Why would you never go out with him?'

Silence while they both thought back, remembering.

It had been no secret that Bradley had been keen on Charlotte. The poetry had been part of years of secret notes, and Bradley's despair, inexpertly disguised and pounced on with glee by his peers and by those younger than him.

Bradley, in his teens, was a spoiled brat and, as far as the rest of the students were concerned, his passion for Charlotte made him fair game. Especially the impover-ished and scorned younger set to which Erin belonged.

More silence.

Normally Charlotte would simply ignore a question such as Erin had just posed. Normally she would just ignore Erin.

But things weren't normal today. Charlotte's social set weren't here— 'Really, darling, cattle shows, you know. Not our scene!' Her two men were both out of reach and Charlotte had to either sit alone in the stands or pretend to talk politely to Erin.

She could do it. Erin had been grooming bulls for hours, both Cecil and others. She looked like a farm hand—someone the elegant Charlotte would employ. So she could spread her finger so the morning sun just glinted on her diamond, and give the impression that her purpose here was to discuss cattle quality with the staff.

And she was feeling so grumpy with Matt, she might as well tell all...

'I could have had both of them,' she confided, and Erin's eyebrows rose. Respectfully. She was playing along for all she was worth here. She could have been a peasant, shocked to the core by the goings-on of aristocracy, and Charlotte's carefully controlled trill of laughter through the stands meant Erin's ploy was working.

'Oh, not both at once,' she continued. 'But yes, Bradley was certainly keen. He's still keen now. He's asked me to marry him—oh, I've lost count of the times.'

'So why not accept? Why pick on... I mean, why did you choose Matt?' Erin asked respectfully, and once again, Charlotte laughed.

'Are you kidding? There's no choice. Matt's family have had their land forever. His grandfather even had a title!'

Charlotte gave Erin her aristocrat to low life look, meaning with her level of intelligence Erin couldn't possibly understand, but Erin did. There were still people to whom the phrase 'old money' meant something, and Charlotte was certainly one of them.

She chose her words carefully. 'So otherwise, you didn't really mind which one you chose?'

'Of course I did.' Charlotte simpered and waggled her diamond bearing finger some more. 'I'm engaged to Matt, aren't I?'

'Of course.'

'And...'

But Erin was no longer listening.

The twins had emerged from the pavilion doors. They were leading Cecil, and Erin was effectively silenced.

So was Charlotte. She puckered her lips in distaste as the twins proudly and solemnly led their charge around the ring. Erin knew that all Charlotte could think of was, why wasn't Matt leading them?

And Erin was thinking of Matt, too, but in a totally different way. Her gaze never left the faces of her two little boys, and all she could feel was gratitude.

She was so grateful she felt like weeping. Damn, she was weeping!

Below her was the purest of pure bloodstock, being led by the cream of the nation's farmers—and in their midst were her two abandoned and unwanted little boys.

They were all she could see, and she could only see them through a mist of tears. They were totally unsmiling, and solemn as judges—every sliver of concentration bent on leading their charge around the arena with the dignity he deserved.

What a gift!

Erin sat absolutely motionless, with every fibre of her being willing nothing to go wrong. Nothing did, and when the boys had taken Cecil twice around the arena and Matt had come forward to help them tug him back through the great pavilion doors, Erin reached for her handkerchief and blew her nose. Hard.

Charlotte shifted sideways in distaste, but Erin couldn't give a toss.

'Well…' Somehow she managed to find her voice. She rose, and the smile she gave Charlotte was tremulous. 'That's it, then. Are you coming to congratulate them?'

'What, congratulate the twins? You have to be kidding!'

'I meant all of them,' Erin said carefully. 'Matt, too.'

But Charlotte was fed up with a Matthew she hadn't been able to boast about. 'Bradley's not out yet,' she said shortly. 'I'll stay and watch the horses. At least Bradley has the sense to lead his own beast out.'

Sense?

Maybe. It wasn't 'sensible' for Matt to let the twins lead Cecil, Erin thought.

It wasn't sensible in the least.

It was just plain wonderful!

It was a subdued set of twins Erin took back to the farm, and it was a very quiet time Erin had of it for the next few days. It was as if they needed time to absorb what had happened to them. They simply couldn't believe it.

The Grand Parade had been televised. Expecting Matt and Cecil to be in it, Shanni had had the forethought to videotape the program. She and Wendy brought the tape out to the farm and the twins watched themselves on television over and over again.

'It's a miracle,' Wendy said frankly, watching the pair of them. Usually unable to sit still for more than two minutes at a time, the twins had been still for more than half an hour, and Shanni was growing more and more incredulous. 'How on earth have you done it?'

'I haven't done anything,' Erin said, a trace of trouble in her voice which her friends could hardly miss. 'It's Matt who's transformed them. They follow him like two little shadows.'

'And that's a problem?'

'I think it may be.'

'Why?' Wendy probed gently. 'Maybe Matt's just what they need.'

'But it's a temporary arrangement.' Erin shook her head and watched the children for a bit longer. 'I just…worry, I guess. At what will happen when they're moved on, yet again.'

'And how about you?'

'I'm sorry?'

'How about you, Erin Douglas?' Wendy hadn't been Erin's friend for years without being able to read her face like a book, and she didn't like what she was reading now. 'How heart-whole and fancy-free are you? When it's time to move on—will you be able to walk away without a backward glance?'

It was two weeks before Charlotte dropped her bombshell, and those two weeks probably ranked as two of the happiest of the twins' lives. And Erin's.

The farm was one huge playground.

Now that Matt had showed his trust in the twins, they repaid him with absolute loyalty. They kept up their allotted duties as Sadie-replacements until Sadie became tired of limping and took her duties back with relish. They obeyed every spoken and unspoken command the wonderful Matt directed at them. Occasionally even Erin was brought up short by the twins' curt command:

'Will Matt think this is okay?'

And Matt usually did, because Matt, too, was enjoying

himself. The twins and Erin herded his cattle. They helped cut and bale his hay. The climbed his haystacks, they swam in his river, they roamed his farm...

And usually he wasn't far behind them. If Erin took the twins down to the river for a swim, ten to one he'd arrive within the hour—'just to check that things are okay'.

'How can they be anything else?' Erin would demand. 'You have the boys hypnotised. Honestly, Matt, they're starting to love you.'

But he didn't see the problem. Only Erin saw it, and she worried about it.

And she worried about herself, too. This was only for six months, she told herself firmly. This was only until the Home was rebuilt.

And then she had to walk away from here. And leave Matt to Charlotte.

But it wasn't to be for six months.

They'd hardly seen Charlotte since Lassendale. Matt had disappeared a couple of times to visit her for dinner, but Erin and the twins were *persona non grata* with Charlotte—and that was the way they liked it.

So it was with some surprise that they saw her car pull up one morning early after breakfast. Charlotte gave the car door a business-like slam and strode purposefully toward the house.

'Uh, oh,' said William, and Erin thought the same. Matt rose to greet his beloved and the three watched with interest. No passionate hugs here, thought Erin. Matt smiled a welcome, but they didn't even touch.

'Hi, Charlotte? What brings you here?'

'Because I've been longing to see you.' That was what she should have said, Erin thought and with a blinding flash of clarity she also thought, that's what I would have said. Instead, Charlotte said no such thing.

'Because I have such good news,' Charlotte told him, not even bothering to greet Erin and the children. 'Priscilla's has had a cancellation and the church is free at the same time!'

'Priscilla's?'

'You know Priscilla's. The great reception house up in the hills behind town. It used to belong to Sir Reginald Chester and his family but they let it go to ruin. The people who've restored it have done such a fantastic job. It's the best, Matthew, and it's the only thing that's been holding up our wedding as I refuse to hold our reception anywhere but at the best. Mummy agrees. But now it's all set. Four weeks from today. Then two weeks' honeymoon on Norfolk Island and back here as man and wife.'

And she looked at Erin for the first time—and beamed.

Erin flinched.

She couldn't live with this woman, she thought, even if she was welcome. And the thought of playing third party to a newly-wed Matt and Charlotte made her feel ill.

'I… That's great,' she managed. Her eyes moved to Matt who was looking distinctly uncomfortable. 'I'll organise something with Tom. If we can stay for those six weeks, we'll be out before you're back from your honeymoon.'

'You're welcome to stay,' Matt started but Charlotte cut in over him.

'Of course you'll stay until we get back from our honeymoon,' she said sweetly. 'But after that… Matt and I have talked about it. Three adults looking after two children is a bit of overkill—wouldn't you say, Erin?'

'Well—'

'Of course it is. And Matt won't hear of moving the children out until the orphanage is rebuilt.' She tucked her arm in his, society hostess approving her slightly eccentric husband's absurd acts of generosity. 'So after we return, I'll play mother to the boys.' She looked doubtfully at Erin. 'I suppose the Orphanage can find somewhere for you to stay.'

She's acting like I'm an orphan myself, Erin thought wildly. Good grief!

'Erin can stay here,' Matt growled but Erin and Charlotte ignored him.

'You're saying you and Matt wish to be the boys' foster parents?' Erin demanded. She felt sick.

Why, though? She had no right to be. The boys weren't hers.

And if Matt loved them then maybe it'd turn out to be a long-term solution for them. They loved Matt so much, and as long as they stayed out of Charlotte's way...

Which wasn't going to happen, she decided, marshalling her thoughts as the twins looked on in confusion. Charlotte had made not the slightest effort to conceal her dislike of the children. How could the twins possibly be expected to ignore that dislike?

They'd cause trouble the minute Erin left.

'You'd be good for us, wouldn't you?' Charlotte asked them, gimlet-eyed. Dear God, Erin thought. Maybe they would, and the thought of subdued twins was almost worse than the thought of naughty ones.

'I'll have to talk to Tom before I can agree,' she managed. 'Tom's the director of Bay Beach Orphanage. Arrangements like this are up to him.'

In answer, Charlotte gave her lovely, soft, carefully cultivated laugh.

'It's a wonderful offer, Erin. How could Tom refuse?'

How indeed?

CHAPTER TEN

'I'M SORRY that was sprung on you.'

Charlotte hadn't stuck around for long. 'With only four weeks to go I have so much to organise. Goodness, Matt, we haven't even sent out the invitations yet. Mother and I have so much to do.' And with that she was gone.

The twins, not understanding a word of what had been said—they'd formed the habit of tuning out whenever Charlotte was around—had left to do their allotted morning tasks, and Erin was left facing Matt.

She felt sick. What had he said? She gave herself a mental shake, hauling her thoughts together. 'I guess you don't have to be sorry. It's been very generous of you to offer to have us this long, and we now have another six weeks.'

'You can all stay for as long as you want,' he said, more forcibly than he'd intended, and Erin gave him a half hearted smile.

'Matt, you know that's not possible. Six weeks will give us time to find…'

'Erin, I want the twins!'

That startled her. She sat back and looked at him, and for the first time saw the pain and the longing behind his eyes.

Pain? Matt? Matt who'd been so careful for his whole life to keep him existence emotion free? Who was marrying Charlotte as yet another way to keep his world ordered and emotionless.

And yet there was definitely pain. And longing.

'You want to keep them?' she asked incredulously and he nodded.

'Yes. Hell, Erin, they're great kids. If I can persuade Charlotte... If I can get her used to them, then I'll adopt them. God knows they deserved better treatment than they've been getting.'

'I look after them,' she said, and got a swift shame-faced smile for her pains.

'Of course you do. I didn't mean to infer that you don't. But you know what Bay Beach is like. Like every local, I've heard their story, and what I didn't know exactly I've heard by asking around. And I think, if Charlotte gets to like them...'

'Do you think she will?'

'They'll be outside with me most of the time.' He gave her a half-hearted grin. 'She knows I want children and this way she won't have to get pregnant to have them. That'll be a bonus.'

A bonus? Was he kidding? Erin thought of the possibility of bearing babies for Matt, and she felt her heart constrict at the thought. There was a wave of almost indescribable longing...

Stop it, Erin, she told herself sharply. There was nothing down that road but pain.

'So you'll have a wife and family with minimum effort,' she managed, and he nodded as if her question was entirely reasonable.

'Yes. I could even enjoy it.'

'You think the boys could, too?'

'I don't see why not?'

'They need a mother.'

'They can get by with just me.'

There. He'd said it. It hung between them, cold and flat,

an expression of what he knew his marriage would be. An expression of all he'd learned the world held.

The twins didn't *need* a mother. He didn't *need* a wife.

Well, he didn't, he thought bleakly, and why the sight of Erin, white-faced and trying desperately to disguise her desperation, should have the power to move him, to make him want to reach out and take her hands in his and hold her...

For comfort, he told himself harshly. For nothing but comfort!

'It won't work, Matt,' Erin said sadly. 'It's a fine offer but the boys need a family.'

'We would be a family.'

'Nope.'

'Erin, you can't keep them forever. You're being selfish.'

'And you're being blind.' She rose, and she felt blind herself. Washed-out and ill. This man was so special, and he was committing himself to a woman who resembled nothing so much as a piece of cold cod fish. And he was committing because Charlotte wouldn't interfere with his life. Because he didn't know what a family could be.

She could show him, she thought wildly. She could teach him.

But her help wasn't being asked for. All she could do was look out for her twins.

'I need to talk to Tom,' she said bleakly. 'I can't make any promises. If Tom says it's okay, then it's none of my business.'

'Let him try.'

'I beg your pardon?'

'You heard what I said?' There were two women and one man seated in the kitchen of Bay Beach Orphanage

Home Number One. The twins were outside with the other kids, and Lori, Erin and Tom were sitting at the kitchen table holding mugs of coffee before them. The mugs were ignored. There was trouble on all of their faces.

Erin had outlined the basic facts. Lori, who'd heard an interesting version of what was happening from Wendy, was wise enough to keep her own counsel, and Tom had reached his own conclusions.

'From what I've heard, Charlotte's not the woman to make the twins happy,' he said. 'But the twins think Matt's great and he can keep them under control. Okay, he's made the offer and it's a good one. We owe it to the boys to see if it'll work.'

'But—'

'I'm not leaving them there indefinitely,' Tom said, raising his hand to silence her. 'Nor am I making other arrangements for you yet, Erin. We've put too much trouble into the boys and seen too much improvement to risk losing all our good work now. What I suggest is that we ask Matt and Charlotte to spend a weekend together before the wedding. With the boys. If, after that, they still want to go ahead with keeping the twins, then we'll assess them as potential foster parents.'

'Tom...'

'It's a gamble,' he said, his wise eyes resting on Erin and seeing things that maybe she didn't even realise she was showing. 'But we'll take it.'

It was a very long shot, Tom thought, and it wasn't entirely the twins' future he was fighting for here. But maybe it was worth the taking.

Erin never found out what means Matt used to persuade Charlotte to spend a weekend of her precious wedding preparations caring for the twins. All she knew was that he had.

'Tom's right. It's sensible,' he told her. 'For us to come back from our honeymoon and have no idea how to care for the boys—well, it'll be less of a shock for everyone if we do it this way.'

'I don't like to leave them,' Erin said doubtfully and Matt thought suddenly that he knew exactly how she felt. He didn't like her leaving either. But that was emotion speaking. If it had to be, then this was the best way.

'You know we're capable of looking after the boys.'

'No one's capable if they make up their minds to be trouble.'

'They behave for me,' Matt told her.

'I know.' But she was still troubled.

And the twins were *not* pleased. 'Why do you have to go?'

She had her reason all worked out. 'You know Shanni? She's expecting another baby, she's tired and her husband's just had an operation. She needs help, and I've offered to give her a little holiday.' That much was the absolute truth. If Erin had to take a break she might as well make herself useful.

'We don't like it when you go away.'

'You know I had breaks as a House Mother. You coped then.'

'But we didn't like it,' Henry said mutinously. 'We always get into trouble when you're away.'

Oh, dear!

'You won't get into trouble when you're staying with me,' Matt told them, clapping his big hands on their shoulders and smiling down at them with a no-nonsense smile. 'Charlotte and I can look after you very well.'

'We don't like Charlotte.'

'You hardly know Charlotte.' This was stupid. Arguing with children?

'Erin, where will you be?' William's eyes filled with tears, and Erin's heart clenched. Heck, they'd wrapped themselves around her heart like a hairy worm. She loved them so much—and she had to set them free. This way was right, she told herself fiercely. This way they had a chance of what they needed most in the world. A family.

'I won't be far,' she told them.

'She'll just be around the other side of the bay,' Matt told them, missing Erin's warning glance. She knew it wasn't safe to be specific as to her whereabouts, but he didn't pick it. 'In fact, if we go down to the beach this afternoon and take the binoculars, you'll be able to see Nick and Shanni's house across the sea.'

'Is it near?'

'Near enough for me to come right back on Sunday night,' Erin told them. 'I'll be gone for two sleeps and then I'll be back. So no problems. Please?'

'They'll be fine.' A heavily pregnant Shanni waddled into her friend's bedroom with two cups of hot chocolate and handed one over to her friend. 'Come on, Erin. It's Friday night at nine o'clock and you're worried already. By Sunday you'll be a nervous wreck.'

'And I should be doing this for you.' Erin took her chocolate and grimaced in guilt.

'Nick made it,' Shanni said placidly. 'He's still on sick leave, and Doc Emily says he might as well make himself useful. Light housework is fine, she told him, and you should have seen his face when she said it. Court appearances are out, but ironing's in.'

Erin chuckled, but her heart wasn't in it.

'If only I could be sure Charlotte would look after them.'

'Hey, she's not a monster.'

'She's close!'

'Matt loves her. She must have something going for her.'

'Matt thinks she won't disturb his life. That's why he's marrying her. She's just like his mother.'

'Hmm.' Shanni plonked herself down on Erin's bed and the bed sagged alarmingly. 'Boy, I'm huge,' she said placidly. 'Not disturbing his life, hey? That's not much of a basis for a marriage.'

'It's what he wants.'

'Is it, I wonder?' Shanni asked. 'Or is it just what he thinks he wants?' She wiggled more comfortably onto the bed and let her mug of chocolate rest on her very pregnant bulge. The baby inside her moved and her hot chocolate splashed onto her robe. She ignored it, as if such events were commonplace.

'Nick used to think he liked being a bachelor,' she added contentedly. 'And here he is and he couldn't be happier. Sometimes…well, sometimes men don't know what they want. Sometimes it's up to us women to show them.'

'I sure don't know how.'

'Hmm,' Shanni said again, and the look she cast at her friend was very thoughtful indeed.

It had to be tonight. Damnation! Just when he wanted to spend the night with the twins, he was forced to leave them with Charlotte.

But he had no choice. One of Matt's prize cows was down with her first calf, and she was in all sorts of trouble. At eight Matt rang the vet, and at ten they were both knee deep in trouble.

From dinner time on, Matt didn't see the twins. There

couldn't be a problem with them though, he told himself, as he worked on into the night. Charlotte had decreed that dinner was to be followed by the twins' bedtime. That should be fine. So when finally his calf was successfully born, he headed wearily for the house with only a little guilt weighing him down.

But he couldn't help thinking it would have been better if he'd been able to say goodnight to the twins himself.

And, at first glance, things were just fine.

Charlotte was sitting placidly in the sitting room waiting for him. This was the vision he'd had when he'd asked her to marry him, he thought as he opened the door. A man should come home to this, rather than what he was accustomed to—solitude and take-away pizza.

Charlotte was looking serene and lovely, and the room was looking beautiful to match. Even though the night hardly warranted it, the wind was getting up and she'd lit the fire. The vases were filled with carefully arranged flowers. She'd waxed the furniture, and all his mother's carefully acquired porcelain pieces had been polished.

The room looked just as it had when his mother had been alive, and he paused on the threshold for a moment to savour it.

Order and calm, and two great kids in bed, sleeping soundly.

This was what he'd always known was right, and, as he crossed the room to give Charlotte a swift kiss of appreciation, he thought finally that he'd done the right thing.

But apparently not completely. Charlotte's nose was wrinkling in distaste.

'Phew. Matthew, you smell.'

'Hey, I've washed and taken off my boots,' he told her, offended. This was good, clean cattle smell after all. 'I thought I'd come and find you before I took a shower.'

'Then think again,' she told him calmly. 'Cattle smells in the living room are unacceptable.'

'But we've succeeded in delivering a great little calf.' He was determined to tell her his good news. 'Mum and calf are both well.'

'Matt…'

'Aren't you interested?'

'After you've showered.'

'Fine.'

Only it wasn't fine. He knew instinctively that if Erin was here she'd be excited for him. Sure, the flowers wouldn't be gorgeously arranged—maybe there'd be a bunch of daisies in a jam jar—and the porcelain wouldn't be polished but…

Hell! This was what he wanted—wasn't it?

'I'll just go and check the twins,' he said and her brow snapped down as if he'd just mentioned something else that was distasteful.

'There's no need. They're asleep.'

'You didn't have any trouble with them?'

'Only a stupid argument about them sleeping in the same bed. They're too old to do that. It seems they both wanted to sleep with that disgusting stuffed toy they insist on sharing. I solved the problem by taking it away from them.'

Silence. Then…

'You took away Tigger?' he said cautiously.

'Is that what they call it?' she said, and her voice was indifferent. 'It's revolting. I locked it in the pantry.'

He guessed he could only be thankful she hadn't burned it! 'But they're asleep anyway?'

'Of course.'

Only, of course, they weren't. When he checked, they weren't even in their beds.

*   *   *

'Erin?'

It was midnight. The phone had echoed through Shanni and Nick's home, shrill with urgency, and Nick had answered it on the third ring. He'd listened in appalled silence, and then come to find Erin. Now, standing in the hall in her bare feet, she heard Matt's fear echoing down the line.

'What is it, Matt?'

'Erin, the twins have gone.'

'Gone.' She took a deep breath, fighting down panic as she forced herself to think it through. Erin hadn't survived this long as a House Mother by giving way to hysterics at every scare. 'You mean they've run away.'

'It looks like it.'

'I...okay, Matt.' She took a deep breath. 'There's no problem. You told them I was just around the bay, remember? They'll be walking on the beach somewhere. I'll come.'

'No.'

'N... No?' She really took on board his fear then, and it was vivid and dreadful. It reached her heart, as his statement that the twins had disappeared had not. 'Why not?'

'I've checked. Like you, I thought of the beach first, so I took the farm bike down there straight away. But I went by the river first. Shanni and Nick's house looks miles by beach, but it looks much closer across the water. The twins will have seen that. Erin, the rowing boat's gone, and the tide's running out at full pace. If they took the boat, they'll now be well out to sea.'

'They promised they wouldn't use the boat,' Matt muttered. 'They promised.'

Quarter of an hour later, Erin and Matt were in the police launch, headed out into the bay—along with half the fishing population of Bay Beach. Every boat that wasn't already out fishing was called into action. Rob McDonald was taking no chances.

'I want them found, and I want them found fast. If they realise they're drifting away from land, there's no telling what they'll do.'

'But they promised,' Matt said again into the night, and there was quiet desperation behind his words. 'Maybe we're wrong to be looking out to sea. Maybe they haven't used the boat. It could have broken away itself. Erin, I trusted them not to break their word.'

'I think they're in the boat—and I don't think they've broken their vow. Or—not on their terms.' Erin's voice was winter-bleak.

'Erin, I heard them promise. I trust them.'

'And you know what I said when they promised?' she whispered into the night. The boat was slipping out of the harbour, a flotilla of fishing boats behind them. 'I said: "While you're living with me you obey my rules." And then I left them.'

He closed his eyes. 'Erin…'

'It's not your fault,' she said bleakly. 'It's mine. I let Tom talk me into this, and I might have known it would end in disaster.'

Dear God…

The sea mist had slipped in over the water. The night was almost eerie in its stillness. They stood alone in the bow, each feeling sick with what they might or might not find before them.

Erin didn't know where Charlotte was. She didn't ask. Once she'd heard about Tigger's removal, it was maybe just as well she didn't know.

Dear God… It was a prayer, said over and over again into the night.

Instinctively, Matt's arm came out and held Erin hard around her waist. For a moment she resisted, but her need for comfort was too great. She let herself be pulled into him, and they stayed that way as the rolling swells of the open sea hit the boat and Rob turned the launch out of the harbour and along the bay toward the tidal outpouring from the river.

Matt and Erin didn't move. They were a man and woman as one. With one prayer...

It was the longest night Erin had ever known.

The flotilla formed a pack. Rob and the most senior of the fishermen worked out a pattern of grid lines based on tides, currents and wind, and each boat was given a course to follow. It was a myriad of criss-crossing lines, with all hands of every boat glued to the guy ropes, and all eyes trying desperately to pierce the fog.

Somewhere in this vast sea were two little boys in a rickety old rowing boat that was never intended to be strong enough to be buffeted by waves like this.

The sea wasn't at its wildest, but it was rough enough to frighten a grown man in an open rowing boat—much less children.

'They don't even have Tigger,' Erin whispered brokenly at one point, and Matt's arm tightened still further. He was trying to instil comfort with every ounce of his being, but at the same time he needed comfort himself.

If only... If only...

He'd been a crazy, blind fool to think this could ever work, he thought. Leaving the twins to Charlotte...

He'd been left with his mother, and he still remembered the coldness. If his father hadn't been there—if he'd had an Erin to run to...

It might have been him in this damned rowing boat, he

thought, and there was something of the lost and lonely child in the look he cast out over the water. Please let the boys be safe, he said to himself and finally out aloud. 'Please…'

'Matt?'

'Mmm.' He could hardly hear. Every ounce of his being was concentrating on trying to pierce the fog. He was willing the boys to appear.

'Whatever happens,' Erin said softly. 'Matt, whatever happens, the boys know that you've loved them. That's meant so much.'

'Not enough,' he managed.

'You're not to blame for this.'

'I am.' He closed his eyes for an instant before pushing them wide to continue searching. 'I am to blame.'

'Why?'

'Because I didn't have the courage to change my life. As I should have done. As I will if I ever have the chance again. Please…'

And finally, just before dawn, they found them.

There was a shout across the water from one of the fishing boats, and then another shout as the boat on the intersecting grid saw what they'd seen.

Immediately every nose of every boat swung into the same point, and Matt and Erin almost fell over the bow in their effort to see.

When they finally did, the fishing boat that had first seen them had seized the rowing boat with a grappling hook and was trying to haul it alongside.

Which was easier said than done. The grappling hook was too short. The rowing boat hit the fishing boat with a sickening crunch, the next wave hit before there was time to lower a man to reach the children, and the fishing boat was forced to pull away. If it hadn't, they ran the risk of crunching the row boat to splinters.

Floodlights played out over the water. The children were crouched low in the boat, clinging to each other in terror.

Rob pulled the police launch in close, but it was so rough he could do nothing. Half filled with water, the old wooden boat was threatening to capsize with every movement. And the twins didn't look up. The men's shouts and the noise of the engines over the roar of the sea was only increasing their terror.

It was too much for Erin. Before anyone could stop her—before anyone could even realise what she intended—she'd grabbed a lifevest and jumped into the water.

One second later, Matt followed.

It took Erin precious minutes to clamber into the rowing boat, and she'd darn near capsized it as she did. But she was born and bred by the sea. The Douglas children had always had boats, mostly home-made by themselves, and there were always too many children in them. She was an expert in keeping old tubs afloat.

And blessedly her self-taught skills didn't let her down. By the time Matt's head appeared, dripping, as he clung to the side, she was holding her two little boys to her as if her life depended on it, and she was able to move backwards to stabilise the boat and let Matt haul himself on board.

And then she had the sense to shift again to the middle. So that once he was safely on board, Matt could take all of them into his arms. It was sandwich squeeze of half-drowned adults and kids, who held each other as if they'd never let each other go again. Forever.

Around them the flotilla of fishermen and police watched with blatant approval and the odd goofy smile. This was the happy ending they'd all wanted so badly.

They should move. They should get the old tub into the lee of the harbour so they could shift the kids out of it.

They should.

But for this moment, no one moved at all. It was as if everyone knew that, right there and then, a family was being forged that would take more power than the sea to split asunder.

CHAPTER ELEVEN

THE children were asleep.

Shocked to the core, they'd been held tight while ropes from the fishing boat tugged them slowly and safely back into the lee of the harbour. Once there, they were transferred to the police launch, William clinging for dear life to Erin, and Henry clinging just as closely to Matt. Then they'd been dried off and brought home.

Charlotte wasn't waiting.

'I said a few unforgivable things to Charlotte,' Matt told Erin briefly, as they put the twins through a warm bath and snuggled them into bed—the same bed—and watched them fall instantly asleep with their precious Tigger between them. 'I don't suppose she'll be back.'

'Oh, Matt, I'm so sorry.'

'Don't be. I've been a fool, and I've been blessed to get out of it as lightly as I have.'

And now, dried and dressed themselves, they were standing in the living room watching the embers of Charlotte's fire die in the grate. The first rays of dawn were breaking over the horizon out to sea.

Erin still hadn't bought herself a decent dressing gown. She was still wearing her huge flannelette welfare handout that made her look about ten years old, and, watching her, Matt thought back to the moment when he'd seen Erin dive from the boat.

Something in him had almost died in that moment. For one awful minute until she surfaced, he'd thought he might lose all of them.

He couldn't bear it. And he couldn't bear to waste another precious minute.

'Marry me, Erin,' he said, and the world held its breath. She stared. 'M... Marry you?'

'That's what I said.' He took the two short steps to bridge the space between them, and he pulled her to him. Somehow he couldn't bear not to, and as her soft body yielded to his he knew that he could never let her go again.

Dear God, he loved her so much. How had he not known it before? He loved her and loved her and loved her.

But she was pushing him away, and her eyes were troubled. 'Matt, it's just the night. It's shock or something. You love Charlotte.'

'I don't love Charlotte.' He glanced down at the beautifully polished coffee table and there was a diamond ring, lying where she'd tossed it in indignation at what he'd said to her. 'And she doesn't love me,' he continued. 'You see? She's given me back my ring. Not that I want it.'

'So now you...' Erin paused, still troubled. 'You want me to wear it?'

He shook his head at that, absolutely definite. 'No way.' Suddenly his arms were holding her again, and a woman would have to have super powers to resist his hold.

'Not that,' he said. 'Charlotte can have it if she wants it, but you're not wearing her ring. You and Charlotte...you're about as different as two women could be and I was a fool to see it. Erin, I love you. The ring we buy, we buy together, and it'll be a ring full of colour and light. Just like you. Sapphires and rubies and... I don't know. Everything. All the colour you've brought into my life.'

Dear heaven... Somewhere deep inside, Erin's heart was starting to sing.

But not now. Not yet. She couldn't!

'Matt...'

He kissed her lightly on her damp hair, and then, because he could resist no longer, he tilted her chin and kissed her deeply on her mouth. The kiss lasted forever, and was a vow all by itself.

'Yes, love?' he said, and his voice was a husky whisper, filled with passion.

'Matt...' She was trying so hard to make herself say what had to be said. She must! Tonight she'd known. As well as loving this man, she had other loves. 'Matt, I can't leave the twins.'

Was that all that was troubling her? With a shout of triumph, he lifted her high and whirled her above his head. 'The twins? You think I don't love the twins like I'll love my own children? They're part of you, my love. A package deal. It's all or nothing, and I want it all!'

'You...' She was swinging dizzily off her feet. 'You mean you'll adopt the twins?'

'*We'll* adopt the twins,' he said simply, and looking down into his gorgeous, loving eyes she knew at last that he spoke the truth. Here then was her happy ever after ending.

Here was her home.

He set her down on her feet, and his voice became surer. He took her hands in his, and their eyes locked.

'So you'll marry me?' he asked.

Yes, her heart screamed but there were things that needed to be said. It was only fair to warn him.

'Matt, your life will be chaos.'

'I've discovered I love chaos.'

'But you love your mother's lovely things!' She looked

around the room. 'This carpet... The porcelain... There'll be accidents. I know the kids. We won't be able to keep the house to the standards you like.'

The answer to that was easy. He lifted one piece of porcelain—a droopy Romeo and Juliet, for heaven's sake—and let it drop. It hit the grate and smashed into a thousand pieces. Then, as Erin gasped in horror, he grabbed the blackened poker from the fire. Very deliberately he walked across the room and drew in huge letters on the once pristine carpet.

MATT LOVES ERIN!

'Matt!' She was shocked to the core. 'That's vandalism. If you were mine, I'd spank you.'

'Hmm...' His loving eyes mocked a challenge. 'You want to try?'

'Matt McKay!'

'Erin Douglas,' he teased right back. 'Now, will you marry me, or do I have to smash every piece of porcelain in the place before you agree?'

'We'd be much better packing it up as a wedding present for Charlotte and Bradley,' Erin said seriously, and Matt gave a whoop of pure joy.

'Very practical.' She was in his arms again. 'Very sensible. You're my own gorgeous, sensible, crazy, House Mother. My love. My heart. My Erin. Now... Are you going to admit that you'll marry me? Or am I going to have to kiss you senseless, and keep right on kissing you until you finally grow so weak you agree?'

And what was a girl to say to that?

'Yes, please,' she said. 'If only to stop you kissing me senseless.'

'I have news for you,' he told her. 'I intend to do that anyway!'

0406/02

MILLS & BOON®

Live the emotion

Tender
romance™

THE CATTLE BARON'S BRIDE *by Margaret Way*

The wilderness of the Australian Northern territory was no
place for city beauty Samantha Langdon. Cattleman Ross
Sunderland wouldn't have agreed to act as guide if he'd known
Sam would be on the trip – he'd vowed to avoid her. But with
danger and beauty all around them, their passion could no
longer be denied…

THE CINDERELLA FACTOR *by Sophie Weston*

The French chateau is the perfect hiding place for Jo – until
its owner, reporter Patrick Burns, comes home… At first
Patrick thinks the secret runaway is a thief, until he sees that
Jo is hiding her painful past. Soon she is a woman he can't live
without. But will her frightening new feelings for Patrick make
Jo run again?

CLAIMING HIS FAMILY *by Barbara Hannay*

Erin has taken her little boy to the Outback to meet his father
– her ex-husband, Luke – whom she hasn't seen for five years.
Erin is not sure how to act around the man she once loved
so deeply. Can Erin find the courage to give their marriage a
second chance – and let them become a family again?

WIFE AND MOTHER WANTED *by Nicola Marsh*

Brody Elliott is a single dad struggling to bring up his
daughter Molly. He's determined to protect his little girl from
heartbreak again. So when Molly befriends their pretty new
neighbour, Carissa Lewis, Brody is wary. If only Brody was
willing to let go of his past and give in to their attraction,
maybe Carissa could be his too…

On sale 5th May 2006

*Available at WHSmith, Tesco, ASDA, Borders, Eason,
Sainsbury's and most bookshops*

www.millsandboon.co.uk

MILLS & BOON®

Live the emotion

0406/01b

Modern
romance™

BOUGHT FOR THE MARRIAGE BED
by Melanie Milburne

Nina will do anything to keep her twin's baby from harm. So when Marc Marcello wants to take his brother's child, Nina lets herself be bought as Marc's bride instead. But what price can be placed on her...in his bed?

THE ITALIAN'S WEDDING ULTIMATUM
by Kim Lawrence

Alessandro Di Livio always protects his family, even seducing gold digging Sam Maguire to keep her away from his brother-in-law! But when passion leads to pregnancy, Alessandro wants to keep Sam as his wife – and their baby as his heir!

THE INNOCENT VIRGIN *by Carole Mortimer*

Abby Freeman is thrilled when she gets a job as a TV chat show host, and who better to grill than famous journalist Max Harding? Max is happy to let Abby get close – but only in private. How can Abby get the story...without losing her innocence?

RUTHLESS REUNION *by Elizabeth Power*

Sanchia has amnesia but when Alex Sabre recognises her, she realises they once knew each other intimately. To unlock her past Sanchia must spend time with Alex. What happens when she learns the truth about the man she's falling in love with...again?

On sale 5th May 2006

Available at WHSmith, Tesco, ASDA, Borders, Eason,
Sainsbury's and most bookshops

www.millsandboon.co.uk

MILLS & BOON®

0406/03b

Live the emotion

Medical
romance™

HER LONGED-FOR FAMILY *by Josie Metcalfe*

Doctor Nick Howell has never forgiven Libby for
running out on him – until she turns up as the new
A&E doctor and it becomes clear that an accident
and resulting amnesia has cut out part of her life.
Now it's up to Nick to help her remember…

*The ffrench Doctors – a family of doctors –
all in the family way*

MISSION: MOUNTAIN RESCUE
by Amy Andrews

Army medic Richard Hollingsworth has devoted
his life to saving others. But his medical skills have
put his life in danger – and that of his beloved Holly.
Now, to escape their mountain captors, they must
submit to the bond they once shared…

*24:7 Feel the heat – every hour…every minute…
every heartbeat*

THE GOOD FATHER *by Maggie Kingsley*

Neonatologist Gabriel Dalgleish is passionate about
his tiny patients. It seems as if they are all he cares
for. Except for Maddie. The new medical secretary
slips through Gabriel's defences, right to his
vulnerable heart!

*THE BABY DOCTORS
Making families is their business!*

On sale 5th May 2006

*Available at WHSmith, Tesco, ASDA, Borders, Eason,
Sainsbury's and most bookshops*

www.millsandboon.co.uk

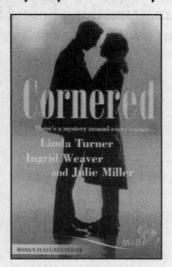